The Clan

Connie,

Hope you enjoy the book!

Dad

The Clan

The Book of Jasher
Part 1

Bill W. Sanford

THE CLAN
THE BOOK OF JASHER

iUniverse books may be ordered through booksellers or by contacting:

iUniverse
1663 Liberty Drive
Bloomington, IN 47403
www.iuniverse.com
1-800-Authors (1-800-288-4677)

Because of the dynamic nature of the Internet, any web addresses or links contained in this book may have changed since publication and may no longer be valid. The views expressed in this work are solely those of the author and do not necessarily reflect the views of the publisher, and the publisher hereby disclaims any responsibility for them.

Any people depicted in stock imagery provided by Thinkstock are models, and such images are being used for illustrative purposes only. Certain stock imagery © Thinkstock.

ISBN: 978-1-4917-9686-3 (sc)
ISBN: 978-1-4917-9685-6 (e)

Library of Congress Control Number: 2016907850

Print information available on the last page.

iUniverse rev. date: 06/23/2016

For Debra,
… always near

Prologue - Perkins, the Extractor

"What is past is prologue."

----- *William Shakespeare*

James Perkins' career could be described as meteoric. Occasionally, when he attempted to extol his quick rise in the Agency, some cynically pointed out he had been basking in the light of Walker Caine's favor for over twenty years. In spite of such talk, he felt his reputation and his particular skill set had made most of that possible. Nonetheless, even he realized when it came right down to where the shit hits the buckwheat, nobody moves up without help and he had received the best a man could have. The downside was that Caine abhorred failure and there was scarcely any room in his world for tolerating it.

Around the Agency some referred to James Perkins as the "Extractor", but few knew exactly how he had come to earn that title and from whence it came. He and Walker Caine had first met when Perkins was on assignment in the Iraq War less than a year after the United States military had blown through the region like a Texas cyclone. At the time he was a young lieutenant working as part of a military counter-intelligence unit that liaised with the Central Intelligence Agency. A few weeks following the capture of Saddam Hussein in December of 2003, he had been assigned to interrogate the ex-Iraqi leader and extract information regarding so-called weapons of mass destruction, or "WMDs". It was beginning to look like the whole justification for the invasion of Iraq had been a hoax and certain parties were anxious and highly motivated to prove it otherwise.

Perkins was getting the interrogation room ready when a man walked in accompanied by two powerfully built men, presumably his bodyguards. The two, no doubt lethal when turned loose, stepped back a respectful, cautionary distance and never took their eyes off the principle. Perkins had never met the visitor and he was curious about his presence during this session; normal protocol required only those directly involved with the interrogation to wait behind the one-way mirror and observe. Perkins stated respectfully, "Sir, I am Lieutenant Perkins. We have never met and I have received no briefing on your purpose during these proceedings. May I know who you are?"

The man was of medium-build, and though his outward appearance was darker than most, his overall physical characteristics typified that of a trim, Caucasian male in his mid to late 30s. Though sporting a well-trimmed beard, an apparent scar was seen along his left cheek that prevented the beard from appearing full. Ignoring Perkins, he waited patiently, and as if inspecting the contents of the room, he scanned it then following his cursory inspection, he signaled one of his men over and briefly whispered something in his ear.

A moment later a senior officer walked briskly through the door. Immediately, Perkins came to attention and saluted the Major, his unit commander. After returning the salute, the Major motioned to the man in the corner and announced, "Lieutenant Perkins, this gentleman is Walker Caine and he will be providing the questions and is here to observe your interrogation of a highly placed political prisoner. You will give him your full cooperation. Is that clearly understood?"

Perkins' reply was crisp and he hoped impressive: "Of course, sir". He had been briefed previously that the prisoner would be political rather than military, but why he had been selected for this interrogation, above all others more senior than himself, had escaped him. His Arabic, he knew, was near fluent and his understanding of contemporary Iraqi politics was better than most, but this was a highly political session. His previous experience had been the interrogation of only military prisoners or low-ranking government officials.

Much to his surprise, two military guards brought in the prisoner in handcuffs with shackles on his ankles, and as he slowly shuffled in, the ankle cuffs clinked miserably across the stone floor announcing his arrival. Though he had been provisioned ill-fitting, tattered prison garb, Perkins had immediately recognized the once proud leader of Iraq, Saddam Hussein. With his disheveled condition, the man now gave the impression of a humble beggar from the dusty slums of Baghdad, which was just the effect the military had wanted. For Perkins, this protocol was unorthodox, in fact, everything up to this point indicated this was to be an unusual session.

Of course, Perkins was aware that this was hardly the first interrogation of Saddam. Word gets around as it usually does in a prison camp, and according to rumor, Hussein was usually placid and cooperative, but when he noticed the dark man sitting quietly in the corner, he began to thrash about and curse. From the brief reaction, it was clear the two men knew one another, but Perkins was unprepared for the words of anger flung in the direction of the visitor. Hussein had mentioned something about a "damned vagabond among men" then had lapsed into colloquial swearing. The dark man seemed unperturbed at the outburst; indeed, he seemed to take it all as a matter of course. He nodded to one of his personal guards, who then walked over to the prisoner and backhanded him hard enough across the face to draw blood. The man then spoke in controlled, fluent Arabic directly to the prisoner as he commanded, "You will be silent, you filthy swine, until you are asked to speak and then you will answer my questions or I will have you cut up and fed to the dogs in that miserable village you call home."

The prisoner was pushed down roughly and then seated opposite Perkins at the interrogation table. This last remark silenced Hussein, but there was still defiance in his eyes. As if to disrupt the built-up tension in the room, Perkins cleared his throat and gazed quietly at the prisoner; he wanted Hussein cooperative, not defiant. Thus, he waited a few moments, giving everyone time to clear the air then he glanced over to the man providing the input and awaited his first question. His job would be to interpret, translate and provide the necessary persuasion when it was required. Nonetheless, it was clear enough that the dark man was fluent in Arabic and would require little, if any, assistance in the interpretation.

"Where are the records?" the prisoner was asked.

"Out of sight and away from your deceitful, filthy hands," he spat.

"I want them. Where are they?"

The prisoner's eyes were defiant as well as his words. "Find them yourself. They are the only reason I remain alive. Why should I hand them over to you?"

"They are worthless to you and I assure you, the moment I think you don't have them, your miserable life will be like a lit candle in a sand storm."

"You promised me that I would be left alone to rule my country as my ancestors before me. Then you invade my country, not once, but twice. Then you depose me and now here I am, treated like a common criminal. Why should I help you?" He then added listlessly, "I am dead already."

The visitor replied, "Yes, I invaded your worthless country twice because I must treat you like a mongrel dog in the street to get your attention. The first time I had my army invade your nation was to send you a message that I was growing tired of your failure to search for my records. And now, yet again, I have been forced to invade, but this time I know you have them." With contempt, he began to harangue, "Have you no idea how much I despise this abominable heap of sand you call a country? You should have realized that your rule would end the moment you refused to turn the records over to me. Remember, I placed you in power and put you under solemn oath for a reason: to find the records and deliver them to me, but what did you do instead? You wasted my time with your ridiculous parades and sabre rattling antics for years. Your posturing, Stalin-like ego has cost me valuable time. As a consequence, you left me no choice, but to invade your miserable, shit heap homeland again. Now, if you want to live, you had better tell me where you have hidden them."

"No, I refuse." Then he was silent.

The dark man nodded to one of his bodyguards and he removed some devices from a large briefcase and placed them carefully on the table then backed away. Walker Caine glanced in the direction of Perkins and asked, "Lieutenant Perkins, are you familiar with the operation and use of the items on the table before you?" Perkins flicked a glance to the Major, his unit commander, for confirmation. When he assented, Perkins responded, "I am, but I think their use is premature at this point."

Walker Caine looked him over and said, "Lieutenant, if you feel you are unable to perform the task, I can find someone else who will."

Attempting to retract his words as a misunderstanding, Perkins replied quickly, "That won't be necessary, sir. I merely expressed my view that we can move onto more persuasive methods as the situation required, but, if you feel the time is right, then I will proceed."

Caine motioned that he was getting impatient, "Then, get on with it. This Iraqi dog is barking and I want him whimpering."

Lieutenant Perkins was well aware of the operation and use of the electrical devices before him. He had seen them used before during interrogations that had proved to be more difficult than was expected, but he personally had never used such techniques. He felt that their use at this point in the session was impulsive, but he guessed correctly that his further input into this matter would go unappreciated. "Guards, hold the prisoner", Perkins ordered. The guards must have known what was coming because they knew exactly how to restrain Hussein long enough to tie him securely to the chair. Perkins picked up two long, pointed nails from the table and walked around the desk.

The prisoner must have realized the interrogation had taken a sudden turn for the worse because his thrashing and cursing recommenced. "Gag him," ordered Perkins and it was done. Further, no doubt the ex-ruler had seen this technique performed before, probably many times, thought Perkins. Placing himself directly in front of the prisoner, he took one long nail in each fist and jabbed downward, punching though flesh and bone directly into the bone marrow of both legs. The reaction from the prisoner was galvanic; an instantaneous muffled scream issued forth through the gag of the condemned man, which could be felt as well as heard by all within the room.

The second phase was to connect an electrical transformer wired to two small jumper cables and plug the device into the wall. After the connections had been set he tested the charge. While the prisoner continued to writhe helplessly in the chair, Perkins touched the metal clips together resulting in a live show of current, and upon seeing this, the prisoner immediately began to thrash about even more. Perkins turned off the current at the transformer and connected the two clips to the two narrow spikes protruding from the prisoner's legs then he quietly walked around the table and sat down. Once he had placed his fingers of his right hand on the transformer switch to regulate the electrical flow, he was then ready to begin. He nodded to the dark man in the corner eagerly awaiting the results for which he had come, and again the prisoner was ungagged by a guard.

"Where are the records?" the initial question was repeated.

Though whimpering in pain, the prisoner refused to respond to the question. With a slight movement, Perkins turned the dial of the transformer slightly and the prisoner experienced an immediate jarring effect. Though he suppressed the scream, notwithstanding his eye balls bulged, the hair on his head began to rise noticeably and his mouth opened, revealing his teeth now clamped together in a rictus of absolute pain. Perkins held the dial in place until the prisoner began bucking and jerking himself forward. The scene continued as he held the dial in place a moment longer then abruptly he backed off the current. The prisoner, now exhausted from enduring the ordeal, allowed his head to loll off to the side. Incredibly, he was still conscious, but then Perkins had yet to apply the maximum dosage and the prisoner knew it.

"Where are the records?" intoned the dark man in the corner.

"Up your rectum," was the murmured response.

Again Perkins applied the current, but this time he increased it and held it in that position for a longer period of time. With the same results, he repeated the process a few more times and in spite of the pain, it was obvious the prisoner was proving more resistant than expected. Finally, after applying a near lethal dose, the prisoner actually passed out when the current was pulled back from the transformer. The guards were ordered to revive the prisoner with water and smelling salts and they complied.

Walker Caine took over the interrogation at that point. He observed with contempt, "You are one foolish Iraqi Arab and believe me I have known my share of fools from your pathetic country. I assure you that this whole process does not offend nor disgust me in the least. So, your discomfort will continue all day long until you die or I get the records. So, which is it going to be?"

The pain was unbearable. Reluctantly, and now in extreme physical distress, he gazed up at his tormentor and quietly declared, "Caine, I have given the records to Jasher."

Caine sputtered, "Why would you do that?"

"Because he asked me and I knew it would piss you off!" He could not resist a taunting smile.

Upon hearing this response Walker Caine rushed over to the prisoner, grabbed him by his tattered shirt and screamed into his face, "You did what? I don't believe you, swine!" He picked up a club from the table and backhanded him so hard with a truncheon that several teeth were broken.

The blood overflowed his mouth and cascaded to the cell floor along with several teeth; his body slumped forward.

The prisoner, owing to the ill treatment, could only muster a grotesque smile, but it was, at least, genuine. "He wanted me to tell you, as usual, you are too late." With that said and still strapped to the chair, he fell limply to the floor.

Now livid and beyond caring, Caine began to pummel the now inert body with his bare fists then the club. When he tired of this, he invited his body guards to finish the prisoner off and they, being creative thugs, waded in with a flourish using their heavy boots.

When it was over, Caine was bent over in the corner panting heavily from the exertion. During the whole scene, Perkins had sat appalled, clearly perplexed by not only the line of questioning, but the extraction methods then the bludgeoning of the prisoner. The Major had quickly exited with the military guards when Caine's thugs had begun the finishing touch to the ex-ruler of Iraq.

When the bodyguards had finished their work and Caine had regained some degree of composure, he ordered the body to be removed: "I want it cut up and fed to the mangiest dogs in his home village." He glanced over to Perkins, and by way of explanation, informed him, "I always try to keep my promises." He took a moment to comb his now disheveled hair and straighten his tie that had gone askew during the sadistic attack on Hussein. As he glanced nonchalantly around the room, his smile was calm, almost beatific.

While the body of the prisoner was dragged unceremoniously by one foot behind each of the two bodyguards, Caine began to follow them to the door. Nonetheless, before leaving, he turned to Perkins then added pointedly, "Well done." Then, he too, walked out.

As the interrogation concluded, Perkins learned that the name of the dark man was Walker Caine or Cain. Although unsure which spelling was more correct, however he was able to place the name with the man and remembered this session the remainder of his life. Perkins left the military soon afterwards and was immediately accepted into the Agency. It would be another decade before he saw Walker Caine again and begin his new role as personal liaison, but he no doubt attributed his rise in the government to the endorsement of this benefactor.

The man in Iraq executed by hanging three years later was a Saddam Hussein look-alike. He was cooperative and especially convincing during the trial. Up until the very end, the fool actually thought he would be set free.

Part 1 – The Records

13 *And the sun stood still, and the moon stayed, until the people had avenged themselves upon their enemies. Is not this written in The Book of Jasher? So the sun stood still in the midst of heaven, and hasted not to go down about a whole day.*

----- Joshua 10:13

17 *And David lamented with this lamentation over Saul and over Jonathan his son:*

18 *(Also he bade them teach the children of Judah the use of the bow: behold, it is written in The Book of Jasher.)*

----- 2nd Samuel 1: 17 – 18

Those who do not remember the past are condemned to repeat it.

----- George Santayana

Chapter 1 – William Bedford, Paleographer

The city of Austin, Texas lies between the two large metropolitan areas of Dallas and San Antonio and, depending upon the person behind the wheel driving the family pick-up, it lies within three hours of Houston. Until 1990, the city was a laid-back mecca for retirees, country and western singers and ex-hippies, all of whom had developed a vital sub-culture which made the city uniquely attractive. Later, those from the northern states migrated south to Austin trying desperately to get out of the snow and the cold and attempted to re-invent the city in their own image, but instead became fully assimilated and converted to the slogan: "Nowhere else but Austin". Now in 2025, all of these groups had found a way for peaceful coexistence that was the envy of most cities in the country. Added to all this was a world-class university that attracted some of the best minds in the world, those who had come to learn and those who came to teach.

The home of Professor William W. Bedford lay nestled within the rolling hills of Northwest Austin in an up-scale neighborhood known as Lago Vista, which had once been quite isolated from the current hustle and bustle of the metropolitan area, but as anyone living in that area will now tell you, the invasion was complete and few prisoners were taken. Though no longer secluded, the area is still well represented by the middle and upper-middle class families of the University as well as the high-tech companies that abound in the surrounding region.

On a warm April afternoon in South Texas, Wesley Bedford, son of Professor William Bedford, leaned unhappily against his car with his arms folded. Though he had mentioned he would make an appearance that day, he had parked outside his father's home and debated whether he should intrude upon his private study. Unkind words had been exchanged during their last meeting, and inconsequence, Wes was worried that what he had to tell him today might jeopardize their already strained relationship. That last argument had precipitated Wes' move from the family home. As his mother and sister had already declared their defection from his side as a result of his parents' recent divorce, he felt what he now had to discuss might actually make things worse. Though he had scarcely wanted to add to his father's sense of abandonment, however, he knew that if he had remained, eventually there would have been the same animosities his father had endured from his mother and sister.

He looked back upon his family life as he had grown up and could see the glaring differences in his life ten years earlier than existed today. Up until the past few years, his father had always been a caring, engaging parent and was determined to insure his family was an integral part of his life. His studies of the past few years, however, had turned him into an introverted recluse. Eventually, everyone close to him began to notice a discernable change in his behavior and no one, least of all his wife, had been able to reach him. His current focus of research was gradually sucking the life from him, reducing him to a person to be pitied and avoided by family and friends alike. Because his latest investigation of his theories had now taken on the tones of an obsession, even his father's long-time colleagues were beginning to distance themselves from his side.

Though reluctantly, Wes had come today to make the break even more permanent. An earlier phone call had alerted his father that he would be dropping by for a visit and the Professor, as usual, would be absorbed with cuneiform manuscripts of an ancient civilization. It was, after all, Wesley pointedly noted, his life's work. He didn't relish disturbing his father's absorbed study, but he had put off this task long enough. Technically, it was still his home, so he simply walked through the unlocked front door into the open foyer and up to the doorway leading to his father's office. So, with some trepidation, he knocked on the open latticed door, walked over to the huge desk filled to overflowing with reference books and archeological journals then sat down opposite his father.

Wesley had been rehearsing what he was going to say. He felt awkward in his father's presence and was reluctant to proceed, even with his father's encouragement to do so. He was determined to be reasonable and affect a tone of understanding; nonetheless, given the circumstances, he felt it was one battle he would lose. He waited patiently a moment then, clearing his throat to get his father's attention, he asked, "Dad, can we talk?"

Professor Bedford had been poring over a parchment manuscript, and noting the arrival of his son, he looked up distractedly, removed his reading glasses then replied with a touch of impatience, "Yes my Son? Please speak your mind."

Wes cleared his throat and replied slowly, "As you know, Dad, I have been accepted for admittance to Rice University to their School of Architecture. I mentioned that I was giving considerable thought to changing my field of focus and I know you have expressed your disappointment with my interest in changing fields, but I have decided to move forward with the application process."

Though his father's endorsement was unneeded to make the change, Professor Bedford readied himself for the question that had been obviously bothering his son for some time. "Dad, will you support me in this decision?"

William Bedford, now a full-professor at the University of Texas in Austin, was a world-renown expert in Anthropology and ancient artifacts. Having ignored the advice of colleagues as well as the Dean of his School, he had made the mistake recently of embracing the idea of historical conspiracy, which in his own field is the equivalent of dabbling in paranormal studies in the field of psychology. Thus, in spite of his past endeavors, his current obsession had eventually resulted in an unofficial censuring within his collegiate community. Though still highly respected among most of his old colleagues, lately his academic career had seemed to have fallen under a dark cloud.

Bedford reflected on the years he and his family had travelled to the Middle-east, and during those extended travels, he had observed his son's inherent ability for learning new languages and adapting to new cultures. He looked sadly over to his son seated in front of him and admitted, "Son", the Professor replied, "you are quite right, I am disappointed. I had hoped that you would be willing to stay in your current course of study in Anthropology here at the University where you could then follow my path in the studies of ancient artifacts and civilizations. You seemed happy and eager to follow that pursuit, and moreover, you have always shown a keen aptitude for languages and a gift for understanding cultural differences." On a note of encouragement, he mentioned, "As you know, I could be very helpful in opening up the doors you would need for success. Have I not encouraged you and repeatedly assured you of this?" It was clear his son was reluctant to answer.

Wesley bent forward, averting his eyes and nervously commented, "Dad, everyone knows you are the acknowledged leader in your field and your endorsements would be the best, but I need to follow my own interests and be at the top in my own field. Otherwise, I risk appearing beholden as the favored son following his father around, everyone expecting me to reach him professionally, but never quite succeeding."

Bedford thought he knew his son better than that. He had explained on several occasions that he needn't worry about trying to fill his shoes and that his own work would eventually speak for itself, thus he realized there was more to this change in direction than Wes was revealing. His father replied with considerably more asperity in his voice than he was accustomed to using, "But Wes, it wouldn't have to be that way, so please think it over." As an afterthought he noted, "As you know I am close to unlocking the key to understanding history from an entirely different social perspective, one which will change the way we look at our society today. This process will take years to complete and I will need an assistant familiar with my work and whose own work will complement my own efforts. Frankly, I was hoping you would be there by my side when I made this discovery." Bedford noted that Wes quickly arose and uncomfortably shuffled his feet then shifted his eyes away from him.

Wes replied, "I'm sorry Dad, but lately I think your interests have become unsound, even confusing. I think you are making a big mistake following this line of research and worse, you will lose your standing in the scientific community. You have worked too long and too hard, sacrificed too much to throw it away on some trivial pursuit."

Bedford realized, without having to mention it, that Wesley blamed him for the breakup of the family. The sacrifice to which he referred was the time he had spent away from his wife and children. The word "recluse" had been used during many marital disputes, until his wife had grown weary of the personal anxiety and had taken their younger daughter to live elsewhere. Subsequently, Wesley had moved out of his home and had been living in an apartment near the University of Texas where he had been attending school the past two years. This was becoming an old argument that Bedford hoped to avoid because it would divert them both from the real reason for this visit.

"Unsound? I don't follow you." But Professor Bedford did, in fact, grasp to what his son had stated so boldly. He had been made aware of this loss of credibility these past months from colleagues he had known, even mentored for years. While attending the Paris Symposium of Ancient Civilizations, others he knew only slightly had been openly caustic in their remarks. He recalled a specific incident that had occurred in the conference center garden where he had been accosted by a few of his old colleagues as well as some much younger.

He recalled, following his most recent presentation, one had scoffed openly, "Professor Bedford, with all due respect, how can you possibly know or even speculate on your theory of a conspiratorial influence on ancient civilizations, especially when these are hundreds, even thousands of years apart. From where do you derive your conclusions when there are no written records anywhere or from anyone that refer to or name such persons or groups?"

Nevertheless, though clearly on the defensive, Bedford had stood by his conclusions when he declared, "Gentlemen, my recent research indicates that there was a shadow group that had insinuated themselves into the different governments at high levels, undermining the social fabric of each kingdom and had contributed to its eventual downfall. The Phoenicians, the Greeks and later the Romans all fell into decline through the implacable influence from without and from within from this same group. Though I am still in the process of examining the data, I suspect that this shadow society even predates those great civilizations." He recollected how a younger colleague had bored in implacably.

"I am sorry, Professor, but your conclusions are specious at best. There is no text or volume of work from those ages that can corroborate your thesis. Neither the scribes nor the great philosophers of those civilizations make any specific mention of this group."

"My findings", pointed out the Professor, "may lack any eye-witness reporting, but my recent research has led me to believe that there were many similarities of their individual declines that can only be attributed to the workings of the same or similar group inside each of the governments."

"Professor Bedford", declared another colleague, "please understand that until an eyewitness or volume of work can be presented to substantiate your research and declarations, your findings will always remain suspect."

With that the ad hoc meeting in the garden adjourned, leaving the Professor now alone and isolated, his work seriously marginalized. And so the debate and eventual censure had proceeded. Whereas once he had been touted, even highly sought after for his erudite opinions, lately he had had to endure the disfavor and criticism from those of his chosen field. Now, in many ways even worse, he felt he was being abandoned by his own son. He felt the unspoken criticism in his averted eyes and the agitated way in which he paced about the room.

Wes raised his head, slowly retook his seat and gazed directly at his father. "Dad, I love you and respect you, we all do, but this line of research you have embraced has brought you the criticism of those whom you respect the most. At the end of the day, it will only be conjecture and opinion, without basis on any solid, scientific body of work. It will marginalize your life's work by turning you into a raving, conspiracy nut!"

The Professor closed his eyes, trying with difficulty to slow the rapid beat of his heart for a moment before responding. He knew Wes had not intended to be so judgmental, but it was clear the events of the past few years had left him bitter and hurt with those choices which had led to his wife and daughter's own defection from his side. Bedford opened his eyes reluctantly and softly declared with less warmth than usual, "I understand your concerns with my work and you do have my blessing to pursue any field of educational interest you desire." His voice rose with a conviction that seemed, even to his own ears, more rehearsed than truthful. "No matter how much evidence I have recently uncovered to support my theories, I do admit that I may now lack the solid evidence, but I am hopeful of a significant breakthrough soon." Bedford made note of the look of resignation on the face of his son.

Scarcely more needed to be said, but before Wes left the office, both father and son arose from their chairs and embraced, though the embrace was hesitant and strained and felt uncomfortable rather than familiar. It was tragic, Bedford reflected, that my work had been misunderstood as an obsession which had brought such a rift between me and those who loved me the most. He watched from the window as his son walked slowly to the driveway. Had Wes detected a cry of desperation in my voice, he asked himself?

It was mild that afternoon in Northern Israel as Professor William Bedford stepped out of the taxi onto a quiet street a few blocks from the bustling market district of the ancient city of Akko, adjacent to the modern city of Haifa. Immediately, the scent of fresh, exotic produce assailed his senses and the aroma, coupled with this visit to the Holy Land, evoked old memories and left him reminiscent. At that time he was doing research for a new book on ancient Biblical scripture written in the Old Aramaic language, and his recollection of the year he and his family had spent in Israel nearly a decade ago had returned unbidden to haunt the present.

His son Wesley, though only fourteen, was even then a gifted young scholar and loved to assist him in the work. The Professor was once again reminded of his son and the disappointingly strained goodbye of three months earlier. There had been scarcely any attempt to reach one another since that day; only short, terse conversations over the phone were now the norm. "If only Wes were here", he muttered. Yes, Wesley would understand and my colleagues would see that my devotion to this cause was justified.

His presentiment was unaccountably strong that this encounter today would change his path and destiny forever. As he hurried to meet his appointment at one of the area's many antiquity shops, he pondered the whirlwind events of the last week. A phone call had awoken him early on Tuesday morning. The persistent ringtone of his phone would normally have driven back his dream state and immediately lift him out of his sleep, but, lately he had been putting in long days and late hours compiling his latest paper for publication, consequently by the time he had retired for the day, he was mentally exhausted and twisted with excitement over recent discoveries. He was about to let the call go to the voice mail when a premonition that something of an unusual nature was about to occur in his life. The Professor had had some experience with these occasional insights and had never regretted following them in the past. So, now fully awake and alert, he reached out to the phone, and using the voice recognition software of his cell, he opened up the connection for the incoming call.

"Hello"? Bedford asked, but somehow he knew what was coming. The impression came to him so fiercely he was momentarily taken back at its strength. *"The time has come"*, he thought.

As if the caller had decided to prolong the experience for the Professor, there was a slight pause on the other end of the line. In retrospect, probably to give him more time to fathom the depth of the event, Bedford decided that was indeed the case. The male voice commented forthrightly,

"Professor William Bedford, we have never met, but I assure you that I am quite familiar with your current work. Moreover, I have in my possession a unique set of ancient writings written on metal plates."

The Professor could detect the pause for effect and could not resist a near audible sigh himself. The caller must have taken that as an acknowledgment, so he pressed on. "The workmanship is quite curious and the language may predate Sumerian, so if you are interested, perhaps we can meet soon and discuss terms of acquisition?"

Professor Bedford heard the sentence inflected as if expecting an assent of approval. Bedford, usually a cautious man and reluctant to accept things at face value, perceived immediately the portent of what was being described by the caller. Nonetheless, some manner of caution was expected and would lend credibility to the conversation, therefore he asked, "Sir, may I know your name and how you know that I would be interested in such a relic?"

The caller paused only a moment and responded, "Professor Bedford, for the purpose of our introductions today, let me simply introduce myself as Benjamin Jasher, an antiquities dealer now living in Haifa, Israel. As to the other, let me assure you that after following your work over the past two years, it is now obvious that you are ready to make the connections you are seeking."

The Professor had a few matters to tie up before he could leave for Israel, but, now intrigued as well as excited, replied, "I can be at your shop by the end of the week. Let us decide on a day and a time, and of course, I will need to know the location of your shop." After agreeing upon the details of the meeting, each exchanged a brief note of salutation then the two men disconnected their lines. Bedford was now fully awake, so after hanging up, he immediately got out of bed and began making preparations for the day. He phoned his office on campus and notified the office aide to post his classes then clear his schedule for the remainder of the week.

As he hung up, a surveillance officer at a central command center in Bethesda, Maryland made a note of the call and relayed the information onward to an Agency office in Washington D.C. James Perkins read the information with increased interest, and after some deliberation, notified a subordinate then later a team was dispatched to follow the professor to Haifa.

Chapter 2 – Benjamin Jasher, the Key

Three things cannot be long hidden: the sun, the moon, and the truth.

----- Budha

So, it had begun with a phone call and now he was standing in front of the door of Benjamin Jasher, Dealer of Antiquities. Professor Bedford reveled in such shops and he was scarcely mid-way through the doorway before the aroma of age beset him with impressions of Man's work suspended in time, now waiting to be unveiled. It was nearing the end of another work day and the man behind the counter was in a serious discussion with a customer. The Professor immediately recognized the voice from the phone conversation of a few days previous, and seeing he had a few minutes before he met the proprietor, he used the time to study the man at some length. Benjamin Jasher was slightly taller in height than most men with a handsome, slightly aquiline nose, tanned face, greenish-blue eyes and light brown hair. Though the man was clearly younger than most antiquities dealers he had known, he commanded a presence at once cultured and intellectual and had an air of authority to which many men strive, but only a few ever achieved. His bearing seemed almost, but not quite, military and he gave the impression of one incredibly self-assured and poised beyond his obvious years. His posture was relaxed, even unconcerned, by the customer's declarations of doubt over the authenticity of a relic he was attempting to buy. Apparently, Mr. Jasher eschewed the fine art of haggling.

Bedford had been to Akko several times over the years doing research, but was unable to recall ever seeing this shop nor did he recognize the proprietor. Like most leaders in any field of endeavor, he prided himself on his knowledge of all those moving in his world, albeit he was puzzled at this lack of personal recognition. Clearly, Professor Bedford thought, he would have remembered him; his style and demeanor were so compelling.

While waiting for the conversation between the proprietor and customer to conclude, the Professor strolled about the room examining the relics on display. Here was no dusty clutter of ancient knick-knacks laid about helter-skelter. After a few minutes of examination of a few articles and a cursory glance about the room, he was struck by the absolute lack of randomness of the display of objects as a whole, as though each had been collected with a common theme in mind. This was no ordinary shop and the owner was obviously no ordinary dealer of authentic relics mingled with Middle-eastern, garage-sale junk. Professor Bedford was pondering over this certainty when he felt a presence approach quietly from behind him. Apparently, negotiations with the customer had come to a conclusion and the man had decided to take his business elsewhere. Without turning he knew it would be the inimitable dealer of antiquities, Benjamin Jasher.

As Bedford turned, Jasher extended his hand of greeting and said, "Thank you for coming Professor Bedford and welcome to my shop. It gives me great satisfaction and relief, I might add, at finally being able to meet you personally."

"He had said "relief". What an odd phrase to use!" thought the Professor. "Mr. Jasher, the pleasure is all mine." replied Bedford. While he continued to speak, his eyes moved around the room and he commented, "I must say I am deeply impressed by your shop. I have travelled the world over and never have I seen an array of items as arresting and uniquely thematic as yours. I trust this was no accident?"

Still firmly clasping William's hand, Jasher's gaze was penetrating as he stated, "There is seldom much about history that is accidental. Would you not agree, Professor Bedford?" At this statement, a slight electric shot wound its way up Bedford's arm.

Something ephemeral, yet undeniably penetrating had passed between the two men, an affirmation of something more than simple, mutual interest or curiosity. Bedford had a premonition that being here with this charismatic, charming man would be the beginning of the discovery of ancient truths he had long sought. "Mr. Jasher, I would indeed agree." With a slight smile the Professor took his left hand and placed it over the clasped hands and gave a slight squeeze. Smiling, Jasher released his grip. It had been so long, thought Bedford, since I have felt anything like that. Reluctantly, Professor Bedford released his grip as well.

"Please excuse me", Jasher politely murmured. He walked over to the door and locked it, flipped around the OPEN sign then pulled down the shades. Now that he and the Professor were alone, Jasher beckoned the Professor toward a closed door then directed, "Please follow me to my office in the back."

With an inner excitement as well as curiosity, Professor Bedford allowed Jasher to escort him to his office in the rear of the shop. On the way he was unable to resist admiring the works of art. Without exception, his collection of delicately honed sculptures and ancient relics appeared unmarred by time and were evident throughout the room. It was amazing; everything he saw was in pristine condition as though each had just been completed by some long ago artisan. Notwithstanding, the musty smell of age still permeated the shop. It was simply a contradiction, yet here it was, he concluded.

Though it should have come as no surprise, the office was immaculate. Undoubtedly, Jasher was a person of controlled outward manner which reflected in all his movements and decisions. The apparel he wore that was tailored precisely and stylishly to fit his trim build exuded confidence and credibility. By comparison, wearing his own hastily arranged and out-of-date, off the rack suit, Professor Bedford felt himself unsophisticated and frumpish. Now in the presence of this man, he suddenly sensed it imperative that Jasher should think of him more highly than he now thought of himself. He felt more like a humble applicant seeking his first appointment and being kept waiting before the Head of the Science Department. Feeling thus self-conscious, he decided to wait to hear what Jasher had to say before he spoke.

Jasher signaled Bedford to be seated in front of an immense, dark oak escritoire of exquisite design and workmanship. Bedford must have conveyed a sense of reticence and anxiety, so instead of seating himself behind the desk, Jasher smoothly lifted a chair of matching size and quality and sat to one side of him. Now removing any barriers to their conversation, he ensured they both sat comfortably as though equals. He clasped his hands comfortably before him on his lap and said, "Professor Bedford, you have come a long way and a man of your obvious reputation will have much to do, so I won't waste any more time than necessary to deliver my message and my gift."

"A gift?" Bedford asked himself. He was under the impression that this was to be an acquisition and having observed the exquisite condition of the other relics in the shop, he doubted that Jasher would deal in anything other than an object untarnished by time and the price would be dear. The Professor made a note of this last bit of information relating to a gift and his heart skipped a beat at its mention. "Mr. Jasher, I don't know why I should feel this way, but I sense you have something to teach me and though it has been some time since I was in that position, I feel inclined to listen and be taught. So, please take your time. I am intrigued."

After a moment, as if to decide the best way to commence, Jasher looked directly at Bedford and asked, "Professor, are you familiar with the so-called lost books of the Bible?"

Bedford smiled inwardly as he finally got the jape between what Jasher was asking and his own surname, Jasher. His name was obviously a jest and only added more mystery to the man. Who was he really? Wishing to avoid offense by appearing flippant, but clearly wanting to impress his host, replied, "Do you make reference, for example, to obscure passages in the Book of Joshua, Chapter 10 and the Book of 2nd Samuel, Chapter 1?" Bedford was unable to resist a slight smile as he cited the connections to the references to Jasher.

Jasher seemed pleased by the response. "I see you know your Old Testament and have understandably arrived upon my little pun." Trying to reassure the Professor, he continued, "It was never meant as a deception, you know, but it is the name I have carried for many years now. The Biblical references are obscure and no one has bothered to ask, so I have never had a reason to admit the connection. That is, until now."

Professor Bedford recalled his own study of these obscure passages in the Old Testament as they are referenced today. The Lost Books of the Bible are those documents that are mentioned in the Bible in such a way that it is evident they were considered authentic and valuable, but that are absent in the Old Testament as it is viewed today. Sometimes known as missing scripture, the Bible makes reference to the Books of Benjamin the Seer, Gad the Seer, Nathan the Prophet and The Book of Jasher, among others.

To Bedford, Jasher appeared quite comfortable and confident as he pressed on with his message. "So, Professor, you would agree then, that there have been writings that have been mentioned in the Bible, but are omitted from Biblical canon as now written?" After Bedford's nodding assent, Jasher continued, "Does it sound unreasonable to hope that not only will this missing scripture be found someday, but perhaps even new documents may be discovered which have never been mentioned in the Bible at all? Professor, I would appreciate hearing your opinions on this matter."

An expression of both wonder and surprise registered now on the Professor's face, however he agreed, "I suppose these newly discovered scriptural documents could shed light on the missing pieces of history and doctrine which seem to be referenced in the Old Testament. Nonetheless, many would consider our current canon to be holy as well as complete as it is now written, but I, for one, find brief comfort at being told that the mysteries and unexplained miracles of the Old Testament are there to test our faith. To me, a miracle is simply an undiscovered truth waiting to burst forth. There is a time to exercise faith, but only after all avenues of discovery for the truth have been examined. In my thirty-two years of study, research and teaching, I have ever sought to bring forth the absolute truth."

Jasher nodded imperceptibly, and said, "For this reason have I reached out to you after so many years of carrying this burden on my own. You, Professor Bedford, have been chosen to assist in the translation and bringing forth of an ancient document which I will call and make reference to henceforth as *The Abridgement*."

The Professor was intrigued, bordering on excited, by what he had just heard, however, he knew from experience that there would be much work ahead in authenticating any such record before he even attempted the work of translation, much less its final publication. Notwithstanding, curiosity had got the better of him and anticipation at viewing the relic was now uppermost in his mind. Before he examined the artifact, however, there was something Jasher had mentioned which would need to be clarified as to the origin of the book and the person who was now in possession of it. "This *Abridgement*, as you call it, does it by any chance make reference to *The Book of Jasher* as is mentioned in the Old Testament?"

The dealer of antiquities steepled his fingers as if considering his answer. He replied, "The mention made in the Old Testament of *The Book of Jasher* refers to a personal volume of historically correct events written by a man some considered to be a holy man or prophet. The artifact in my possession represents an abridgement of many records written many years before and since that book, including historical observations made by the same Jasher. So, in some respects, they are one in the same."

Professor Bedford nodded his understanding of the distinction and his interest was etched clearly across his face. Jasher silently arose from his seat and walked toward an armoire in the corner of the room. At the cabinet, he was careful to ensure his back was to the Professor while his fingers played over the side of the closet. A tiny switch was located and depressed which allowed a small door to swing outward slightly, now allowing apparent entrance to the contents. He opened the door, but Bedford could clearly see that it was still bare inside. Jasher found, yet, another small switch on the other side of the armoire, depressed it, revealing finally the contents he was looking for.

Professor Bedford's brow creased slightly as he was momentarily taken back by this latest discovery. A false wall had been built into the back of the cabinet. Apparently, Jasher not only felt the need to keep this treasure within his reach, but likewise took great pains to ensure its security, even if the security he used seemed more mysterious than assured.

Jasher carefully pulled out a medium sized wooden object that was similar in design to the Qajar wooden box of the Tabriz Museum in Iran, but was considerably larger. As he sat the box down in front of the Professor, Bedford's mind registered the ornately colored and lacquered characters of Azerbaijan royalty. While Bedford gazed on in wonder at the singular beauty of the artifact, he wondered where Jasher had acquired it. The box had two hinges on the side so as to allow the top of the box to be swung upward, thus revealing its contents within.

The Professor arose from his seat and bent over the box now on the desk, waiting for Jasher to complete this process. As though anticipating Bedford's evident interest, he swung open the box and within was a solid, square-like object covered with an oil cloth for protection. He lifted the object tenderly out of the box, still covered by the protective cloth, and placed it carefully upon the desk. Ensuring that no harm came to the object, he removed the cloth covering fastidiously, revealing a bright, untarnished metal artifact with metal leaves, each connected to rings as you would see a book binder, thus allowing the leaves to be turned without taking them out of the relic.

"Mr. Jasher", stammered the Professor, "of what metal is this object? It appears to be gold, but can it be brass?" Jasher must have anticipated Bedford's obvious need to touch the plates. He handed him surgical gloves allowing him to touch then carefully turn a few leaves of the book without marring it in any way. The Professor knew from his experience and metallurgical research that compositions of early brass objects are an alloy of copper and zinc and most of the early relics usually have zinc contents of between 5% and 15% of the weight. If this object were truly brass with such a glossy shine, then the zinc content would have to be much higher, which would result in a distinctive golden color. Moreover, he reflected, it would explain its untarnished, non-corrosive condition.

"Professor Bedford," explained Jasher, "the object is made of a high quality brass smelted and designed by an artisan of exemplary skill and dedication." He quietly added, "I hesitate, for the present time, to refer to him by name, but he was truly a master at his craft, unequaled in his day. My gift to you this day is not the object you see, but an opportunity to carefully study and translate it first-hand. As you will see, it is unequalled by comparison to any other artifact you have ever examined."

The Professor noted the degree of respect in Jasher's voice at his mention of this now long-deceased craftsman. There were so many questions he had for this unusual man and vowed to ask them all, but now, with anticipation, Professor Bedford began examining the cuneiform characters written on the brass leaves. The characters were similar of the Sumerian-Akkadian type, yet different. With dawning realization, he comprehended two things immediately: that these cuneiform characters predated anything he had ever examined and that he was going to need assistance or perhaps a key to translate these characters accurately. Obviously, he could draw from his current understanding of ancient Sumerian, but he would have to use either some reverse-extrapolation process to make some sense of these more ancient characters or he would need to work with someone with the right background. The accuracy would be suspect until he had completed a long process of re-editing and cross verification by others in his field;

barring this, the process would be extremely costly in time. He raised his head and looked directly at his host to explain this, but before Bedford could relay his initial reactions, Jasher related, "I should inform you that the translation of the writings needs to be completed as expeditiously as possible."

The Professor began hesitantly: "Mr. Jasher, the characters appear to be authentic Sumerian, but…" he paused as if to add more. "They predate anything that I or any of my colleagues have ever examined or translated and without a key or the assistance of someone already well versed in the language, the process of translation will be long and tedious."

Jasher must have anticipated the inherent difficulties to which Bedford had pointed out, so he said, "Sir, it so happens that I have a special means to assist you with this project. Before today I would have been reluctant to reveal this, but the time has come for the world to discover and know the contents of this book. And I can ill afford to have the records in the open for any protracted length of time."

Professor Bedford was grateful for the intuition of this man and it appeared that both were anxious to begin this work. "Thank you, sir, and this special means?" pressed the professor, now happy that this could be provided.

Benjamin Jasher, antiquities dealer, slowly bowed and with a slight smile, revealed, "Professor Bedford, I am the key, the authority that you seek".

Chapter 3 – The Escape

There are only two mistakes one can make along the road to truth; not going all the way, and not starting.

----- *Budha*

Skopos theory is the process of translation that focuses on translation as an activity with an aim or purpose, and on the intended addressee or audience of the translation. The idea of this process of translation is to produce a target text in a target setting for a target purpose for target recipients given target circumstances. One has to look at the offering of source information which the translator turns into as an offer of information for the target audience.

Paul Kussmaul writes about a functional approach to this theory: "the functional approach has a great affinity with Skopos theory. The function of a translation depends on the knowledge, expectations, values and norms of the target readers, again influenced by the situation they are in and by the culture. These considerations determine whether the function of the source text or passages in the source text can be preserved or have to be modified or even changed."

Professor Bedford was quite familiar with the *Skopos* method of translation. Therefore, much consideration would have to be given to how the target audience might receive the rendering. The biggest challenge to the actual translation, though, thought Bedford, was insuring the original text was translated in a way that the writer had intended. The closer the translator could come to the intention to the original writer, the truer the translation. Jasher had mentioned that he was the key. *"What does that mean?"* he asked himself. The Professor knew that the time had come to get answers to some of the questions that had been troubling him about this man.

"Mr. Jasher, you will need to explain what you mean by you being the *key*. Moreover", the Professor added, "I should like to know more about the man that declares he is the *key*."

Jasher sat back comfortably in his seat and proceeded to explain. "Professor Bedford, I am well versed in the language that these ancient characters represent. I have made it my life's work to maintain a study of several ancient languages, including this one, and that makes me imminently qualified to introduce this material. Furthermore," he added, "I have spoken it".

"Spoken it with whom?" Bedford responded incredulously.

"With many and over a period of many years", Jasher replied.

"Mr. Jasher," responded the Professor slowly and reasonably, "I don't doubt your intellect nor your dedication to this work, but what I doubt is your years of expertise which you declare to have. Sir, how could someone as youthful as yourself have achieved so much in such a short period of time and without drawing the attention of the scholars of the world? Undoubtedly, these same scholars would have been your teachers and mentors, a short list I can assure you. I would no doubt have known many of them personally yet I have never heard of you before our meeting today."

Jasher remarked agreeably, "Professor, I understand your reluctance to believe me, but you must understand that, in spite of my visible youth, I am well versed in this language, therefore the translation will be an accurate and true rendering. If it will ease your mind, I will state simply that men of my father's lineage are long-lived and don't appreciably age the way others do. Thus, I am much older than I appear. I began my studies well before the turn of the last century. And that should be sufficient explanation for now."

With some effort, Professor Bedford attempted to reign in the surprise look of doubt he felt was clearly visible on his face. He was, in fact, attempting to appease his host and encourage further explanations, so he replied with what he hoped was a reasonable smile. "If you are so knowledgeable regarding this language, why do you need me? Couldn't you just as easily translate it yourself?"

Benjamin Jasher reflected over the hours he had spent the last few weeks preparing for this moment. Thus, when the time had come to answer the questions Professor Bedford had directed him, he had realized he had anticipated many of them, but after so many years of maintaining his secrets, he still felt a reluctance to be completely forthcoming. Yet, he was still left with the decision of how much to tell him now: too much too soon and it might leave the Professor overly skeptical; being too cautious with too little information and it might affect his commitment and neither must occur. So, with this dilemma in his mind, Jasher closed his eyes for a moment in quiet meditation, and began the process of seeking guidance and receiving answers. After analyzing both sides of the dilemma, he came to a decision. Once he had made a decision, he waited for the sure answer to come as it always had so many times before. The confirmation was seldom long in coming and this time was no exception. A palpable peace of mind came over him and he now knew what had to be done.

His voice was apologetic as he explained, "Professor I know I appear overly cautious and what must seem to you to be melodramatically mysterious. Once we begin our work and you understand the scope of our endeavor, however, you will quickly understand why, for safety and security reasons, I must be careful and circumspect in all my actions. Even now, after so many years of waiting for this day and when I know you are clearly the one to whom I have been guided to reach out with this project, it still gives me anxiety to reveal this message. Sir, I am in the way of knowing you are ready to hear the truth, all of it and everything about me. What you are about to hear may seem incredible and entirely ludicrous to much of the world at large. I assure you if you are ready to receive the truth, you shall hear it."

Jasher noted Professor Bedford now appeared attentive and anxious. He felt the nerve endings thrumming throughout his body as though his spirit were alive and demanding to share something unseen, hidden by time.

"Please proceed", Bedford whispered.

"Sir, as I am sure, you are familiar with the Biblical story of Adam and Eve. They had many sons and daughters, but the three sons I wish to talk about are, indeed, revealed in the abridgement before you: Cain, Abel his younger brother, and Seth. Seth was, of course, the son with whom Adam and Eve were blessed following the murder of Abel at the hands of Cain. From the beginning, Adam was given the responsibility of writing the history of his family. Later, and now being very old with age, Adam called Seth to his side and turned this responsibility over to him with an added charge: it was to keep an accurate record of all the actions of his elder brother Cain and the impact that his nefarious influence would have over future generations and the civilizations of Man. The time would eventually come when he, Seth, would deliver his records over to the next in his lineage and the process of recording these events would continue. The writings that we now have in the Old Testament of the Holy Bible represent a different type of recording; they were religious or instructional guidelines. Nevertheless, this additional calling of recording these other events was primarily of an historical nature. Seth was a holy man empowered with a holy calling and as such, was permitted to live much longer than the Bible suggests. This was done to ensure a continuity and clarity of observations by one person alone. As a translator, you should know how much simpler the process can be when only one person is involved with the writing of the original source text."

Jasher continued, "Some years before the Great Flood, Seth delivered all of these historical records to Lamech, father of Noah. The records contained incriminating evidence of Cain's influence in the decline of civilization down through the time of Lamech, just prior to the Great Flood. Lamech was put under solemn oath to ensure these historical records would be maintained and that only he and Noah, his son, would be aware of them until a time and place designated by the Creator. Eventually, Lamech was directed to deliver these records to a safe location and he hid them up in a mountain vault. What eventually became of Seth, I doubt even Lamech knew precisely except to say that he was "caught up in the spirit and was seen no more by anyone."

"Following the Flood, life began again and Noah and his wife, his sons and their wives had many sons and daughters. Noah, a holy man, was instructed to locate one of his descendants born following the Flood and entrust him with the records and this sacred responsibility of carrying on the work of Seth. Professor, I am Jasher, great-grandson of Noah. I am one of the few select record keepers and chroniclers of the fall of all civilizations since the time of Noah, my great-grandfather. Are you willing to assist me with this project?"

Jasher watched as Professor Bedford listened to the last of this revelation and was unsurprised as he physically recoiled at the possibility of what he was hearing, but he sensed that because of the strength of his declaration,

Bedford's doubts may have been minimized. He noted the Professor had difficulty articulating his feelings, but patiently awaited his response.

With obvious distress, Bedford found the words and said, "Jasher, I hope I may now call you that, I feel overwhelmed by what you have said and wonder that I can be equal to the task at hand, but, of course I accept." With a slight grin, he added, "Regardless of your brash claim of being the great-grandson of Noah, assuming it was authentic, you may very well have the hidden answers to the puzzle I have sought for so long and should be contained in this record." Though the excitement could be easily detected on Bedford's face, Jasher knew there were still many questions he had for him.

Jasher now felt a rush of relief that his inspired intuition about this man had been realized. "Professor I have come to present my work to you, a man having influence in the world of science, who can give credibility to the historical message of this book. You are a known figure, and because of this, the world will have to take notice. Sir, so that you may grasp the importance of what we will be doing, please permit me to outline to you our roles in this endeavor. This must appear before the world that you have acquired a document of ancient origin from an antiquities dealer who wishes to remain anonymous and you will be completing the task of translation yourself, all of which is true. You have hired me to ensure the safety of all those involved, including the records, and to oversee all aspects of security. With your permission and without giving offense, I will be staying with you at your residence to best provide these services. Once the authentication process of the records is complete, we will begin translation in earnest. As soon as the translation has been rendered and all editing has been completed, we will secure a reputable publishing house for publication."

Professor Bedford slowly nodded his head as if in agreement and replied, "Jasher, assuming you don't mind the usual clutter of a scientist who performs most of his work from his study, of course, you will be welcome in my home. But, might this be better handled by playing down the security end so as to give our project the appearance of a natural, normal translation process? I have never had problems of security before, so why draw undue attention?"

Jasher seemed to consider what Bedford had said and being careful neither to appear overly dramatic nor critical responded, "I can assure you that this degree of security is equal to the importance of the project. As you have no experience with the confrontations of dedicated malevolence as I have, I can assure you that once certain parties learn of what we are translating, they will spare no expense or effort to block our work. These persons have considerable resources at their disposal, not only from business circles, but from religious and social societies as well. Allow me to explain what they may do: the first step will be to attempt to discredit your work and marginalize your past successes; they will then try to vilify you by attacking your personal life, especially vulnerable will be your relationship with your family; if they cannot convince you to abandon this project altogether, then you can expect threats of personal harm to your family and finally, they will inflict bodily harm on you and those you love. Believe me, I know of what I speak."

Jasher could imagine how difficult this project would appear to someone who was accustomed to a more sedate life-style. Gone was the initial excitement of acquiring a new, remarkable document to translate and to begin a watershed project for his career. His enthusiasm would now acquire a bitter taste and he would wonder if this endeavor would be worth the personal risk that had just been described, but Jasher knew that total honesty at this point was prudent and necessary if they were to move forward in this collaboration. Jasher, reading the now troubled look in the Professor's face added, "Professor, please understand that this undertaking will be dissimilar to any work you have ever accomplished in the past. Any past roadblocks to your advancement or criticisms you may have had to endure early or even later in your career will not begin to measure up to what you are now likely to face. I will assure you, however, that you will never be alone. This work is far too important and I will be using all the considerable resources I have to keep us one step ahead of the opposition. We will succeed, but only if we can avoid underestimating the dedication of our enemies."

Jasher glanced down at his watch and noticed the time for their departure was growing near. Until now, he had refrained from alerting the man to the escape, but now seemed the prudent time. "Professor, this may appear abrupt, but it is necessary. Since you have accepted this collaboration, we now must remove ourselves with the records and depart the city." Jasher calmly arose and replaced the records back into the protective box. He turned with the box in his arms, pushed the cabinet aside and opened a concealed door directly behind it. He realized that his movements appeared more to the effect of an episode of a classic *cine noire* movie, but time was running out and the records were now officially out in the open.

"Jasher, what is happening here?" Bedford exclaimed.

He explained quickly, though apologetically, "I am sorry Professor, but we must now make good our escape." With that he led Bedford down a short hallway to an alley in back of the store. They then crossed the alleyway into what appeared to be the back of a deserted shop, whereupon Jasher quickly unlocked the door and the two men slipped into the dark without notice from anyone in the alley. A moment later, he pulled a cell phone from the inside pocket of his jacket, opened a connection and whispered a number to be dialed. A voice on the other end answered with one phrase, "code word". Jasher, without hesitation, whispered in response, "Jericho". He then quickly broke off the connection, dropped the cell phone then crushed it under the heel of his shoe. The two men continued through the deserted shop and through what appeared to be at least two other similar stores, equally dark, to the street beyond that led to a bustling market place.

After quickly blending in with shoppers and venders alike, they finally emerged on the other side of the market where three cars were parked and awaiting them. They slid into the back seat of the middle SUV and all three drivers sped off in three different directions. Their car took an incredibly circuitous route through the city then, at one point, another car suddenly pulled in directly behind them. As if expecting it, the driver of Jasher's car quickly registered the identity of the unknown car. He then nodded to his partner in the passenger side and said only three words: "It's Perkins' men".

The other man ordered, "Find a quiet alley and do it quickly!"

The driver sped up then quickly turned the next corner into an alleyway while the other man on the passenger side jerked opened his door and rolled out onto the street just inside the alley. With Benjamin Jasher and William Bedford still safely in the back seat, the lead car never stopped and raced on in the gloaming darkness of sunset. A few moments later, automatic gunfire could be heard and a sudden explosion rocked the intersection inside the alley from where they had just driven.

Dov Hacohen was ex-Mossad and highly trained in matters relating to what he and his comrades would describe as *smash-and-grab*. The principles had been collected and now it was his job to ensure they arrived to their destination safely. When the Agency car had pulled in behind them from a side street, he had immediately readied himself to take the offensive, so, after the driver turned the corner into the alleyway, he had jerked the door open and rolled out onto the alley then pulled up to a firing position. He found a nearby dumpster on the corner to brace himself against the backlash concussion of the Tavor-2 9mm and unloaded on the chase car as it went into the turn through the alley. Another of Hacohen's SUV's pulled in behind the chase car, blocking the exit and snaring the chase car in a cross-fire. Two men from the SUV exited and began firing from the rear.

Perkins' men in the chase car were suddenly riddled with the impact of the shells of Hacohen's automatic weapon from the front and his team's weapons from the rear. While glass blew out of the side windows, both men in the front seat were ripped apart by the 9mm bullets. The driver, his arms and head now a mass of blood, lost control and plowed into a nearby wall. Sensing some movement in the back seat as he was racing by, Hacohen pulled out a fragmentation grenade from his belt and rolled it under the remains of the bullet-riddled car. Immediately, he and his other two men returned to the waiting SUV and just as he closed the door of their car, Dov noticed the chase car containing Perkins' detail was ablaze from the ignited fuel from the assault and subsequent crash. As Hacohen's SUV backed down the street, half the alleyway was consumed with exploding grenade fragments that blew out and flipped Perkins' chase car over to its side. Hacohen, now driving the second car, led the race to the Haifa airport to provide cover support for the car containing the principles.

Until now, Professor Bedford had never in his life experienced a moment that he worried for his personal safety. His heart was beating much too quickly and he worried that his ex-wife might have been correct about his weight and lack of exercise. Everything had happened too quickly to make much sense of it all, but he knew that his life was in danger for the first time. He had heard the automatic fire and had turned to witness the explosion and subsequent billow of fire and smoke so the reality of his brush with death was undeniable.

Five minutes later the van containing Jasher and Professor Bedford pulled up onto the tarmac of a small corporate airport. Up ahead they could see a Learjet being prepped for departure. Jasher and Bedford quickly exited the van and made their way up the ramp to the awaiting plane and within minutes they were airborne. A few minutes after take-off, the cover vans squealed to a halt on the tarmac. Hacohen quickly pulled out his phone, and watching the plane's departure, speed-dialed a number then relayed two words "extraction complete" to his remaining detail covering the back door to the airport.

They were thirty minutes out of Haifa when Professor Bedford, still clearly shaken from their hasty departure from Israel, turned to Jasher from his seat and asked the obvious question: "Jasher, what in heaven's name happened back there?"

"Professor Bedford, those were the forces I was telling you about," Jasher explained. "It was a bit dicey back there, but I assure you that at no time were my men out of our sight."

"A bit dicey!" exclaimed Bedford. "That would be an understatement. Is life always like this with you?" The professor was starting to believe Jasher was a dangerous man to be around; at least that part of the story was thus far correct.

"It is only when the records are in the open, and fortunately they seldom are." He explained, "This is the reason I seldom take the risk of exposing them in this manner. Our observers, those who surveil me on a regular basis, got nervous when they were unable to account for our whereabouts. So, they foolishly tipped their hand and now they know that I know they are on our trail. It is a game of high stakes that I have had to play for many years now and without my security team I could never keep pace with these forces."

The professor had many more questions, but, assuming there weren't more altercations awaiting them in Austin, he reluctantly agreed that there would be time for them later. When the shock had worn off, the adrenalin rush he felt earlier during their mad rush through Akko and later in Haifa had left him unsurprisingly weary and exhausted; within moments he was asleep. Before he drifted off, however, he wondered if the enigmatic Benjamin Jasher could truly be that closely related to Noah, and if so what other surprises might lie ahead.

After making a few refueling stops along the way as well as making a change in planes for the transatlantic flight, Professor Bedford and Jasher finally arrived at a small corporate airport outside the city of Austin the next day. Jasher had mentioned he had considerable resources and he was as good as his word, for he had made a few phone calls and the box had passed through customs without delay. Accordingly, along with the box containing the brass plates, the two men arrived later that evening at the Bedford home in northwest Austin. Now rested from their travel and unusual departure from Haifa, both sat down in Bedford's office and began to discuss and plan out the next step in their collaboration.

Over the past twenty-four hours, Professor Bedford had pondered over several points he wished to discuss with Jasher. His restive posture indicated anxiety over what he might learn from his guest, but not withstanding his reluctance to probe, he carefully turned the conversation around to what had been bothering him the most. The Professor began his question hesitantly, "Mr. Jasher, there is one thing that you have mentioned which has concerned me since you revealed it." His curiosity and need to understand all aspects of this project were far from satiated.

As if reading Bedford's mind, Jasher spoke for him. "It's about my age, isn't it?"

Now grateful he was out of harm's way, Bedford's fear had gradually given way to curiosity, even perplexity over what Jasher had thus far revealed to him. He briefly smiled, slowly assented and replied, "Jasher, how is it that you claim to be so old and yet look scarcely middle age or, perhaps better put, how is it you could possibly be the great-grandson of Noah, the prophet in the Old Testament?"

"Professor, at the risk of seeming evasive, let me just say that the length of a man's life is relative to the man's mission in life. I am sure you have read in the Old Testament of those prophets who were considered, at least by the standards of today, as being long-lived. I can assure that those accounts were not the least bit exaggerated; Adam lived over nine hundred years, Methuselah nearly a thousand and yet there were many who could have and actually did live longer. There are varying reasons why this occurred, not the least of which was that mankind had been commanded literally to populate the earth and a short life span was simply not a practical way to bring this about, but the real reason may rest more with the needs of the Creator. It is my opinion that those same men who lived to a very old age had a very special mission which required a long life to accomplish a specific calling. Consequently, their days were lengthened to expedite that process. Since I, too, fall into that category, I can speculate with a high degree of certainty that the mission was the determining factor. I am long-lived because my calling requires it and that is all that needs to be said for the time being."

Bedford was still skeptical, but the man was convincing. He concluded, however, that if Jasher was exactly who he claimed to be, then those records would be authentic and his search for the answers to his questions were about to be provided. He would have to be patient, it would seem, until Jasher was prepared to share more of his colorful past.

Chapter 4 – The Consultant

*Great deeds give choice of many tales. Choose a slight tale,
enrich it large, and then let wise men listen.*

----- Pindar, Ancient Greek lyric poet

*Paleography is the study of ancient and historical documents, as well as
processes of handwriting. Sometimes included in the discipline is the practice of
deciphering, reading, and dating historical manuscripts. It can be an essential
skill for historians, as it addresses two main difficulties. First, since the style of
a single alphabet in each given language has evolved constantly, it is necessary
to know how to decipher its individual characters as they existed in various
eras. Second, scribes often used many abbreviations, usually so as to write more
quickly and sometimes to save space, so the specialist-paleographer must know
how to interpret them. The paleographer must know, first, the language of
the text and second, the historical usages of various styles of handwriting and
common writing customs. Moreover, the language, vocabulary, and grammar
generally used at a given time or place can help paleographers identify ancient
authentic documents.*

*Knowledge of writing materials is also essential to the study of handwriting
and to the identification of the periods in which a document or manuscript
may have been produced. An important goal may be to assign the text a date
and a place of origin. This is why the paleographer must take into account the
style and formation of the manuscript and the handwriting used in it.*

Jasher was well aware that for a process of translation of this magnitude
to be credible, the exhaustive verification of the material upon which the
text has been written would add authentication to the rendering of the
final translation. This would have to be considered and weighed against
the security of the project. Eventually, this would have to be accomplished,
but that phase would have to move forward more cautiously. Professor
William Bedford was well versed as an expert in his field of paleography
so he could make preliminary tests upon the records, but the project

required the services of trained technicians as well as an independent, yet respected linguist of ancient languages who could lend credibility to his latest endeavor.

Jasher pondered over what lay ahead, and after a few moments of quiet reflection, came to a decision. The time had come to outline the best approach to enlist the help of an independent scientist for authentication and translation of the writing on the plates. "Professor Bedford," he began, "this phase will be critical to the endeavor, but because it will be the only time the project will be completely exposed to anyone outside this room, it will likewise be the most dangerous. The selection of the consultant will have to be carefully considered. Only someone absolutely trustworthy that would avoid divulging the contents and the details of these records could be selected. If the consultant even inadvertently let slip any vital point prematurely, then the project would be compromised."

"Jasher," began Bedford, "I am not quite following you. You say that the project could now be compromised and yet we have scarcely begun the work?"

"William, at the risk of appearing paranoid, let me offer you a brief explanation of whom and what we are up against. There is a movement, an actual society, in our world which has existed for many centuries that is committed to prevent the account from *The Abridgment* from coming to light. This Society is the selfsame organization which you have been trying to identify for years in your research, but up until now have been unsuccessful at making the connections. Consequently, if I know the opposition, and I do, then they have already mobilized considerable forces to be on the alert. The leadership of this Brotherhood still only has pieces of the puzzle, but they are highly cunning and deductive and there is little, if anything, they will leave to chance."

Even after their wild ride thorough Haifa it was evident on Bedford's face that he remained unconvinced. "Are you sure we aren't being prematurely over-reactive about their understanding of our project at this stage?"

Jasher remarked, "Professor, please try to imagine a world in which one society turns the geopolitical forces in the palms of its hands. Regardless of which government or the level of government, a phone call is made and their bidding is immediately followed. They will want to undermine our project; Inconsequence, we must prevent them from gaining access to the information we translate or they will have it translated in a way that will suit their agenda then our translation will be deemed weaker by comparison and our message marginalized." Jasher was hesitant to appear overly concerned, but Bedford had the right to know how serious the opposition was. He advised, "Regardless of how careful we are, they are sure to be alerted when you meet your consultant, so you have to ensure that he will be the right one and he is well inclined to help us. Unless he is immediately disposed to commit to the project, once he is involved, he could easily be coerced or threatened to release the translation prematurely. If that should occur then our work would be invalidated."

Finally, after some discussion of possible candidates, both agreed that a Professor Isaac Levinson, now on staff at the local university, was the ideal consultant. He was not only well respected in his field of ancient languages, but he was an old colleague and friend of William Bedford. The two men had spent many years cultivating a lasting trust and friendship based on a knowledge and respect of the other's work. Isaac Levinson was American-born and a son of Rachel and Herschel Levinson, both immigrants and survivors of the European holocaust of World War II. He was a gifted linguist of several European languages, including Hebrew, which he learned at the knee of his grandfather, also a holocaust survivor. Both parents had been university linguists living in Warsaw at the outset of the War in 1939, so it was natural that they should instruct their only child in the art of languages. Educated at Harvard and later at Cambridge, Levinson was highly adept at understanding ancient languages and so was a natural selection for Jasher's project.

As Professor Bedford had known Levinson since his own days at Harvard and later Cambridge, he had set out to make an appointment to visit his old and trusted colleague. Given he had worked with him on several projects over the past thirty years, it was agreed he was a logical choice for the task and there was a good chance he would be amenable to approach, however, following the security protocol of Jasher, Bedford avoided using phones and computer mail to make his appointment. To this end, having known the campus office where Levinson worked, he seated himself under the hanging branches of an ancient live oak at a nearby bench to await his old friend and colleague and approach him in that manner. While Bedford sat expectantly near the path leading from Levinson's building, near noon, his old friend and colleague emerged from the building as if to eat lunch.

Professor Isaac Levinson bore a close resemblance to an actor, Herbert Lom, and indeed had known the actor personally in his youth. It was said that Levinson even had many of the actor's mannerisms. He was shorter than most men, but he carried the unmistakable bearing of an intellectual, professorial character, complete with slightly long hair and grey, bushy brows. He was seldom seen in public without a three-piece suit and conservative dark bow ties. He truly enjoyed the persona of the stereotypical old-school college academic. His wife, now deceased nearly two years, often commented on these affectations, but Isaac was always quick to point out that his students could hardly be expected to take him seriously unless he did also.

Bedford arose, and trying to be casual, approached Levinson and greeted him, "Isaac, my old friend, it's been far too long. How have you been?"

With a look of surprised recognition, Levinson replied genially with a smile, "William, it's been far too long, you look wonderful. I wish I could say the same for myself," he added with good natured levity. The two shook hands and embraced as old and dear friends will do.

"Isaac, we must talk." He looked around furtively as if to ensure their meeting on the common sidewalk had avoided undue attention. His eyes, now cautious, rested on Levinson and he added "Can I interrupt your lunch hour for a few moments and talk about a new project I am anxious to begin?"

"William, my dear friend, of course," responded Levinson immediately. Inwardly, Professor Levinson was more than just mildly intrigued by this chance meeting to discuss a project with his old colleague. It had been many months since their last discussion, no doubt due to Bedford's recent project. Isaac had heard rumors of Bedford's obsession lately and, of course, his recent divorce had been a topic that had found its way into many staff parties and lounge discussions of late. Nonetheless, Levinson reflected, the two of them had always enjoyed an open, relaxed relationship, but there was something circumspect, even guarded about William's manner today.

The two scientists retired to the same bench where Professor Bedford had been seated before. So, still a trifle tense, Bedford began to speak and after trading news of the other's family and other friendly amenities of career discussion, he appeared anxious, almost uncertain how to start.

Levinson, sensing his old colleague wanted to confide in him, but lacked the confidence to proceed, gently urged him to begin, "William, I am intrigued, please tell me about your latest project."

Jasher and Bedford had discussed the issue of how best to approach Levinson the night before. As security was of paramount concern for the project, it was agreed that only minimal information regarding the undertaking could be revealed until Levinson had agreed to a full commitment. "My dear Isaac", he began the story. Though he did omit the incredible information of Jasher's origin, and of course, the car-chase and narrow escape through the back streets of Akko and Haifa, he did report in broad strokes all that he had recently experienced. He went on to request the consultation and assistance of Professor Levinson with the process of authentication of the characters and plates. He declined to answer any specific questions from Levinson as to the description of the relic he had acquired. "Isaac, please understand that for reasons I am unable yet divulge, I must decline to provide any more information today. Would you be available to come by my home tomorrow morning and assist me? As you know, I have an extensive reference library to facilitate our process and render an honest evaluation, but please feel free to bring any references or materials you feel would be needed for the project."

Levinson, with enthusiasm, confided that he could clear his schedule for the next morning and arrive at Bedford's home around 9:00. The two men shook hands amiably then Bedford turned and strode away down the footpath toward the parking lot. Musing over the strangeness of this short encounter, Levinson sat back down and watched his friend's departure. William, usually quite loquacious and open about his work, was obviously reluctant to discuss anything about it except in general terms. Levinson brooded a few minutes and finally concluded that Bedford must have something extraordinary indeed or he would have been more willing to satisfy the curiosity of an old comrade.

In keen anticipation of viewing the relic to which William had alluded, Levinson arrived early before 9:00 the next morning and knocked on the door of the Bedford home. William greeted him warmly at the door and showed him directly to the study. On the way, Bedford reiterated his thanks to Levinson for coming and offering his expertise with this project. As Levinson entered the library cum study, he noticed seated to one side a rather tall, handsome man nearing middle age. As the man arose, Professor Bedford looked at his old friend and signaled to Jasher, formally introducing them. "Isaac, this is Benjamin Jasher. Turning to Jasher, he said, "Benjamin, it gives me pleasure to introduce my oldest friend and colleague, Isaac Levinson."

Jasher met Isaac half way and with a smile extended his hand of friendship. "Professor, Dr. Bedford has spoken of you so highly and so often I feel as though I already know you. Thank you so much for coming." Jasher then began commenting on some of Dr. Levinson's recent papers and made several extremely erudite points. Levinson, listening with a trained ear, prided himself on identifying regional dialects. Nonetheless, the urbane manner and cultured accent of the man he had just met had left him momentarily disconcerted; he had found it difficult to place the birth of origin. Though his accent was nearly flawless, English was definitely not his first language, he decided, but he was not continental European either. If he had to guess, he suppose he would have to conclude that the man Jasher was middle-eastern and probably Iranian because of his light Caucasian skin, though his eye color and facial characteristics were a mystery if he were Iranian. He was definitely not Slavic, he concluded, then what, Israeli, perhaps? And if that were true then he and his new acquaintance might have more in common than language.

Genially, Bedford said, "Isaac, please be seated and we will discuss our project". All three sat down and faced one another. Each settled in to their seats and as potential work companions will often do, they began measuring the other and anticipating how events would unfold.

During this brief pause, Jasher reflected back over the many years he had spent in his mission. Most times he felt fortunate to be so trusted to be one of the few historians of Man's civilizations. He had always gone where he was asked or felt there was a need and never questioned the reasons, but invariably, his assignments seldom brought anything more than disappointment. Each civilization had begun with the best intentions and ultimately had ended disastrously because of the same corrupting influence. Even when he was permitted to interject a modicum of sanity and hope, the rulers inevitably rejected it, and though were warned of the consequences, they preferred instead to choose their own short-sighted self-interests. The rights of the citizens to exercise their right of choice and self-determination were usually the first compromises that were made. Right up until the end, each ruler felt he could replace what had been lost, but before they could regain the advantage, assuming they were disposed and most were not, they had discovered the citizens were beyond caring. They were content to follow their leaders into the same pit of self-destruction, wallowing in their own ignorance. At such moments he was always reminded that it was not his assignment to call them to renounce their behavior; there were others assigned to do that. His was only to record the historical facts. Now finally, here he was at the end of times, yet nowhere near accomplished was this final labor.

As he had had so many confrontations with Levinson's ancestors over the centuries, Levinson, the Jewish scholar sitting opposite him contributed to the final irony. In spite of their moral values, Jewish leaders had shown a disappointing disposition towards insulating their people and encouraging non-involvement with social changes. What a waste, he thought, for they could have been a force and a voice for positive change and reason. In their defense, they had always argued that non-involvement was their only means of survival in a hostile world, so instead of actively reaching out to their communities, they buried themselves in their traditions and chose to remain a people apart. Ironically, that course of action had nearly annihilated them. Jasher knew Levinson as a Levite, a descendant of the keepers of the temple, highly versed in all the outward ordinances of those affairs. He hoped Levinson would prove useful in this last effort to halt the inevitable depraved influence he had seen and recorded time and time again. He felt strongly this civilization would be the last, and at long last, he had been permitted to reveal the entire workings of the Clan.

Levinson inclined his head toward the stranger and appraised the man once again. His charisma was unmistakable and clearly he leant a tone of significance to the meeting, but in what way? Musing, he wondered if Jasher was, indeed, his name or was it being used as an artful contrivance? Being a Biblical scholar, he knew of only one Jasher. He smiled inwardly and wondered if the man was putting them on, then concluded that he would undoubtedly explain himself in his own time.

Professor Bedford, as host, began to explain the scope of the project, including the part Jasher would play. Levinson, always a good listener, allowed his friend to complete his explanation of the facets of the project before he interjected a question. "William, I am honored to be a part of this endeavor," he began, ", but exactly how does *Mr. Jasher* fit into all of this?" He paused at the mention of Jasher's name and offered a brief smile.

Benjamin Jasher, ever one to intuit the feelings and intent of others, returned the smile to Professor Levinson and interjected, "Dr. Bedford, if I may, I would like to speak on my own behalf at this juncture." He inclined his head over to Levinson and said, "Benjamin Jasher is my name, though most of my life I have simply gone under the name of Jasher. As you have correctly deduced, Professor Levinson, my name is Biblical in its origin and I can testify without equivocation that I am descended from an ancient Hebrew tribe that proceeded from before the time of Isaac, your namesake. As our time together progresses, you will no doubt see the relevance of my name to the project."

By way of explanation of their proposed collaboration, he boldly stated, "Sir, I have provided you and Professor Bedford with a metallic manuscript upon which you will see ancient writings. While you two evaluate the relic and complete the process of authentication, I will be here to insure your interruptions and distractions are held to a minimum. I apologize in advance for what you may consider melodrama, but Professor Bedford and I both expect that this work will attract the attention of many persons, some of who are highly committed to preventing this discovery from seeing the light of day. For this reason it will be necessary to expedite the completion of our project. Dr. Levinson, I hope we may count on your discretion and forbearance until we have completed the process of translation and are ready for a full disclosure of this project to the world." There was no inflection in the man's voice signaling a question. It had been an emphatic statement of fact.

Professor Levinson, intrigued by what he had just heard and of course impressed beyond measure by the inimitable style of this younger man, assented, "Mr. Jasher, you and William may count on my discretion in this matter."

Now relieved Levinson had accepted their invitation, Professor Bedford arose from his seat then invited both men to his adjoining study. As they proceeded to enter, inside on the writing desk sat a box and within it a relic of curious workmanship upon which were written ancient characters that traced the early history of mankind.

With casual strides, Jasher walked around the desk and faced the other two men. He carefully lifted the plates out of the box, still covered with oilcloth, and placed the relic on the table. He uncovered the cloth and revealed the artifact within. Jasher pushed the brass records across the desk toward the two professors and quietly declared, "Professor Bedford, Professor Levinson, I present to you *The Abridgement*."

Chapter 5 – Callings

I believe God takes the things in our lives, family, background, education, and uses them as part of his calling. It might not be to become a pastor, but I don't think God wastes anything.

----- *Eugene H. Peterson*

Noah and his great-grandson, Jasher, walked along the valley floor in the cool of the evening. Their own land lay almost seven months to the west on foot and it had taken them nearly two days to find the northern pass that led through the mountains to the valley they sought. Over three hundred years had passed since the Flood and game had begun to reappear in multitudes. It was now common to see an abundance of deer and other wildlife feeding on the grasses and shrubs; it was a lovely place, full of spring flowers and trees of all types beginning to bloom. Nature, in all its myriad forms, had begun to prosper prolifically.

On both sides of the valley there was a long cordillera of mountains. The two men were arriving from the north and so they paid only brief notice that others inhabited the valley farther to the south. Notwithstanding, Noah knew they were there, but said nothing to Jasher. It was not time for him to become aware of them, but that day would come, perhaps much sooner than later. He would need to become aware of the records and those who had watched over them for so long. Noah could sense the forces of darkness already forming and shooting out their nefarious tentacles among men and it was for that reason that he had sought out his grandson and had made the arduous and tiring trek across the continent with him.

To the south and east Noah could see the mountain he sought. It had been many years, but he never doubted he would see it once again. Memories came rushing back to him as he became aware of the gentle slope of the mount as it connected with natural footpaths above the glacis. Eventually, with patience, the footpaths would lead them to an unusually curious cave near the apex. The cave was their destination and by tomorrow morning they would reach it. There lay the records of his fathers and there would they remain until the days of men were completed at a time many years in the future. His father, Lamech, as well as a distant kinsman, Seth, had begun storing them there since many years before the Great Flood. Before being taken by the flood waters, Lamech had not only bestowed a special charge to Noah to oversee and maintain them, but had been shown the location where they were to be deposited and stored.

Jasher, glancing over at Noah, suggested, "Grandfather, I am tired. Let us rest here and make our way up the mountain in the morning." He could have pushed easily on to the top, but he could see just how weary the old man was.

Noah had reached a point in age where he was still physically able to do move about with much difficulty, assuming he had sufficient rest, but he paid for it dearly by the end of the day. His feet and back were sore and he missed his bed; inconsequence, he realized that this trip would definitely be his last. He smiled, "Very well, Jasher, if we must. This is probably a better location than others. While I rest my aging bones, please find wood for our campfire." In reality, Noah understood on a primal level that he was being supported physically by the Creator. Indeed, his journey this far would have been impossible without it, but that help was dependent upon his exercising wisdom at the right moment. He intended to see this trip through to the end so he allowed Jasher to persuade him of the need for a stopping point for the evening.

Jasher had watched Noah grow wearier with each passing day, and as they trekked up the mountain on the morrow, he made a mental note to keep a close eye on him. He wasn't sure what would be found and still could not yet fathom its significance, but his grandfather had reassured him on several occasions that the journey had to be done and would directly affect him the rest of his life. That had been enough for Jasher, but regardless of the reasons involved, he realized that it was still a long, tedious journey for a man of his age.

After a light meal of bread and dried fruit, Noah fell immediately asleep. Jasher, still awake, and noting the curious game which had come to investigate the intrusion on their home, smiled in amusement at his grandfather's snores that had eventually frightened them away. He watched as the stars in all their glory appeared and wondered, hardly for the first time, if he would ever understand their movements. To punctuate his musings, a shooting star streaked across the night sky then after a few minutes, he too, fell into a deep sleep.

The climb up the mountain the next day had proven more arduous than Jasher had expected, but he observed that somehow Noah had found the strength to match him step for step. He didn't know where he had found the stamina, but perhaps it had something to do with the mission before them. He became aware of more spring in Noah's step that morning, but guessed that was just because of his excitement at being so close to the end of their journey. By the time they had reached the entrance of the cave, however, it was obvious to Jasher that it was something else entirely. He had seen Noah touched by the Creator before, but never had it been so obvious; the years had seemed to drop off him with each passing step he had walked that morning. He now seemed to stand before Jasher a much younger man; even the timbre of his voice had deepened without the inevitable slur of old age.

Noah's voice broke his reverie as he announced, "Jasher, yonder there is the entrance to the cave." He avoided further explanation then, closely followed by his grandson, he walked through the entrance and down the short walkway to the main opening. In the corner, a large round covering could be seen as though it had been rolled away from the entrance. Having seen very few caves, Jasher was now completely amazed at the vastness of this one and the unexpected natural light that seemed to emanate from the walls. Noah led him effortlessly through the main cavern to the sub-caverns within and it was here that Jasher received his first view of the records that had been so fastidiously written and maintained by his ancestors and had later been collected by Seth and delivered to Noah's father, Lamech. Eventually, all the records had been deposited here in this cavern prior to the Flood.

"Grandfather," he stammered, "I had no idea of the vastness of the records. They are evident in every room of the cave. To what purpose were they written?"

"Jasher, my son, they are of two types. Those that speak to the spiritual needs of the people and those that serve as historical documents of the times and seasons of all known civilizations of man. While others will be responsible for those that are spiritual in nature, it will be your mission to observe the events of men and record and maintain the historical records." Now, with growing strength, which could be seen as well as felt, Noah directed, "My son, please kneel before me and receive your calling and a blessing."

Obediently, Jasher knelt before his grandfather. Noah now laid his hands upon Jasher's head and delivered a sacred pronouncement that would govern him all the days of his life. Noah spoke with strength and passion. He promised of things to come both from the earth and from the heavens above and left him a blessing of long life and strength to persevere in the face of personal tragedy and despair. Jasher would forever remember this moment throughout his long life and when moments of trial did appear, he would recall Noah's blessing and draw strength from its message meant for him and for him alone.

Having reviewed the plates for the first time, Levinson reigned in his astonishment and delved into the work for which he had so assiduously trained. The two professors realized from the outset they were examining an historical document without equal and the careful sifting of information and note-taking lasted the better part of the day. Later, as the work level intensified and the two labored continuously to ensure they were both satisfied of their findings, they adjourned for a small lunch, but so eager were they to return to their task, the food was scarcely eaten.

Once they had completed the meticulous process of validation, including the use of a few basic methods to test the plates for composition, Professors Bedford and Levinson retired to the living area with the observations each had made of the characters and writing style of the author. The artifact itself would need to be tested by a more intense metallurgical process, but even their basic methods seemed consistent with what they had observed regarding the characters. Amazingly, there was absolute concurrence in the conclusions that both had reached. Jasher was already seated and had been awaiting their arrival for several minutes. After all were comfortably seated, Professor Levinson cleared his throat and began:

"Gentlemen, in all my days of research in the fields of paleography and linguistics I have never viewed any document to equal what I have seen today. It would be valuable beyond belief, assuming a price could even be attached to it. The characters are clear and precise and obviously predate any other cuneiform writing that has ever been discovered. The workmanship of the metallic plates on which they have been written is unusually skilled, perhaps unsurpassed, and undoubtedly the reason for the condition of the characters after so many years. Many of the characters are Sumerian, which should facilitate our work of translation, yet there are many that are unique and would relate to an earlier alphabet: I would place the date of the characters at 4000-3500 BCE. Though our translation is far from complete, what I have found most compelling is that the sampling of the texts I have examined seem to have been written by more than one person, each with a distinct style of writing, though I will be uncertain until a more extensive translation has been rendered. That is my general opinion with details to be included in my final report." Levinson, now beside himself with interest and curiosity, blurted, "William, exactly what have you found? What in God's name did I just validate?"

Bedford glanced over to Jasher for a response to Levinson's plea. Jasher nodded slightly as if to accept control for the moment. Bedford replied to his colleague, "Isaac my friend, I will need to defer to Mr. Jasher's counsel at this point. Up until a few days ago, the plates were solely in his possession. It is likely he has owned these plates for many, many years".

Levinson glanced over toward Jasher who seemed to be in quiet meditation as he had closed his eyes. He wondered how it could be that this man could have acquired the plates and have had them for as long as William had seemed to imply. Jasher could scarcely be forty years of age. What was he withholding here? He wondered. The longer the pause was drawn out, the more charged the air in the room seemed to intensify. He could feel and verify the strength of the static electricity building by the hairs on his arms, hair and neck. Isaac looked toward Bedford and it was obvious by his reaction that he, too, was feeling something peculiar. Their hearts were beating more rapidly than normal and their eyes were fully dilated as they helplessly steeled themselves for something extraordinary to come.

Jasher slowly opened his eyes and gazed directly at the two men. "Gentlemen," Jasher began slowly. His voice had taken on a deeper, more resonant timbre; his face had a distinct glow about it. "I am in the way of knowing that there is something you both must now know before you begin this translation. "William, your lineage is of the House of Ephraim and you are a direct descendant of Abraham, Isaac and Joseph and as such you are entitled to all the blessings and privileges pertaining to that great lineage, one of which, as it has been revealed to me, is the gift of translation. You have a great work ahead of you that will encompass the remainder of your life. You are charged to fulfil this responsibility and will be accountable for your actions, but if you remain faithful to this calling, you will be assisted in your work by forces above and upon the earth to ensure your success."

Tears were streaming down the face of Professor Isaac Levinson as Jasher's penetrating eyes turned to meet his. After a moment, Jasher continued to earnestly testify, "Isaac, you are to assume a larger role in this matter than had been previously considered. It has as much to do with your lineage as your expertise in matters of linguistics. You are a direct descendent through the House of Levi who served Moses and Aaron in the wilderness. Your ancestors were keepers of the Temple of Solomon down though the time of Zechariah, father of John the Baptist. You are, in fact, a direct descendent of the father of Zechariah. You shall serve as scribe to William, and like William, you are charged to fulfill this responsibility and will be accountable for your actions but, if you will remain faithful to these duties, your understanding of the skills necessary for success will increase ten-fold."

"William and Isaac", he added solemnly, "If you are true to the callings that the two of you have received, your thoughts and your actions to perform this great work will be heightened beyond anything you have ever experienced. Because of your dedication to this work, your understanding will grow even as the work grows beyond our current project. I am both grateful and humbled by your years of preparation as I extend you these callings." He smiled and then went silent as though allowing each man an opportunity to ponder these pronouncements. He slowly closed his eyes, his breathing slowed and he seemed to pull within himself in quiet meditation.

A few moments later, Professor Levinson was the first to speak following this profound event. He looked over to his friend and colleague and whispered fiercely, "William, this man, Jasher, is he what I think he is? Many years ago my grandfather, a rabbi, taught me from the Talmud about such men. He would have referred to them as Holy Men of God. Is Jasher a prophet? Is he the same Jasher mentioned in the Old Testament? Is that even possible?"

William Bedford responded slowly, but emphatically, "Isaac, I think he must be! Did you not feel the absolute certainty at what he said? He told me that he was long-lived, but until now I simply was unable to comprehend his claim."

Jasher slowly regained his consciousness and refocused on the two professors sitting across from him. He leaned forward slightly and quietly declared, "Gentlemen, in all my years in preparation for this project, I have never felt the degree of certainty I have felt as I made these pronouncements this day. Isaac, you have something to share with us; am I correct?"

Levinson, now surprised, but visibly moved that Jasher had somehow discerned a deeper, more personal connection to the project confided, "I want to share something with you both that I have never told another person about my grandfather, Ezra Levinson. At the age of twelve, as I was preparing myself for my upcoming *bar mitzvah*, he and I were discussing a passage in the Talmud when he suddenly grew quiet. My grandfather was well past eighty at the time and I thought he had simply dropped off to sleep as he occasionally did. His face became pensive then gradually it took on a special glow I had never seen again until this day. "Isaac," he intoned, "before you die, a holy man will enter your life and bestow on you a special calling and a blessing. From this day forward you must study earnestly the ancient languages and texts of the Talmud and what the gentiles refer to as The Holy Bible to prepare yourself for that great day. Mention this to no one, but never forget it." Then with emphasis, he added fiercely, "Will you promise?" I nodded my head and said I did. Then, my grandfather blinked as if waking from a dream and resumed his explanation of the passage of the Talmud as if nothing of importance had just occurred, but my grandfather remembered, because just before his death a few years later, he called me to his bedside and reminded me of my promise on that special day when, as he put it, we were both taught."

Professors Levinson and Bedford now sat somberly as they pondered the meaning of what they had just experienced. Bedford was the first to speak, as he asked, "Isaac, how do you feel about being my scribe in this endeavor?"

Levinson, remembering the promise he had made to his grandfather so long ago, reflected, "It seems my whole life has been a prelude to this event. I have long studied with the intent of preparing myself for this purpose and I can assure you that my promise to my grandfather is as binding this moment as it was when I was a young man. I only hope that my labor all these years will prove to be sufficient for the task before us."

The next few minutes passed as Isaac and William both watched silently, yet curiously, at the strange man seated before them. Jasher seemed to break slowly from his internal reverie then smiled warmly and confided with a touch of understatement, "Isaac, thank you for sharing that message. Gentlemen, I would apologize for my lapse of attention, but it would seem sadly misplaced in view of the information I have revealed to you and your personal thoughts you have just shared with me." This brought smiles to all in the room. A brotherhood and a bond had just been struck, one which would serve to strengthen each as the coming darkness threatened their sanity and peace of mind.

Chapter 6 – The Translation, a beginning

While the two men had been busy validating the plates, Jasher had contemplated the next steps in the process. Concerned for security as well as their safety, he had decided that the fewer persons who were aware of their venture, the less worry they would all have and could stay focused on the task at hand. "Gentlemen, before we begin, I want to discuss with you a matter of the utmost importance. During periods of translation, security will be almost as important as what we are translating. Until now, I have been operating under the presumption that should an issue arose that could compromise the completion of our work, there would always be time to pull out and re-group at a different time and place. Though that option may still exist, it will indicate that a serious degree of danger had entered into the decision. Thus, we must minimize doing anything which might precipitate that circumstance. William, I will have to impose once again on your hospitality by inviting Isaac to stay with us here at your home. While our work is in progress, we can feed ourselves and do all the cleaning necessary to maintain order. Furthermore, once we begin our work, no one is to leave the premises." He glanced over to Levinson and said, "Isaac, I know this request seems abrupt and for that I apologize and hope that this will not inconvenience you too dearly. I know the two of you are single men, but you still have family and your absence will be noticed, so please make whatever arrangements you feel necessary to minimize your distractions during this process. Gentlemen, please feel free to comment on these guidelines."

Bedford was the first to comment. "Jasher, of course I would be delighted to open my home for my dear friend. You have informed me already of our need for security and for good reasons, however, Isaac may still misunderstand the forces that we are dealing with here and may seriously doubt that your security measures are warranted."

"Since I have *volunteered*," Isaac commented with a smile, "it would be helpful if I understand the need for such security."

Jasher paused a moment as if pondering how best to proceed. "Once the two of you enter the phase of translation you will begin to comprehend that the degree of security is equal to the task at hand. There are powerful and dangerous parties whose world-wide operations would be severely compromised if the truths contained in *The Abridgement* were ever uncovered before the world. I assure you that this is not mere melodrama. If these persons knew what we were about to commence, they would spare no expense and no effort to prevent this from happening. Your careers, your reputations, even the well-being of your families could be in jeopardy. Once we go public, however, then the advantage reverts to us and then they go on the defensive. They can ill afford exposure to the light of day by men of reputation and credibility, which is why you have both been chosen. So, please make the necessary adjustments to your schedules today to accommodate this arrangement. Every day that goes by before we go public is a day to their advantage and a day in which the records are technically in the open and relatively unprotected."

The two scientists, following Jasher's instructions, prepared themselves and Bedford's home for the work of translation. Later, both men notified their Deans of School of an emergency sabbatical that would interrupt their teaching schedules. In addition to retrieving additional reference books from his home, Levinson returned that same evening with sufficient clothing and toiletries to see him through the project. Unbeknownst to the two men, their movements as well as any outside calls were immediately tracked and passed on to waiting, interested groups.

The next day, the work of translation began in earnest. Jasher, having first-hand knowledge of the language on the records, would provide key translations to unknown characters. And so it had proceeded, while Jasher confirmed the veracity of each word, Bedford translated each character. Meanwhile, Levinson wrote each word and once a sentence had been completed, they all confirmed its proper intention in context with all previous sentences. For Bedford and Levinson, these would be days never to be forgotten. They translated by day and Jasher presented explanations of the translation in the evening after work had been completed for the day. Thus, by the end of the first few weeks, the translation was all, but complete. It was now time to piece everything together in a cogent, written text that could be versified with chapters and proper punctuation.

One thing that the professors agreed upon and confirmed by Jasher was that the book they were translating was never meant as a record for theological instruction, rather it was an abridgement of historical accounts of the rise and fall of Man's first organized civilizations, with its governments, rulers and citizens. Jasher also confirmed that this book was intended to be an earthly witness that would be used at some future date when all men would be judged. Presumably, all men, including rulers, will be judged and held accountable for their actions in upholding the freedoms of mankind. An excerpt from the translated text regarding the mission of Seth seemed to support these conclusions:

And I, Seth, son of Adam and Eve our first parents, have been taught after the language and manner of my father Adam. And knowing that he would soon die, Adam entrusted me with the records of his family from the time of his expulsion from the Garden with my mother Eve to the present.

The records of Adam were largely written with regard to the spiritual matters of his family and his instructions to them toward righteous behavior. These, he entrusted to me to be passed on to my son Enos and later his descendants. With an added commission I was to create my own records and to primarily write the history of Man's first civilizations.

As was his way, my father expounded on the need to maintain such records so that all righteousness might be fulfilled; that all acts of Man, both good and evil, might be recorded on earth to stand as an earthly witness at the Day of Judgment so that all flesh might be justified according to the Laws of God and the Agency of Man.

Some points of discussion arose from this passage when William commented, "Jasher, how is it that judgment will depend upon these records? If the truth is so important," he paused trying to grasp the *bon mot,* then proceeded, "might it be more beneficial to record these actions in a more *heavenly location* away from the common grasp of men?"

Jasher pointed out, "Actually, William, these records are maintained in heavenly sanctuaries and they will be made available at the right time and opportunity." He added, "But, our earthly records must likewise be maintained and be used as an additional witness against those who would willfully disabuse us of our need for personal choice. Isaac, surely you know that your ancient Hebrew texts remind us of a need for two or more witnesses to satisfy the demands of justice?"

Isaac nodded his approval and acceptance of this comment. "I am beginning to see why these records would make some individuals quite uncomfortable."

"Quite right!" exclaimed Bedford.

After a moment, Jasher added, "Please believe me, those who would deny us our basic freedoms in order to gratify their own selfish pleasures understand this principle and are highly motivated to remove as much evidence from being presented as possible."

Part 2 – The Origin of Cain

And the Lord said unto Cain, Where is Abel thy brother? And he said, I know not: Am I My Brother's keeper?

----- Genesis 4:9

And Cain loved Lucifer more than God, the Creator. And after Cain had slain his brother Abel, the Lord said unto Cain, Where is Abel thy brother?

And Cain said, I know not, am I then My Brother's keeper?

----- The Abridgement, Chapter 2.

Better to reign in Hell, than to serve in Heaven.

----- John Milton, author of <u>Paradise Lost</u>

Chapter 1 – The First Family

In every conceivable manner, the family is link to our past, bridge to our future.

----- Alex Haley, author of Roots

It had been a long, hard day working with the livestock. A few cows had recently birthed and some horses had foaled colts so the new ones had needed special tending. Even though he had remained to finish up the work for the day, Adam had sent his sons, those who worked with him, onward to the house to be rested and fed for the evening. After their dismissal, a few minutes passed away when, unsurprisingly, he became aware that Abel had quietly joined him and had begun to help without any encouragement. He found him busy in the corner of the barn pitching the hay at the feet of the cows that had been restlessly milling about, looking for food. Adam called over and said, "Abel, the horses have been fed, but as long as you are here, when you have finished with the cows, please dump some food into the troughs for the pigs."

"Will do, Father", he replied cheerily. Work had never been a struggle for Abel, Adam reflected; he simply accepted it as part of life and necessary to maintain the needs of the family. Abel's normal duties included tending the goats and sheep, but when he finished up his tasks with them at the end of the day, he often joined his father, especially if he knew Adam was working longer than usual. It was a special time for both of them and so, for Abel, the time was well spent.

Adam was a tall man. He had a roughly hewn, square face and rugged handsomeness about him that seemed contradictory to his personality. Usually quite affable, even gregarious at times, he kept his family entertained with his humor as well as his wisdom in his more introspective moments. Adam, though tired, made an effort to engage Abel in conversation and so asked, "Abel, how are things at the corral?" The goats and sheep were kept locked up at the end of the day to keep them from wandering too far astray.

Adam and Eve had seventeen sons who still lived with them at home and Abel was near the middle of this group in age. He was shorter in stature than his father, but never felt diminished by his father's height advantage. His hair was the same light brown as his mother's, his eyes a dark blue, almost violet. Though lacking in the physical gifts of his father, he more than made up for it in an innate intelligence and high degree of commitment to his stewardship. He replied cheerfully, "All have been accounted for and rounded up for the day. I sent the twins on ahead so that mother will not worry if she doesn't see them at the dinner table." With a smile, he added, "I told them to go directly home and avoid distractions or mother would be cross with them and likely beat them with a soup spoon." The twins, Michael and Gabriel, had a tendency to wander off together, but the idea of their mother being angry with them was, of course ridiculous, but it was a private jest between Abel and Adam.

Adam had a sense of humor and appreciated his son's overplay of Eve's anger, which as everyone knew, was non-existent. Adam, too, appreciated this special time with his son who had grown to manhood with so little effort. He tried hard to avoid obvious comparisons between Abel and Cain then draw unfair conclusions, but Adam realized that the biggest difference was their outlook on life. Abel was always positive and helpful; he saw life as a wonderful experience for personal growth through service to others. Cain always saw things, and especially people, as consequential only if they were in his service or under his control and especially if he stood to gain from that control. Naturally gentle and patient with all animals, Abel had been made overseer of the flocks and light livestock. On the other hand, Cain had always worked the fields and to show his appreciation for his dedication, Adam had made him chief supervisor over his brothers in that labor.

Adam inwardly sighed as he reflected that, while in the field that morning, he had had to reprimand his son Cain, yet again, for failure to see to the needs of his brothers. Adam and three of his sons took care of the larger livestock whereas Abel oversaw the twins who worked with him with the goats and sheep. Cain was the overseer of the other ten sons who worked the fields. Though Adam was impressed with the work being done in the fields, he did not appreciate the way Cain tended to neglect the needs of his brothers who reported to him. Today, Adam had been walking through the fields and observed one son, Jared, clearly exhausted from the heat, and asked him when he had last drank water or had eaten. Jared had responded that Cain had purposely withheld water and food and had not allowed them a break. He excused his son and admonished him to get some rest and told him he would go looking for nourishment, though he suspected Cain had hoarded the food and water nearby and so he went looking for him. Unsurprisingly, he found him on a nearby hill overlooking the progress of his brothers, with arms folded and eyes hooded with disdain.

Cain was closer to his father in physical attributes. Though his eyes were blue, more like those of Eve, he seemed to have inherited his father's darkness of hair. His head was thickly covered with deep-black wavy curls that he normally had to tie back out of his face, but seldom bothered to do. His head conveyed the impression of angularity and squareness as though built up out of a sharply angular plane surface. Unlike his father, Cain was more like an unfinished piece of sculpture with sharp edges not yet rounded off. If was not just a sense of massiveness, which would allow him to be so intimidating in years to come, but a sense that he would not soften with age, his flesh would refuse to become gross with fat. He would give the impression of being designed more by a good draftsman than a fine artist. As to his personality, it was driven by furious anger.

"Cain, I would talk with you, if you please?" Adam always found it wise to speak respectfully to all his children and especially since Cain was no longer a child, but the eldest and a full adult.

Cain had noticed when his father had entered the field, and as he saw him coming in his direction, his anger began to seethe. That feckless fool of a brother, Jared, must have cried big tears to his dear daddy, he thought angrily, and now, once again, I will be forced to deal with Father. He turned slowly, but refused to meet him half-way, thus compelling Adam to climb the remainder of the steep rise of the hill. Finally, as Adam reached the top, Cain declared insolently, "Yes, Father, what is it can help you with today?"

Without returning his son's greeting, Adam slowly began to walk around the top of the hill then stopped abruptly when he observed that Cain had stored all the water gourds and food under a nearby tree. He was trying hard to conceal his anger as he patiently pointed out, "Cain, your brothers have been working hard all morning and afternoon in the heat of the day and yet you have prevented them to break for food or water." He attempted to control his voice, but found it hard. "Why have you denied them nourishment and drink?" he asked.

Cain's expression changed from one of bored insolence to hardness around the eyes and jaw. He replied flippantly, "I see that lazy fool Jared has been busy falsifying the truth again. I made the decision to deny him food and drink until he picked up his level of work. It would have set a bad precedent to the others if I had encouraged his slothfulness." He finished his comment defensively, "If they don't work, they don't eat or drink; they all know my rules."

It would not be the first time that Cain had misunderstood his role. Now, trying to appeal to his sense of fairness, Adam remarked, "Cain, this is no way to treat your brothers. From where I stand, they are all doing a fine job as are you. Please remember that in our family we must show love and respect for one another. Are you unable to put yourself in their position and feel their need for food and drink after so much work in the heat?"

While the discussion continued from the top of the hill with Cain, all work stopped down below. Shaking his head in disgust at the work stoppage, Cain looked out over his brothers, and cried, "Father, look at what your meddling interference in this matter has resulted." He grabbed his father by the arm and pointed, "My Brothers have stopped working and now I will have to deal with their laziness the rest of the day!"

Now tiring of the argument, Adam was angry. "Cain, do you never listen? I am calling in your brothers for them to rest and receive nourishment. And when you have properly rested them, then you may direct them to return to the fields, but not before." He turned to his sons below them in the field and called them to break for a late lunch.

Cain was mortified that his father had publicly usurped his authority in this manner. He swung around to his father and growled, "Very well, Father, but don't blame me if these lazy dolts refuse to finish the work for the day." With that, he turned and strode angrily down the hill where he could be alone. The boys tiredly trudged up the hill and fell down nearly too exhausted to eat, but they did manage to have their fill of the water.

They quietly watched Cain stalking away muttering threats under his breath and knew he would eventually take his anger out on them.

Adam looked over his tired sons and his heart went out to them. "Boys, I am sorry you had to work so hard in the heat without proper rest. I will be by each day at noon to ensure your brother Cain is treating you fairly."

Jared gazed up at his father and shrugged between bites of food. "Cain will take it out on us if you drop by too often, Father. It would be best if you simply reminded him each morning and came by every few days."

Adam was taken back by the off-handed remark. "What do you mean he will take it out on you?"

Jared was a peace-keeper and a realist. "As long as he remains overseer, he will feel a need to exert control over us. His verbal insults do as much harm as his oversights to our needs for nourishment."

Now standing at the bottom of the hill, his arms folded, his back to Adam and his brothers, Cain waited impatiently while his brothers rested. Adam gazed for a moment in Cain's direction, turned around then looked down at his tired son and said, "Jared, at the end of every day, I want you to personally report to me everything that is said and goes on out here." He looked around at the boys and realized that none of them were children anymore. All were now young adults, most old enough to have families of their own soon. "When you have rested, finish up the work for the day. I will instruct Cain to set you free at sundown."

Adam walked down the hill and before he could reach Cain, his son turned around and impudently asked, "Well, have those sniveling, snot-nosed little babies had enough rest yet or do they need their mommy to wet-nurse them as well?"

Adam was in no mood for anymore verbal sparring with his son. "Cain, your brothers will rest for an hour. They will work until sundown and you will dismiss them at that time for dinner. Is this all clearly understood?"

"Of course, Father. Will there be anything else I can do for you today?" he asked with thinly veiled contempt.

Adam tiredly shook his head. "No. Just see that it is done." He turned and trudged apathetically away toward the barn. He felt exhausted and there was still much to do. Talking with Cain was more taxing than any hard labor he could imagine.

Adam's experience with his eldest son earlier that afternoon had left him in a sour mood. Abel sensed his father's annoyance and knowing his father normally to be easy-going and agreeable, he quickly concluded that he must have had another run-in with Cain. So, he tried to lift his spirits by giving him a complement. "Father, the mare was having a difficult time foaling, but thanks to your care, the new colt will be strong and healthy and will serve us well. You certainly have a way with the horses."

Adam was quick to give the mare the complement. "The mother was already strong and healthy herself. It just took some loving care with just the right encouragement." After a moment he added sadly, "If only people could be as easy to persuade."

Abel heard the concern in his father's voice and quietly asked, "Cain again, Father?"

Adam felt a need to talk, but was reluctant to unload his burdens upon him. Finally, he explained, "Son, the fault with Cain is mine alone to carry. I just can't seem to reach him and my lack of understanding is just encouraging his rebellious behavior."

Abel quickly came to his defense. "I would doubt that, Father. Cain is an adult and quite capable of making decisions on his own. If he is dissatisfied with those around him, he should change his actions. As I recall it was you that was fond of saying, "If you want to affect change in others, you have to be willing to make change in yourself first."

Adam sighed, "Yes, I am quite fond of saying many things, my son."

Abel disliked seeing his father berate himself so he decided to help out. "Father, I will try also to reach out to him and between the two of us, I am sure we will be successful. On the morrow, I will make a concerted effort to engage him in conversation and complement him on his fine work in the field."

And Adam knew that if anyone could reach him, it would be Abel because he saw only the good in people, never the bad. With a quick smile he agreed. "That's a wonderful idea, son. We will yet succeed in bringing him around." After a pause, he concluded, "We must teach Cain by love and example."

He and Abel spent the next hour finishing up the evening chores and discussing family matters then finally the two men made their way tiredly back home.

After a late meal and personal washing Adam tiredly slipped into bed next to his wife. He was almost asleep when he felt Eve stir slightly. "Adam, we must talk." There was worry in her voice, so it had to do with one or more of the children and he had a good idea which one. He had always been highly attuned to the needs of Eve and knew without having to ask whether this moment was the time for a discussion and that tone told him it was.

"I am listening, Eve." Adam could detect the sigh of her breath and sensed that it was more than just worry. It was Cain, of course; his eldest son seemed to have been born willful and stubborn. From an early age, everything he was asked to do was returned with a caustic remark or a rebellious determination to do the task with minimal interest and effort as possible. Regardless of how well he had been taught, Cain invariably felt that honest labor was somehow beneath him. After the other children were born, he had been quick to bully his younger siblings into doing the work for him.

There was a reluctant silence from Eve then a catch in her voice before she spoke. She whispered, not caring to have the conversation overheard, "Cain is abusing the other children, especially his brothers in the field."

At hearing her use the word "abuse", Adam winced as he realized that Cain's behavior might now be beyond his control. He knew about the neglect, but abuse? With quiet insistence, Adam asked, "Abusing. I don't understand Eve, who has told you this?"

"Sariah has witnessed this behavior and mentioned it to me today. At first I couldn't believe such a thing was possible, so I went with her into the fields this evening before sundown and saw it for myself. Adam, Cain was using a whip to threaten our sons". The last statement trailed off with sobs.

Adam was aghast and mortified at the thought and so replied, "A whip? Where would he get such an idea? I don't even use one on our horses and donkeys."

"Sariah says he must have made it and I am worried that his cruelty is getting out of control; she informed me that the other children now fear being around him. This should not be happening, Adam, and we must do something about his behavior. As his father, you must speak with him," she pled.

Adam then recalled the incident which had occurred on the hill that afternoon, and as he lay in bed holding his worried wife, he silently rebuked his son for causing his mother so much emotional pain. "Eve, I will speak with him in the morning. Meantime, you must get some rest," he soothed. His comforting arm went around her tighter and she snuggled in close; nonetheless, for the two parents, sleep came slow that night.

While the dawn of a new day broke over the horizon in the east, Cain walked barefoot over the morning dew from the stone outhouse that had been constructed many years before. It was a well-built privy and his mother and sisters had done their best to ensure that any odor was well hidden with scented herbs of rosemary, jasmine and other fragrant flowers that grew in profusion about their home.

As he reached the porch of the rambling family home, Cain began to review the daily work schedule. It was going to be another warm day and his brothers would have to be pushed harder to get the work done early before it got too hot to work, otherwise, per his father's wishes, he would have to dismiss them before they completed the day's labor. Or, he could simply push them until they dropped of exhaustion then report to his father that they were shirking and needed to work longer and harder to make up for lost time.

He no longer cared nor sought his father's approval for his behavior and so was hardly concerned he would have to account for his neglect of their well-being. Though the whip was used mostly for show to satisfy his curiosity at how much verbal abuse the poor fools could endure under threat, he doubted his father was aware he had been using it lately to persuade them. In any event, they wouldn't dare report his threats back to his parents as they knew this would result in the use of his fist and his whip. Lately, he seemed interested with the concept of inflicting pain on them and how it might make him feel if he personally administered it. So, with anticipation at what the new day would bring, as he entered the house, there was a spring in his step and a smile on his face. It was good to look forward to the day.

During Cain's approach to the house, Adam had thoughtfully observed his son through the window. Even as a child, he reflected, Cain had always been lacking in natural affection, but since entering adulthood his behavior had become increasingly violent with his younger siblings. He glanced over at his wife cooking the morning breakfast and knew that Cain worried her greatly. If recent talks with Eve confirmed what Adam already suspected as well as what he had personally witnessed, unless Cain could control his anger and behavior, Adam felt he would have to make changes that would result in his expulsion from the home. Always a sensitive and loving man with his family, Adam was loath to take this final step, but Cain had been an adult now for a number of years and one day he would be a husband and father himself. It was time he became more personally accountable for his actions.

Eve knew without turning from the cookpot that Adam was watching her son. Cain's morning ritual was predictable, which seemed to be about the only thing about his behavior these past few months that was. His erratic behavior, constant irritability and harshness of words with everyone with whom he interacted had created havoc with the harmony in their home. As a loving and attentive mother she was highly sensitive to the needs of her large family and she took great strides to ensure everyone felt comfortable and loved and made a contribution to the success of their home life.

Sariah, the eldest daughter still living at home, watched her parents and sensed something was afoot and knew it had something to do with her elder brother Cain. She had known him all her life, not as a parent, but as a sister, and so her view of him was unlike her mother and father. Even as a young child she recollected how Cain would tease her unmercifully until she was crying. Only when she was sad, apologetic or subservient did he even seem satisfied to be around her. Her misery was his joy, but in spite of his abuse, it did not change her love she had for being near him.

That all changed as one day, when still an adolescent, she had observed that her brother seemed especially happy, and wanting to be with him, she quietly followed him into the woods. It had been a lovely spring day, the flowers were in full bloom and she had intended to pick a bouquet for her mother and she hoped Cain would join her. Sariah had just crested a small hill and entered a small copse of trees when she spotted him afar off. She was about to call out his name, when she abruptly stopped as something curious had caught her eye, momentarily putting a halt to her greeting. With mounting fear she became aware he had caught a squirrel in a trap and was poking it with his knife, teasing it and occasionally chuckling at its futile efforts to get away from the knife. After a while, Cain must have grown bored with its agitated efforts and simply stabbed the poor creature with his knife. Immediately, his face lit up, diffused with simple joy and satisfaction. Knowing his anger and what he might do to her, Sariah quietly backed away from this sight and returned home, now shaken. She never mentioned this incident to anyone for many years, but she never forgot it and from that day forward she kept her brother at a distance. Nevertheless, he never seemed to miss their companionship, such as it was and never made any effort to reconcile the strain in the relationship. If only Cain could be more like Abel, she thought for the thousandth time.

Abel, always attentive to the needs of his sisters and brothers, but especially to Sariah whom he loved dearly above all others, noticed she appeared distressed this morning. Wanting to lighten her mood, he gave her a morning hug and kiss on the cheek which always improved her spirits. Nonetheless, this morning his show of attention didn't seem to have its usual effect on her so he sat down and tried to engage her with light and breezy talk. He became quickly aware she was distracted and occasionally glanced toward the door; it would be Cain, of course and he now understood her mood. To Abel, his older brother was an enigma and a challenge to love, but he made the daily effort to offer a serious attempt, and since his talk with his father yesterday evening, he had recommitted himself to that effort.

Announcing in his own way his emerging pre-eminence in the home, Cain made his usual boisterous entrance. Now ignoring his father at the window, his eyes slid contemptuously over his younger brother. "Abel, My Brother, I see you are awake finally", he began his usual bantering, hectoring tone he reserved especially for Abel who he considered feckless as well as useless. "Will you be joining us in the fields today for some real manly work or, as usual, will you content yourself with dallying about with your little sheep?"

Wishing to avoid an angry response to his brother's tone of scorn, Abel replied jovially, "Cain, of course, I would be happy to join you. I can turn my duties over to the twins, Michael and Gabriel, this morning. They seem to have caught on to their responsibilities with the flock quickly."

Cain shook his head scornfully and sneered, "On second thought, don't bother. I will need real men in the field today and you, my Brother, do not qualify." This last comment resulted in a rich guffaw of laughter which only he seemed to appreciate.

Sariah and Eve were both appalled by this level of offensive talk and it showed on their faces. Eve glanced over to her husband for him to step into the discussion and get this uneasy banter under control. As Adam, too, was offended by the snide remark, she need not have worried.

His father, still behind him at the window, cleared his throat and said with a sterner voice than usual, "Cain that will be enough!"

Cain whirled around, eyes blazing and retorted, "Father, when I need your counsel, I will seek it, otherwise, I will say as I will when I so desire. I am no longer a child anymore to be pushed about by you and Mother at your whims." He then deliberately turned his back on his father and made as if to walk toward his bedroom. Adam, trying desperately to quell his rising anger at the contemptuous tone Cain had used against Eve, his wife, caught him by the arm.

"Cain, "Adam pleaded quietly, "We need to talk. There are things that need to be discussed."

Cain angrily jerked his arm out of his father's hand. "Oh, so this is to be another family council, I presume?" he hooted derisively. "I will, of course, be the center of the discussion and all my faults will be brought forward and tallied for future reference. Sorry, dear Father, some other time would be more convenient", he retorted breezily. "As you know, I have the daily chore to rouse my lazy brothers for their labor in the fields and direct them onward. Without me to remind them they would be totally useless instead of only partly so."

"No", responded Adam with rising anger, "this conversation will be between just you and me. When you are dressed and have your brothers dismissed for their work assignments, we will talk."

Cain always sought the final word in every discussion. "Of course, Father whatever you say, but do try to keep it short", he added sarcastically.

"I have much work to perform and my brothers work best when they are properly motivated by my presence." At the mention of the motivation he had in mind for them that day, his eyes gleamed with the luster of anticipation.

After he sauntered arrogantly out of the room, Adam walked over near the hearth and brooded a moment, his arms crossed over his chest, pondering what he could say to Cain to penetrate his rebellious exterior. Eve, having witnessed the scene between her husband and eldest child, slowly became aware of the concern on his face and realized what was bothering him. He was doing what he said he would do the night before and Cain, as usual, was being difficult, as well as insulting. Knowing what Adam needed, she put down the utensil she had been using to stir the food and walked quietly over and stood in front of him. Without a word, she moved forward and clasped her hands around his neck. They remained there, her eyes looking up slightly and searching his until he placed his arms around her waist, his eyes now finally locked with hers. Once she had his attention a small smile played along her lips and finally he, too, smiled in return. They embraced and swayed slightly together for a few moments and as it always seemed to happen when they were holding one another, the answer naturally came. Adam, now understanding his course of action, relaxed and with playful glee gently blew air into his wife's ear. This always caused Eve to break up into giggles of happiness and desire. Thus, they were in the process of showing their love, oblivious of the watchful eyes of their two children seated at the nearby table.

These two children, now in early adulthood and so similar in nature and disposition, were never happier except when their mother and father were together and showing their love for one another. Sariah and Abel didn't have to be taught by precept the importance of a happy marriage, they had only to observe their parents together and see how complete their bond was to one another. What their parents had was what they both desired when the time came to find their own special companion and friend. When Eve began to laugh and playfully pat Adam's cheek, both children wore radiant smiles.

Chapter 2 – The Rebellion

Rebellion without truth is like spring in a bleak, arid desert.

----- Khalil Gibran, writer

Later that morning, Cain announced the day's duty assignments for work to his brothers, and with a flick of his whip, disdainfully dismissed them all to perform their labors. He couldn't resist the temptation to punctuate certain points of his instruction with the business end of his whip across a nearby tree trunk. As he was watching them leave, he contemplated the possibility of adding small flint edged stones to the tips of the whip and wondered what that might look like across the back of his brothers. While his mind played over this new possibility, he took out his fine honed knife and began slashing marks into the tree. He was smiling slightly when he noticed his father approaching from the southern end of the field.

Cain slowly sheathed his knife and tucked the whip inside his belt; he didn't bother to hide it, though. He had voiced his opinion before his brothers that it was well past time his father understood who the real man was around here, anyway. His smile vanished as he anticipated the confrontation with Adam, and accordingly he assumed a relaxed, haughty posture of one both bored and disdainful of authority.

As Adam approached, he waved his hand in greeting, and with a smile on his face, he walked up to his eldest son. He looked around and with genuine admiration exclaimed, "Cain, you have done a marvelous job with the corn and wheat crops, moreover, the orchards and gardens have never looked better. Since we have truly been blessed with the right amount of rain and sunshine, we should remember the Lord and offer oblations to him this Sabbath day. Will you please join Abel and me, along with the rest of the family, with the ritual sacrifices?" Ever since the early days when Adam and Eve had left the Garden to begin their family, each member of the family who had reached the age of accountability was taught the law of sacrifice and maintained their own personal flock of sacrificial lambs. Thus, only the finest, unblemished lambs would be chosen when the time arrived for the ritual.

Adam always looked forward to this rite with his family. All those involved with the ritual would place sheep on their own altars then each would spill the blood of the unspotted lamb, light the fire of the altar, and while the sacrificial lamb burned, each praised the Lord their God. Being together with his family while in the act of praising God in this manner, was, for Adam, the ultimate demonstration of his willingness to be obedient and offer thanks to his Creator. From the day Adam and Eve had received these instructions from the Creator, they had faithfully taught all their children the importance of performing this ritual correctly. As his sons would one day be patriarchs of their own homes, he ensured that each son clearly understood the ritual so that each, in turn, could teach his own family the correct manner of the rite.

After Adam had made this request for his son to join them, Cain laid his hand over the whip handle in his belt and disdainfully proclaimed, "The Creator doesn't seem to appreciate my sacrifices, Father. He has been unreceptive of late, wouldn't you say?" When the Lord has accepted the sacrifice, a glowing plume of smoke appeared to signal His approval. If He doesn't approve, no glow appears. The last ritual sacrifice had ended this way at Cain's altar, whereas at the altars of Adam and the other sons, the smoke emanated a bright orange. Mortified at this rejection beyond words, Cain had furiously stalked away kicking stones out of his path without even a backward glance to his family.

As Adam reflected on the day of the incident, he was pained that he would have to remind him. "My son, I begged you to select only the unblemished and healthy lamb and you offered instead the oldest and sickly of your flock. Can you blame the Lord for rejecting your sacrifice when you willfully disobeyed his instructions? Please, join us and perform the ritual correctly this Sabbath. The whole family will want to attend and give thanks to the Lord for our bounty."

Reluctantly, and primarily to halt what he considered an inane litany from his father, Cain agreed to attend. "Very well, Father. I will attend. Obviously, I am no judge of the correct offering, so please ask my brother Abel to provide a sacrificial lamb of his choosing." He was about to walk off, but offered a personal remark instead. "After, all, I would not want to offend the Creator," he added sardonically.

After embracing his son, Adam again thanked him for agreeing to join with the family on the Sabbath to perform the sacrifice. Cain, for his part, was just glad this little meeting was over and the relief was evident on his face.

As Adam walked away from the fields, he pondered all he had said to Cain and was elated at the results. He felt strongly that the ritual performed by himself and his sons would have a healing effect on Cain and would restore order and harmony to his home. The idea had come to him while he and Eve embraced in the kitchen. He thought of how Eve had somehow known how to calm his spirit such that he could receive inspiration for this idea. Tears welled up in his eyes as he thought of how much he loved her and depended on her counsel and so he offered a silent praise to the Lord for providing him this companion and help-meet. The Creator must have understood that she would complement me in so many ways, he thought. Realizing that Eve would want to know of Cain's decision to join them on the Sabbath, He decided to share his joy with his wife before beginning the daily chores.

Meanwhile, as Adam was giving praise, Cain was busy berating himself vocally for accepting this invitation. "Does my father take me for a fool?" he furiously asked himself? Am I so pathetically dependent upon the approval of my parents and God that I would reopen myself for further humiliations?" He was thus in this act of furious and pitiful self-abasement when a feeling of heightened awareness suddenly came upon him.

"Cain" a voice gently called him from within the copse of oaks directly behind him. He had, of course, felt this presence and heard the voice many times before, but never so loud and never so intimately. So, out of curiosity, he whirled around. "Show yourself", cried Cain fearlessly. As if awaiting this request, a figure, first translucent then gradually more solid, pushed his way through the bushes and stood boldly before him. Wearing a scarlet robe with a black sash, the being became increasingly more "there" until he assumed what appeared to be a near solid shape.

The man, if you could call him that after such an entrance, was not much taller than Cain and had a face that at once appeared disarming and then the next moment cunningly intelligent. His eyes were a piercing blue and his beard and hair, cut short, had a dark ebony sheen. He wore an expression of suppressed mirth, as if he were about to deliver a fascinating, yet humorous story. He looked directly into the eyes of Cain and his gaze seemed almost to pierce and finally penetrate his normally veiled exterior then, with a jovial, silken voice, he announced. "Well, Cain, we finally meet in person". After a moment he added thoughtfully, "I think it's time we got better acquainted." The being paused a moment and with a short, charming bow announced, "Please excuse my rudeness if I don't shake your hand as the results would only serve to confuse you and confusion is not the message I have brought for you today. I am here today to bring you clarity and reason and my name, as you may have already surmised, is Lucifer."

"Lucifer? Of course," thought Cain. Then, after recovering from his initial surprise, he now replied, "My father has spoken of you, but you don't seem to fit the description I had imagined and was told to expect. You seem, well, composed and friendly."

A look of subdued disappointment came over the face of the being. Lucifer audibly sighed and shook his head with mock sorrow. "I freely admit my last meeting with Adam went badly; I blame myself completely" he confided. With feigned deep regret he added, "False accusations were thrown about and harsh words were exchanged, leaving the two of us with hurt feelings which still remain unhealed to this day. If only he would listen, I could make life here so much better for him and his family, but he is obdurate and refuses to listen to reason." He added somewhat peeved, "The only thing I would ask in return is simple recognition and gratitude for my services."

Cautiously, Cain asked, "What are you offering? Maybe I can convince him." Cain was sick of this life with so much hard, back breaking work, and for what? So, he could grow older and bruised under the yoke of daily toil, underappreciated by his family and rejected by God, while he watched with futility as Abel grew stronger and more favored by the day?

Again, Lucifer shook his head, and replied, "Cain, I am afraid your father, well intentioned man that he is, has been deceived for so long he now refuses to see reason. He would rather allow his family to suffer needlessly than accept my counsel and suggestions. Since all my efforts to reach him have failed, I would prefer to work with you and allow you to be my agent in this matter." With a slight pause for emphasis, he added, "After all, you are the eldest and the favored son and will eventually inherit all that your father has." He paused ever so slightly for effect, then added courteously, "Is this not so or should I be talking to Abel, your younger brother?"

Suddenly, Cain saw for the first time the reason for his incessant anger and frustration. For so long he had endured his father's dreary homilies and Abel's ill-intentioned efforts to befriend him. It had all been a carefully planned ruse to convince him of their feigned love for him, but, in reality, they had plotted to demean and disinherit him all along. They would steal from him his birthright, his patriarchal right to ascend to the leading role of the family and inherit all. With mounting fury, Cain was beside himself with anger and swore he would destroy his brother Abel. With steel in his voice he slowly replied, "No, you are talking to the right person." Cain was unaware that only one more small push would seal his fate.

Lucifer responded dejectedly, "I suppose you are right, but I have to wonder." He seemed to ponder over this dilemma and then, as though coming up with a solution, calmly explained, "Cain, you must plant in the minds of your family your worthiness to lead, but, even more important, this acceptance must come from the Creator. You must show Him that you are a man of resolve and strength, independent and self-assured, better in every way than your blindly obedient, flaccid excuse of a father and your misbegotten, puling brother Abel."

"Yes," Cain eagerly agreed, "but how do I do that so that it is evident to all?"

Lucifer pretended to think it over. "I have seen your suffering and have observed the unfair way you have been treated all your life. Ironically, your own father has provided the means for you to prove yourself once and for all, not only to the whole family, but to the Creator Himself. Do you not recall the ritual sacrifices your father has set for celebrating the Sabbath?"

"Of course, the ritual sacrifices!" cried Cain. "Even if I must steal it from my brother's flock, I must find the finest sacrificial lamb!"

Lucifer seemed to weigh Cain's well-meaning suggestion then shook his head no. "Sadly, this would be insufficient and it would scarcely reflect the greatness of your effort. Are you not the tiller of the fields, even the overseer and therefore responsible for the success of the crops which feed your family? Why are you then making a sacrifice of the fatted lamb? That is what your younger brother Abel would do. Should you not instead be offering that which reflects your great contributions and intellect? Bring, instead, the best of your crops then observe how the Lord will accept and reward you."

Cain was overwhelmed with gratitude at the magnitude of this suggestion. "Lucifer, I thank you for your counsel. No one has ever shown me such love before and I do accept your offer to be an agent on your behalf for my family."

"Cain," replied Lucifer. "Just as I have helped you I am willing to help all of your family and, as I have asserted, I have come to bring clarity and reason. Regrettably, however, I fear that even with the Creator's acceptance, there may be resistance from your father and brother. An example of your strength may have to be made for the greater good of your family."

"Lucifer", testified Cain with grim determination, "I will do whatever is necessary."

"That will do fine," replied Lucifer. "We will meet again soon" he promised. With that being said, Lucifer turned and then walked back into the copse of trees, slowly disappearing.

After his discussion with Lucifer, Cain proceeded on to the fields. As he walked slowly through the orchards that morning, he was deep in thought over the encounter with his unexpected visitor and he had to admit, as far as he was concerned, Lucifer's advice did seem sound and his insights had hit the mark. It was high time for a change of direction, he reasoned, and if his father refused to be persuaded to accept these changes then, for the good of the family, his authority to preside should be wrested from him. His ascendance to preside over the family, Cain concluded, was both necessary as well as inevitable. Thus, by the time he had arrived at the fields, Cain had made his decision, and observing that his brothers were already hard at work, he had decided the time had come to firmly establish his authority over family matters.

As overseer of the crops, he could supervise the quality of their work at his leisure and clearly he was the master over his domain so why should his stewardship not be added upon in due time? With obvious pride at the abundance of the yield, he didn't need his father or anyone, for that matter, to validate his superb husbandry and management. If it weren't for my leadership, he concluded, his loutish brothers would no doubt have already failed us all and we would have all gone hungry; all they needed, really, was an occasional reminder of my control. Accordingly, he took out his whip and strolled over to his brother Avram who was busily leaning over the morning task he had been assigned. With a disarming smile, Cain observed, "Well done, my Brother, I see you have been hoeing the furrows of the carrots. What then of the cabbages?"

His brother, of equal size and weight as Cain, wearily looked up and wiped his brow. It was already hot and he was in no mood to listen to any insults Cain might have stored away for the moment. He replied testily, "Cain, as you know, we have just now entered the fields. I am now tending the carrots, so the cabbages will have to wait." As a result of his long toils of the day before, Avram was weary, and to add insult, he had had to endure the constant threats of his brother. So, he was sore and had not slept well during the night, thus his impertinence was understandable, though ill advised. After making his sullen comment, he resumed the task of weeding the rows of carrots and so missed the look of anger which flared up suddenly on Cain's face.

Avram had unwittingly provided Cain the perfect alibi to send a clear message of his preeminence over his domain. The initial anger turned quickly to obvious glee at his brother's remark. "You dare talk to me in that tone, you worthless ass?" Cain spat. "For your lack of manners and gratitude, you need a lesson in justice from him controlling these fields!" With that said, his arm swung out and the whip caught his brother full in the face. Suddenly, Cain felt an almost erotic charge flow through this body and he realized immediately that never had he felt as alive as that moment when he had struck his brother with the whip. Now, totally beyond all caring, he was raising his arm and whipping his brother over and over.

Seeing their brother Avram on the ground being flogged by Cain, the two brothers working nearby came running over. Trying to protect their wounded brother, they threw themselves between Cain and Avram, and in doing so, they likewise received the business end of the whip until Cain's arm became too tired to lift. He abruptly stopped, his breathing now labored from the whipping he had administered, but his joy at seeing his brothers rolling about like whipped dogs more than made up for the soreness in his arm. Looking at his cringing brothers now laying on the ground and bleeding, he kicked out at them and shouted, "Let that be a lesson to you all! Get back to work you shiftless louts! I should have you all work through your water and lunch breaks!" With that he turned on his heels and strode to the far end of the field to see who else was shirking his duties.

With fright and in obvious pain at Cain's outburst the three silently watched as he strode off in search for someone else to punish. "I am tired of Cain's threats and his abuse", cried Avram. "Father must know what he has done to us today!" They had bathed their cuts and bruises in a nearby stream and were now on their way to talk with their other brothers.

His elder brother Jared pointed out, "Avram, we must not involve Father; it would only upset him. Let us confront Cain and demand he stop this abuse."

The three had just topped the hill when they saw Cain, his arm again raised with the hated whip in his hand standing over another brother laid out on the ground. He was about to swing the whip again when Jared shouted, "Cain, that is enough!"

Jared, with his two brothers trailing behind him, was almost upon him when Cain abruptly turned around and his arm shot out, backhanding Jared across the face and knocking him to the ground. Cain gazed malevolently at Jared lying at his feet and announced contemptuously, "I am tired of reminding you fools that I rule these fields. Soon you will know that I rule it all! Now, get back to work unless you need further persuasion!" He thrust his whip into his belt and angrily pushed through the crowd of brothers who had formed to hear his declaration.

"We must inform Father", Avram repeated his threat. The others agreed, but deferred to Jared for a final decision.

Jared had a sobering suggestion. "No, tomorrow is the Sabbath and we must prepare for it, therefore I suggest we avoid any discussion of this matter with Father that will distress him before the ritual sacrifice. As you know, our married brothers and sisters and their families will be in attendance on the morrow as well. Once we have discussed the matter with them first then, if need be, we will then bring this up before Father for his counsel."

The Sabbath Day dawned gloriously mild and sunny. It had been over two hundred years since the first parents had left the Garden, and including children, grandchildren and great-grandchildren, the family had grown to well over four hundred persons. As Father Adam and Mother Eve led their progeny up the winding path to the three altars at the top of the hill behind their home, Adam remarked to his wife on the number, and holding the hand of his companion, squeezed it in affection and she, in return, gave his hand a squeeze. Sometimes she worried about growing old and finally dying even though she had no frame of reference for such concepts; no one had yet died of old age. Even so, she decided to tease Adam a little and looking up at his face, she smiled and asked with mock seriousness, "Adam, my wonderful husband, I will be yours forever. Will you still love me even after I grow old?" Adam, though quite serious, he nonetheless returned her smile and replied, "Eve, my beautiful wife, I will always love you, worlds without end." To Adam and Eve it was the perfect start to a glorious Sabbath day of thanks.

The progeny of Adam and Eve had indeed waxed prolific. Several sons and daughters had left home years earlier to begin their own families, and though they were all younger than Cain, but older than Abel and Sariah, their homesteads were within walking distance of the original home. Each maintained farms, livestock and flocks of their own, but the original home and properties of Adam and Eve were much larger and better established. It was for this difference that Cain had remained at home content and self-assured that one day he would inherit all his father had; that was, until lately.

If Adam could have predicted how this disastrous day would unfold, he would have reversed his steps and led his entire family back down the hill until reason prevailed between Adam and Cain. The hill on which the altars rested was hallowed, holy ground and had been consecrated specifically for the purpose of honoring the Lord God. Consequently, it was hardly a place for family disputes or a place for disrespect of that which was sacred.

As the party reached the top of the hill, it was evident that Cain had arrived earlier and had already made his preparations for the sacrifice. When all had gathered at the apex and could see what was being sacrificed, a collective cry of concern emanated throughout the throng. Abel, his brother, had tethered three unblemished ewe lambs to be used for the sacrifices and was approaching the altars with his Father when they heard the commotion ahead. Cain had just completed laying his sacrifice upon the center altar when he heard his father and brother approaching from the bottom of the hill. "Father", announced Cain in a booming voice, "so good of you to arrive. I will now begin the ritual with my sacrifice." As he turned around, all could clearly see that, instead of a fatted lamb upon the altar, Cain had laid out various fruits and vegetables which he had taken from the fields.

Adam, now too stunned at what he was seeing, could only stammer, "My son, what is this you are doing?" Cain had not only usurped the authority of his father by beginning the rite himself, in like manner, he had desecrated holy ground by attempting to burn that which was not specified in the ritual. Clearly appalled at what they were witnessing, Eve and Sariah quickly appealed to Adam and Abel to do something about the abomination before them. In shame, they had covered their faces in the hopes of blotting out the blasphemy.

Cain responded with sardonic contempt, "Father, I am doing that which I should have been doing all along, offering a sacrifice to the Lord according to my contribution. I till the fields so my sacrifice will represent the fruit of my labor. You can take that fatted lamb you have brought for me and toss it off the mountain." With that said he turned around and lit the pyre.

As the sacrifice ignited, all could see the glee of success on the face of Cain. He began swaying and dancing about the altar as if in the throes of ecstasy. Adam, sickened by the mockery of the ritual that he was witnessing, attempted to move forward through the crowd to put a stop to the profanity. Before he could do so, however, strong arms reached out and restrained him, thus preventing his intervention of the scene. He loudly protested, "Let me through, I must put a stop to this!" Now mesmerized by the scene in front of them, a collective madness had descended upon his family and many responded, "Not so, let Cain finish!" While Eve and Sariah were both weeping openly as the obscenity dragged on, Adam looked pleadingly over at his son Abel for help, but he too had been restrained. As if beseeching some unseen force to accept his atrocious offering, Cain was now loudly howling and screaming at the sky.

When it happened, it occurred violently. Instead of the controlled, gradual change of color, which had always signaled the acceptance of the sacrifice, the entire altar blew up and out over the side of the mountain. There was utter silence as everyone stared in stunned disbelief at the destruction. Cain, now visibly sick with disappointment at the rejection of his sacrifice, slipped to his knees and began to wail in frustration.

Then, a quiet, firm voice was heard everywhere at once. *"Cain, why art thou wroth? And why is thy countenance fallen? If thou doest well, shalt thou not be accepted? And if thou doest not well, sin lieth at the door. Satan desireth to have thee, and except thou shalt hearken unto my commands, I will deliver thee up, and it shall be unto thee according to his desire, and thou shalt rule over him."*

Cain, now hearing the voice of the Lord God, unsteadily arose to his feet. The words that he heard, instead of softening his heart and bringing regret of the abomination he had instigated, brought only pure livid hate. Adam and Abel knew Cain and realized that he was about to say something irreversible, thus, the two men rushed forward to try to convince him to humble himself and ask the Lord's forgiveness for the misunderstanding. "Please Cain", they begged. "Submit yourself to the Lord's counsel!"

Cain gazed about the stunned crowd with a look of hurt betrayal and shouted, "You have all been deceived by your father and brother Abel! They have been plotting against me and you for years, to deny me my rightful birthright as the first-born." Cain pointed an accusing finger of outrage at them and continued his harangue. "They would have you blind to the truth and lead you about by your noses to keep you foolish and easy to manage by feeding you lies disguised as commandments." With palpable scorn, he declared his final epithet with a sneering smile of hate, "They pretend love, but they want only to control you and deny you a simpler, easier life. I am weary of their constant lies and deceptions and now I will be taking control of my own life. I am leaving and any of you who feel as I do should follow me." He purposely pushed past Adam and Abel and strode through the crowd and many of the sons and daughters of Adam and Eve followed him down the hill that day.

Chapter 3 – The Translation, continued

Jasher, William and Isaac were all three seated around the dining table and had just finished the evening meal when William commented, "Jasher, I can understand that Cain's sacrifice would be rejected if his heart was not in the right place. What puzzles me is that it seems the offering was unaccepted because it was insufficient as an offering. Was not Cain correct in offering the fruit of the fields? He was, after all, a *tiller of the ground.*"

"William", began Jasher, "Adam had taught his children the principle of sacrifice not because he thought it was just a good thing to do, but because he had been taught the principle first-hand from a messenger of God. Not only was he instructed how the ritual was to be performed, but specifically what was to be used in the ritual, an unspotted lamb. Furthermore, Adam was taught that the rite was a necessary remembrance that one day the blood of the unblemished Messiah would be spilt on behalf of Mankind. When Adam taught his family this principle, he acted out of a perfect understanding and a full knowledge of what he was doing and he was quite thorough and detailed about teaching this principle to all his children. Thus, when Cain committed this obvious heresy, he was not acting out of ignorance, but a willful rebellion of the principles lain down in the ritual."

Isaac was also quick to comment on the day's translation. "Jasher, the translation seems to indicate that God's lack of acceptance to Cain's offering was the catalyst to his rebellion and subsequent murder of his brother Abel. Did Cain lack a full understanding of the consequences of this action?"

Jasher paused momentarily before responding. "Isaac, this question has been debated many times over the years. Obedience to the Law of Sacrifice involved the shedding of blood and could only be demonstrated if the blood of the pure and unspotted lamb was used as the sacrifice. As you both know, Abraham practiced this ritual as well as all the Old Testament prophets and later the priests in the Temple of Solomon; they were all quite aware of what they were doing and what it symbolized. Cain's offering was rejected because what he laid upon the altar was of the fruits of the field, not an unblemished lamb, therefore not a proper symbol according to the guidelines of the ritual. If he had performed the rite correctly, he would have been complemented and his sacrifice accepted, but, since he willfully disobeyed, his sacrifice was rejected and he was reproved for disobedience. No doubt this public humiliation led him to a complete break with his family and any future interest he might have with the Creator. His only commiseration for his disobedience came from Lucifer and this encouraged his eventual allegiance with him. Having lived during the times in which animal sacrifices were the norm among the early Hebrew people, I suspect that the offering of sacrifices was a regular routine in Adam's home and it was his duty to teach it properly. I know it was in mine."

Levinson then turned the conversation slightly. "I see by the translation that what we have rendered differs slightly with the account found in the Old Testament. Since Seth was not actually a witness to Cain's break with his family over this incident with the ritual sacrifice, I suppose it would follow that this account, as well as the event surrounding the murder of Abel, would provide a slightly different slant on matters than those which exist in the Old Testament. How do we interpret them?"

Jasher responded, "Although unborn at the time of the event, Seth was still well versed in the tragedy that befell his family with regards to his elder brothers Cain and Abel. The event as described in *The Abridgement* is similar to what we now find in the Book of Genesis today except that Seth intended to focus on the personalities involved as well as the actual cause and circumstances that led up to Abel's murder and the eventual effect that this act would have on all generations that followed. Seth was simply journaling a historical incident and made no attempt to comment on the spiritual implications of the actions; those accounts were left to others to write. Seth was directed to write a historical account of the Family of Adam, especially as it pertained to Cain's involvement with Adam's children and progeny. This, by the way, is also the same mandate which I received at my calling."

Chapter 4 – A Family Divided

Sariah sat stunned along with the rest of the family, but it was obvious from her lack of response to any questions from concerned family that she was the most traumatized by what she had witnessed that morning at the holy altar. She was a dreamer and so never felt constrained when faced with a narrow set of guidelines. Though she could accept them, and did, if there were other truths to be found outside, she had no trouble accepting them either. Her mind was always active and she seemed quite capable of thinking and performing many tasks simultaneously. She was what psychologists would someday term "an acute multiple imager" and because she was also a dreamer, she always wore her heart upon on her shoulder, which made her an easy target for someone cruel and cunning. Nothing in her psychological development had prepared her for what had just occurred with her family that day.

Sariah was not the oldest of the children; she had older brothers and sisters already married with families of their own, but her younger brothers and sisters were numerous. Thus seeing her mother so overburdened with caring for them and the home, she had postponed her own marriage and family and had stayed at home to help. Of all the family members, she was probably the most observant of Cain's cruelty, but her nature simply rejected the possibility that he was beyond help. Over the years, every attempt she made to reach him lovingly or to reason with him to abandon his cruelty and rebelliousness was met with anger or scorn. In spite of this, she never permitted her past failures to deter her love for her brother. Of course, she was aware of his mistreatment to animals and lately to her brothers, but today had been different. Her family was her whole life and Cain had just ripped it apart without any consideration for what it would do to Father and Mother. She began to wonder if there was something inherently wrong with him, something outside the love and caring influence of family. For the first time in her life she felt the gnawing horror of fear and it had shaken her to her very soul.

Eve was an unusual woman. Some would say, "Well of course. She would have to be." But that would grossly underplay her influence upon the role she willingly assumed as mother and wife. Her patience, intelligence and optimism went beyond what most women and men could achieve in a lifetime. This says volumes when one considers she had never had earthly parents of her own to use as role models. She had progressed degree by degree with minimal digression and so to say she was the matriarch of the family was understated. She was what all her daughters had hoped to become. Eve was what her sons had looked for in a marriage partner, but, like Sariah, there was little in her experience which could have prepared her for what Cain had done this day. Even though over two hundred years had passed away since his birth and many other children had followed, she still recalled the unique experience of bringing him into this life. Never had she felt so complete, so at one with her nature and special calling. And even when Cain had acted as a rebellious child, her heart still had a special place for him. He was her first and felt she would always love him in spite of his unbridled anger and cruelty, but today she had begun to have doubts, and like Sariah, it had shaken her unlike anything else had ever done before.

Eve was sick with despair and Adam was unable to give her much comfort. He hated to see his beloved this way, but since the scene on the mountain, he, too, had been visibly shaken by the loss of his precious children. Such a rebellion within his family was inconceivable to him. Had those other children who left with Cain to join his camp always felt as he? Soon after the incident on the mountain, reports of pagan ritualism among Cain and his brethren contributed to further anxiety between their parents and moreover, Cain had pointedly rejected to ask Adam his blessing when he had taken one of his brother's daughters to wife. Lately, Adam glumly plodded through all the now vacant rooms of this large home he had so carefully and lovingly built for his family over the years. What would the Lord think of his stewardship? He felt so unworthy.

The family council held the next week was doleful and unlike any which Adam and Eve had ever before convened. Adam had dispatched one of the twins, Michael, to invite Cain and those at his camp to attend so that grievances could be heard and differences ironed out. Michael had returned with the despondent news that no one would be attending from Cain's group. Adam would have gone himself, but all efforts to reach Cain and the others had failed miserably that week and had ended with angry words and insults from his children.

After praise and thanks had been given to the Creator, they began the meeting with various reports from those who worked the fields and livestock. Adam had recently assigned Jared the job as overseer of the fields and orchards and it was clear that this change had been accepted wholeheartedly by his brothers who worked along beside him. Adam winced as he saw his son rise to present his report. Jared still bore the marks delivered by the cruelty of his brother as did Avram, but if Jared was ashamed he refused to show it.

"Father" he began, "our crops this season are more bounteous than ever. The corn and wheat are growing well and will be harvested on time. The fruit from the orchards will soon be ready for picking. I look forward to Mother's preserves over the winter", he added with a smile. More specifics were announced as well as the work schedule for the week. Within a few minutes he had completed his report and was seated.

Adam was thrilled that Jared was working out so well in this role. It was clear that Jared led by example and his love for his brothers would always be his first concern. He turned to Abel and announced, "Abel will now give us a report on the livestock."

Abel, always exuberant and a family favorite at the councils, was uncharacteristically subdued that evening. Of all the children of Adam, he knew his father better than anyone except his mother. All of his life he could be seen side by side with Adam, and even though as a small boy he had had to run to keep up with him, if he had felt any impatience, he never showed it. He loved his mother dearly, but he had always been his father's son. With the exception of Cain who loathed him, his older brothers and sisters had looked upon him with fondness and forbearance. Abel simply loved life and his love was contagious, moreover, everyone saw him as a peacekeeper and someone who could be counted on to find something positive about every situation. Being around him was usually enough to brighten anyone's disposition because he made an effort to know something special about every member of the family. When extra understanding was needed to heal a bruised ego, he reached out and found a different approach then persisted until the problem was resolved and the brother or sister was smiling again.

Yes, everyone loved him except Cain. No matter how hard he tried, and he was never more persistent than around his older brother, he could never penetrate the hate and scorn. And now, what was to be done about the rift Cain had caused within the family? It was enough to make even Abel morose. He arose from his seat and prepared to deliver his report, but tonight his heart was heavy with all that had occurred.

After the council, Eve found her husband alone on the porch looking up at the stars. She joined him, but said nothing. The two parents could hear the laughter inside and knew Abel and Sariah had the others playing a game. Finally, Adam murmured, "I love to hear them play. You can almost forget that most of them are no longer children. Even the smaller ones are growing faster than we can keep up with them."

Eve smiled and squeezed her husband's hand. She meant to be light-hearted, but instead her question came out subdued, pensive. "Did you ever think it would happen this way? I mean, our children growing up and leaving us? Wanting to do things their own way, even if that way meant misery and despair?"

Adam had been thinking about those same questions for some time now and he still had been unable to reconcile his feelings. Finally, he responded, "We can teach them to make good choices, but we cannot learn the importance of that lesson for them nor can we force them to accept what we know to be true. We are one, you and I, and it has always been that way from the beginning. The correct course of action has only been easier for us because we have chosen to act together for the good of everyone, but that was a conscious decision on our part. Our children will have to learn the importance of agency the hard way, through opposition and many times alone." This last pronouncement led to an inspired thought: "Our agency to choose is meaningless unless we learn to use it justly, but without it, we would have no chance of learning to act justly at all and there would be no growth without it." He placed his arm around his wife as if to comfort her and she came into his arms. There were tears in her eyes, but she understood his counsel.

If the episode on the mountain had struck Cain's parents numb with worry and anxiety, it was having the reverse effect on him. Now drunk with power and completely embolden by what he considered his new found emancipation from the rule of tyranny he had suffered under his parents, he was now reveling in his new found authority over his brothers and sisters who had followed him on that day. With the help of Lucifer, who had counseled him of the importance to maintain dominance over his followers, he had embraced a new set of commandments which he was quick to indoctrinate among his new family. In his mind, the new arrangements he had instituted had freed them all from the numbing mediocrity of living the mandates of the Creator. They were now free to act for themselves and try anything and everything they desired, and as Lucifer had assured him, there was no end to the many wonderful and varied things to try.

One day a month later, Cain sent one of his sisters, Rachel, to the home of his parents to negotiate, as he had so cynically put it, "an arrangement." It seems his rapid departure and the defection of his brothers and sisters was made in such haste that they neglected to provision themselves properly, so now they were running out of food and other resources to sustain their new-found freedom. The arrangement was simple enough to Cain: Adam would give Cain half the crops from the field or, if necessary, they would take it by force. He reasoned, as he had sweated and toiled so long to make the land fruitful, half should belong to him and his new family anyway. Adam readily agreed to this compromise, but Adam wanted to see him first. He hoped that an opportunity, such as this, would present itself to make peace with his son and convince him and his brothers and sisters to come back home and reconcile their differences.

When Rachel appeared, Adam was alone in the barn tending to the livestock, and while he pondered over the loss of his family, upon seeing her, he saw the opportunity to arrange a meeting to discuss a rapprochement with his estranged children. After hearing his appeal, she looked upon him with utter contempt and said, "Father, Cain will neither talk with you nor listen to any more of your lies. We will have this our way or we will take what is already rightfully ours to have." She then proceeded to list their demands and the consequences should Adam resist.

Adam responded with despair, "My Daughter, you are breaking my heart, please come back home to us." He walked over to her in an attempt to embrace her.

She brushed him off and smiled sardonically at his attempt to dissuade her then retorted, "Cain has taught me a simpler, better way to live. Why should I listen to you and Mother?" With this said, she turned about to leave. As she was walking out the door, she called over her shoulder, "Say good-by to Mother for me. I will not be coming back." Rachel reported back to Cain all which had occurred between her and Adam. She had grown wanton and lascivious in just a few short weeks and her report to Cain reflected the contempt she felt toward those who remained at home with her parents. "The fools all beseech us to return" she reported with a sly grin, "But I told our father to give us what we want or we will take it."

Cain's grin was no less self-abasing. "They will soon understand that we control things now. What was his response to the ultimatum?"

She laughed. "What do you think? The dolt actually believed he had the power to negotiate with us; I set him straight on that account. He will deliver what we ask in the north field at the end of the day tomorrow. I told him be gone before we arrived, just leave the food." At this sally, she tittered with laughter.

Cain realized his sister Rachel was really quite attractive after all.

Cain was absolutely livid with fury. Two months had now passed since their previous demands to their father and Cain and his new family needed more meat. Their continuous gluttony had caused them to over hunt their new homeland and winter had begun to set in; local game had suddenly become scarce. He had once again sent a sister as an emissary to the home of his parents to talk about the next peace negotiation. On this occasion, however, Adam refused to agree to his pointed demands unless he, Cain, made a personal appearance to talk. So, when his sister returned with Adam's message, Cain flew into a tirade of cursing and blasphemy that surprised even Lucifer in its color and variety. His terrified sister, in tears, had fled his presence.

"That foolish twit!" he fumed. "I should have sent Rachel!" As he shouted profanities at any and all within his range of sight and hearing, Cain was shaking as if with palsy. They all fled to a place as far removed as possible between them and his rage. He was thus swallowed up in angry self-pity when Lucifer appeared suddenly at his side. Lucifer, always one to listen to friends and extend them judicial counsel, pretended to listen and commiserate with Cain's plight. He watched patiently as Cain paced up and down the hovel where he and some of his brothers and sisters, including his new wife, had been wallowing in their filth for weeks. Though he was still breathing heavily, finally Cain had spent his rage and was ready to listen.

"So, Cain", began Lucifer, "It appears your father would have you crawl back and bow before him in humble obeisance. I suppose he might likewise invite you to meekly wash the feet of your younger brother, Abel."

"Tell me something I don't already know," growled Cain in response. He was still angry, but now alert. Lucifer would tell him what he needed to do. His counsel was always exactly what he needed to hear.

"The time has come, Cain, for me to teach you the ways of truth that will always exist in the world that you live. This life is hard and brutal and doesn't forgive the mistakes of fools like Adam and your brother, Abel. Your father's way would have you immerse yourself in tired homilies designed to prepare you for the next life, but do pathetically little to help you in the present one. Once I have taught you then you can teach others and be the master over them all, for that has always been the way of the world."

Now that he had Cain's full attention, Lucifer continued his lecture. "There will be many facets to learn, but the first one is the most important: in order to gain the allegiance and loyalty of others you must find a way to ensure they compromise their supposed values; once their values have been sufficiently set aside, you must make it obvious they will need you as a close friend or confederate to prevent exposure of their wrongdoings before others. Most will be willing to pledge themselves to you with hardly any encouragement because a shared confederation will always be appealing to those who wish to operate their true aims outside the light of prying eyes. It tends to either spread the blame or give an alibi of support in the event they are both discovered. This confederation must be sealed with a solemn oath of allegiance to a select fraternity of persons who want to share a common destiny of power over others. The allegiance may never be broken except on pain of death and only those willing to exercise true power and control deserve to lead in this manner. Everything else is just empty words and weakness."

Lucifer asked him pointedly, "Are you ready to covenant with me by your throat and by the living God that you will not reveal my creed to anyone outside my society or suffer death? If you so agree, I will covenant to be your protector and deliver your brother Abel into your hands this day."

Cain responded with a resounding, "Yes".

Lucifer smiled beatifically. "That is good. Now go to your brethren and have them swear the same."

Cain's defection from his parent's home had placed his birthright in considerable question and he was anxious to ensure that he could lay claim to what was rightfully his without coming again under his parent's direct control. Cain suddenly realized he had just been given the answer to his current dilemma. He began to mentally review the steps he would need to accomplish that goal: he must select a few trusted brothers and put them under the oath of this fraternity; then he will inform them of their father's stubborn refusal to help them through this current crisis and insist that they all must take drastic measures to regain what has been thoughtlessly denied them; they will go to their father and pretend repentance, desiring to come back home; while they keep him occupied with hope, he will visit Abel tending his flocks and there he will engage Abel and kill him when he least expects it; later, he will testify that a regrettable accident had taken his life and then playing the penitent and bereaving son, he will then report this tragedy to his father and the old fool will anoint him future leader over the family. Yes, he thought, *"If I play this right, I will inherit everything, including the fields and flocks of my feckless brothers. Eventually, there will be another regrettable accident, this time befalling our poor father. Cain, the anointed one will step forward and claim his well-deserved throne."*

He nodded his head in appreciation of the plan, but before putting it into effect, though, he determined to first put his confederate brethren under oath to ensure no one ever suspects his hand in this conspiracy. Furthermore, he would insist that the idea of his ascendancy to patriarch of the family come from them. As they will all be under solemn oath, none will ever speak of this again outside the alliance. He happily concluded that he could pass this precept along and teach it as many times as he desired. "I will be known as Master Mahan", he marveled aloud at his new name.

Lucifer was quite aware of Cain's thoughts and so interjected an occasional point to clarify the concepts then he congratulated Cain on his choice of title, though of course he had put it in his mind.

Cain gathered a dozen of his most trusted brothers around him. The campfire provided what light and warmth was needed, but still a few of them were reminded of the hearth that awaited them back at home with their parents. Cain was well aware that there had been murmurings of late among his new family and had been assured by Lucifer that this covenant would strengthen their resolve to remain together.

Cain recalled everything which Lucifer had taught and carefully explained the covenant process that each was to make to him and to their new society. One by one they stepped forward and made a blood oath covenant and swore an allegiance which bound them all to Cain and to one another and were then welcomed as full members of this fraternity of murder and secrets.

A few days later, the plan was laid and the trap was set. All that was needed was the will to see it all through. Once the oath was made, though, any reticence they had quickly flew away and besides, they reasoned, what else could be done? They had made a covenant to stand by Cain, thus returning to the home of their parents was no longer an option, moreover, as they were out of food, neither was starvation.

Chapter 5 – And Cain Slew Abel

And Cain talked with Abel his brother: and it came to pass, when they were in the field, that Cain rose up against Abel his brother, and slew him.

----- Genesis 4:8

And Satan covenanted unto Cain: Swear unto me by thy throat, and if thou tell it thou shalt die; and covenant with thy brethren by their heads, and by the living God, that they tell it not; for if they reveal it, they shall surely die; and this that thy father may not discover it; and this day I will deliver up thy brother Abel into thine hands.

And Satan covenanted unto Cain that he would do according to all his commands. And all these things of darkness were done in secret.

----- The Abridgement, Chapter 2

None are so fond of secrets as those who do not mean to keep them.

----- Charles Caleb Colton

The evening gloaming had begun and Abel watched as the daylight began to fade. Since the defection of his brothers to the camp of Cain, Abel had stepped up and had been helping his father with the larger livestock. The cows had been safely led to the barns and the horses had already been carefully corralled for the day. His younger brothers had just completed the evening work with the goats and sheep and as Abel made his way back to the sheep corral, the light had finally begun to dim into night. He signaled his two younger brothers, the twins, over to his side and complemented them. "Michael and Gabriel, your work was excellent today and it is time to halt our labors, so you may go. I will lock up everything and join you at home."

The twins brightened as they heard they could leave early. "Thanks, Abel" they both exclaimed as they started down the hill to the house.

Abel loved his brothers and although his parents had other twins that were fraternal, Michael and Gabriel were identical male twins and therefore unique and were yet the only such twins of the family and extended family. Abel looked upon them fondly as they were always together, did everything together even spoke together. He envied them their absolute natural bond to one other. Smiling, Abel exclaimed, "Boys, tell Mother I will be along soon and look forward to her famous stew. Try not to eat it all before I arrive."

In unison the two boys sang out, "We'll try!" Then off they ran down the hill.

Cain was a man with a purpose. It was now twilight and the stars were beginning to lighten up the darkening sky, and in anticipation of consummating his long-awaited goal, Cain walked briskly up the path to the top of a nearby hill. He noted his brother Abel was standing next to the fence and knew from experience that, in all probability, Abel had already locked up the fences and was preparing to leave for the day. Cain glanced around the clearing to ensure the fool was alone, and as he had hoped, Abel had sent his brothers back home while he finished up the daily chores. Yes, there he was staring up at the night sky, as usual dreaming his feckless life away. "Abel," called out Cain in greeting, "it is I, your brother."

For Abel, the end of the day was his favorite time to contemplate the majesty of the Creator's works and designs. The night sky was now in full spectacle before him and he had been stargazing at the wonder of it all. As were all of the sons of Adam, he had been taught of the movements of the sun, the moon and the stars in the heavens as they pertained to the daily needs of the family, but Abel, however, had expressed an opinion to his father there must be much more beyond their practical import and was intrigued that there might be other purposes involved with their creation. While he was thus pondering these possibilities, he heard a voice and with a surprised look of joy, he turned around at hearing Cain's greeting.

"Brother, it has been too long and it's so good to see you," replied Abel with total sincerity. He rushed up to Cain and embraced him tightly, and then pulling away he became aware that Cain's countenance had darkened. He knew of his brother's rejection of the family, of course, but he still loved him as they all did. Perhaps he might convince Cain to return home. Why else had he come to see him if not to reconcile differences? Mother and Father will be thrilled, he concluded with joy. Abel opened his mouth to extend the invitation when he felt something sharp penetrate the underside of his throat in a lateral movement.

Cain was immediately soaked in the blood of the brother he had long detested. Abel dropped to his knees then fell forward to the ground as though he had lost his balance. Cain watched with mounting glee as Abel thrashed about before him on the hard, rocky soil, finally rolling over onto his back, and never having seen a person die before in this manner, he was anxious to witness the event. In fact, he felt an inexplicable need to record the event in his mind forever, so he bent forward, squatting down next to him for a closer view. Though tragically no more could be heard except desperate gurgles, his larynx having been severed, Abel was now clutching at the gaping slice across his throat while trying uselessly to call out for help.

As Abel's hands slackened and fell from his neck, the blood from the wound coursed upward in rich, red fountains. While his death throes became feebler, the air grew thick with the rich coppery scent of fresh blood and now the moment that Cain had long awaited was near at hand. Because of his proximity to his dying brother, Cain was now soaked with Abel's blood upon his face, his hands and clothing, yet he reveled in the cloying wetness of it. While his own heart was beating desperately in counterpoint to his brother's slackening heartbeat, Cain could sense that the time for the end was coming fast. Thereupon, Cain bent over to look into the eyes of his brother for one last time and smiled with victory. Abel's eyes seemed to rest upon something over Cain's shoulder then gradually closed. Cain arose over the prostrated body of his dead brother and raised both his blood-soaked hands high over his head. "It's over," he exulted in pure ecstasy. "Surely my brother's flocks will now belong to me!" With utter contempt for his brother's memory, he kicked the body and then threw it off the hill then with fascination he watched as it rolled limply down into the draw. Having expended all further interest with him, he strode down the hill back to his camp.

Adam was deep in thought and unaccountably in a somber mood this evening. As he watched the sun setting in the west, he was only faintly aware of Eve and his daughters preparing the evening meal. The smell of the stew wafted throughout the house and the men and boys that had put in a full day on the farm and fields, though resting, were immediately roused when they knew meal time was approaching. This had always been when the family gathered for food and fellowship, to discuss the day and plan for the next and for Adam, it had always been his favorite time of the day, though recently, he reflected sadly, there had been unsurprisingly little to look forward to. Today, for some reason, was especially bad. He was about to turn from the window when he spied figures walking toward the house. Adam walked outside to get a better look and ensure that his eyes were truly seeing his sons and that it was not just wishful thinking. With a boundless joy, he rushed from the porch and ran to them, calling each by name.

"Father," they cried. "We are here for a visit. In truth, we are hungry," they joked. But Adam could see that they had all lost weight and so he was not fooled by this false joviality.

With a love so deep he could hardly contain it, Adam invited them all inside for the evening meal. "Come inside, my sons. Your mother will be happy to see you." They followed him through the front door to be greeted joyously by their brothers and sisters.

"Eve, our sons who were lost are now found. Can it be so?" exclaimed Adam.

Eve nearly dropped the crock ware she was carrying to the long table. "My boys," she cried and ran to them, embracing each. "Please come inside and be seated. I have just now completed dinner and you have arrived on time."

It was the first real meal the men had eaten since they walked off behind Cain down the mountain nearly three months earlier. They had their fill of food and family love and much later excused themselves, insisting that they must talk with their brothers and sisters over reuniting the family. For the first time in months, Adam and Eve felt their hopes soar.

Now back at the campsite, Cain met with his fellow conspirators. He had reviewed mentally the events of the night before and had found the results well above expectations. He was now eager to hear what his brothers had accomplished. "Simeon, report what you have done."

The leader of the group, Simeon, now turned to him to relate all that had happened that night and proudly reported, "Cain, our father Adam, to our surprise, had seen us approaching from the window and had gone out to meet us. And can you believe it? He embraced us as though we had been gone for years instead of only a few months." Then his tone turned subdued and incredulous. "Our Father had accepted our pardons and readily forgave us of all that had occurred on that Sabbath. He then had invited us for the dinner meal where our mother doted and clucked over us like a mother hen. Everyone was so happy that no one took notice of the absence of Abel until much later when we were making our departure."

Cain listened attentively and marveled at how well their plan had been executed. "Well done, brothers! Anything else?" he asked anxiously.

Simeon added, "We left them with a promise to return with more of our brothers and sisters."

Cain nodded his approval and then excitedly related the murder he had committed step by step, omitting none of the particulars. "You should have seen him bleed!" he crowed with delight. "The moment I cut his scrawny neck, the blood spewed out of him like a stuck pig! It was glorious", he added contentedly as though remembering a delicious meal.

His brothers, though relieved the deed was done, were disinclined to dwell on the grisly details as Cain had. In fact, they seemed sickened by the account. One of them changed the subject a tad too quickly, "So, Brother what is next?"

Cain registered their disinterest and it angered him. He suspected they were secretly judging him for having the stomach to do what had to be done. Being careful to avoid endangering the alliance, he smothered a biting comment. He replied smoothly, "You will *accidentally* stumble upon the body in the morning and unless it has been carried off by some wild beast, you should find it at the bottom of the hill in the ravine near the corral, well bled out by then, I suppose. Take it back to Father and Mother. There will no doubt be weeping and wailing for the loss of someone so precious and dear, but mention to them that all of us will be present for the funeral, including myself, and we will discuss a long overdue reconciliation."

Simeon was well aware of his part in their ruse to have his family look the other way while Cain murdered Abel. In fact, he was getting concerned that this whole mess might come crashing down upon them all. "Do you think they will suspect you, Cain?" Simeon ventured to ask.

Cain, characteristically impatient at the inanity of his dullard brother, reacted with an exasperated shout. "Of course they will you fool! You all must vouch for my whereabouts during the night!" Before separating, he once again reminded them of the blood oath and covenant to their Brotherhood. For Cain it had been a highly successful day and a good beginning to recover that which had clearly been stolen from him, namely his birthright and the possessions that came with it.

Cain awoke the following morning, refreshed and ready to proceed with the next phase of the operation. If his brothers had stayed on task according to the plan he had outlined, they should be on their way back to the home of their parents with the body of his feeble-minded brother in tow. So, now stepping lightly down the path with visions of his inheritance now insured, he whistled a tune under his breath. He had walked no more than a mile when he noted where there was once birdsong, now only silence. Suddenly, from within a copse of tall bushes just to the right of the pathway, he heard a voice:

"Cain, where is Abel, thy brother?" The Voice was calm, yet insistent.

Now recognizing the voice and wanting to appear casual, even though clearly he was alarmed that his plan had been discovered so quickly, Cain said, "I know not. Am I then my Brother's keeper?" he added flippantly.

And the Voice asked plaintively, "What hast thou done? The voice of thy brother's blood cries unto me from the ground!"

Now speechless and powerless over the presence emanating from the bushes, Cain could only listen in horror as the Lord God cursed him for the murder of Abel, his younger brother. "And now thou shalt be cursed from the earth. She now opens her mouth to receive thy brother's blood shed from thy hand. From henceforth when thou tillest the ground it shall not produce unto thee her strength. Thou will be cast out and live as a fugitive and a vagabond among men cursed to walk the earth alone."

Reeling from the condemnation that he had just received, he managed to stammer out in his defense, "Lucifer came tempting me because of my brother's flocks. And I was wroth also at Abel for his offering thou didst accept and not mine." Openly wailing in shame and fear, Cain cried out in spiritual agony, "I cannot bear this punishment!"

The voice from the bushes was silent as if waiting to hear more of Cain's useless excuses and denials.

Cain sniveled out a petulant sob, "Behold thou hast driven me out so from this day I am hid from the face of the Lord, and I shall be a fugitive and a vagabond despised of all in the earth; and it shall happen, that he that findeth me will desire to slay me, because of the record of mine iniquities, for these things will not be hid from the Lord."

The voiced assured him with a voice like thunder, "Whosoever shall slay thee, he will know my vengeance and it shall be taken on him sevenfold! And I the Lord will set a mark upon thy face, Cain, lest any finding thee should desire to kill thee."

An unseen, but powerful force threw Cain to the ground where he writhed in pain. Then suddenly the voice was silent and the presence departed. Quiet, but tentative bird-song resumed from the nearby forest. As his hand shakily slid across his left jaw and the blood slowly trickled onto his chin, Cain was now trembling from fear. A deep gash had appeared where once there had been a thick growth of beard and only later would his brothers further comment on the sudden darkness of his skin. At last, now more frightened than humbled and still smarting from the wound, he pulled himself up and staggered back to his camp.

At no time in the human experience had such an event occurred. As parents, Adam and Eve had known death of their children and progeny. There was the occasional accident inherent to all families who live in the wild without the benefit of modern medicine or procedures to treat severe wounds: Children will drown and others will be mortally injured while working in the fields or, owing to illness at childbirth, grandchildren will be born and die shortly thereafter. Our experience in mortality is rife with accidental death or unexpected illness, conditions which have remained regretfully unchanged since the beginning of time. Murder, however, was unknown to the first family, and its aftermath was both traumatic as well as personal.

When Abel's return had grown later than usual for the evening meal the night before, Adam had begun to be concerned. Later, only after the departure of his sons following the meal, did his concern turned to worry. He would forever wonder whether the outcome would have been different if he had followed his initial feelings of disquiet, but the joyous arrival of his sons had temporarily disconnected him from the promptings he had received. For the rest of his long life he would sometimes inexplicably reflect upon that night and berate himself because he had been too slow to act. Since Abel had not returned home the night before, in an effort to determine his whereabouts, at first light Adam and his sons had set off down the pathway leading to the corral and holding pens for the livestock. His premonition was stronger than he had ever felt before and it was terrible; images of Abel, his beloved son, injured at the bottom of some wash came unbidden to his mind.

They had almost reached the holding area for the livestock when he saw coming up the road the other sons he had entertained the night before. Behind them, two were pulling a cart, a third pushing from behind. From where Adam stood, it looked as though there was something or someone inside. Then with a horror so great he could scarcely express it, his only word was: "Abel"!

He and his sons raced forward until they met up with the others beside the cart. Inside laid out was the body of his son, Abel, bruised and bloody, utterly lifeless. As he took the body of his son in his arms, Adam wept openly while his sons who had been part of their father's search were too stunned to believe what had occurred and so looked on in morbid silence. Young Michael, confused by the scene asked quietly, "Father, why is our brother Abel so cut and bruised? Can you not awaken him?"

The answer came from Jared, much older, but nonetheless equally bewildered and traumatized by the sight. "Abel, our brother, is dead", he replied in a subdued tone.

Adam suddenly fell to the ground to his knees in profound grief over the loss of his beloved son. He sagged forward helplessly, grasping at the body of his dead son. He could only shake his head in abject despair. Suddenly, a feeling of vertigo overcame him and to prevent a violent sickness he closed his eyes. The self-awareness of being nearby with his sons was gradually dissipating, slowly fading until suddenly he seemed at one with a new reality outside of himself. Images appeared with lightning speed as a blur then began to slow down, down until he could grasp them. Suddenly, even though he was conscious of having his eyes tightly closed, a panoramic view of a landscape sprang before him. Sound had a wasp-like humming quality as it, too, began to slow down, down until it gradually tuned such that audible clarity was acquired.

He had a sense of being in a faraway place or time?? The smell of moisture and salt were gravid and heavily assaulting to his senses. It was a slate dark morning, overcast and slightly misting. He felt he was in a powerful device such as a cart, but constructed of some type of heavy material that conveyed him over a large body of water. Around him worried and frightened young men arrayed in strange clothing were seated and waiting some type of confrontation. In their hands they carried what he supposed were weapons of war that each intended to use in what he intuited to be a battle of some sort. A man appearing to be his own age began speaking and Adam listened intently to what seemed to be his battle orders. As he had no reference from which to draw, none of what Adam saw should have made any sense, nonetheless he knew, or felt, what was about to happen and perceived what the man was thinking:

Lieutenant Barrows wearily gazed over the men he had been training for over a year in England. They had all been waiting the day of invasion known as Operation Overlord and last minute planning had contributed to an unfortunate lack of sleep the night before among the whole platoon. Barrows was tired and the closer they approached the coastline the more palpable the anxiety was felt and the more he became convinced of the disaster that awaited them. Struggling to be heard over the roar of the landing vessel, he shouted, "Men, the beaches have to be cleared of obstacles and it is up to us to do the job. You have all had the best training any soldier has ever received before battle. If you remember your training, you will survive. I will see you on the beach."

Though slightly foggy, the outline of the French coast of Normandy could be clearly seen a thousand yards ahead. Their beach carried the name of Omaha and once hitting the coastline they would establish a beachhead for subsequent landing vessels. Later, they would work their way inland to link with the British landings at Gold Beach to the east and later linking up with VII Corps at Utah Beach.

Then suddenly, the landing vessel door opened up revealing the last fifty yards of water still to be forded before they could attain the beach. Before the men could exit the craft, however, machine gun fire could be seen, yet unheard from bunkers overlooking the beach. Rapid zinging, then plunking sounds seemed to assail them as projectiles began to ricochet off the launch. The first dozen men scarcely knew what hit them as the 94 mm machine gun rounds from the German bunkers raked across the front of the vessel cutting most of them in half, throwing blood and body parts across the faces of those behind them. Barrows shouted, "Get over the side, now!" and those quick enough to react threw themselves over the side of the boat, but the rest met similar fates as their comrades.

In spite of the machine gun fire spitting death all around him, Lieutenant Barrows quickly pushed the remainder of his cowering, drenched men to the beach, but he could see that those landings from the other vessels had encountered the same deadly resistance. Once on the beach, a barrage of mortar fire begun to rain death down upon them from all sides and whatever semblance of control he had once had then slipped as his men ran helter-skelter to avoid the deadly trap into which they had fallen. He pushed and shoved as many as he could toward relative safety of the nearby dunes, but before reaching their destination, a soldier tripped a land mine and Barrows, as well as what remained of his platoon, were consumed in an explosion of shrapnel that sliced through them like a scythe through ripened wheat.

Adam felt a rush of outrage and despair as he gazed upon the scenes of horror before him. It was unforgivable that young men could be capable of such depravity and death. He wanted it to end, but was helpless to prevent the ear-shattering noise that assailed him and the nightmare landscape of scrambling, screaming men as they died brutally before his eyes. At length, mercifully there seemed to be a merging of time and space; a quick moment of vertigo then everything slid back into place. He was back on the road slowly swaying over the body of his son and he knew with a certainty who had been responsible for the death of Abel and who would be responsible for setting in motion all the murders to come.

Adam shakily arose and laid the body carefully back into the cart and turned to his sons. "Fetch water from the stream. We must clean him before we arrive home. I will not permit his mother and sisters to see him this way." After water and clean wash cloths were brought, he lovingly washed the grime and blood from the face and neck of his son and covered the neck wound as best he could. Finally, he murmured, "It is time for his mother to greet her son for the last time."

It was a silent, moribund procession that made its way silently down the hill to their home. Death had just arrived into the world in a way that was both incomprehensible and horrifying. Much later, after thousands of years had passed, death and murder would become an all too familiar and common place occurrence. It would be something to be casually discussed over breakfast and by noon forgotten, usually replaced the next day by news of still more of the same. Wars of aggression and terror would rage and young men would return home maimed, battered and traumatized at having witnessed murder first-hand and in many cases had dealt it out. As the procession continued silently, Adam sadly reflected that he had clearly seen all the murder and destruction to come and openly wept at the utter senselessness of the events he saw in the vision. *"So," he thought miserably, "this is only the beginning. It is not to be borne!"*

As they cleared the copse of bushes which separated the road from their home, Adam could see Eve and his daughters crowded around together in front of the entrance. He thought it unsurprising that Eve had felt the same presentiment as he had. They had always been close and as one and after today, they would have to be even closer.

Chapter 6 – Division and Reconciliation

The weak can never forgive. Forgiveness is the attribute of the strong.

----- *Mahatma Gandhi*

Many family members, married and unmarried, including many from the camp of their brother Cain, had come quietly and respectfully to the burial site at the foot of their holy mountain. All had come to pay their respects except for Cain and a small coterie of his loyal followers. Each, in his own way, silently reviewed the life of Abel and the influence he had had on them. None could ever recall any offense done or words uttered that reflected badly upon their brother; he had died innocent and pure.

Tears sprung from Sariah's eyes and dropped quietly down her cheeks as she openly wept for her personal loss. She remembered an incident that best exemplified the life of her brother. It had occurred a few years earlier while she, Abel and the twins, Michael and Gabriel, had all gone out to look for wild berries for their mother. They had envisioned the fresh berry tarts and cobbler, so each was highly motivated to find as much as they could. It had been a beautiful day and the land was rich with berries and fruits of all variety. Since each had pails they had divided up, thinking they could make better time that day and their harvest would be even greater. So, they had separated and gone their own way, though, of course, the twins were inseparable so they had dashed off together.

Abel had found a bountiful patch of blackberries and was in the process of plucking them carefully from the bush when he heard a still, small voice. He knew the voice well and was careful to listen when it came. "Abel, thy sister Sariah is in danger. Go to her now." Without further thought, he set off in the direction in which they had separated a half-hour earlier. He had found a path through a copse of dense bushes when he realized that he was going the wrong direction, whereupon he abruptly turned to the right and hurried up a small hill. There in the clearing, he could see his sister with her back against the wall of the hillside, and in front of her and closing in, was a large female mountain lion. Abel realized that Sariah had inadvertently entered the lair of this mountain cat, and feeling threatened, the cat was simply defending her young.

Abel quietly moved forward carefully and slowly so as not to distress the lion. Glancing toward his sister, he whispered, "Sariah, remain perfectly still and make no sudden moves."

Sariah was, of course, terrified, but, seeing Abel moving quietly in her direction, she gradually began to calm herself. Hearing his quiet instructions, she assented without saying a word and resisted a sudden desire to dash for safety into the nearby trees.

The mountain cat had heard his words of encouragement and had turned in Abel's direction, but, instead of reacting violently to the intrusion of another person, she seemed to be waiting for him to speak. She cocked an ear in his direction as if curious, yet unthreatened.

All the while humming a familiar tune in a peaceful, soothing tone, Abel quietly walked up to the great cat. The mountain lion appeared fascinated and allowed Abel to touch her and brush her flanks with his hand then he quietly bent over close to her ear and whispered something only he and the cat could hear. The mountain cat seemed to nod her approval and abruptly sidled off into the nearby bushes.

Sariah observed all this with utter disbelief. She had wandered into the area after spotting some promising berry bushes from afar. Excited at having found them, she was completely unaware of the mountain lion and her cubs nearby. When the cat showed herself suddenly, Sariah was nowhere near an escape. All she could do was back up and hope the cat would leave her in peace. When she heard the aggressive growl, however, Sariah knew she was in trouble and was still backing away when she heard her brother approach. And now she was safe and when this thought flooded over her she ran to Abel and held him tight. He had saved her and yet she wondered how this had happened. "Abel, what did you say to her?" she exclaimed, nearly in tears.

He took her hand and quietly led her back down the hill. At the bottom, he turned to her and said quite blandly, "I told her you were too boney and it would be a waste of time and effort to eat you."

Even though he had related to her his premonition of her imminent danger, she never learned what he had said to the mountain lion that day.

Every time she asked, his reply was flippant, followed by a laugh. And now, she reflected, she would never know. *He saved my life and now my days will be less bright because of his absence.* How was she to be consoled in this loss? She looked over at her mother and weeping sisters and realized that her only comfort would come in consoling them. Without saying a word she walked over to the group of females, put her arms around her mother and sisters and helped them weep out their sorrow. She was hardly surprised that it had helped more than she could have hoped. They had always been close and now they would draw even closer.

At the end of the funeral, Adam added a benedictory statement to all his children present at the event: "Each of us has come this day to remember the life of our beloved son and brother, Abel. Before his death, he had expressed his deepest hope that the rift among us would be healed. If his death has any meaning at all, it should be that we could all come back together as a family out of love and respect." Adam paused to steel himself for what he was about to utter, then he continued, "If I could trade places with him this day, I would gladly do it without hesitation. I say that not just as a father, but because I knew him, and I know he would have willingly given his life for me and any of you here today, including his brother Cain who slew him so horribly."

A sudden gasp shuddered through the gathered family members. Some murmured, "Cain has killed our brother? How was that possible? And Why?"

Adam fought back his personal loss of not one, but two sons. "Each of you will need to choose for yourselves how you wish to deal with this truth, but from this day forward, none of you must allow Cain into your homes. He is to be shunned and put out on the road as a vagabond among men. His name is to be a hiss and by-word throughout all time." Adam choked back a sob of loss and personal grief, "He is my son no more." With a finality that comes only with a perfect knowledge, he added sadly, "The Creator, the Father of us all, has so willed it."

Cain had considered a number of ways to remind his brothers of their covenant to him and to his master, Lucifer. He had dismissed them all as being ineffective and lacking the outward sign of the importance of their vows. Ironically, the answer came to him while he contemplated over how he was to recover from the damnable curse he had received. Over the past few weeks he had developed the annoying habit of rubbing the scar that ran down his left cheek. Though it had healed quickly enough, he was nonetheless aware of it as a constant reminder of being rejected by God and family. When he became nervous or was deep in thought, he tended to rub it as though it were a constant itch that he could scarcely satisfy. It was during this process of reflection that it occurred to him that his brethren, if they were to share this covenant, should likewise carry a similar mark as a visible sign of their loyalty.

Later that afternoon, accompanied by a small group of his most trusted brothers, Cain climbed to the top of a hill overlooking the camp. Each of his loyal conspirators looked at him somewhat uneasily. The consensus opinion among them was that perhaps they had been overzealous in their alliance with him. They had arrived at that conclusion as they heard some of their brothers and sisters remonstrating quietly then more vocally with their concerns over the way Cain was managing their lives.

Cain looked them over disdainfully, and candidly reminded them, "You have all made a covenant with me and with him who I serve and who serves me." He unsheathed his knife and, with a quick motion, he flicked the wrist of his right hand along the left side of the face of his brother on his right, slicing a small wound where the blade had cut. His brother yelped in surprise and immediately blood began to dribble down his beard. They all looked at Cain expectantly as though mesmerized by the cut of their brother, and none moved away. Cain continued to hold the blade in his hand and stated, "Each of you will wear a similar mark to remind you of your oath to me as your master. You will honor this or I will gut you like a pig then your blood on my blade will mingle with the blood of our worthless brother, Abel. From now and henceforth, I will carry another name, Master Mahan, and that name will remind you that I am your master and no one else."

One by one each brother lined up to have the mark placed upon him to seal the oath and covenant that each had made. When it was over, Cain, now feeling the control he had so ardently sought, gazed upon each with an amiable smile. He concluded their meeting with a note of encouragement. "Brothers, as members of My Brotherhood which I will call the Clan of the Scar, there is much to plan and each of you will share in my legacy. I will teach you all the ways of this world and what I don't know, I will ask and we will all learn together."

Within a few days, a deep break occurred within the camp of Cain's new family. Now knowing, no longer merely suspecting what Cain had done to their defenseless brother Abel, many came to a decision that split the camp in half. A discussion led to loud disputations and accusations. Many raised their obvious desire to reconcile differences with their parents. Finally, Cain in a furious frenzy hurled threats at those who would dare accuse him of murder and go crawling back home.

"Get out", he screamed dementedly at those who now tormented him with their pathetic appeals to make peace with their parents. "Haven't you heard, you fools, that I am shunned and to be a vagabond among men. Our own parents have forbidden me back in their home, even if I so wanted, and just as well. Our father would simply return to his old habits of empty persuasion to lull us back into his addled ways. Good riddance, I say, so if that is what you want then get out!"

Those who listened were clearly appalled at this senseless harangue and lately his brutish behavior had become unbearable. With dawning realization, many decided that they would prefer to associate with a loving and forgiving family than live around an angry man having no respect for anyone, including himself. It was far better to live with overbearing, yet loving parents than a murdering monster.

That day a small exodus started from the camp of Cain and ended back to their birth home. Adam and Eve, when they saw the group approach, ran out to them and welcomed them back with open arms. With love and affection these two fine parents assured each of the returning children as well as their married children that a place in their home would always be there for them and all the angry words and recriminations had been forgotten; it was as though nothing had ever occurred to pull them apart. By common, yet unspoken consent the name of their brother Cain was scrupulously avoided in all conversations.

Now repentant of her behavior, Rachel had held herself back from the group, so ashamed that it had made her physically ill. Sariah observed her reticence and embraced her as a sister and Rachel, now in tears, asked her,

"Dear Sariah, after all that has been said and done, how can all this love and forgiveness be possible?"

She could think of little else to say except, "It was Abel's parting gift." They walked inside the home of their birth and were greeted with warm welcomes and hugs.

Adam and Eve were the last to enter. The two first parents walked back into the home, now holding hands, where children and adults were bustling and shuffling about getting ready for the evening meal. Smiles and laughter and good natured banter abounded. There would always be an empty space where Abel's life should have been, but knowing him the way they did, they knew he would want them to move on. Eve looked up at Adam with a smile and observed, "My Husband, it is time to serve the children dinner. They are hungry and await us."

Chapter 7 – The Translation, continued

"Jasher," began Bedford, "our translation indicates the formation of a Brotherhood or Society that Cain created for the purpose of murdering his brother, Abel, which he used not only to cover up the murder, but to enlist others to help him with the act then to keep the secret. There seems to be something vaguely familiar about how this society operates and what some historians have speculated as to how world events have unfolded, particularly in the destruction of governments as a result of coups and assassinations. Do you see a tie in our day and age to that same ancient conspiracy?"

Jasher paused slightly as he began his explanation. "The tie is there and is deliberate, but to simply say that this society is conspiratorial in nature and leave it at that is to underplay its true role. The Society then and now serves a greater purpose for those who would attempt to deny us of our agency for choice. Perhaps now would be a good time to explain the necessity for this work in which we are now engaged and how Cain was and is still involved." Both scientists were immediately startled at the implications of the last statement and Jasher, anticipating their questions as well as their doubts, slightly raised his hand and remarked, "Please let me continue, then your questions will be answered."

"Lucifer, known as Satan or the Devil to many, has from the beginning wanted complete control over mankind to satisfy his own ego and personal glorification. He has deceived himself and his followers, Cain being principle among them, that there is still a chance to prove the Creator's plan of agency or personal choice as unworkable, which of course, is absurd. Our translation will reveal to the world that this Society exists and has been the means to undermine and destroy all historically significant civilizations since the beginning of time and replace them with Cain's own brand of government bent on removing our personal agency of choice. In order to cover his tracks, since the beginning, Cain has been busily destroying all record of his nefarious influence and the havoc it has caused, and that effort is ongoing today."

Both Isaac and William remained stunned at the implications of Jasher's latest revelation. Isaac was the first to verbalize what they were both thinking. "Are you saying that Cain, who murdered Abel of the Old Testament, still walks the earth?"

Jasher slowly nodded his head and sadly commented, "Cain was cursed to wander the earth among men as a vagabond, but there has never been any mention in any scriptural or historical text I have read where he actually died. I, too, was stunned when I heard this from my great-great grandfather, Noah, and gave it little credence at the time until I met the man personally soon after I had been called to this mission."

Bedford slowly shook his head in wonder at this latest revelation to their project. With some consternation he asked, "If this man still lives on, how is it he has managed to be so successful at gaining power and maintaining it where others in history have failed?"

After a moment of deliberation, Jasher commented, "Most of us embrace a life of limited possibilities. It isn't really our fault because, according to our natures, we tend to compartmentalize our daily routines and so we live for the day: We arise in the morning, prepare ourselves to get through the day, perform our daily work, retire for the evening, sleep and start the same process over again the next morning. Most long term planning is never considered until it is too late. However, if you thought you were never going to die then your possibilities for planning for success would eventually force you to see well beyond the day. If you didn't, your daily routine would become so mundane it would eventually drive you mad. I can say this from personal experience."

"Cain's long life has produced a creature completely amoral that lives according to his own laws and gives allegiance only to the father of his lies. He is cunning beyond your imagination and lives only to traffic in power and misery. Imagine a person, if you can, who never makes a move without considering several counter-moves, much like a chess-master, except on a much larger scale. To him, there is no short-term daily plan and no sense of permanent defeat, only a strategic withdrawal using countermoves to succeed the next time so as to get one step closer to his end-game. Now that he is close to global control over most world governments, he has finally managed to take this game to the next level. This is the only game he plays and its consequences extend well beyond this life as we know it."

Bedford and Levinson were both still doubtful, but by the looks on their faces, they were beginning to believe that there was much more involved in this project than either had ever dreamed could exist.

Isaac then asked, "Assuming we can put this discussion of Cain on hold for the time being, just how do you and we fit into all this? Aside from their obvious historical value, why maintain the records, especially in view of the dangers involved?"

"I have spent most of my life struggling to understand this same question. I have concluded that there are things we are permitted to know for a certainty and others we must act on in faith until we are ready for the full truth. My only answer I have been permitted is that we maintain the records as a witness to ensure that the Creator's justice will be swift and sure and that Cain and his followers do not escape the judgment they deserve."

Chapter 8 – The Report, New York

In New York City there is a nondescript ten-story office building in Mid-town Manhattan overlooking the East River. Though its design and color are unobtrusive externally, the inside has been luxuriously appointed with art work and sculptures designed at once to project power and instill a sense of intimidation. No one who enters this austere, sterile building can ever leave without feeling the loss of personal control on some level. Multiple visits have stripped many would-be politicians or corporate executives from any delusion of retaining what they had foolishly considered as control over their own destinies.

The CIA Section Chief over the Middle East, James Perkins, was paralyzed with fear. He had every right to be fearful not only for his career, but possibly even his life. It was his painful duty to enter that building overlooking the river and stand not sit, in front of the only man he had ever met that could reduce him to a babbling, stammering fool. On this day he had been summoned there to personally deliver a report over the latest intelligence gathered from Israel concerning a dealer in antiquities, Benjamin Jasher.

Perkins was now sitting in a small anteroom in which a severe, but no doubt highly qualified secretary was typing constantly on a computer keyboard. Occasionally she had answered phone calls and had spoken in at least three different languages he could understand and one that he was unable to identify, and for him that was unusual.

Suddenly, a voice came over the intercom. "Send him in" was all that was said. The secretary glanced with a cool arch of her eyes in his direction. Her gaze told him that his appearance was required and any other decision was inadvisable.

With silent dread he walked down a long, dark paneled hallway. At the end was a heavy oak door with an emblem embossed in the middle and face-high. Following his initial meeting in the building, his curiosity had driven him to discover the meaning of the symbol, and after some research he had consulted a middle-eastern expert on Sumerian who related to him that the symbol had reference to a walking man or a vagabond.

Perkins hesitated at the door, but there was no turning back and running. Where could he hide where this man wouldn't find him? Most reputations, he had discovered, were more myth than fact, mere affectations to inflate the reputation or ego. This man was the one exception to the general rule and Perkins needed this report to go well, otherwise being demoted might be the least of his worries. He remembered all too well the interrogation room in Baghdad. That was the first time he had worked with Walker Caine and the first time he had heard the name of Benjamin Jasher.

He was about to knock when he heard from within, "Mr. Perkins", the voice was calm, yet commanding, "Please join me." There was no inflected question indicating courtesy, but a simple flat statement of fact.

Even after four visits, Perkins was still surprised at how starkly intimidating this office was. For one thing it was smaller than most executive offices, though he suspected that aspect only lent to the intimidation factor because one felt upon entering boxed-in or trapped, eaten alive. At one end where Caine sat was a large desk and matching chair, both of solid mahogany and rococo workmanship. The carpet was immaculate, ivory-hued, the curtains a bright red. The walls were of expensively papered silk with cuneiform characters over a desert tone shade of light brown. Opposite his desk on the other side of the office was a gilt framed replica (or perhaps the original?) of William Blake's *The Great Red Dragon and the Woman Clothed in Sun*. In front of his desk there was an absence of anything resembling a chair.

Perkins' mind retreated over thirty years to the time he was a young 2nd Lieutenant in the US Army. His commanding officer never had a chair in front of his desk either. The possibility of loitering in his office was never a possibility, thus a chair was unneeded. You were expected to march smartly to the front of the desk, salute then report. He was tempted to do the same, though the man behind this desk might wonder whether he was attempting to be facetious. Since he didn't feel facetious, he waited nervously at the doorway to be invited farther into the room.

Finally the man behind the desk, probably reading his mind, signaled for him to enter and walk to the front of the desk. He said only one word,

"Report." His eyes rested upon Perkins, and the CIA Section Chief handed him a printed out three-page summary, double-spaced, and began to speak.

"Sir, he began, "Our operatives for the last year have been keeping close surveillance on the man Benjamin Jasher. Moreover, we have been monitoring his movements and our reports indicate Jasher is a total recluse and, during the time we have been surveilling him, he primarily remained in his office, visited no one socially and had no regular associations except those delivering his merchandise. We have done background checks on every customer who has entered his shop over the past year and you will see this list in my report. Further, we have monitored all phone conversations in and out of his shop and have done a similar background check on each of those with whom he has met and that list has likewise been included in the report."

Now he came to the part of the report that would decide his fate. He paused slightly, then continued, "ten days ago, Jasher walked into an artist's shop in the Ein Hod art and market district in Haifa and managed to elude our surveillance. He re-emerged ten minutes later two blocks away then took a taxi and returned to his shop in Akko. If he met with anyone it would have been during the period we lost him in the art district. Three days later he had a visit from a well-known expert of paleography, a Professor William Bedford of the University of Texas at Austin. After the professor entered his shop, they retired to his office in the back where they had a private conversation that lasted approximately thirty minutes. Though we don't know yet how he did it, we were unable to make any audio and video record of the meeting; Jasher must have found a way to scramble our surveillance devices. Then, abruptly, he and the American professor made good an escape through a back door to his shop, of which we were unaware, and they were observed later a few blocks away entering a dark, SUV van. Other identical vans were likewise in play, so somewhere along their routes they may have crossed one another to throw us off the trail. We picked them up again a half mile from the Haifa airport, but they must have realized we were on to them because someone rolled out of the lead van and the next van came up behind our chase car. There was an incident, a firefight. Our car was blown apart with a fragmentation device and all men were lost before backup could arrive. Bodies were strewn all over the street and in the confusion, this professor, Jasher and his men slipped away."

"After they escaped, our team broke into his apartment and found nothing which could link him to his probable destination. We suspect he used a fake passport and entered another country, probably the United States under an assumed name. A copy of the passport he used does bear some resemblance to the man we may be looking for. Since this Professor Bedford was the last person to see him, we may conclude that Jasher accompanied him on the same private plane used for his own escape. Presumably, Jasher is with the professor and is now staying with him in his home in Austin, Texas. Our surveillance cameras indicated that another Professor, Isaac Levinson, was seen entering Bedford's home a week ago, but once he re-entered the home a day later with some luggage, he has remained in the residence since that day. Another person has likewise been seen inside the residence, but he avoids the windows so we haven't been able to get a good identification, but our best guess is that it's Jasher. I say guess because, again, we have been unable to make a positive identification. Jasher has employed a most impressive device that has been jamming our best surveillance equipment."

During the entire report, there were no questions, no comments, no interjections of any sort, only a stony silence. Slowly Caine closed his eyes and sighed deeply. Swearing softly under his breath, the man arose and walked over to the window. His hands were clasped tightly behind his back as he gazed out the window to the river below him. Without turning around, he said only, "You may leave".

Walker Caine, as he was now calling himself, watched a cargo ship make its way slowly up the river and he realized that this simple exercise had a correspondingly calming effect upon him which only he could appreciate. The man standing at the window bore no emotional resemblance to the anger-filled creature of so long ago yet, coincidentally, his physical appearance had changed hardly a whit and in spite of the shortness of his hair and beard, his own mother would have recognized him. Nevertheless, that despicable scar he carried with him across the left side of his face had always been an annoying reminder of who he really was. Once, long ago, he had sported the scar boldly about. When asked about the scar he would invariably call it an old war wound then he would break up into gales of laughter. It was, of course, a private joke he carried with him like old baggage, and as the real truth would never be believed, he just invented a story everyone wanted to hear.

For the longest time, he recalled, it had bothered him that he was unable to make friends or if he did, he was never able to keep them for long. Over time he simply accepted the curse and began to use it to his advantage. For the most part, except on few exceptions, he had wrested control over his most obvious weakness, his anger, and was amazed at the intuition that began to flow to him. He became an observer of human nature and used his ancient art to weave his tapestry of deceit and manipulation to gain wealth and power. The advancement in technology over the past century had permitted him to quickly and efficiently consolidate his empire of control he had begun over five thousand years earlier by trial and error. His ability to learn was no greater than the next, but because he was long-lived he had had many years to examine, experiment and perfect various styles of social control. He knew which social experiment would work and under which circumstances it could be employed successfully and the application of the correct logistics to maintain it. If not for that accursed flood, he reflected, he would have achieved his goal long ago.

Now in this time, he had been on the verge of absolute success when Jasher had again unexpectedly arrived on the scene. "Damn him," he muttered under his breath. The only other person he had ever known to have brought out so much anger in him was Seth, his meddlesome brother. He reflected that Seth would always show up just when he had executed his best line of offense then he had to turn on the defensive and waste valuable time trying to anticipate Seth's next move; thus the cleanup was always so costly in time and effort. He began to recall his earliest experiences with him and the recollection always contributed to his inner turmoil.

Part 3 – The Clan of the Scar

17 And Cain knew his wife; and she conceived, and bare Enoch: and he builded a city, and called the name of the city, after the name of his son, Enoch.

18 And unto Enoch was born Irad: and Irad begat Mejujael: and Mejujael begat Methusael: and Methusael begat Lamech.

19 And Lamech took unto him two wives: the name of the one was Adah, and the name of the other Zillah.

20 And Adah bare Jabal: he was the father of such as dwell in tents, and of such as have cattle.

21 And his brother's name was Jubal: he was the father of all such as handle the harp and organ.

22 And Zillah, she also bare Asshur-cain, an instructer of every artificer in brass and iron: and the sister of Asshur-cain was Naamah.

23 And Lamech said unto his wives, Adah and Zillah, Hear my voice; ye wives of Lamech, hearken unto my speech: for I have slain a man to my wounding, and a young man to my hurt.

24 If Cain shall be avenged sevenfold, truly Lamech seventy and sevenfold.

----- Genesis 4: 17 - 24

For, from the days of Cain a secret combination, a Brotherhood, was had among men and their works were in darkness. Each man was placed under oath and each knew his brother for the oath's sake. For each man placed under oath knew the covenant of secrets and for the oath's sake none dared reveal the works of this Society. And this was done for riches and to gain power over the hearts of men.

Wherefore Lamech and his household were cursed for he had covenanted with Lucifer and Cain; for this oath they kept not the commandments of God and their works were abominations in the land under his rule. And in time Lamech anointed himself Master Mahan, the father of lies and this oath and his influence began to spread among all those in the land.

And among women the oath and covenant of this Brotherhood was unknown. But Lamech in his pride had spoken the secrets unto his wives and when they rebelled against him, they declared these things throughout the land and had no compassion for his sake.

----- The Abridgement, Chapter 6

Chapter 1 – Ashur's Report

In the days of Lamech, king of Enoch, the realm was divided among the kingdoms of Cush to the far west near the Western ocean, and Shinar, Calah, Sharon, Heth, Nod, Enoch, Shulon and Cainan toward the Eastern Ocean in that order. To the south, there was a large extensive territory, sparsely inhabited, known as Hesh.

Barak, grandson of King Perazim of Nod, had been foolish and far too impetuous for his own good. It seems King Lamech had been foolishly indiscreet with his explanations to his wives concerning the aims of the Clan and Barak was looking for revenge on the group who had murdered his cousin. After being told about the workings of the Clan by his mother Zillah, wife of Lamech, Barak had attempted to enlist his kinsmen to help him avenge their cousin. But, the king heard of Barak's plan to expose Cain's Society and so had personally, and quite literally, cut Barak's life short in the marketplace with his own sword. Unfortunately for Lamech, Barak just so happened to be the favorite grandson of his worst enemy.

Ashur, acting as Cain's personal messenger, had just arrived from the land of Enoch, and the news was bad. He had been on the road for over a week now with insufficient sleep and he was weary from his travels, but Cain would want to know the news much sooner than later. Moreover, he feared that because of the singular nature of the event, he feared the reports would reach Cain's ears before he could get to him first. Knowing Cain's legendary temper better than most, he was highly motivated to avoid that outcome.

It was almost a fortnight ago when Ashur had first begun to hear of disquieting rumors in Enoch. He was staying with a kinsman, his brother and court adviser, Eber, and the subject of Lamech, the ruler over Enoch, had first come up over lunch. "You do realize Ashur," began his brother Eber, "that before long King Lamech will have the whole land of Enoch and most of the other kingdoms calling him by his new name, Master Mahan." This was said almost facetiously, but Ashur detected a hint of worry in his brother's voice.

"Why do you say that, Brother?" he asked, now instantly on the alert. As Ashur was the personal envoy to the court of Enoch, he was considered a personal representative of Cain. The mention of Cain's Society name, Master Mahan, had taken him by surprise.

As a court adviser to Lamech, Eber knew of his brother's position and relationship with Cain and he was hoping to elicit his help cautiously without compromising his loyalty to Lamech. Accordingly, acting in his best diplomatic interest, he declared, "The king is quite serious, or so I have heard. Since he killed Barak, one of his wife's sons, for the sake of the Clan's oath, he has become obsessed with claiming that he was the first to take such a bold action."

"What bold action, Eber?" This was something new and he wondered where it was going.

"Ashur, we are both members of Cain's Society and as such we are required to avenge our brothers when they have been offended, but no one has ever been murdered simply because he was foolish enough to spread the details of the oaths and covenants around the kingdom. Barak was given details of our oaths and like a moronic fool, began to bandy them about trying in a desperate attempt to avenge his cousin's murder by divulging those details. Lamech, like a good member, silenced his wagging tongue and everything else attached to it. Unfortunately, Lamech was the cause of his knowing the details in the first place and further, he took the poor dullard's head in the public market place."

Since such actions were normally performed in secret or somewhere less conspicuous, a public murder was indeed news, especially one involving the Clan and affecting one of its members. "And where do you see this going, Eber?" Ashur persisted.

Eber replied, "Barak, as you may know, was a kinsman of King Perazim of Nod and he took the murder of his grandson personally. There is talk now of war unless the King of Nod can be mollified. Owing to the fact that he is also a member of the Clan, your Master, Cain, might be able to persuade Perazim to back down. War is the last thing our kingdoms need, especially over something as trivial as this."

"Brother, we both know wars have begun over far less than this," Ashur glibly commented. But, Ashur, to be on the safe side, had stayed a few more days to ensure the story he was getting was verifiable.

The next day he made an appointment with the king's executive secretary to appear before King Lamech. As personal liaison to his court from Cain, he should have been accorded that privilege immediately, but he discovered that Lamech was less than excited about giving him audience. He was turned away a number of times, but finally Ashur made it clear that unless he could see the King, he would have to make a report to Cain without the benefit of hearing Lamech's official account of Barak's public murder. With reluctance, the King gave him leave to appear before him the next morning and so, after a few delays, Ashur found himself being escorted into his audience chamber.

Lamech, son of Methusael and ruler of the kingdom of Enoch, was sitting comfortably on his throne enjoying wine recently pressed but thoroughly fermented from his vineyard. As usual, he was drunk, but content. He had everything he wanted, of course, but there were things a man needed that went beyond mere creature comforts, such as respect and recognition, for example. A king should avoid being thought of as a fool or a simpleton, but he was convinced his wives and children considered him as both, and lately he had likewise suspected many at his court had held this same low opinion. Before long, he reasoned, his enemies within and outside of Enoch would hear of this presumptive attitude and grow embolden to attack his kingdom and depose him as the true leader.

He ordered a servant to bring more wine. At some point, he mused, a king has to exert a strong show of force. Reluctantly, or so he remembered, it had been necessary to send a clear message that he was in control and that careless fool Barak had presented the perfect opportunity he had needed. The impudent pup had had the nerve to broadcast the secrets of the Clan to his kinsmen and nearby communities. Eventually, if he had not had the foresight to intervene, the entire kingdom would have been privy to our oaths. I had every justification, he reflected, to take Barak's worthless life and now, perhaps, I will get the recognition and respect I deserve. As it has a certain justifiable ring to it, he reflected, he had been using the title Master Mahan since the incident and it suited him perfectly and, for that cause, he began to practice using the title publicly. Since speaking always made him thirsty, he decided to order more wine from his servant.

While he was thus engaged in practicing his new title between bouts of wine, his secretary respectfully entered the throne room and announced Ashur, first ambassador of Cain. Ashur, Lamech knew, would be quick to report back to Cain the particulars of the incident with Barak. For some reason lately, Lamech had been having trouble focusing on problems and so it had taken him a few days to formulate a story to present to Ashur. Everything he had done was justifiable, of course, but still it would improve his chances for a favorable outcome if he was well prepared. He took the next needed gulp and relished the taste as the wine slid comfortably down his throat.

"Ashur, my old friend and adviser!" bellowed King Lamech." His flushed face spread into a mask of welcome so broad it was grotesque. "You must be parched, please be seated and have some wine. It is fresh from my vineyards" he slurred. The man was drunk, his face slack and his eyes bloodshot.

Ashur had heard rumors that the king was a drunkard, but never had he appeared thus in an official capacity while giving audience. "No, thank you sire," he replied respectfully, "I must be on the road today by the noon hour. Our master will want to hear word of the recent developments here in your kingdom as soon as possible. He will no doubt render you a favorable decision on this matter of Barak, but I want to ensure he receives the truth directly from you so there are no misunderstandings later on."

Lamech blinked a few times as if uncertain how to take Ashur's last statement. "Of course, I would be happy to relate the incident just as it occurred", Lamech slurred with a bleary voice. He tried to focus then he bellowed toward the doorway, "Bring more wine!" His eyes were hooded, now brooding. "Where is that worthless servant?" he asked to no one in particular. After he was served another round and the cup was drained, he threw the glass goblet against the stone fireplace next to his throne. It shattered into hundreds of pieces. He glared at the mess then appearing to come to a decision, he nodded, turned back toward Ashur and declared, "That is what I think of Barak." The king had the pinched, furtive look of the long-time drunkard and he now stared at Ashur as though he was having difficulty focusing. Finally, the last relay switch in his brain kicked over and then he added distractedly, "I need a nap." And with that the

King of Enoch arose unsteadily from his throne and stumbled slowly past Ashur to his bed chamber. A door slammed; the audience was now over.

When Ashur arrived in the courtyard of Cain a few days later, he was deep in agitated conversation with his chief security adviser, Gilgal. Ashur, now loathe to interrupt his master, remained at a discreet distance near a small fountain to await Cain's permission to approach.

Cain furiously pointed an accusing finger directly at Gilgal and clinching his teeth muttered in threatening tones, "It was your job, your only job, to make sure that Seth, my interfering brother, was watched. Did I not make myself clear to you? I told you, I have to know where he is at all times. If he is observed writing, he must be stopped and his records destroyed. Did I not tell you to have someone inserted into his household to monitor his movements?"

"But master," gibbered Gilgal, "It was done, even as you ordered. But, the incompetent wench I paid to befriend his wife and children must have let slip her true identify, because Seth, including his whole household are now gone."

"Fool! So where did he go?" countered Cain, now angry with frustration.

Cain's security officer, mortified at having displeased his master, reluctantly revealed, "Sire, I followed the trail and his family is now living with his father-in-law in Shulon. As to Seth, no one knew of his whereabouts. I took a detail and questioned them all quite thoroughly and used the usual threats to extract the information, but they said they awoke one morning and he was simply gone. Given his disposition for disappearances when it suits his needs, I am inclined to agree with them."

Cain was in no mood to hear a lame excuse. "Gilgal, must I mention that there are more persuasive ways to extract needed information from reluctant peasants. I am beginning to believe you lack the stomach for this work", he added contemptuously.

"Master, you must understand that Seth's father-in-law is not a peasant but an important man in the district over Shulon and Cainan; he is, after all, a court adviser. I feared it unwise to be too vigorous with my questioning."

"Gilgal, the only person you ever have to fear is me." He was very aware that Seth's father-in-Law, Aram, was yet unaffiliated with the Clan, and so was beyond the usual persuasions reserved for a member. "Did you search both premises?" Cain persisted.

His security captain, nearly blubbering with fear, remarked defensively, "My men and I searched his home and the home of his in-laws, but we could find no trace of any records."

"That's because he has the records with him, you plodding dolt," snapped Cain. "And he needs to be alone and undisturbed to write a fuller account." He paused, catching his breath then yelled, "I need to think. Get out of my sight before I have you hung up by your heels in the middle of the courtyard."

Gilgal was now happy to be leaving with his life and quickly retired from the courtyard and out of sight. Perhaps, he thought, it was time to find another master, preferably one on the other side of the realm.

Cain, now aware his ambassador to Enoch stood at the nearby fountain, beckoned him over. He would hear what Ashur had to report then retire to his bed to rest. Perhaps the answer to Seth's location would come. Whenever he had time to think, it usually did. He walked over to a quiet, cool corner of the courtyard under a shaded tree and motioned Ashur to be seated next to him.

"So, Ashur," began Cain, "why are you not in Enoch?" Ashur's official position in Enoch was first emissary to the ruler, Lamech, as well as direct liaison to Cain who provided counsel to Lamech. Actually, he used Ashur to keep an eye on the kingdom and convey his demands to Lamech while, in reality, Cain was the de facto ruler of Enoch and always had been.

Ashur, fearing the worst as no one liked to be the messenger of bad news, reluctantly made his report. "Sire, I am afraid I have to report that Lamech has murdered Barak, grandson of Perazim, your kinsman and ally of the land of Nod. Perazim now demands revenge for the murder of his favorite grandson while Lamech goes about openly boasting that he is now Master Mahan. To make matters worse, Barak was the son of Zillah, one of Lamech's wives and her tongue is wagging about the land telling anyone who bothers to listen to her that Lamech is a leader of the Clan. After delays, I was finally permitted an audience to hear his defense of his actions against Barak. The man was so drunkenly incoherent he was unable to slur more than a few words together without passing out before he stumbled out of the room to his bed chamber. This whole court intrigue was spiraling out of control so I knew you would want to know as soon as possible."

Cain would no doubt blame him for allowing this situation to unravel as quickly as it had. In his whole service as court adviser to that bumbling, incompetent King Lamech, he had never feared for his life until now. As that imbecile king was more than capable of doing something rash like this, he should have foreseen this coming. It was, after all, his job to prevent an incident such as this from happening and now that drunken fool couldn't control his wives and he couldn't control his mouth.

Ashur closed his eyes to brace himself for the well-deserved slap that he knew must be coming. Cain had struck him before, but this time he hoped that was all he received. Therefore, he was surprised that Cain had yet to respond, so he cautiously opened his eyes and saw Cain in deep thought, staring vacantly over his right shoulder. Remaining motionless, Ashur awaited his master's response.

Cain muttered, "So that was why my brother disappeared. He had gone to Enoch to make record of this debacle and was, of course, going to lay the blame for this mess at my doorstep." After a few moments of contemplation and with mounting concern he came to a decision. "Ashur, fetch my councilors and inform them that I am convening a special session to discuss the matter of Lamech and his bungling rule over Enoch. After that, bring me Gilgal and a contingent of guards," he ordered. "We are going to Enoch and take this problem in hand. I will restore order where that fool Lamech has created chaos and if my brother Seth steps in the way, I will do with him as I did with my brother Abel."

A few minutes later, Cain walked over to the window overlooking his courtyard and began to plan his upcoming trip to Enoch. As he was contemplating Lamech's fate and how he would deal with his prying brother Seth, an ephemeral entity coalesced in the room. Cain turned and, not for the first time, noted a chill in the air as if it emanated from the form of his mentor. Now curious, though he suspected that it might have something to do with his current dilemma, he awaited the message from Lucifer. "Cain, your business in Enoch, though urgent, should not exceed the limitations of our agreement that we have established with the Creator."

Cain replied with disdain, "By that you mean that I should roll over like a whipped dog whenever my brother Seth demands it?"

His mentor replied patiently, "As long as he maintains the records, neither he nor his family is to be harmed in any way. If the records are in the open, you may indulge in whatever action you deem necessary to prevent them from being maintained or hidden, but he is not to be harmed. Doing him violence or any that follow him nullifies our agreement with the Creator and that will shut down our plans to expand our Society. As long as we abide by this agreement, you will live a long life and provide us the means to disseminate our message to future generations."

Cain murmured menacingly, "This agreement is absurd and places me in a position of weakness that I refuse to tolerate. You must renegotiate the terms."

Lucifer, knowing Cain's temper, attempted to placate his anger. "Cain, you are cunning and more that equal to the challenge of the agreement. Step up your surveillance of the man, have him followed and remove his records; it is a simple thing."

Cain suspected his mentor was far weaker than he ever let on and so replied with a cutting remark. "Lucifer, are you so feeble that we must continually bow and scrape in humble obeisance before the Creator?"

"Cain, I am telling you, this is the only way. Do not harm your brother or your life will immediately be forfeit. Take care of your business with Lamech, but allow your brother to move about in peace; he can't disrupt our plans. It is a small thing to allow him his delusions."

As Cain paced about the room, he fumed, knowing that as long as his brother was favored, he would always have the advantage now and in the future. "You are right, I will deal with this, but my patience is wearing thin and as long as Seth is a constant thorn in my sandal, he will be a distraction that neither of us can afford to tolerate."

Since the earliest days of the Clan, Cain had always surrounded himself with trusted advisers to help him make the decisions that needed to be made on behalf of his expanding interests. Of course, the final decision was always his and the number of advisers in his inner circle was always the perfect number 6 so that in the event there was a lack of consensus, his was always the tie-breaker. Before leaving for Enoch to deal with the

King, he called an ad-hoc meeting to determine whether Lamech should retain his kingdom. Though, in his own mind, he had already made the decision, he nevertheless needed the absolute loyalty of his inner circle of advisers and so sought their counsel.

A day later sat six of Cain's most trusted councilors in a room around a large table specifically set aside for just such a council meeting of the Clan of the Scar. He reflected that it was an extraordinary group, unlike the brothers who had hunkered down uncertainly around a campfire awaiting his next directive so long ago. These men were sought out, not because they were ruthless and violent, but because they were intelligent and thoughtful, not given over to petty jealousies and emotional tirades. Furthermore, unlike the general rank-and-file of other members of the Clan, these men could be trusted with his innermost secrets and they wore his mark on the left cheek to seal their devotion to his cause. Cain began his address with an apology. "Brothers, I am sorry to have called you away from your business but a matter has come up regarding the king of Enoch, Lamech. He has publicly executed a grandson of a respected member of the Society, Perazim the King of Nod, without permission from our Council. Brothers, I would appreciate your views on the matter before we take a vote on his final disposition as King of Enoch."

A serious, though dispassionate discussion followed in which each council member expressed an opinion over the matter and each weighed the possibility of Cain's suggestion whether Lamech should himself be publicly dispatched. At length, the adviser with the most tenure of the group summed up what they all had concluded: that, though well-intentioned, the King of Enoch, Lamech, had acted precipitously, no doubt the result of his drunken state of mind. Furthermore, he had committed this act against a relative of a member of the Society without permission. According to the laws of the Clan, therefore, the King should be removed from his throne. He further commented, "Sire, we, your councilors feel you should grant leniency to Lamech. Though an incompetent drunkard, he was acting according to the best spirit of our Society by ensuring our secrets and activities remained out of the public eye. Additionally, we, too, agree with your conclusion that a thorough investigation should take place to determine the extent of damage that was done to the reputation of our Brotherhood."

Cain had concurred with his councilors and now, satisfied of his final decision on the matter, gathered his personal guards as well as Ashur, adviser to the court of Enoch, and made preparations to return to his old homeland of Enoch.

Cain, along with his entourage, had arrived post-haste to the land of his first settlement, Enoch. He would always have fond recollections of how he and his new family of brothers and sisters had built up this kingdom out of little more than desire and hard work, no thanks to his father Adam and his gutless brothers who refused to stand up for him. When he had turned this kingdom over to Lamech's great-grandfather this land had been a paradise and a model for all future kingdoms he would raise up. Now just look at the state of affairs to which it had been reduced! It sickened him that Lamech's stewardship of Enoch had been reduced to this slovenly condition. Where was the man's pride?

Tradition required that Lamech would receive the inheritance of the first-born as well as entrance into the Clan's process of initiation as his fathers before him. Cain murmured under this breath in exasperation, "I had known this pompous fool throughout his life and I should have prevented his initiation into our Society. His father, though, had been adamant about his entrance and had vouched personally for his son's conduct." He continued his thought, *"Against my better judgment, I allowed the old horse's ass to talk me into it. I should have realized that someday Lamech would forsake his oath and I would regret that decision. And here I am, cleaning up this cretin's mess."*

Chapter 2 – Adah and Zillah

"Truth is stranger than fiction, but it is because fiction is obliged to stick to possibilities; truth isn't."

--- Mark Twain

Adah and Zillah were both wed to the same man. If Lamech had ever attempted to be an ideal husband, the two hapless women would have found reason to be jealous of one another. As it turned out, jealously never seriously entered into the equation. Rather, for the past several years they more often than not had turned to the other for solace at their clear misfortune. Their husband was not only a loutish boor but likewise a hopeless drunkard and today was turning out to be more of the same. It was unfortunate, but inevitable, that events from this day would result in so much political intrigue and loss of stature for the King and his wives.

The three were seated and being served the noon day meal around a large dining table. Adah glanced at the servants having a devil of a time keeping up with the demand for wine that their husband had been guzzling since the meal began. His only contribution to the table-talk was an occasional belch followed by a strident pounding of his empty goblet next to his scarcely touched meal. Adah glanced at her sister, Zillah, now demurely sipping at her wine serving while eating small portions of veal and potatoes. That girl, thought Adah, eats like a squirrel and has the brain capacity to match. Am I the only one here disgusted by our husband's boorish behavior?

Adah cleared her throat, and trying to avoid a shrewish comment, interjected, "Lamech, do try the veal. The cooks have done a splendid job and should be complemented."

Lamech's eyes narrowed waspishly as if trying to comprehend Adah's request. He belched. After deciding that debate over the lunch meal was beyond his current capacity, he returned to his favorite pastime, trying to drink himself under the table.

Adah kicked out under the table to her sister in an attempt to solicit help with their husband before he collapsed yet again into his dinner plate. Zillah got the message after the second kick and affected a coquettish manner. She purred, "Sire, your meal is getting cold. Do finish it as I have plans for you this afternoon. I have missed your warmth in my bed." She smiled her best *come hither* look which earlier in their marriage had never failed to illicit his attention. These days only one thing seemed to get his attention and he was drinking it.

Lamech slowly turned his head toward Zillah and grunted, "Zillah, be a good girl and shut up." He waved the goblet around for another round of wine. The servant immediately rushed to his side to deliver the next drink to extend the bout. All the while drinking, he occasionally picked up a shank of veal and began to slowly munch.

Adah sighed inwardly at the uselessness of her efforts. She had a drunken lout for a husband and a twit for a sister. Perhaps she should get him to talk about something that might interest him. "Husband, I heard in the market today that there was an uprising last week in the kingdom of Hesh. A neighboring army was sent south to quell the disturbances."

Lamech, as if coming to life, glanced in her direction, leaned back in his chair and explained, "It wasn't just any army. It was Cain's personal coterie of specially trained assassins. Their work was quick and vicious and no one in Hesh responsible for the uprising survived. Their king was deposed and fed to his own dogs for being irresponsible; it was foolish of him to fail the Clan."

Adah's interest was now piqued and her face grew pensive. "What's this about Cain and a private army?" Everyone knew of Cain, of course, but it had never occurred to her that he might be that powerful.

Concurrently, Zillah had been slurping her soup and in mid-slurp abruptly laid down her spoon; even she was intrigued so, she pressed for Lamech to proceed. "I have heard of the Clan; my first husband had mentioned that Society, but no one seems to know much about it and who controls it. Do explain, Husband."

Explanations always seemed to increase his thirst lately so he ordered another round of wine. Lamech had always felt that Cain was underutilizing his talents. He knew he was capable of more responsibility and it flattered

Lamech to think that as a member of the Clan he might step up to be a regent of the realm one day, perhaps even become the Master Mahan. So with justifiable pride at his eventual advancements, he felt he could reveal a few things to his wives in view of his inevitable honors to come. His voice, now thick with drink, slurred, "Cain is the titular head of the Clan and calls himself the Master Mahan. Whenever anything happens in the realm of any significance, you can bet he is behind it. His specially trained army terrorizes kingdoms and deposes any king who thinks he can displease the Clan and live."

Adah sat back in wonder. She asked incredulously, "Husband, are you saying that there are kings that are members of this secret society?"

Lamech rumbled his response, "Woman, we all are. No one becomes a king in this realm unless they swear a blood oath to Cain's Society." He then went on to describe the oaths in general terms. To make a further point he added, "But, it goes beyond mere kings. Every adviser to every court and every general in the field is likewise sworn to the Clan; he has spies and assassins everywhere."

Zillah asked, "Husband, why are these oaths administered?"

Lamech thought for a moment. The wine had blindsided his reasoning and his thinking was bleary and slow; no doubt this had clouded his sense of discretion as well. Unaware of the dangerous trap he was setting for himself, he continued, "It's all about power and control and getting gain. Notwithstanding, in the end the hardest part for a king is keeping what has been gained, but the Society takes care of its own and ensures that everyone loyal keeps what they are either given or have taken."

Adah added, "Moreover, I have heard that they kill without remorse anyone who dares to offend them or gives offense to the Clan."

"Yes, my darling Wife, they act with impunity because no one dares to prosecute the killers." He added cynically, "I, for one, find the whole business to my taste." As an afterthought he followed, "I also find the wine to my taste!" he bellowed and began beating his fist on the table in obvious drunken glee over his wit. He ordered still another round of wine. Apparently, the discussion had increased his thirst so the lesson for the day was now over.

Within a quarter hour, his face was again anointed by the gravy in his dinner plate. Adah and Zillah reluctantly carried their besotted husband to his bed chamber and laid him across the bed. Within moments, he was snoring away his latest drunk.

Later that evening, Zillah ran into her son, Barak, at the market center and asked him to dine with her and Adah for the noon meal the following day. After the usual banter of accusing her son of breaking the hearts of so many women in Enoch, Barak reluctantly agreed to attend. Zillah reflected she would always save a special place in her heart for her playful, handsome son.

The next day, Barak arrived at the noon hour to find her mother and Adah had prepared him a fine repast. Zillah had personally supervised the cooks to ensure that her son's favorite foods were prepared to his taste. Knowing that men sometimes tend to overdrink wine at the meal, she was careful to provide only the minimum amount with instructions to the servants to provide no more than what was on the table. Their husband, Lamech, would be absent as he had already eaten, or perhaps it should be said, he had already drunk his noon meal and was already busily sleeping it off in his bed chamber.

Barak, always the complementary guest, asked, "Mother, where is Lamech our King and your husband? I should like to greet him."

Zillah was too mortified to admit her husband's drunken behavior so she appeared disappointed and simply explained that he was *indisposed*. She added, "He may join us later if he is feeling better."

Her act did not fool Barak. He knew from personal observation his step-father's propensity to overdrink. The drunken fool had fallen on his ass enough times in his presence to make that abundantly clear. But, allaying his dear mother's fear of this knowledge was part of Barak's charm and love. "Of course, Mother. We all hope he is feeling better" he sincerely replied.

They were all seated at the table, Barak at the head as the honored guest. The meal had progressed well with Barak complementing the women on their taste at selecting each course. Finally, Adah kicked out at her sister under the table to indicate that it was time to begin their special item of conversation. Apparently, their interest from yesterday's conversation regarding the Clan had only intensified. Since Barak was a popular gallant of the kingdom, it was assumed he would probably know more. The women had decided beforehand to pick his brain at the noon meal.

Zillah smiled warmly at her son, obviously with motherly pride and asked innocently, "My Son, what do you know of the Society of the Clan? Our husband, Lamech, mentioned it to us at the lunch table yesterday, but seemed hesitant to reveal much information. What have you heard?"

Barak had just picked up his wine glass for a sip then he abruptly laid it down. His jovial, gregarious mood had been quickly set aside and now he was calmly appraising his mother. He said, "Very little, but perhaps if you could fill me in on what you already know, I might be able to provide you with the rest."

Adah and Zillah then repeated everything Lamech had mentioned the day before. As the ladies began to describe the workings of the Clan, Barak became angrier by the moment. At the completion of their story, Barak sat silently brooding for a few moments.

"Barak, my Son," exclaimed Zillah, "what is the matter"?

Barak arose from his seat, threw his place napkin over the plate and formally said, "Please excuse me, ladies, but I must go. There is an urgent matter to which I need to attend." With that he stalked angrily out of the dining hall. It was the last time either of them saw Barak alive.

Unbeknownst to Zillah, Barak had lost a cousin who had given offense to a member of the Clan there in Enoch and had been cut down during the evening meal in his home in front of his family. The meal, though badly burned by his cousin's wife, was still the highlight of the evening as the assassin had bolted through the back door soon after jamming the carving knife through the throat of his hapless kinsman. Consequently, once Barak had learned of Lamech's affiliation with the Clan, he had sought out his other cousins from Shulon to recruit them to assist him in exposing the oaths and covenants of their Society. He had found them staying with a kinsman in Enoch and met them in the courtyard overlooking the market.

"So, Jacob, my cousin, will you help me with my revenge? These swine think they can come and go as they please and do whatever they want regardless of the harm it does to the families of our communities" Barak pointed out, hoping to persuade them to help.

"Barak, are you insane? No one speaks out against the Clan and lives", responded Jacob incredulously. All the other cousins agreed, but were likewise eager to hear the details. "Please tell us more of the oaths. You say Lamech is a member? What about the other kings of the realm?"

Barak replied, "I know regrettably little of the specifics of their oaths, but I did learn from my mother that nearly all the kings are members as well as most of the court advisers as are the army commanders in the field. Their numbers are few, but their influence reaches throughout the realm".

"And these oaths, how are they administered?" asked the second cousin.

"According to my mother, these are blood oaths given to the membership for the sake of attaining and maintaining power over the citizens. Furthermore, these oaths are never to be divulged on pain of death. As you can imagine, they are serious and our cousin was unlucky enough to offend one of them. So, he was murdered in his own home and no one has come forward to exact justice. He must be avenged!"

"Not from us cousin," responded Jacob. "But, the information is appreciated."

Barak harangued his cousins awhile longer, but it was clear they wanted nothing to do with giving offense to the Clan. Now disgusted with their cowardice, he strode angrily from the courtyard into the market square.

"I will throttle Lamech in his own bed," thought Barak angrily. *"It was he who should have exacted justice for my cousin's murder, but instead chose to support the Clan's oath. My mother hates him anyway. The drunken lout deserves no less."*

He was crossing the market and formulating his plans when a figure stepped out behind a vender's store. "Barak, I hear you have been talking about things that are forbidden. That was foolish and you must now pay the price." It was Lamech with sword in hand and he had caught Barak out in the open and completely exposed. Unfortunately for Lamech, if he had been thinking more intelligently he would have confronted Barak in a less public place. Thinking, however, was not one of Lamech's strong suits.

Barak, when he heard Lamech's voice, turned to face his adversary. His first reaction, however, should have been to turn and run because Lamech felt scant obligation to provide Barak with a fair fight. Lamech's sword sliced quickly down through the air and caught Barak's arm as he was reaching for his own blade. The arm fell uselessly to the ground and where it had been severed was now a constant fountain of blood spraying over venders and passersby alike. Trying to avoid getting spattered with Barak's blood, the onlookers quickly scattered.

With an animal scream which permeated throughout the market square, Barak looked on stupidly as the stump continued to pour blood everywhere. Meanwhile, Lamech looked on placidly trying to decide how he should finish off this fool and shut him up. After a moment's deliberation he shrugged and swung his broadsword with both hands and caught Barak high on the jaw and decapitated him, cutting him off in mid scream.

"That's better", commented Lamech. "The fool had a big mouth and now he has none", he guffawed at the wit of his own sally. Lamech sheathed his sword, turned around and muttered to a servant, "Clean this mess up." He kicked the severed head into the gutter as he strode through the gathering throng who had come to witness the commotion. The servant gazed upon the decapitated body still bleeding and occasionally twitching. He was nearly able to avoid becoming violently ill… nearly.

Adah was keeping a close watch on her sister, Zillah, whose son Barak had been murdered by their husband. Zillah was openly weeping for her loss and screaming out threats against Lamech. Zillah, trying to evoke sympathy from her sister, cried out, "If only Lamech would show some remorse for what he did, but instead he struts around our home gloating over his outrage to my precious son." Her precious son was the result of a previous marriage. Her first husband had had the bad luck of selecting a beautiful, though slightly simple-minded woman to wed. One day, while hunting with Lamech, who had been eying his wife for some time, he had met with an unfortunate accident that took his life. Within the month, Zillah had been elevated to queen status.

"Zillah", replied Adah sarcastically, "your precious son was a grown man that should have known better than test the patience of the Clan. His foolish, wagging tongue has resulted in his own death. Now look what has occurred. Barak's grandfather has now taken offense and threatens to invade the kingdom unless Lamech is punished. Our husband is a fool, granted, but it is now obvious these men take their oaths and vows to their inane society seriously. What is done is done and over and we have ourselves to think about now. Remember, we told that imbecile son of yours everything we had heard and witnessed personally about the Clan and if our husband was insane enough to murder a man in public who had important kinsmen then had the bad taste to boast about it, just think what their Brotherhood will do to us. We are women and they will treat us like bitches tied up helplessly to some court yard gate."

That last comment hit home and abruptly cut off Zillah's incessant weeping. She was usually offended by her sister's crude language, but Adah did have a point. What were they going to do when Cain arrives? His tactics of terror and cruelty were legendary. And if Lamech was to be believed, Cain was titular head of the Clan and would take an unfavorable view to their husband's self-proclaimed ascension as Master Mahan. She and Adah were going to have to create a believable story that Cain would accept, nonetheless, her precious son was murdered and Adah acted as if she was solely to blame for their husband's lowbred public display.

"Adah", she huffed, "You act like this whole bungle was my fault. Your tongue was wagging just as fast as mine," she reminded her. "Maybe if you had been more accustomed to using your tongue for more than idle gossip, neither of us would be in this dilemma", insinuated Zillah with her most sneering smile.

"What's that supposed to mean, dear Sister?" demanded Adah.

"We both know what you have denied our husband from the beginning", countered Zillah. "It's clear he prefers me over you. I have four sons from the bandy little rooster. How many do you have?" she spat.

"Just because I won't straddle him in the hallway or service him in the kitchen as you do, doesn't mean I am any less a wife than you," she brazenly countered. Zillah recoiled at her sister's crude sally. This argument was getting them nowhere. "Look, Sister," Adah pointed out, "We have to keep our wits about us or we are going to end up losing our heads just like your feckless son. When Cain arrives, we must say that our husband was drunk, as usual, and we overheard him boasting that he was going to be the next Master Mahan. Out of simple curiosity we asked him to what he was referring. He replied, "Chief Keeper of the Clan." Then he drunkenly continued to inform us of all details without any further encouragement from us. We didn't know whether it was the truth or not. Later, we invited Barak to join us for the noon meal and we asked him if any of this nonsense rang true. Barak, upon hearing what we told him, immediately ran from the room swearing he was going to inform his cousins. One of Lamech's security officers, patrolling near the market, overheard Barak's tirade against Lamech and he reported this incident to him. The next thing we know, Barak is lying dead in the street and Lamech is claiming responsibility for the murder. A few days later he is publicly referring to himself as Master Mahan. Outside of that, we know little more." Adah ended her tale of fiction with a smug smile on her face. It was simple and mostly true; that had always seemed good enough for Adah.

Chapter 3 – The Lamentations of Lamech

Beware of false knowledge; it is more dangerous than ignorance.

----- George Bernard Shaw

Lamech was trying to recover from his latest visit to the wine cellar, said visit having lasted two days this trip. Though all attempts had been unsuccessful, he was trying to remember all he had done in an effort to put some perspective on what he now must do to extricate himself from his current dilemma. With a gnawing despair, he desperately hoped he had not completely crossed a line of no return; even in his present stupor of mind, he felt he had.

He recalled how his father, Methusael, knowing that he must soon die, called Lamech to his side and disclosed to him what was expected as a member of Cain's Order. The oath and covenant of the Clan was held very sacred to those inducted, and once in, you were always a member until death. The oath you took was to Cain, the Master Mahan and agent to Lucifer. Signs were a part of the initiatory oath and you must remember them so you would be able to recognize a fellow brother and revealing these signs to those outside the Brotherhood was forbidden and punishable by death. The covenant was to Lucifer so that as you obeyed the voice and authority of Master Mahan and abided by your oath, you would be assured riches, power and authority over other men. As a member you were under solemn oath to protect your fellow brothers of the Clan even to the shedding of blood.

Lamech smiled fondly of the day in which he became part of something greater than himself and his whole kingdom. His life and rule would now be protected from all outside interference. He only had to worry about the ambitions of his brothers. Accordingly, after his ascension, wishing to curry their favor and support, he had generously bequeathed each of them a small fiefdom of the kingdom in which they could rule so long as they always reported to him and delivered their tribute taxes on time. Thus far, this far-sighted plan to rule and to maintain his power, yet keep his kingdom free from family intrigues, had succeeded. He had had Adah to thank for that idea.

Lamech's memory was coming back a little at a time, and he began to piece together recent events by recollecting snippets of his younger days, including a childhood beset with continuous abuse from his father and contempt from his younger, ambitious brothers. Lamech was the eldest of fifteen brothers and nineteen sisters. His father's five wives had been prolific and each had wanted only the best for their brood; that is all but one, his own slut of a mother. Being his first wife, she above all others should have been his father's favorite and closest confidant. Instead, she had been weak and unable to tolerate his father's incessant need for women both in and out of the home. She retaliated by having a public affair with a distant cousin. His father, in a fit of rage at her blatant infidelity, banished her from their home, and when she threated to expose the Brotherhood, he had her chopped up, along with her lover and fed to the pigs.

Later in adulthood, his brothers knew from an early age that he, Lamech, was in line to inherit all and be inducted into the Brotherhood after his ascendancy. As a consequence, the only chance that any of them had to circumvent this tradition was to either kill Lamech outright or undermine his growing influence with their father. Lamech remembered the culminating point of his adulthood like it was yesterday and he smiled at his own cunning at thwarting his brothers' foolish attempts to achieve that aim. Yes, he had been very clever or perhaps it had been Adah who had been the cunning one and he was merely the pawn. Nonetheless, as he recalled, the incident had brought the two of them together and as he began to reflect on those days with fond recollections, he had to admit, she had certainly come through for him on that occasion.

His young brother, Gideon, had ineptly attempted to wrest away from him his legal birthright and induction into the Clan. Along with his two other younger brothers Calah and Asher, Gideon had secretly conspired to implicate him in the theft of his father's gold shipment. During the theft, Calah and Asher had been murdered by the thieves Gideon had hired for the occasion. His brothers had been dispatched to make the theft more damning to Lamech and would have elevated Gideon to the position of favored son and heir had not Adah's son, Jabal, witnessed the crime and had been party to the theft. Realizing his own life might be at risk when he had completed his part of the plot, Jabal decided to alert his mother, Adah, the night before the theft and both agreed there might be more benefit in bringing Lamech into the plan and altering the outcome. Consequently, the three had met and Adah had outlined her stratagem in broad strokes and Lamech had agreed to play the outraged, innocent son when Gideon attempted to implicate him in the theft and murders.

Due to the success of Adah's cunning strategy and the assistance of her two sons, Jabal and Jubal, Gideon's plan had been thwarted and he was found guilty of the theft and subsequent murders of his brothers. After Gideon had been exposed, later that night, Adah had met with Lamech in the outer room of his residence and after both had been seated, he could hardly contain his satisfaction.

"Adah, your plan was perfect and the denunciation of Gideon was a master stroke," he gloated. "Please explain the details and how you pulled it off."

Adah, now trying hard to contain her soaring aspirations, demurely replied, "Surely, My Lord, you would have thought of it yourself had you the opportunity to see Gideon's deception more clearly." She continued, "After Gideon's filthy betrayal of your brothers in the market square, according to plan, my son Jabal loaded up the treasure in the cart and he pulled it down the road along the square. He made a switch with Jubal, his twin brother so, instead of the gold being stashed in your bed chambers, it ended up in Gideon's. A box full of junk was delivered to your quarters by the other son."

"How did you manage the switch? Surely Gideon would have Jabal followed."

Adah nodded her head in agreement. "When I saw that Jabal was being followed, I stepped out of the alley in front of Naaman, Gideon's servant, who had been sent to follow Jabal, and blatantly accosted Naaman oh so salaciously. I thought the old goat would die! Clearly he was having trouble deciding whether he wanted me more than to do his duty by his master. Thankfully for us all, he overcame his lust and chose Gideon."

"While Naaman was thus deciding, though, my other son, Jubal was busy making the switch, taking the treasure and putting it on his own cart.

He replaced the treasure with a similar box which contained mostly junk in Jabal's cart. Jabal continued as if nothing had occurred and eventually ended up in your quarters and placed the box of junk in your closet. Jubal pushed the treasure box to Gideon's residence and hid the box under his bed. Naaman witnessed what we wanted him to see and later the next day, the box with the stolen gold was discovered by your guards and now Gideon languishes away in your father's dungeon." With that she could contain herself no more and roared laughter.

Immediately, Lamech joined her and a bond between the two had been struck. Lamech, now quite content asked her pointedly, "Tell me Adah, how do I repay you for coming to me with Gideon's plan and thwarting it so expertly? Moreover, you may have heard, my father has made me official heir and recipient of his birthright. I am now in a position to be magnanimous with my favors, so how can I help you and your cunning sons?" By now Lamech was looking her over in a different light. He began to see in Adah the confidant and cunning companion he should have had with his mother, but due to her idiotic infidelity he had been deprived. Adah was a little older than he preferred his women, but she was still quite lovely. Further, her cunning and intelligence were without equal.

Adah observed Lamech as she pretended to give his offer some thought. In reality she had been hoping for an opportunity like this for many years and knew exactly what to ask for if given the chance. "Sire," she began slowly, "if I have impressed you even remotely, perhaps I may be of service to you in the future, along with my sons, of course. It may sound bold, but as your wife I could be very useful to you. You have many brothers who are waiting in the wings and even if the die has been cast in your favor, they will still expect a parcel of what rightfully should belong to you. You will need someone nearby to shield you from their machinations and ambitions and keep you informed of any intrigues they might concoct for your downfall." She was afraid she had overstepped her place, but this might be her only chance and she was not going to lose it for her sons.

Lamech nodded his head in agreement. "I think it is time we made our arrangement permanent. I will notify my father immediately of our engagement."

His mood now changed from justifiable pride to one of self-pity as he miserably thought of the repercussions of having done his duty. Lamech thoughtfully concluded, for over sixty years now, his kingdom had experienced peace and prosperity. That was until a week earlier when that loud-mouthed imbecile Barak had broken the peace of my home and my kingdom by spreading foul rumors that I had broken the covenant of the Clan by speaking of its secrets to those outside the Order. Those deceitful, back-stabbing wives of mine had been at the forefront of this dilemma. Why had they so willfully involved me in this scandalous outrage by talking to that infernal miscreant son of Zillah? Barak had been not only the eldest son of Zillah, but the favorite grandson of one of my oldest enemies, Perazim, ruler of the kingdom of Nod. How was I supposed to know that pox-ridden oaf was the old fool's favorite grandson?

"Of course I had to halt his filthy tongue from wagging!" he protested sullenly to the silent walls of his room. Finally, after a few more minutes of besotted logic, he reasoned that Barak had really given him no alternative, whereupon he fell back onto his pillow and resumed his nap. Within a few moments, he was snoring loudly and deeply the sleep of the morally vindicated.

Chapter 4 – Seth, Son of Adam

Seth, son of Adam, was an unusual man living in challenging times. He was born in Cainan, as were all the sons and daughters of Adam and Eve, but while his parents were middle-aged. Seth's most arresting, physical characteristic was that he was in the absolute, express image of his father Adam. Those who knew the two men, Adam in his youth and Seth, himself now in middle age, would have been unable to distinguish them apart. The only significant difference between their physical appearances now was the age difference which had gradually taken its toll on Adam. Seth, now growing older, had begun to enjoy a slight silver tinge to his hair that enhanced his air of trust and intellect.

Aside from his attractive outward appearance, what truly set him apart was his extraordinary intelligence. When most of his kinsmen in Cainan and distant cousins living throughout the realm were eking out a living by the sweat of their brow, he was innovating new ways to cultivate more food growth. He was a keen observer of the seasons and heavens and had written an accurate almanac based upon the planet Venus and the Moon.

While many lived in broken down hovels, Seth had developed plans for new tools and instruments and had artisans mold them into workable implements used in the construction of family homes. Inconsequence, his family home was a showcase of the most advanced use of stone and wood. Furthermore, He developed and installed the first water-proof lime plaster cistern for his home to ensure the collection and storage of fresh water. Later, to ensure the surrounding communities had adequate reserves, he supervised the building of an elaborate aqueduct system constructed of rounded river rocks made mostly of volcanic rock. The architecture of his home was both admired and used as the standard for other homes, including the home of his father-in-law who heralded Seth's genius to as many as would listen. Many did, in fact.

His innate understanding of chemistry had led to many breakthroughs in glass manufacture, glassblowing, metallurgy and other practical skills. His genius had spread throughout the realm and had inspired others to further innovations. If he had lived five thousand years later, he would have rivaled Thomas Edison and other inventors of the modern age. He was in large part the reason civilization had made such significant progress in the first seven hundred years.

If asked to comment, however, on his greatest achievement, he would invariably respond, "My family." In spite of his obvious genius, Seth was a humble man, but when it came to his family, he was justifiably proud and never passed up an opportunity to boast of his children's accomplishments. He had fifteen children, nine boys, six girls and each, he proudly declared, was special and he never tired of broadcasting it. His sons were not just farmers, but like himself, farm innovators for he taught them advanced animal husbandry and crop cultivation as well as the use of the latest tools and measurements. His daughters were not merely wives and mothers, but gifted musicians of many instruments, some of which Seth had personally crafted on his own. His wife, Deborah, he confided, was the real genius. She could hold everything together with her love and familial ingenuity. He would speak of his wife tenderly and never complain.

Yes, Seth was a genius and innovator, but he likewise had a special calling and he vividly recollected the day in which his Father Adam had extended it to him. It was fifty-three years earlier, and he was at his birth home visiting his parents when he noticed his father slowly moving around the house, limping occasionally. Eve, his mother, also in advanced age signaled her son to help Adam into a comfortable chair. After he was seated, he began speaking. "Seth, your mother thinks I am getting too old to move around on my own. Actually, I'm just sore. I can't put in a day in the fields as I once did, but if I rest often enough, I can usually get most things done." He added with a smile, "Your brothers stop over regularly to help out, but I really don't need it."

"Ho, ho!" quipped his mother from the next room.

Adam added dryly, "Well, I never turn them away. They come by just to eat your mother's cooking anyway." After a brief chuckle over his last comment, Adam began talking about the family records. "As you know, Seth, I have been tasked since the beginning to keep a record of family events, births and a complete genealogy. I have also added my spiritual insights, such as they are, but of late, it has grown increasingly difficult to keep up with these records and remain current. I feel inspired to turn these records over to you and for you to add to them as you see fit and maintain them for future generations. When the time arrives and seems appropriate, you must pass these records on to your first son, Enos, who will pass it on to his first born son and so on each receiving the same assignment."

Seth knew of his father's calling and was unaccountably surprised that he, instead of his older brothers, would have that responsibility fall to him. Moreover, his father was still a robust man, though elderly, so he didn't think it would come that soon. His father was correct, though, the family was growing faster than any one person could keep up and the task would need someone more mobile to keep pace with it. He replied, "Of course, Father, it would be an honor to preserve the records."

Adam responded, "Thank you, my son. The Creator has indicated that this calling was his will and it pleases me that you have done so well to be worthy to accept it."

Thus, for the last fifty-three years Seth had faithfully fulfilled that role and his travels had taken him throughout the land where he discovered that most of Adam's descendants were gratified to learn that someone was keeping up with this task.

Seth loved his parents and had used them as role models for his own family. His own wife, a second cousin from Shulon, never tired of watching how these two interacted and so easily complemented one another. Ironically, it would be Eve, not Adam who would pass away first. It was now fifty-three years later and Seth and his family had recently visited his father who now, a widower, lived contentedly with his sister Sariah and her family who occupied the original homestead. Within a few minutes of their arrival, his older sister took him aside and informed him, "Seth, Father has been distracted, even maudlin at times and lately has started to berate himself over the loss of Abel. Also, he won't mention Cain's name, but I know he must be on his mind as he continues to dwell over the past and what he terms "missed opportunities". He misses Mother desperately and if she were here, no doubt she could reach him and calm his worries; his depression concerns us all. Perhaps, Little Brother, you can reach him where we have failed."

Seth pondered over the request. He, like everyone else, had just assumed that Adam, the patriarch of the family, would just live on forever.

Though he was well aware that life in mortality was finite and eventually has an ending, it was a severe blow to be informed of his father's declining health and state of mind. His reply was typically Seth, genial and positive. "Of course, Sariah, our father may simply need someone different to talk through his concerns and remind him that our brother's death was not of his doing. We will speak alone and I will encourage him to open up and relieve his anxieties."

Sariah looked at Seth and realized that he had become the brother who had been taken so viciously away from her so many years ago in her youth. Nevertheless, her love for Abel and the loss she felt over his absence had never wavered in spite of the passage of time. For more times than she remembered she had asked herself, could love for someone be so strong? Her eyes suddenly misted over at the recollection of how Abel had saved her life that day and she reached out to Seth and embraced him, knowing he was not Abel, but he was very close. "Thank you, Seth. Mother would be happy to know you were here and helped out with Father."

Sariah was correct, of course, Adam desperately missed Eve, but he maintained confidently that the separation would be temporary. While the cousins and the women were engaged in family interests and catching up on recent events, Adam found time to speak seriously with Seth regarding an additional matter related to his genealogical task Seth had received years before. It was during the second day of the visit when he had asked Seth to walk with him up to the corral that contained the sheep and goats. As the two ambled up to the pens, Seth observed that Adam had been pensive and uncharacteristically withdrawn all morning, seldom adding more than an occasional comment to their conversation. Seth, cognizant of his father's slowly deteriorating mobility, insured that the walk was careful and deliberate. As he would be the attentive listener, he intended to encourage his father to speak his mind.

Finally, they reached the corral and they both looked silently over the well-kept herd then spent a few minutes watching the sheep milling about seemingly oblivious of their surroundings, but Adam knew better. When he spoke it was with strength of understanding that comes from years of experience and accumulated wisdom. Seth looked unsure whether Adam was addressing him or simply musing aloud, but his tone was instructional, consequently, Seth was keen to listen and so prepared himself to be taught. Adam continued his gaze out over the pen while commenting, "You might think the sheep have no idea of who we are nor their function to our lives. After all, you may reason, they are only dumb animals, good for nothing more than to be pushed about and exploited according to our needs." Adam turned his head and glanced over to his son and added quietly, but fiercely, "Nothing could be farther from the truth and anyone who spends his days harboring such feelings has missed a fundamental point of our existence." Adam paused then explained, "We are all here, Our God's children, to learn who we are and act upon that knowledge so that we may become more than we are now. That is how we learn to fulfill the measure of our existence. The animals around us already know who they are and understand their function, so in many respects there is more to respect in them than most men, especially those who boast when they should listen. Any intelligent person can see our Creator's hand in the majesty of these beasts as they go about fulfilling the fullest measure of their existence every day with little teaching and encouragement from us. So, we would do well to respect these creatures and admire them, perhaps even to learn from them."

Adam knew he was getting closer to his point and he hoped he could express it without becoming overly emotional, but he suspected it might be a battle he would lose. He choked back a sob and declared, "Your brother Abel knew these things and taught me these principles many years before you were born. There was so much more he could have taught us all, but his life was cut abominably short and so we must all stumble about without his wisdom to guide us." Adam had now hung his head low and warm tears of sorrow were now coursing down his cheeks as he thought of the two sons he had lost on that day. Seth placed an arm of comfort about his father's shoulder and remained silent; he knew how much his father had blamed himself for that loss.

After a few minutes of quiet introspection, Adam turned to face Seth who, though not his eldest, was the most complete and prepared of any of his sons for the task that lay ahead. As if reluctant to speak, Adam grew sadder by the moment then finally he could postpone it no longer. "Seth, you have been chosen for one additional calling as regards the records. As I have mentioned before, the family records you must pass to your son

Enos when you feel the time has arrived to do so in accordance with the Creator's will." He paused. "The additional calling is equally necessary, but I fear you will find scant joy in fulfilling it. Frankly, had Abel still been alive, this calling would have fallen to him, but I have watched your sober-minded, positive attitude toward life and have recommended you to the Creator for his consideration." Adam now paused in his careful deliberation of the matter. His smile was reluctant, but he gazed at his son encouragingly. "The Creator has called you to record the efforts of your brother Cain in his unrelenting effort to undermine the agency of Man. Specifically, you must make a complete, detailed account of his dealings with regard to that abominable secret society he has created under the inspiration of Lucifer, the common enemy of our family now and down throughout the ages. His influence, as well as that of his agent Cain, will continue to grow until all men have been seduced by the force of this ill-conceived society he has foisted upon us. These records are to be used to stand as a witness against your brother and his followers on the Day of Judgment. Furthermore, they will prove that Lucifer's plan to eliminate the agency of mankind is unworkable. Without these records, Lucifer and Cain may gain some success in altering the outcome we fought so hard to resist from the beginning."

Adam went on to point out, "Cain has been permitted a special dispensation to live on in spite of the passing of time. He will work passionately to destroy these records and will make every attempt to persuade others to help him. He has been denied permission to harm you unto death nor any who follow you in this sacred charge, but he will have power to destroy the records. You must always be aware that, once he discovers what you are doing, he will make every effort to prevent you, as well as those who follow you, from fulfilling this mandate."

Adam, now a widower, and cognizant of his own personal loss and separation of his beloved Eve, was loathe to mention that Seth, too, would have to endure a similar separation. Reluctantly, he continued. "Moreover, to maintain the continuity of the records, you have been given a longer life span than most men. I am sorry, my son, but you will live to see your sons and daughters and your lovely wife pass over to the next life before you. Do you understand all that I have said, Seth?" Adam quietly waited for Seth to express his feelings on this additional calling he would carry the remainder of his life.

Seth now understood what had been bothering his father that Sariah had mentioned. Nodding his agreement, he, too was sobered by this calling and knew that it would put him in occasional contact with the brother shunned by the family for the murder of his brother Abel. "Yes, Father, I understand and you are right, this calling will no doubt bring me sorrow, but it must be done." As he looked back over the many years since that day, he reflected that there had been more successes than failures, but Cain had still managed to destroy many of the records. He constantly had to be on the alert and think one step ahead of his clever, devious brother.

For the past few days Seth had received the strongest impression he should travel to the land of Enoch and make a record of the events that were going on there. Unable to shake the impression, he decided the time was right for the preparation for the journey westward but an issue had arisen and he had felt it necessary to discuss the matter with his wife Deborah before departing. Accordingly, he had approached his wife, now busy mending clothes with a special sewing device Seth had devised. "Deborah, how is the sewing machine working?" he asked as he watched his wife carefully making repairs on the children's clothing.

Seth's machine was a lockstitch. The device was made of wood and used a barbed needle which passed downward through the cloth to grab the thread and pull it up to form a loop to be locked by the next loop. The machine used an eye-pointed needle, with the eye and the point on the same end, carrying the upper thread and a falling shuttle carrying the lower thread. The curved needle moved through the fabric horizontally, leaving the loop as it withdrew. The shuttle passed through the loop, interlocking the thread.

"Wonderfully, Seth" she exclaimed. "The neighborhood wives are so jealous! It has saved me countless hours of work, especially my eyesight. Many women have already talked with their husbands to speak to you about the device."

"I am happy." But he was likewise anxious, so he brooded about the room for a moment, trying to find the words to explain why he had sought her out for her counsel.

Deborah realized something was bothering her husband. "Seth, you have something on your mind?"

"Why do you ask?" he replied distractedly.

Deborah arched her eyes as though Seth should know by now he had an obvious tell when he was nervous. "You are pacing about the room like an old mother cat."

"It's that obvious, is it?"

She replied matter-of-factly, "You get this way each time you have to leave on a recording trip."

"This time it's different. I think the new housekeeper is more spy than cook."

Deborah abruptly stopped work and went over to the door and closed it. She turned and whispered, "Do you mean Elina?"

Seth nodded and whispered back. "I do."

"But why?" she asked incredulously. "Does it have something to do with your new assignment?"

"Yes. It's Cain's way of keeping an eye on me and my movements."

Deborah thought for a moment then commented, "I think it is time my parents had a visit and saw their grandchildren."

Seth smiled at his wife's way with words. He had pondered this dilemma over for a few days but needed Deborah to confirm his plan. "When Elina leaves tomorrow afternoon for her home, we will take the children living at home with us and visit the home of your parents in Shulon. When she arrives the next day, we will be gone, and until she asks around, she will have no idea to where we have escaped."

Deborah thought it over and could find no flaw. "The plan will work, my Husband, but if Cain suspects we have fled because we have discovered his spy, he will be angry and may decide to take revenge on our family living nearby."

"We will leave word with our adult children that we had to quickly depart because your father was feeling ill and your mother needed help caring for him. Considering his chronic back problems, our story will have just enough truth to throw off any suspicion of our true intention. The important thing is that we get a head start so that I can settle you and the children in to your parent's home before I depart for my assignment. This way I can leave without being followed."

Seth and Enos, his son, were walking down a mountain path at a brisk pace. In contrast, their donkey, now laden with recording materials, as well as food and water for a few days, walked slowly behind them a few paces. Spruce and other evergreens had lent a bracing aroma to the still, cool air, and at this altitude it was refreshing now, but the two men knew when they reached the foot of the mountain, the air would be warmer and more humid. Enos, the eldest son, was an adult with a family of his own and eventually would have to assume his calling as the family record keeper. As a consequence, when the opportunity arose, Seth had decided to have his son accompany him to Enoch. Seth was grateful, though, that the special calling he had been assigned to record Cain's influence upon the realm, his son would never have to endure.

Always an astute scholar and keen observer of details, Seth had quickly learned the writing and language of his people, as well as the intricacies of higher mathematics, particularly as it applied to the movements of the sun, moon and stars in the night sky. All these things he had assiduously taught to all of his children, including his daughters because he intended for them all to be complete help-meets for their future husbands. After all, he reasoned, a father and patriarch in his home carried a solemn, holy responsibility to teach and lead his family justly and help them plan for a successful life. All these concepts were to be taught and passed on to his children who would then pass them down through their lineage.

Seth began to reflect on the singular responsibilities which the Creator had set for him and for all men who would call themselves a father. He had been taught of the importance of patriarchal authority and succession at the knee of Father Adam from the time he was old enough to understand. Perhaps more than any man alive, except his father, Seth understood that each patriarch of his home was accountable to the Creator for the success of his family, which is the primary stewardship of all fathers. As the extended family was growing larger by the day and events of an unsettling nature were occurring more often, Enos would be asked to assume the duties of family recorder which would free Seth up to be fully dedicated to his primary calling, that of historian.

After all, that was the reason he had been directed to the land of Enoch. He was on his way there to investigate and record Cain's latest involvement which had caused serious consequences in the land. He clearly understood his special calling to record these events for the sake of historical accuracy and a true judgment upon those who would fight against the Creator's plan. Aside from all this, Seth reflected, he enjoyed his son's companionship and this presented an excellent opportunity to teach and bond further with him and, thinking of this, he gave his son a friendly slap to the shoulder. After a while, he began to whistle a tune he had heard his daughters, Leah and Hannah, play. Both, of course, were gifted musicians of the harp and organ and each had been taught well to play these instruments by his lovely, intelligent wife, Deborah. Thinking of them, he smiled spontaneously at the thought of his wife and children. Seth was a contented, happy man.

Chapter 5 – Confrontations

As it turned out, Seth and Enos had arrived a few days ahead of Cain and his entourage. Upon arrival, Seth had made a few enquiries around the market square and had rapidly concluded that those who best to talk to about the current incident were the now worried wives of Lamech, Adah and Zillah. The two women were reluctant to speak initially, but quickly warmed to the subject of their erstwhile husband and made their home available for the discussion.

The four had retired to a cooler location within the inner court of the residence and now, seated around a large table that could accommodate all of them, including the writing materials, Seth sought to make the ladies more comfortable and at ease. He observed the room was high-ceilinged and built to allow the maximum amount of sunlight to stream through and provide a natural light source and so commented, "Ladies, you have a beautiful residence and it is obvious that your good taste permeates the room." He deliberately looked about the room, making further observations on the design of certain sculptures and flower arrangements and finally encouraged them to talk about their grandchildren. The women were clearly impressed by Seth's manner and his attention to homely details; thus, they were profuse with their thanks with each of his well-timed complements. Within a few minutes he had broken down any reluctance or regrets they might have had to cooperate with him.

Enos looked on in silent amusement and admiration. As he had seen his father perform this act of appeasement many times before, the results were unsurprising. Once he had asked cynically how he was able to conduct this act with such ease and his reply was guileless and typically Seth: "Enos, my Son, what act?"

Seth now held their complete attention. He summed up quickly their business that day, which was to make a record of the incident in question so that others would understand the truth and minimize the tendency for idle gossip. Having now set the ladies at ease, Seth asked, "Lady Zillah,

I know this is difficult for you, but could you tell us what you remember about Lamech's behavior on the day of Barak's death?"

Zillah, having been well coached by her sister, realized that the story Adah had concocted was actually quite close to what this handsome stranger was asking her to state for his records. As she was still in the midst of her period of mourning, the thought of Barak being murdered in the street by her pig of a husband still brought tears to her eyes. She slowly began to speak then added more emotion as her story unfolded:

"Our husband, Lamech, had been drinking heavily that day and when he drank he tended toward garrulousness. He was speaking all manner of idle rubbish about how he was being cheated by his brothers and how they refused to tax their citizens sufficiently enough to bring him more revenue. He then began ranting about how he was going to see Cain and demand additional land to be added to his kingdom. Adah and I had no idea that Cain could possibly control something like that, so we asked Lamech to explain what he meant. He went on a rambling explanation of the workings of the Clan, as he called it, and after a few minutes he then revealed that Cain, known as Master Mahan, was the titular head of this Society and the most powerful man in the realm. To our surprise, Lamech drunkenly boasted that he was just as capable of being Master Mahan as Cain. He then staggered from the room and passed out drunk in the hallway outside his bedroom. We had experienced these episodes before so we picked him up and carried him to the bed chamber where he quickly fell asleep and began snoring away the remainder of the afternoon." Zillah glanced toward her sister and pleaded for her to continue with the story. "Adah, I can't recount the murder of my precious Barak. Please relate the story from this point." Zillah began to sniffle.

Seth, now realizing how difficult this must be for Zillah, produced a small cloth which he offered to her for comfort. While Zillah dabbed at her eyes and thanked him, Adah looked on, trying to commiserate with her sister's loss, but also knowing that her doe-eyed son's carelessness had put them all at risk. So, attempting to soften the impression she had of Barak, Adah continued the story.

"After our husband's drunken exit, we were curious about some of the things Lamech had said about the members of the Clan. Zillah's eldest son,

Barak, had mentioned to us in passing once that he had heard rumors of the workings of the Clan, accordingly, as we were still curious about this Brotherhood, we asked Barak to join us the next day for the noon meal and he accepted. At noon day, while our husband was sleeping off his latest drunk, Barak arrived and joined us and over food and drink we asked him about the Clan. He became quiet and pensive then asked, "What have you heard? What has Lamech told you?"

"We related everything our husband talked about, especially the comments about Cain. Thinking that most of what he said was silly, drunken bravado, we paid Lamech little attention, but we were curious about the Society he called the Clan. Barak listened intently to all we related, then he got angry and said Lamech would pay for the insults to his family. He arose and ran out the door without as much as a backward glance. Alas, that was the last we saw of him. The next thing we know Barak lay dead in the street, minus an arm and a head, and our husband was standing over him, shouting to anyone who would listen that now he was Master Mahan." With this last statement, Zillah's quiet sniffling became raw sobs of fresh grief.

Seth, recognizing the loss of her son had been difficult on Zillah, sympathized with her and extended his condolences. While he allowed Enos to clear up the writing materials and pack them away, he murmured his thanks for their cooperation and complemented them both on their courage. Slowly, the air in the room seemed to take on a slight charge and a sub-aural thrumming could be felt, if unheard. Seth, now gazing at the two anxious women, took them both by the hand and said, "My Ladies, I have felt your worry and concern over your part in this incident. I feel inspired to tell the two of you that no harm will come to either of you and that Cain will leave you in peace." The two women felt something warm and tingling shoot up their arms as Seth made this pronouncement; it left them surprisingly light-headed but very happy. Tears welled up in their eyes as they wished the men a safe journey.

Seth and Enos walked silently down the dusty road to the market. It was a mild day and the birds in the trees seemed especially intent on sharing their songs of greeting. Still feeling the effect of his father's words of encouragement to the women, Enos was reluctant to speak aloud what he, too, had experienced and was at a loss as to how to state the question he wanted to ask. Patiently, as Seth was in no hurry to rush him, he awaited his son's question and finally Enos asked quietly, "Father, what happened back there?"

Seth, now deep in thought, was a long time in answering and Enos was afraid he might have to prompt him again. Finally, he commented, "It was a reminder that our Creator loves every one of us and knows our trials and our fears. My Son, when the occasion warrants it, God reaches out in a special way and reassures us that we are not alone. If you are prepared, you will feel this power again and it will work for you even as it did for me today."

Enos was quiet for a moment then replied, "I, too, felt their concern, Father, but could their story have been exaggerated somewhat?"

Seth commented, "Of course, and for that reason we now go to interview Barak's cousins living here in Enoch to get their impressions of the incident in the market. Our final report will represent an unbiased rendering of the influence of the Clan from many perspectives." He glanced over to his son and laid a hand on his arm and declared, "But, none of that will diminish what I felt and conveyed to the wives of Lamech. Cain will not be permitted to harm them."

It was the next day when Cain and his entourage arrived in the City of Lamech as it was now called since the death of his father, Methusael. Cain was worried that his brother, Seth, would arrive before he had a chance to call Lamech and his household together. He wanted to interview each of them thoroughly to insure that all had the same story and that it did not involve the Clan, thus he began to review his options and consider his plan of action. Primarily, he had in his mind to either stop his brother before he arrived or destroy his recordings if he had been too late to intercept him. This business with Lamech was quickly spiraling out of control and he did not need Seth to add to his worries that he would record an exaggerated account of the Clan's involvement and then spread them about like so much manure in a peasant's garden.

A few hours later, after receiving word from his advisers and spies within the city, it wasn't long before Cain deduced that he had been too late and he would now have to confront his brother Seth after the fact.

He had decided it was time to make a public display of his power and he intended to make his brother out to be the fool that he knew him to be.

Seth had just completed his interviews with Barak's kinsmen as well as several venders in the market. He had carefully hidden the records in a safe place and was now crossing the square when he became aware of Cain's arrival. It was, of course, he reflected, an ostentatious show of power designed to instill fear, not respect; in short, it was one worthy of an evil, embittered man. As he suspected Cain would lose little time in spewing his invective on him in front of his son, Enos, Seth had hoped that a public confrontation could be avoided. Nonetheless, as Cain had already decided beforehand that a confrontation in the open was his plan, the meeting in front of the market was inevitable.

Cain, now seeing his brother walking toward him, motioned to his followers to remain twenty paces behind so that he could have a personal, though public, debate with his brother. Even though his face looked friendly enough, Cain wore a mask of false joviality that did not fool Seth for a moment; his eyes were dark and the light never reached them. While the two brothers squared off near the main gate of the market entrance, Seth instructed Enos to halt likewise, nearly out of hearing range. Having no mask and no desire to dissemble, Seth walked slowly forward a few paces then simply waited impassively to see what his brother had to say.

As Cain began moving forward, he absently rubbed the scar on his left jaw all the while grinning impishly at this brother. After a moment, he sidled arrogantly up in front of Seth, dropping his hand carelessly from his face then he casually commented, "Well, Seth my Brother, you look well. Please tell me about the family. It has been many years since I last had the pleasure of their company." A false look of sorrow passed over his face as he continued. "I understand our dear mother has died recently. A pity I was unable to attend the funeral, but unfortunately I was omitted from the invitation list, was I not? I am sure it was just an oversight and not meant as an offense. And our esteemed father, I am sure that he is still as hale and hearty as always. Still full of juice, I assume?" He chuckled with good natured humor. Cain knew Adam was feeling his age and was tired most of the time, now requiring a cane to move about, but he couldn't help adding the comment as an added dig to Seth's discomfort.

My brother is a fiend, Seth thought scarcely for the first time. Wishing only to remove himself and Enos from his presence, Seth responded with loathing, "Cain, you are too late. I have made my record of your latest attempt to spread chaos throughout the land. The records have been well hidden and now out of your slimy grasp."

Seth's acerbic comment hit Cain like a backward slap to the face. His false countenance was removed and replaced by the face of an embittered, damned man. He readied himself for a choleric response and glancing in the direction of Enos, he seethed, "Seth I see it is too late to convince you of our father's lies, but there is plenty of time to reach Enos, though." This last biting comment was followed by a leering smile in Enos' direction.

Wishing now to avoid any more of Cain's reviling, Seth turned to go, but added, "One other thing Cain, I know you are intent on interrogating the women of Lamech. No harm is to come to them."

"And why not, if I so choose? Who is to stop me, Brother?" snapped Cain, now visibly livid over Seth's impertinence.

Seth was loath for any further discussion but patiently proclaimed, "Cain, I have been instructed to inform you of this. You well know from whom this message comes and what the consequences can mean if you are disobedient." Seth glanced at the left side of Cain's face; the scar was now a vivid red. Cain noted the direction of the look and glared malevolently at Seth. With that Seth quickly turned on his heels, figuratively dusting off the dirt from his sandals as he did so.

Cain stood impotently there in the square, so angry now that he was shaking. His soldiers ran up to him to help, but he angrily shoved them away and shouted, "I have already wasted enough time this morning and I am now ready to see Lamech. Bring him to me along with his wives." His pompous exit from the square was less significant than that of Seth's and he was keenly aware of it.

Cain carried with him a certain celebrity aura wherever he appeared. Since his appearance usually meant trouble, however, most people made it a point to be elsewhere when he arrived. Unfortunately, this was impossible for Lamech and his household.

Cain was always accompanied by a small, but fierce contingent of highly trained body guards who would protect him with their lives if necessary. The guards had a dual purpose: in addition to personal protection they further provided an intimidating presence that could be applied to interrogation, which they had performed on many occasions before. It was this presence that he hoped to impress upon Lamech and his wives. Cain may have been warned that no harm was to come to the women, but he could and was willing to use intimidation.

Now seated on Lamech's throne, Cain had ordered everyone brought before him, including the servants, to the audience room and ordered them all to kneel, which they immediately did without hesitation. Wanting the pressure and anxiety to build up in their minds so that they would be more compliant to his requests, while Cain sat silently, he compelled them to remain uncomfortably in that position for some time. At length, he gave them leave to stand then ordered everyone out of the room except Adah and Zillah. While the others were filing out, he took the opportunity to look over the two women. It had been many years since he had last seen them, but they both still appeared robust and quite lovely. *"Ladies, what have you been up to?"* he wondered silently.

The ladies felt his discerning gaze upon them and now, quite uncomfortable, they lowered their eyes in humility. Once the room had been cleared except for the women and his guards, Cain, now using his smoothest, courteous voice coaxed, "Dear Ladies, please tell me everything you know regarding Barak's death. Omit nothing."

Cain was a master at interrogation and prided himself on his ability to extract information quickly and efficiently. Adah began with her rehearsed story and Cain never interrupted her. When she had completed, he had Zillah relate her story and when she had concluded her recitation, as if deep in thought, Cain steepled his fingers under his chin. He then asked Adah to repeat her story, this time listening for any inconsistencies between the two women. Then, he requested Zillah retell hers, likewise listening for any contrivances that might exist in her version. When he was satisfied that their stories had meshed without too much inconsistency or too little, he instructed the guards to bring two chairs and the women were seated.

Cain then began the laborious process of separating the relevant details from the useless information they were all too willing to share. At length, he came to the conclusion that Lamech's wives had allowed their curiosity to get the better of them and had unfortunately asked the wrong questions at the wrong time to the wrong person, namely that idiotic husband of theirs. He would have enjoyed allowing his guards to interrogate them more vigorously, but apparently he would be denied that added bonus. Seth had said nothing, however, about any limitations on what he could do to Lamech and he was the problem anyway and always had been.

With a grim smile and a flourish of his hand, he beckoned that they leave. "Ladies, you may leave, but with a stern warning. You know much more about my Society than anyone outside the Clan should ever know. I will spare your lives only because I have been forbidden to do you harm, but if I ever hear of your tongues wagging again about this subject, I will personally make sure you no longer have tongues to wag."

Adah and Zillah walked out of the room as if suspended off the floor. Their lives had been spared by a man that never made that concession once he had determined your guilt. As they had correctly concluded that it was Seth to whom they owed their lives, each woman in her own way silently blessed him for his intervention. On their way past the door, they heard Cain sardonically bark the order, "Guard, send in Master Mahan. He and I have an important matter to discuss."

Lamech, son of Methusael, wished now that he had requested the use of the title of Master Mahan instead of assuming it. Standing before Cain, he felt more like a child who had misbehaved and now awaited punishment. He stammered, "Please, Cain, I can explain everything. It was all a misunderstanding, I assure you!"

While Lamech sweated fear and alcohol from every pore of his body, Cain sat behind the table and stared disgustedly at this wretch, now getting angrier and more offended by the moment at the man he considered a misbegotten son of a fool. With disdain, Cain ordered, "Start explaining your actions from the time you decided to murder the grandson of an old ally to the point you were standing boldly over his dead body in the market place bellowing to all who would listen that you had assumed your new title." For added emphasis, Cain stonily intoned, "Omit nothing."

"Sire", Lamech blubbered, "I was only trying to protect the name of the Clan that Barak had sullied by spreading his damnable lies." When he saw that Cain remained unmoved by his protestations to protect the honor of their Brotherhood, he reluctantly pressed on from the beginning. When he had concluded his story, Cain had ordered him to repeat it, then again.

Cain observed him critically, though silently, throughout this replay of his story. He was measuring Lamech's story against what his wives had reported and what witnesses had stated from the market on the day of the murder. There were several egregious omissions that he had failed to relate. Cain began a series of quickly fired questions to test the confidence of Lamech's story.

"Were you drunk with wine on the day your wives asked questions regarding the Clan?"

He was reluctant to admit it but Cain's face told him he already knew the answer. Lamech replied limply, "Yes."

"Did you reveal the information about the oath and covenant?"

"I don't remember", he stammered. Cain looked at him balefully. "Yes", he sobbed.

Now Cain leveled at him the truly damning question. "Did you kill Barak in the market place without first getting permission from the Clan?"

With dawning horror, Lamech realized that no murders against relatives of their Fraternity members are permitted without permission from the Council. This point had slipped his mind and he had failed to consider it before he had acted in the market. "I supposed I did not," he admitted miserably.

Cain was weary of the smell of this oaf and loath to ask a final question and, of course, he already knew the answer. "Who gave you leave to publicly claim my official title of Master Mahan as your own?"

"No one", Lamech whispered.

Cain, now thoroughly disgusted with the utter stupidity of this cretinous clod, was so exasperated he could hardly speak. With finality in his voice, he stated, "Lamech, I convened a council of the Clan before I left to investigate this disaster you singlehandedly created and so I can speak on behalf of the members. You have forfeited all your rights to lead this kingdom. It will be given to another in due time. As to you personally, your punishment will be banishment. The only reason you are still alive is that you were too besotted to realize what you were doing when you killed the grandson of a member of our Society. You will be unwelcome in any part of my realm. If anyone takes you in, provides you shelter or accommodates you in any way, he will incur my wrath and my justice will be swift."

"But, is there no appeal?" he sobbed.

"There is none. Lamech, get out of my sight before I have my guards set upon you."

With total misery, Lamech exclaimed, "As you, Cain, were assured to be avenged seven times if anyone attempted to harm you, surely, if any man attempts to do me harm for what I sacrificed for the Clan, I will be avenged seventy times seven."

Cain, with thinly veiled contempt, stonily pronounced, "Lamech, do not begin to compare yourself with me after the damage you have caused here. You are unworthy to even kiss my feet, assuming I would even permit such an offense to my person." "Guards", he shouted, "Escort Lamech to the street and make sure he gets on his way down the road."

Chapter 6 – The Translation, continued

Jasher silently walked through the downstairs hallway into the study. He was feeling tired, but fulfilled as a successful day had been completed. The two professors, Bedford and Levinson, were already there poring over the latest translation pertaining to Lamech. The two scientists were deep in conversation, but paused as Jasher entered.

Professor Levinson's face turned quizzical as he asked, "Jasher, we are perplexed over the phrase, *oath and covenant*. Obviously, we know in general terms the dictionary definition of the two words, but used together, how do they apply to the involvement of the Clan?"

"Gentlemen," explained Jasher, "the first thing you should understand about the Clan of the Scar, as they call it, is that this society is an aberration and its precepts are anathema of existing truths; they are an offense to all things holy. The oaths and covenants of the Clan signify their allegiance to a false being who has no power to give any legitimate validity to their oaths nor is he in any position to bind any covenant, no matter how much they honor him. In short, what Lucifer and Cain, his agent, offer is a lie. They traffic in power as a means to subvert the agency of man then wrap it up in a false cloak of legitimacy by calling it the Clan."

After having been informed that Cain was still very much alive, Levinson had been initially skeptical, as would anyone given the details. But, he was mystified over a point which had bothered him and so prompted a question. "How is it that Cain has been so successful? Does God care so little that he would avoid any intervention into this madness?"

Jasher paused to reflect whether Levinson, a man of science, could follow his logic. He inwardly shrugged and proceeded. "Isaac," he countered, "you may as well be asking why bad things happen to good people or why the rich and powerful persist while the humble are trampled over and exploited." He asserted, "The agency of Man is inviolate and has been given to us since the beginning, even before our existence here in mortality. Our comprehension of our ultimate gift of immortality would be useless without it. But, there is much yet that we lack in understanding so we must accept the omniscience of God the Creator. All conditions that exist that may affect the decisions of men and women, regardless of whether they are used to do good or evil, are an extension of His will and I can assure you that His will is being played out today, in this home, this very moment."

Levinson pondered over what had been revealed to them, but one question, for now, still remained. "How is it you seem to know Cain so well?"

Jasher replied regrettably, "Cain and I do not share a common lineage, but it amuses him to consider me a brother and, in a real sense, I suppose our ancestral ties are close enough to be considered brothers. At least in our chance meetings I have permitted him to address me in this manner, though I doubt I could stop him if I tried. I know him quite well not just by his reputation but as an historical recorder of his works."

Professor Bedford pondered over the power of this Society and quietly asked, "Jasher, much of what you have described to us regarding this society seems to corroborate my findings regarding the downfall of many great civilizations throughout history. Is this Society among us today?"

"William, this society has always existed, though over the centuries it may have gone underground for short periods of time, only to experience a renewed resurgence of strength later. I can assure you, though, since the middle of the fifteenth century, it has ever grown stronger and its influence can be felt at every level of government in every nation of the world today. A more modern version of Cain's society now exists and, as I have mentioned, *The Abridgement* will so testify that Cain is still at the helm. In our day, Cain's Society is not just secretive, it is invisible. It is the very opposite of public and its influence has been insinuated at all levels of government as well as the corporate-controlled media. Notwithstanding, our modern world has evolved and even Cain has been forced to remove his activities from the public light into what it is today, a shadow society."

Part 4 – The Days of Noah

5   And God saw that the wickedness of man was great in the
     earth, and that every imagination of the thoughts of his heart
     was only evil continually.

6   And it repented the Lord that he had made man on the earth,
     and it grieved him at his heart.

7   And the Lord said, I will destroy man whom I have created from
     the face of the earth; both man, and beast, and the creeping
     thing, and the fowls of the air; for it repenteth me that I have
     made them.

8   But Noah found grace in the eyes of the Lord.

----- *Genesis 6: 5 – 8*

And it was that Noah prophesied among the children of
men and called them that they should repent, but they neither
listened unto his words nor hearkened unto his counsel;

And after that they had heard him speak, they came to him
boldly saying: Behold, we are all the sons of God and do we not
take unto ourselves the daughters of men to marriage? And do
we not eat and drink and marry and give in marriage when we
please? And our wives bear unto us children and are they not
mighty men? Have we not come forth from mighty men and do
we not appear as men of old, men of great renown? And they
rejected the words and counsel of Noah.

----- *The Abridgement, Chapter 10*

A man's conscience, like a warning line on the highway, tells him what he shouldn't do – but it does not keep him from doing it.

----- Frank A. Clark

Chapter 1 – The Mountain

On the east of the land of Cainan stands a tall mountain, much taller than the surrounding peaks of the region. Those who remember the old legends would tell you, if you took the time to listen, that there had always been something timeless, even sacred about its location. From time immemorial there had been those who had walked past its gentle glacis and ventured up its rugged paths then finally past the glacier that could be seen year round even during years of drought. They came for different reasons, of course, and unless they had a good reason for the ascent, many held the opinion that the sheer height of the mount would discourage all but the most experienced from the climb. Others, who saw the mountain as hallowed, would make the climb to satisfy some inner need to commune with that which was sacred. The latter reason hardly applied to the current era where men were more actively engaged in violence than to appreciate something as peaceful as a holy pilgrimage or the discharge of a holy calling.

Nonetheless, there were those who had made the journey and at least one had come back with a fascinating discovery: the mountain was the home of a large cave. There was hardly anything new about this, of course. Men had been discovering caves for many years and some of them were quite extraordinary, even beautiful, but none discovered had ever been suitable enough to protect and serve as a long term habitation for those seeking shelter from a cataclysm. This one, however, either due to a geological quirk or provenance, had a natural light source as well as an abundant source of geothermal heat, and most important for survival, it had water.

It was a cool crisp autumn day as two elderly men could be seen emerging the mountain cave. Though they were advanced in age, one was actually much older than he looked and it was evident that he was now struggling to keep up with the other. After Seth had revealed to Lamech that he was to accompany him eastward, Lamech had spent most of the last month with him on this trek to the homeland of their fathers. Lamech had been aware of the existence of his distant kinsman, but had never met him before this journey, so it was with a keen interest that he had finally made acquaintance with a legend. There was much he had learned and even more that he ever expected to learn.

Now, having completed their tasks in the mountain cave, they had descended and had reached the foot of the mountain. Lamech had discovered a pathway south, and supposing Seth was just behind him, he began walking in that direction. Realizing he had just finished a long mission and had little energy to continue, Seth had stopped, however, and had decided he could go on no farther. Consequently, as they entered the path towards the southern end of the valley, he tiredly sat down on a nearby boulder, and calling to his travelling companion, said, "Lamech, my Brother, this is where we must part."

Surprised, Lamech turned and saw that Seth was seated and breathing with difficulty. Attempting a note of encouragement, he pointed out, "Seth, there is a community towards the south that we observed coming down the mountain. Surely, we can make it there by nightfall."

"Most assuredly you will continue south, but without me" Seth added tiredly with a smile.

Lamech was puzzled. His companion was wearied, but surely they both had the stamina to reach their destination before it got too late. "Seth, I do not understand."

Patiently, and now near exhaustion, he replied, "Lamech, my mission is finally at an end. The only task I had remaining was to show you the depository for our records and that has been done. You and your son Noah will complete the process of delivering your records in due time before the end."

Lamech was confused by this conversation, but he was especially struck by the sense of finality in Seth's declaration. "Seth, you say Noah and I will complete the process? To what end are you referring?"

A shadow seemed to come over Seth's face and Lamech could see that he was pained by something. "Lamech, something catastrophic is about to befall mankind. It has been decreed that only your son Noah and his family and only a handful of others will survive the disaster to come." Seth paused a moment to gather the last of his remaining strength. He noted,

"My age appears to be catching up to me all at once, so there is no more time to waste. The specifics of this event will be revealed to you and your son at a later time, but for me, what I have seen suggests the world will be cleansed with water and few will survive and those surviving will have to begin anew. The records must be safeguarded to ensure the survivors are given a chance to understand their history and their language. It is my hope that future generations will learn from our mistakes."

Lamech was astounded at this declaration. "But Noah, my son, will survive, you say?"

"Yes, there is a survival plan and he plays a large part in it; further, those who live in this valley play a part as well. At the southern end of the valley you will meet a girl whose name is Sariah. You will find a time to talk with her alone and you will reveal to her the whereabouts of the cave which contains our records. This will plant an idea in her mind that will manifest itself when she reaches adulthood and feels a need to climb the mountain then investigate the depository for herself. She should keep the contents of the cave a secret until a time in the future when your son will return to this valley and prepare the people here for the disaster that is to come. As all things will be revealed in the due time of our Creator, be patient, my Brother. Above all, remember, the records must be protected; they are the key to the future of our family."

"So, for us, this is a farewell?" Now dreading the reply, Lamech had asked.

Seth was exhausted. "Lamech, I have longed for many years to be reunited with my wife and family. For me, the hardest part of my mission was burying my children; a father should never have to do that. You must go on and fulfill what you have been pre-ordained to do just as I have done." He exclaimed, "Brother, the time is near. I have a sense of joy unknown to me for many years. Let us embrace one last time in life then you must be on your way."

It was said that Seth was in the express image of his father. For Lamech, the embrace was as close as he would ever come in life to have ever known their Father Adam. After the embrace, Lamech shook his head incredulously and replied, "Seth, how can you expect me to just abandon you here at the foot of this mountain."

Seth smiled wearily, replying "The Creator has always cared for me. I rather doubt he will abandon me at this point. Farewell, Brother. Please be on your way."

It was a bittersweet parting as Lamech turned to begin the journey south and to wherever his mission in life was to take him. At a bend in the road ahead, Lamech turned to wave one last farewell, but instead got a glimpse of a light opening up in front of Seth as he eagerly stepped forward into it then disappeared.

No one from the valley had discovered the cave, but it was said that, even as a child of eleven, Sariah could recall the day when an elderly man had walked through their valley from the north on his way from the mountain. Claiming to be a kinsman, he had stopped at the farm for rest, food and water then he had spoken reassuring words of gratitude to the family. As he was about to make his leave, he asked the man of the house a special request. "Avram, as I have said, I am Lamech, a distant cousin of your family and I thank you all for your hospitality this day."

"It was our pleasure twice-fold since you are a kinsman" Avram replied.

"Avram, would you indulge an old man a parting favor?" Lamech asked, still smiling.

"Of course" The response was immediate and sincere.

"Could Sariah, your daughter, accompany me a short way down the path to ensure I don't stray too far from my cut-off through the mountain?"

Sariah was easily within hearing range when this request was made so she quickly positioned herself next to her father. "Well, Sariah, would you like to guide Lamech to the next farm?"

Sariah was a precocious child and quickly assented not just because it was polite, but because she sensed there was something this man wanted to share with her. "Yes, Father. Shall we go, Lamech?" She was obviously excited and anxious to know what would develop.

Grinning at the excitement from his daughter, Avram made his final farewell and Lamech, now accompanied by Sariah, made their way down the road. After a few miles Lamech motioned her over to a fence for rest under a tree. He studied her open face for a moment and asked her pointedly. "Sariah, do you know of the mountain north of here?"

"The large one?" she asked.

"That's the one" responded Lamech with an indulgent grin.

"They say it's special, even sacred" she informed him.

"They are correct." was his reply and added, "But it's more than that. It is a place where our people have been storing records since the days of Seth. I will tell you of this place, but you should refrain from speaking to anyone about it until you are old enough to see it for yourself."

Lamech went on to discuss at length the location of the cave with Sariah as well as the details of its inner rooms and the contents therein. The last thing he said was: "Sariah, one day this knowledge will be of great worth to you and your people and the cavern will serve as a refuge in the event of imminent disaster. Keep all I have said safe within your heart and mind until that day arrives. Can you do this?"

Sariah gently smiled and responded matter-of-factly, "Of course, it is my mountain." It would not be until decades later, after she had grown into adulthood that she had occasion to think again of Lamech.

Several years had passed since the family of Seth had convened a reunion. Of course, Seth had been gone nearly one hundred years, but the gathering was a strong family tradition, one which reaffirmed their love and continuity. Two elderly men of Seth's lineage, Lamech and his father, Methuselah stood against a stone wall near an old maple tree. It was in the late fall of the year, the leaves had all fallen from the trees and they could feel the inevitable approach of winter. Although other family members danced and frolicked with wild abandon, completely indifferent and uncaring of the danger to come, the finality of the season seemed to reflect the somber mood that prevailed between the two men.

Earlier in the day, the two patriarchs had stood before the group and had given them a stern warning, rebuking many because of their wayward behavior from the Creator's precepts and a consequential, impending disaster unless they reversed their ways of living. The two then instructed their family that their message was to be shared with other family members and friends at their homes and towns in Cainan. They were both saddened that their words had been met with laughter and doubt, many disbelieving and expressing openly their opinion that these two patriarchs were addled. Though none of the other family members were aware of it, both men were keenly aware that this reunion would be their last.

While his father and grandfather were deep in discussion, Noah had sighted them then slowly weaved his way through the thronging, festive relatives. His dream of the night before had been disturbing and he knew of only two persons who could help him discern and clarify his impressions, thus he had sought their counsel.

Methuselah was the first to observe his approach and so had extended an embrace before Lamech could respond. "Noah, it is wonderful to have you back in our midst."

Lamech likewise embraced his son, but now noticed his somber, somewhat reflective mood. "Son, welcome to the reunion! I see by your countenance there is something that worries you beyond what your grandfather and I have announced this day. Your worry is well-founded and I truly wish that other members of our family had taken our warning as soberly as you had."

Noah was eager to share the specifics of his dream, but simply had no idea how to interpret them without help. "Father, Grandfather, your message today has clarified in many ways what I had experienced on my mission to the realm. The people I visited were unwilling to renounce their ways of corruption and now I see that my own family has been contaminated by that same influence. If it were possible to do so, I fear that this darkness may grow now even worse." At this juncture he paused slightly as if to comprehend the magnitude of what he was about to declare. "Father, I have seen the end. For me it is no longer an abstraction to be shared as a general, impending threat. According to my dream, there is to be a flood and nearly all will perish."

The two patriarchs glanced at one another knowingly as if something of immeasurable value had just passed between them. Methuselah turned to Noah and murmured softly, "I see it is true and so does your father. You and your family must prepare for the end and you will begin a project designed to preserve our lineage and our records. The specifics will be revealed to you upon your arrival back to your home, but before you begin this labor you will have to warn the people once again. It is imperative that this be done as a second witness to them so that this destruction of the Creator's children will be justified."

Sariah was a lively child, and if you listened to her friends and family, she had a heart of gold. She was one of those special persons who come into this world with a mission and she spent her days anxiously engaged in discovering what it was. There was no challenge too great, no intellectual point she was unprepared to search in order to grasp an understanding of her purpose. Though she was raised in an isolated area of the realm, the life with her family and neighbors was nearly ideal for it permitted her growth without barriers. Though the valley was remote and little news got in and very seldom did anyone ever venture out, the people living in the valley were not intellectually inferior farmers. Since they were of the lineage of Seth, they had immigrated here generations before and they brought with them the collective knowledge of their society and had passed it along to their children as was the custom of Seth's family. Thus, each had been educated in the language and writing of their fathers and had developed an appreciation of knowledge as well as a collective written history. Additionally, on those occasional visits Seth made to the valley, he invariably shared much of his knowledge with them, and as can be imagined, it was considerable.

One day, about twenty years after the time she had bid farewell to Lamech, Sariah was helping her father, Avram, with the livestock. For some time now she had been obsessed with a new challenge, but she wasn't certain how her father would react to it. Since there was an element of danger, he might forbid it, but in Sariah's usual bold manner, she felt sure that she could wear him down.

It was near the end of the day and the two had finished up the gathering and feeding of their herd of horses. Sariah, sensing that the time was right announced, "Father, I wish to climb the mountain."

Her father, now washing his heads from a nearby bucket, knew which of the mountains she referred, but notwithstanding replied blandly, "Really, which one?"

"Don't tease" countered his daughter. "You know there is only one mountain worth climbing." She pointed to the tallest mountain in the range that ran along the northern end of the valley. "The one Lamech talked about. He said it contained a cave and he was quite specific where it could be found. I have to find it and see for myself."

"And what will you do with that knowledge?" her father prodded, knowing that to Sariah, once she decided on something, she was slow to put it aside. As a consequence, it would do little good to try to talk her out of it. "Lamech, the old man and our kinsman, said that one day the family would need this for our survival. I think it is time that one of us went up the mountain to verify that the cave exists and assess what can be done if we do need it."

While he thought about approving his daughter's latest adventure, Avram continued his cleanup of the day's work. Finally, he replied, "Sariah, Lamech said a lot of things, many of which were probably just the maunderings of an old man. I have always indulged your interests because you have always seen a thing through once you have started it. I know once you have commenced this climb, you will avoid backing down even when common sense suggests you should. And that is the problem. You don't know when to quit."

"So, I should be a quitter?" she smiled impishly.

"I doubt you would know how to be" he replied seriously, still reluctant to take the bait and smile with her.

"You know I am old enough to decide for myself," she slowly pointed out.

"I know you are, but that doesn't lessen my worry." He realized it was pointless to argue with his head-strung daughter once she had made up her mind about a thing. He gave it some additional thought and came to a decision. "Ok, permission granted, but you are not to go up there unprepared. You are to dress warmly and you must wear proper foot wear and take whatever provisions you can carry with you. You should not be gone for more than five days. If you are gone longer, your mother will be worried and she will send me and your brothers up that mountain looking for you. Understood?"

Sariah could barely contain her excitement. She clapped and danced around her father and then gave him a hug.

He smiled at this daughter he adored, but clearly would never understand. He grumbled, "I don't know why I bother to try to talk you out of anything."

She smugly remarked, "Because Father, I always listen."

By the second day of her trek she realized she was near the top. And now, quite winded, Sariah stopped to catch her breath. The air was cooler and much thinner up here, the vegetation and tree line were now well below her. Lamech had said to look for a large outcropping in the shape of a cat's head then look directly below it. It took her a few minutes walking around the summit of the mount to get just the right viewpoint. She carefully gazed in every direction then spied what appeared to be a large boulder in the shape of an animal and on closer inspection concluded that it must be that of a cat's head; the head was canted to the side instead of overlooking the valley floor. From her vantage point, it appeared that a pathway had been cut by someone many years before and the path led directly to the entrance. It was now clear why no one had ever noticed it before because the falling rock debris from above had partly blocked the opening, leaving it unnoticed from the valley far below. As she got closer, though, it was clear that an opening did exist. She simply followed the pathway and carefully pushed off the larger boulders to one side and tossed the smaller ones over the cliff. The entrance to the cave was now fully exposed.

Before beginning the climb, Sariah had created a torch, and as she entered the cave, she lit it to provide light. She walked a few paces inside with the torch in front of her to cut back the dimness of the interior opening, but, after a few moments, she became aware that instead of getting darker, which one would expect, there was a dull, but discernable light emanating from the walls. After noting the light, it was obvious that she really didn't need the torch, so she extinguished it to try to get a better impression of the natural light of the cave. The small pathway from the cave entrance quickly gave way to a wider one that led to an opening into a large room. The room was wide and extremely tall with long rocky projectiles hanging from the ceiling as well as coming up from the floor. The same glowing mineral rock that had lit the pathway from the entrance was in obvious abundance here in the inner cavern for it was lit up as any room of a house at mid-day. There were exits off the inner cavern that presumably led to other rooms and it could be clearly observed that these, too, were lit up by the same rock walls. Then her mind registered something, which when all things considered, was even more astonishing: it was actually warmer inside the cave than it was outside. In fact, as she walked into the other rooms off the main cavern, the cold seemed to dissipate the farther into the inner rooms that she walked. Remarkably still, in one of the deeper caves that she explored she found a warm spring of fresh water bubbling up from below the floor as well as a large, deep pond of cold fresh water that formed as a result of water dripping from the ceiling. Being perceptive, she reasoned that this dripping water from above was a result of the melting from the small glacier she had noticed while climbing up that side of the mountain.

The last room she discovered, though clearly there were many more, was the most curious of all. As she walked through its entrance, she observed the room was covered from the floor upwards to several meters with what appeared to be metallic tablets. Upon closer inspection of one of these, she noted the inscription was of the writing of her people and she was able to understand much of it in spite of the small differences of syntax. With an eager excitement, she began to read and discovered that the writings belonged to her distant relative, Seth. The writings of each metallic record she picked up contained a preface followed by an historical account. Upon further exploration, she discovered still more rooms full of these metallic objects.

She spent most of that afternoon inside the cavern exploring new rooms and poring over records from the adjoining rooms until the inner voice of her father seemed to tell her to curb her enthusiasm and that it was time to turn back toward the entrance before she got lost. She didn't always listen to that voice, but she sensed that this might be a good time to do so. Carefully, and making a mental note of the size and attributes of the cave, she walked back to the entrance, but became aware of something highly unusual she had missed as she first entered the inner room off the cave entrance. To her right, propped up again the wall of the cave was a huge rock sculpted in the shape of a wheel, but without the hole for the axil. She took a few moments and examined the heavy object and wondered for what purpose it had been sculpted and by whom. She looked over at the cave entrance and smiled. She envisioned how the wheel might fit over the inner doorway if enough force and strength could be gathered to push it over in that direction. She had made the possible connection to the entrance, but the reason for its use as yet held no meaning, so with an inward shrug, she turned away from the wheel then walked out of the cave and into the afternoon sunshine of a beautiful day. Two days later she was back at her home and when asked to relate her discoveries, she remembered Lamech's warning and so refrained from giving details of the records and any speculation of the use for the cave. That seemed to satisfy even the most inquisitive among her family and friends so, for the time being at least, the real purpose of the cave would remain a secret.

Over one hundred ten years had passed since that day she had discovered the secrets of the mountain and she now had a family and home of her own. Quite understandably, she had encouraged her husband to build their homestead at the foot of the mountain at the northern end of the valley and well within walking distance of the cave. Owing to the continuous conflicts that disturbed the rest of the realm, few ventured eastward to pay homage to the mountain as they once had and so, apparently, even rumor of its existence had faded with time. Eventually, Sariah gradually got used to calling it her mountain, though, in truth, she was unable to recall a time when she had looked upon it in any other way, but, down through the years, she often recalled the words of Lamech and still wondered if the day would ever come when they all might have to find refuge there.

Thus, over time, their valley remained remote and seldom travelled. In fact, to her knowledge, only one family had bothered to return to the turmoil to the west, leaving their peaceful valley behind. Her closest childhood friend, Elisheba, and her family had left many years earlier. She said her father had grown tired of farming and it was unlikely they would ever return. Lately, however, Sariah had been thinking of her childhood friend and began to wonder if they would ever meet again.

Chapter 2 – Giddiel the Robber King

Men rise from one ambition to another. First, they seek to secure themselves against attack, and then they attack others.

----- Niccolo Machiavelli

The landscape of the kingdoms and the boundaries under the control of the Clan had changed only slightly since the time of Enoch the Prophet some three hundred years earlier. What had changed were the tactics Cain used to consolidate his empire. For hundreds of years, the use of limited warfare had been employed primarily as a means to subjugate the people with the use of minimum force. Known only to Cain and a few trusted advisers, an equally important reason for this tactic was the discovery and confiscation of any and all records that were found during the temporary occupations of Cain's armies. Cain had all records destroyed that might connect him or his Society directly to the collapse of kingdoms and the eventual subjugation of the citizenry. Over the years, after careful interrogations and making exhaustive investigations, he now had every reason to believe that the primary cache of records lay somewhere in the kingdom of Cainan far to the eastern edge of the realm under the rule of King Menahem.

His tactics had now changed from trying to rule a loose confederation of independent kingdoms to govern a consolidation of all kingdoms under one common ruler. And now, finally, after over one hundred years of conflict and reorganization, Cain was one kingdom away from achieving that goal. Because of its location in the center of the realm, the kingdom of Nod had always been the logical place from which to centralize and control his government of the realm. For that reason Cain had always used it to maintain his power base and from there his influence could be promulgated to all directions of his empire. Following the conquest of each kingdom, puppet kings, who were members of the Clan, had been set up in each to disseminate the directives and edicts of Cain and his Society. These kings realized, however, that they could be easily replaced on a whim, that their election was based more upon simple expediency than any sense of gratitude from the Society. Much of the time they spent establishing their own power base as well as a standing army to protect what little they had been given from Cain. Thus, their sense of loyalty to the Clan seldom ran deeply. The real power lay in the Regent Governor of the realm to whom all the kings paid homage and he was accountable only to Cain.

Owing to his ruthless nature, Giddiel, king of Nod, was chosen by Cain to act as Regent, the chief enforcer of the realm as well as its nominal governor and with Cain's approval was now close to being undisputed master over the entire continent. Having just conquered one of the last independent kingdoms and its citizens, Cain could now turn his efforts and complete attention to the overthrow and subjugation of Cainan, ruled by Menahem. This kingdom remained the only region of the realm with limited dealings with the Clan and therefore the last bastion in which there existed nominal self-determination. Moreover, and equally important to Cain, he felt that Cainan was the location of a large cache of historical records that must be discovered and destroyed at all costs.

Zadok, third son of King Giddiel, was disgusted by what he had just witnessed. His father, Giddiel the Robber King, as he was known, had just completed his final victory over his rival from the kingdom of Hamazi. Zadok was a general of the army of the kingdom of Nod and he had, in fact, served for over thirty years in that capacity in support of his father's incessant quest to bring the realm under one ruler, which of course, in time would be he. In spite of his training and long service, Zadok now regretted his association with Giddiel. The fighting of the last few years had been less about consolidation of the realm and more about instilling fear and terror.

And now the ruling populace of Hamazi would be next to be put to the sword. Giddiel, never a gracious winner and always an intolerable loser, had made sure that a clear message had been sent to all of the kingdoms in the realm that there would be no further obstruction to his absolute rule. Since he was usually pitiless towards those he conquered, the entire genealogical line of the rulers of Hamazi were beheaded; their heads had been mounted on pikes that now adorned the entrance way of their principal city. Zadok had tried in vain to convince his father that this savage act on the populace was unnecessary, that the king and his family were well under control with no further desire to contest his rule. Giddiel had contemptuously gazed at his son under hooded eyes and stonily told him to obey his orders and if he was unable to stomach them, he would find someone else who could. Under the protests of his chief captains, Zadok had removed his men from the field of battle and marched them back to the capitol of Nod that same day. He left the beheadings up to a more accommodating general who shared his father's similar ideas of battlefield glory.

The following month, now on the throne and firmly in control of the realm save one kingdom, Giddiel had ordered Zadok to appear before him to discuss the conquest of Cainan. As Giddiel's most successful general, his tactics in the field had turned many battles from near defeat into absolute routs, thus saving many unnecessary casualties and deaths, but Zadok was weary of war and had begun to look forward to the day when the realm was peacefully established under one ruler, thus he fought for peace and honor. Following a victory, he refused to allow his men to disgrace themselves by looting, pillaging and raping and though his men grumbled at this lost opportunity of spoils, the realm was always in a better position to recover when General Zadok had taken the field of battle. Though Giddiel scarcely cared a whit for his son's moral inclinations, so long as he remained successful on the battlefield, Giddiel tolerated his impertinence.

There remained only the kingdom of Cainan in the far eastern region of the realm that had dared resist Giddiel's expansionist designs. Menahem had a formidable army under his command and would no doubt put up strong resistance to any organized attack from the west. Though Giddiel by temperament was loath to employ subterfuge as a ploy for conquest, he had nonetheless been instructed by Cain to develop and execute a plan that involved such a strategy. The plan, in broad strokes, was to keep King Menahem of Cainan off balanced and uncertain long enough for a full-scale attack to be successful. Thus, the King had to be convinced it was in his best interest to postpone or at least hesitate at the precise moment to commit his troops to a confrontation until it was too late. That strategy would require the right person to perform the ruse, and though Giddiel doubted his son could pull it off, Cain had determined its success would require the help of Zadok.

Giddiel was no fool and knew of his son's contempt toward him, thus he despised the idea of appearing friendly when he should have broken him for his insubordination during the last campaign. He had assured Cain, however, that he would make every effort to convince Zadok to accept his part in the deception.

Concurrently, Zadok knew his father's ruthless, conniving nature, so he was wary of any intrigue his father may have brewing that would involve him in such actions and was suspicious of any overtures to involve him in any matters of state. Accordingly, when he appeared before Giddiel he was careful to avoid discussions that might lead to his involvement of betrayal or fraud.

"Zadok, how is your home and family?" Giddiel asked solicitously.

"Sire, my wife and children are all fine and healthy and send you their greetings and love." Zadok detested his father and loathed having to play this game of civility with the cretin, especially when it involved his family.

"And their loyalty?" added Giddiel sardonically.

"It is, like my own, absolute Sire." Zadok replied, acting the dutiful son.

Giddiel seemed to ponder over this response for several moments. As if coming to a decision, he announced, "Zadok, you are hereby relieved of your status and commission as a field general in my army. Another has been found and has been placed in your stead. I need you now to fulfill an equally important role as First Ambassador to my throne to all kingdoms under my rule. Once you have delivered my edicts to each of them, you must ensure that all the ruling kings understand my statutes and insure they become the law of the land. You will be escorted by a company of your finest and most trusted soldiers and you will be empowered to enforce my laws under your jurisdiction, if necessary. Once you have completed this task, it will be your honor to represent my authority as my personal envoy to the kingdom of Cainan on the eastern reaches of my realm. King Menahem is the last and most powerful of all my enemies, but I want to avoid open confrontation with this man; I need an alliance. Will you accept this appointment?"

Zadok despised court intrigue and was unable to envision acting in this role. "Sire, I am unconvinced our methods of enforcement are entirely compatible. Would not someone more in keeping with your usual ideals be more to your liking?"

The king rankled under the veiled criticism of his son's last comment. He held his temper and pressed on. "No, I need peace and you are a peacekeeper. If anyone can bring tranquility to this war-torn land it would be you. Will you help me?"

Zadok had to play for time and stall his father. "Sire, I will, of course, give your offer serious consideration, but I will need time to think it over. Once I have discussed this matter with my wife, I will personally deliver to you my decision."

Giddiel replied with some umbrage at this obvious attempt to deflect this great honor. "Zadok, why do you insist on consulting with your wife? She is but a woman and should follow her husband regardless of the matter at hand. Was it not thus in our home while in your youth? Just order her and insist she obey. You are the head of your household, are you not?" he asked with unveiled sarcasm.

Zadok countered, "Sire, I may be the head, but her counsel has always served me well. It would be foolish of me to ignore her on a matter of this much importance. Besides, she is quite outspoken with her opinions."

Giddiel replied with a snide remark. "Yes, her opinions are quite well known. I am sure she inherited those fine qualities from her bloodline."

"I am well aware she is a direct descendant of Seth from Cainan, but her advice has always served me well," replied Zadok with some irritation.

"See that it does. I want your answer within a week. I will be disappointed if you decline this appointment, my son. Please see to it."

Giddiel's parting remark was meant as a dismissal as well as a threat. As Zadok turned and walked toward the palace gates, he was unable yet to fathom why his father had singled him out for this dubious honor, but it would bear close examination. He had been a military man all of his adult life and now he was expected to be an ambassador. It made no sense. With growing anxiety over this dilemma, he hurried his step so as to arrive earlier at his home and once there, his wife, Elisheba, would counsel with him on this matter.

While Zadok and his father had been deep in discussion, Cain had been standing in a dark corner of the room. He heard the counter remarks between the two and decided that a few things needed to be clarified to Giddiel. After Zadok left, Cain walked out of the shadows and stood before the king. "Do you think he will accept the appointment?" Cain asked.

Giddiel had never been able to understand him. Zadok, a middle child, would never be the favored son, and because he never expected more, it was impossible to manipulate him in the same manner as his elder sons. "Who knows? My son can be stubborn and hard to control. If he feels there is something to be gained by it, I am confident he will accept." Giddiel asked pointedly, "Why has he not been approached with an offer for membership into the Clan? All the other field generals have been extended membership and each has accepted. His acceptance would make him more pliable to our plan."

Cain had likewise come to the same conclusion many years earlier. He remarked pointedly, "Membership was extended to him except that he refused to accept. He was approached first obliquely then later more directly, but his attitude is obdurate; he sees no advantage to it. At the present time, it serves our goal better if he remains unaffiliated."

Giddiel was lost when it came to the intricacies of subterfuge so his question was anticipated even as he asked, "How does his non-affiliation serve us?"

With a sigh, Cain explained, "The success of our plan depends upon you son's complete commitment and belief in his role as ambassador. We both know that King Menahem of Cainan will be suspicious of your offer for an alliance. He will desperately want it to be true, but in his heart he will think it a trap, which of course, it is. It will be Zadok's role, even if he does it unwittingly, to ensure that Menahem will let down his guard long enough for us to move against him. Your son, after all, has a reputation throughout the realm as being fair minded and just in his dealings, so we can use that to lure Menahem into believing the alliance will last. Moreover, his lack of connections to our Society serves to allay Menahem's doubts whether the truce will last and that Zadok intends to introduce a hidden agenda on our orders."

Cain placed his hands behind his back and began to pace as he continued to explain, "To further enhance his reputation, Zadok must believe he has been given complete control to ensure peace with the other kings I have placed around the realm. They all, of course, are beholden to only me for their positions, but Zadok doesn't know that and he must feel that he has accomplished his mission so that when he becomes official ambassador to Cainan, he can assure King Menahem with total sincerity he carries authority to ensure a lasting peace. We want Zadok reassuring Menahem right to the very end that all is well and you would be the last to break the alliance."

Giddiel's response was typically dense and his point was more offense than he had intended. "And this is what the Clan expects? That Menahem will be so easily led down the path of this deception that he will allow us to simply walk over him?"

In exasperation over the man's inability to see the vision, Cain laid it out simply and explained, "Giddiel, when will you realize that I am the Clan? Menahem can and will be deceived and it will be done my way. His kingdom has enjoyed peace for many years and prosperity has abounded, so unless he feels directly threatened he will hesitate to order his army into the field and risk losing all he has worked so long to establish. He is the last and the strongest of the kings still unaffiliated and his reign must be terminated and this is the only chance we have of a complete victory without throwing the entire realm into open warfare. The other kings of the realm, if they see my army fully occupied in Cainan, may use it as an excuse to break their vows with me and reinstate their own armies to restore their power we have worked so hard to remove. Now, when the time comes after the kingdom of Cainan falls, you may indulge yourself in whatever public display amuses you, just never forget who put you where you are now and who can and will remove you. Do we understand one another?"

With obvious disgust over the use of subterfuge, Giddiel reluctantly replied, "Cain, of course you are most wise and it will be done according to your plan, but have you tried lately to approach Menahem with acceptance into the Clan? Surely this would be a better solution, especially if you gave him no other recourse to prevent an invasion. Personally, I despise the man for his airs of superiority, but it would make our goal more achievable."

Cain replied pointedly, "Unfortunately, he lacks our vision to consolidate the realm under one master, thus he has rebuffed my offer repeatedly and that has made my efforts all the harder. His continued reticence is setting a dangerous precedent to the other kings and an example must be set or others may decide to follow his lead."

Giddiel was reminded of his last social encounter with the King of Cainan. He had felt the man's condescending attitude of superiority and had been intimidated by his intellect and breeding. Giddiel snarled, "That hardly surprises me. Menahem is an *effete* snob!" He arose from his throne as he seethed, "He boasts the kingdom of Cainan under his rule is so enlightened that they have scarcely any need for the counsel of our Society. He struts about contemptuously of all other kingdoms in the realm." Giddiel paused to catch his breath then shouted, "I long to have my blade at his throat!"

Cain was weary of listening to this cretin. "Yes, yes, of course he is, but I must have his kingdom and the next ruler must be placed in his stead immediately and this must be accomplished without a prolonged campaign of open warfare. Giddiel, it will be your responsibility to take your armies into the field against him and obliterate his rule once and for all. Do not allow your blood lust to blind you to what I really want from that kingdom. I want those records."

In reality Cain had other reasons for the assault on Cainan. He was reluctant to share them completely with Giddiel because he was convinced the ignorant lout would simply have misunderstood. Cainan was the last stronghold of the descendants of Seth. With the exception of one kingdom, Cainan, Cain had scoured the entire realm and had removed any trace of all records of the deeds of the Clan. He knew without a doubt the remaining records were located there in that kingdom and if his end goal were to succeed, all of them would have to be destroyed and all the descendants of Seth along with them. He smiled in anticipation of his long-awaited victory, which he knew was truly within his grasp for the first time.

Owing to the constant warring among rival kingdoms, Elisheba had seldom seen much of her husband the past several years. She, more than Zadok, had wanted the peace that would come with the consolidation of the realm, but for more selfish reasons. Though she knew that her husband was an able general, she worried that each time he went out to battle, it would be the last she would see him alive. So, what he was explaining to her now about this new appointment seemed to be a perfect solution.

"Elisheba, after the realm is stable with all kings reporting to my father, I will be free to ensure the success of the alliance with the King of Cainan, Menahem. If I can reassure Menahem that a lasting accord is possible, then perhaps the realm can enjoy peace for the first time in over a hundred years."

She was doubtful. "Will the King of Cainan trust you?"

"He doesn't want open warfare with Giddiel; that is a war no one can win. Even if Giddiel were to defeat him, it would come at too great a cost; the realm would dissolve into chaos without our army to hold it together. No, Menahem will want this alliance as much as my father. He will trust me because he knows my word is my bond and if I extend the branch of peace, he will accept the truce."

A few days later, Zadok was again summoned to stand before his father. He glanced around the room, and satisfying himself they were alone, he began, "Sire, I have the response you have been expecting for this appointment. Though I have proven myself a loyal and effective general in your service, if you feel it is in the best interest of the realm for me to now serve as ambassador to the kingdom of Cainan, then I will accept."

"My son, you have no need to fear that you lack the formal training as a diplomat. You have a natural gift for diplomacy. Thank you for accepting and please make ready to leave as soon as possible. Once you have established yourself in Cainan, feel free to send for your family. More than anything else, this will convince Menahem of my sincere intentions."

Zadok responded, "I am sure your generous gesture will please Elisheba." He added with a smile, "After all, she is from the kingdom of Cainan and looks forward to reuniting with her kinsmen".

As he was leaving the room, Zadok could scarcely brush aside the feeling that he and his father were being watched and their conversation had been overheard. He tried to dismiss an old soldier's intuition for unseen danger, but it nonetheless lingered with him as he exited the palace.

As he walked from the shadows, Cain muttered, "Well, there he goes." He turned to face Giddiel. "Your son will be the perfect dupe. I told you that allowing his family to be at his side in Cainan would allay any lingering doubts he may have had. It was a master stroke."

Giddiel shook his head in disgust. "They could have been used as hostages to his loyalty. When he realizes what we are up to, he may decide to change our plans."

Cain assented, but added, "By the time he realizes that, it will be too late for anything he might do. Besides, his family, when they join him, will immediately become hostages of Menahem. In any event, Zadok will be highly motivated to follow our agenda once he becomes completely aware of it and how his defiance would place his family in danger. Our advisers have been briefed regarding our long-term plans for Cainan and they will be sent with him to insure that he understands what must be done when the time is near for our invasion. If he tries to interfere, he will be informed that his family will meet the same fate as the rest of the kingdom of Cainan."

The last several months had been busy for Zadok. As official envoy, his goal to reassure the other kings of the realm and bring them into line with his father's wishes had been successful. They had all been reluctant in one way or another to surrender their autonomy to Giddiel, but in the end, each had realized that they were still free to rule their kingdoms in their own fashion so long as they were subservient to his father and continued to pay yearly tribute. To emphasize his point, Zadok had threatened each of them that if they ever attempted an insurrection, Giddiel's army would crush them. Furthermore, they would be executed along with their families and the other rulers would be placed over their kingdoms. He was unhappy at having to use coercion, but he realized that these men were cut from the same cloth as his father and would only respond to threats.

Regardless of the tactics he felt constrained to use in other kingdoms of the realm, Zadok's role in Cainan was quite different, thus his approach would be different. As an official ambassador to the court of Menahem, he was to establish an official alliance and ensure that it remained unbroken. Additionally, he was to reassure Menahem that Giddiel would refuse to be the one to break the peace. Once he reached the kingdom of Cainan he realized, however, that he had entered a land unlike all others. His advisers had cautioned him that King Menahem was a cunning ruler and his ideas about government were anathema to the rule of his father, King Giddiel. Even now as he stood before King Menahem, he wondered if the peace could be maintained. His rule of government was so different from any other in the realm that sooner or later he was bound to come under attack as a threat.

The King of Cainan began his greeting amiably enough. "General Zadok, or should I now call you Ambassador Zadok, your reputation for fairness precedes you, but am I now addressing the General or the Ambassador?"

Zadok replied reassuringly, "I can assure you Sire, that in all matters pertaining to my role in your court, I will be pleased to act as ambassador. There is no one more useless than an old general in peacetime," he replied with a smile.

Menahem was seldom easily appeased by mere words or flattery. "And this is what your father expects me to believe, that you are here to extend the olive branch of peace and forge a peaceful alliance? I can see how that will benefit me, but knowing your father for the murdering tyrant that he is, I wonder how long an alliance will satisfy his lust for power?" If he had expected to goad Zadok into saying something brash and defiant to reply to this open insult to his father, Menahem was mistaken.

"Sire, I realize that your trust will have to be earned and that it will take time. I am here to ensure that the alliance will be maintained by my father," assured Zadok. He added, "Moreover, while I am here, I will expend all my energy to remain open to your suggestions. Your concerns will become mine."

The king pondered what Zadok had just said. "Zadok, I think that in time you will earn my trust. Moreover, allowing your family to accompany you on this mission goes a long way to convince me of your sincerity and your faith in a peaceful agreement. A man that has surrendered his loved ones to become hostages may well work especially hard to maintain the peace. This gesture of faith is far more impressive than any words you have said." He signaled to a servant to bring Zadok a chair and when it was brought, the King said, "Please be seated and let us talk of my kingdom."

"Thank you, my King. There is much I should know."

The land of Cainan was a benign monarchy with limited representation of the public in areas of basic services, such as care for the poor, construction of roads, housing and other such necessities. Taxation of the citizenry went toward these services as well as for maintaining the king, his court and a standing army. The army was well trained and used to not only police the kingdom, but to provide basic defense in the event of imminent invasion from aggressive neighbors. Cainan's greatest deterrent from invasion consisted of this well-trained standing army, as well as a large contingent of reserve soldiers that could be called up from the local citizenry. In an emergency, the reserve contingent could be placed along the northern and southern borders of the realm, thus an invading army would have only limited success as it could not easily encircle the more populated areas for a long siege. While the main army contended from the front, cavalry units from the reserves could be wheeled around an invading army and attack from the flanks. Nonetheless, the size of Giddiel's army as well as the overall strategy, which he and Cain had planned, would obviate any precaution for siege that Menahem had considered. Assuming they could lull Menahem into a false sense of complacency, Cain preferred a quick, decisive frontal attack and overrun what forces Menahem could throw in their path; thus, they had not bothered to prepare for a long-term campaign, which was the reason for the ruse of peace they had hoped Menahem would accept.

Several months had passed since that initial meeting of Zadok and Menahem and during that time an uneasy peace had been established in the realm. Then, during the fourth month of the year, an adviser from Giddiel's court from the kingdom of Nod, acting as messenger, had ridden up to the gates of Cainan on horseback with instructions from Giddiel to Ambassador Zadok. After meeting secretly with Giddiel's other advisers, the messenger was eventually admitted into the residence of Zadok and he presented the message then was dismissed. Along with his wife and a few trusted members of his advising staff, Zadok sat and discussed the ramifications of what they had just been informed. The kingdoms of Shulon and Hesh, the two kingdoms to the west of Cainan, were squaring off against one another over an alleged offense that the king of Shulon had taken against his neighbors from Hesh and this offense had escalated into a declaration of war.

Zadok began the discussion with a succinct comment. "So, my father is to invade Shulon, directly to the west, ostensibly to protect the peace of his realm." After a brief pause he asked, "Can this be the only reason?"

Shimeon, his military adviser and long-time friend was the first to reply. "Zadok, at this point, we can only convey to King Menahem what we know and try to allay any suspicions he may have. That is our first directive." His other three political advisers were quick to agree with Shimeon, but of course, they were on Cain's payroll and were eager to maintain the status quo regardless of Zadok's and Shimeon's suspicions.

Elisheba, always quick to observe subtle changes in policy, replied, "Shimeon is correct. Your first order of business is to inform Menahem of your father's overt intentions and mollify his fears. But, we know your father is cunning and if he is planning any deception, we should know about it much sooner than later; our lives may well depend upon it."

Zadok shook his head in agreement. "Shimeon, Elisheba is quite right about my father. His ambitions have no boundaries. Please arrange for a few members of my military staff to visit our neighbors to the west and find out what is really happening then have them report back to us when they have learned all they can that is related to the disturbance of the realm. Thank you all for your counsel and now I must convince King Menahem that all is well and that my father has intentions only on the kingdom of Shulon."

After the ad hoc session had adjourned, the three court advisers gathered together for their own strategy meeting. Gilgal, being the senior adviser, had the most to lose from Zadok's premature discovery of the subterfuge being presented. "We must inform Giddiel of Zadok's suspicions. If he concludes that the invasion on Shulon is merely a ruse to bring his army closer to Cainan, Giddiel may lose the element of surprise."

Gad, the second adviser, was in close agreement, but warned that if Giddiel moves too quickly to counter any suspicions of the ruse, then the invasion would be less prepared and have less a chance for success. "I agree, but our message to Giddiel should be cautionary only." He looked over to the other adviser and asked, "What is your suggestion, Rueben?"

The third adviser leaned more toward Gad's viewpoint, but pointed out, "We have been given authority to divulge the entire plot to Zadok, if necessary, but I think we would all agree that his allegiance has turned toward Menahem and if we tip him off to what Giddiel really has planned, he will undermine whatever element of surprise his father has counted on for victory. Let us simply inform Giddiel to place his forces on alert, ready to move quickly should Zadok fall onto the true attack plan." He further added, "Knowing Zadok the way we do, he may attempt something dangerously heroic, which will not only place us all in danger, but it could alter the overall campaign strategy. If that should occur, Cain will be very displeased at our failure."

It was agreed that Gilgal would quickly dispatch a messenger in the direction of Giddiel's invading army and inform him of Zadok's suspicions. The three advisers then talked freely and passionately well into the night to plan an escape should they be caught in the middle of any unplanned debacle. They finally broke up the meeting, but felt only moderately better about their chances for survival. If Giddiel invaded, King Menahem would undoubtedly begin looking around for those responsible and would expend minimal time and thought at reaching the conclusion that Zadok's court advisers were in on the deception.

A few hours later, Zadok was presented to the King of Cainan. "King Menahem," he began, "Giddiel, King of Nod, has been informed by his security detail that the kingdom of Shulon, directly to your west, is planning to invade the neighboring kingdom of Hesh, ruled by King Japheth, and may attempt to claim the lands that now fall under my father's control without his permission. I have received word directly from King Giddiel to officially inform you, my King, Giddiel intends to quell this uprising by placing his army in position to block and defend any aggressive move on the part of the King of Shulon, Nathaniel, and invade that kingdom if necessary. Furthermore, I have been instructed to assure you that this confrontation need not concern you nor make you unduly anxious to get involved. This internal matter is under his control and is to be handled by King Giddiel to safeguard the populace in the event the king of Shulon intends unwarranted expansion into neighboring kingdoms.

King Menahem was no fool, but he desperately wanted to believe that what Zadok was telling him was the truth. "So, Ambassador Zadok, should I then wait until your father's army has invaded Shulon and he places his forces near my western borders on my doorstep before I take any action?"

Zadok would need to tread very carefully at this point to reassure Menahem of Giddiel's sincere desire to maintain the peace at all costs. "Sire, my father would consider it a violation of the alliance between our two kingdoms if you put your army into the field and proceeded to the border of Shulon. I urge you to take no overt action at this time that would send an aggressive message of your battle intentions. I counsel you to simply place your army on alert and allow my father to deal with the army of Shulon on his terms. It is hoped that any protracted confrontation can be completely avoided and Giddiel can address this issue with minimal bloodshed."

Menahem was intelligent enough to see the possible trap being set. He was not assuaged by Zadok's assurances. "Suppose this insurrection in Shulon spills over into my kingdom?" countered Menahem.

Zadok was adamant and gave his counsel not only as an ambassador, but as a former military man. "Again, let me urge you to avoid any action that cannot be recalled. I counsel you to observe only and allow my father to handle this matter."

Reluctantly and with obvious reservations, Menahem agreed to order a stand down to his generals, but, he was hardly so much the fool that he would let his guard down completely; as a consequence, he placed his army on alert and sent several spies to the land of Shulon to ascertain the actual designs of the ruler there, King Nathaniel.

The eastern provinces of the realm included Hesh, Shulon and Cainan from west to east. The King of Shulon, Nathaniel, was unhappy that Giddiel was using his kingdom as a staging area for an invasion. He had been appeased when told that he would share in the spoils, but it still made him nervous at the size of the army that Menahem could place into the field and throw against him should he suspect treachery on his part. All of these plans against the kingdom of Cainan had left him suspicious that he would be the one to suffer the most from this deception. After all, the invasion of Cainan would be staged from his kingdom. He had remembered vividly the last meeting with Cain and Giddiel several months earlier. He had been in a heated debate with them over the particulars of the invasion and what they said had left him unsurprisingly skeptical at their intentions. Cain had just laid out the justifications for the invasion as well as Nathaniel's part in the ruse. "Cain," countered Nathaniel, "suppose Menahem learns of my secret pact with Giddiel. So, instead of us having the advantage of surprise, Menahem unleashes his army upon my kingdom pre-emptively instead."

"If you do exactly as I say, when I say it, he will remain unsuspecting until it is too late for him to do anything except surrender his kingdom," responded Cain. He went on to outline the plan: The two kings of Hesh and Shulon were to allow Giddiel to use their kingdoms as a staging area for an attack on Cainan, supposedly to allow Giddiel an opportunity to get close enough to Cainan without alerting Menahem to his intentions. When the time was right, Giddiel would attempt an attack ostensibly on Shulon but instead of giving battle, he would combine his army with that of Hesh and Shulon and attack Cainan in force. Cain had then directed, "Since Menahem has repeatedly rebuffed each request to join the Clan under one consolidated realm, you will deny him any petition for a peaceful surrender nor show any mercy. His whole family, his court and his army must be completely destroyed."

Nathaniel, King of Shulon, remained unappeased by the staged invasion. He asked, "And the Ruler of Hesh, King Japheth? Is he likewise in on the deception?"

Cain's voice was soothing, even reassuring, but quite adamant. "Yes, and he will do as he is told as will you. He would not be seated on his throne without my help any more than you and he well understands that he must assist our Fraternity to achieve our end goal. I will send you word by messenger when to begin. In the meantime, Nathaniel, you must convince Menahem that your intention to invade Hesh is genuine. He will undoubtedly send spies to verify the story and you must appear highly committed to the invasion. If you can play this role convincingly, you stand to inherit a large portion of the land of Cainan."

After Nathaniel had left, Giddiel and Cain were left to discuss other matters. Giddiel inspected the map before him and then looked over to Cain and asked, "Do you think Nathaniel will suspect that the combined armies, after we have dispatched Cainan, will move against him and take over not only the kingdom of Hesh, but his as well?"

Cain responded confidently. "For the time being, Nathaniel has been promised the kingdom of Cainan, more spoils than he ever could have hoped for in his lifetime. He will set his mind on that and only that. His army will follow my generals and in the end, his kingdom of Shulon and that of Japheth, the kingdom of Hesh, will be swallowed up and eventually fall under your rule. It is regrettable, of course, that it has come to that, but both kings are showing signs of discontent and lately have attempted to adopt the ways of Cainan against the advice of their advisers. This superficial loyalty to our Society cannot be tolerated, so their kingdoms will be forfeit."

The true consequences Cain intended to keep from Giddiel, at least until his services had been rendered. Cain had no intention to maintain Giddiel in a position of absolute ruler over the realm any longer than it was necessary to attain the goal of the Clan. Cain's true intentions, known only to his inner advisory council, were to consolidate the whole realm under his undisputed control as Emperor without a Regent. Cain knew that being emperor was Giddiel's lodestone all along, but Giddiel, after all was a weak, despotic head crusher good for only one thing, ruthless action. When the realm was finally consolidated, his usefulness would be at an end.

Giddiel nodded his understanding, but one other matter remained. "At what point will I communicate to my son, Zadok, he is to remove himself and his household from Cainan, including his advisers?"

Cain had already come to a conclusion on this matter. "Up to the very end, he, his family and advisers must stay in place and reassure Menahem. If they flee just before the invasion, they will tip Menahem of my intentions and that we cannot allow. Unfortunately, if Menahem attempts to use them as hostages, you will have to leave them to their fate. The consolidation of my realm under one supreme ruler must take priority over all other considerations. Giddiel, since you stand to gain so much from this plan, you need not be overly concerned for the loss of one son, especially one who has proven to be so independently minded," he pointed out.

"Of course, Sire, these were my thoughts exactly," responded Giddiel. He knew once this unification was finally in place, there would be room for only one supreme ruler and he intended it to be himself, not Cain. After all, Cain was long overdue for an accident.

Chapter 3 – Noah's Last Mission

And whosoever shall not receive you, nor hear you, when ye depart thence, shake off the dust under your feet for a testimony against them. Verily I say unto you, it shall be more tolerable for Sodom and Gomorrha in the Day of Judgment, than for that city.

----- *Mark 6: 11*

Noah knew that his mission was nearing an end. Deciding to get an early start on the day, he awoke early, well before first light. He had been on this long trek back to the land of Cainan, the ancient kingdom of his fathers, for nearly three months. Following the counsel of his father and grandfather, he had left over twenty years earlier on a second mission of warning to the people of the land and the dreams he had before leaving his home had compelled him to begin work on an incredible project that would take him and his sons many years to complete. He had been on hand to begin the work, but his assignment to carry his message on a second mission to the realm had interrupted that project for him, so he had had to leave its completion with his sons and grandsons.

During those years he had traveled all over the realm, but few had bothered to listen to his message and most had scoffed at his efforts. Some had even plotted to take his life, but he had been quick to observe when the signs had come. And each time this rejection occurred, he had had to perform the ritual dusting off of his feet as he left each town and kingdom as a witness to their disobedience and that rite had assured their inevitable punishment. He no longer asked himself why this ritual was so necessary; the people were completely beyond saving and he knew their end was near. The rite was merely a way to place the official stamp to the Creator's judgment. They could have chosen to listen and make this unnecessary, but with each rejection in each city and kingdom they had instead sealed their fate. Still, it was a difficult burden he was being asked to perform.

He crossed over into the land of Cainan on a late afternoon in the fifth month of the year, and as he was setting up camp in the open field, he spied in the distance a figure walking slowly toward him from the east. Since it was near dusk, the stranger was difficult to identify, but as he drew nearer there was something familiar about his gait, which was slow with a slight limp. Now realizing with some astonishment that it was his father, Lamech, Noah rushed from his camp site out to meet him.

Lamech had been on the road for a few days now and was weary from his walk. He raised his hand in greeting and said, "So, my son, we meet for the last time." Father and son embraced with genuine affection. It had been many years since last they had spoken at the family reunion.

Though apparently well enough to walk the back roads of Cainan, upon closer inspection, Noah could see how much his father had aged and marveled that he was still alive. Noah escorted Lamech back to the camp near an old oak. "So, the time is that short?" replied Noah with an inward shudder of apprehension.

The aging man carefully sat down with the aid of Noah and leaned back against the oak. "Yes, Noah" answered Lamech with regret. "We have much to discuss now that you are home. Your grandfather passed on quietly to his death a few years ago. I miss his counsel terribly." He meditated for some time and Noah wondered if he had been so wearied by his travel that he had simply nodded off to sleep.

Noah had run into a kinsman in Shulon that had related to him the death of Methuselah so he had known of his passing. He reflected that his grandfather had died a very old man that had seen and endured much, but, like Lamech, he did miss the man's wisdom. Noah knew his father Lamech as an arresting, normally talkative man, usually quick with a poignant story or anecdote, so this quiet, reflective behavior was out of character with the man he had known. Granted, it had been many years and the passing of Methuselah had affected him, but clearly Lamech had changed and this was probably due to his carrying a heavy, emotional burden. With concern in his voice, Noah asked, "Father, are you all right? Can I get you water or something to eat?"

After a moment Lamech replied, "Thank you, Son. Perhaps some water and bread, then I must rest; we will talk in the morning." Lamech finished his meager meal, laid back on his bedroll and was quickly asleep within minutes. With a foreboding that his father's brooding behavior was somehow connected to the project that he had left his sons, Noah lay back on his bedroll and began to speculate. After a few minutes, Noah was aware that the night had grown cooler so he took the extra blanket from his pack and gently covered his father from the night air. He then found his own spot under the same tree and watched as the night stars began to appear until he likewise grew drowsy and fell into a deep slumber.

In the morning, Lamech was the first to arise and was gazing at the sunrise of a new day when Noah awoke. Wishing to avoid rushing his father any faster than he was ready to speak, he began to prepare their simple breakfast of dates and some water which he collected from gourds at a nearby stream. After a few minutes of silence, Lamech began to teach. "Noah, as you are already aware, very little in this world happens by accident and nothing is left to chance; there is always a plan. In many ways it is comforting to know that our Creator is mindful of all we do and takes all things into consideration before He acts. Regrettably, our minds are too shallow to comprehend fully His plans and too quick to reject them if they seem too harsh to our limited understanding. So, He must parcel things out to us in small measures like a mother bird feeding her young. Eventually, if we are patient and most of us continually struggle with this, I included, we eventually arrive at understanding His will. As you know, I have lived my whole life trying to comprehend His will as my father Methuselah and his father, Enoch, before him. I have tried to prepare myself for the destruction that is to come, but even now the magnitude of it overwhelms me."

Noah's dream nearly twenty years earlier was the reason he had set out to build the ark. He was convinced that it was the only thing that would stand between his family and complete annihilation. With resignation Noah's shoulders seemed to slump forward. With head bowed, he whispered, "Then the destruction is to be total. Just as I dreamed it would be."

Lamech quietly assented at his son's assessment. Reluctantly, he continued, "For this reason you were instructed to begin work on a large ship, an ark, before you left again on your second mission to warn the people to forsake their rebellious ways. Your sons, grandsons and their families have been busy constructing it in your absence and have now nearly completed it. I have been directed to speak with you concerning your role in this plan. First, I am here to verify again that your dreams were true; the destruction will reach nearly every man, woman and child on our world. Very few will survive."

Noah recalled that the specifics of his dream did not reveal the reasons, only the results and the results were more than enough to convince him to take action. After years among his people, however, he had concluded that their rebellious and unrepentant behavior had sealed their fate, but still the punishment seemed so drastic and final. Noah shook his head in despair and asked, "Father how can this be and why?"

Lamech turned to gaze at the now rising sun in the east. "There are too few mornings which remain of my life and I am loathe in disturbing the beauty of the scene with words of despair." At some length he turned to his son and continued, "Noah, you have spent the last several years away from your home and family and lived among the people of the realm. You know of their corrupted nature even as I. We have both warned them and then later you were again sent to warn them one last time and it is clear that our words of warning have fallen on deaf ears. They have embraced the ways of darkness and no longer desire or recognize the truth and light, the doctrine of Our Creator. Further, I know that you have performed the ritual dusting off on each kingdom in accordance with the Creator's will and now their doom has been irrevocably sealed. He has decreed that He will wash them from off the face of our world and I speak as a second witness to your vision and conclusions. You must prepare yourself now for your final roles."

This was unexpected to Noah's ears. The ark was nearly completed, but if the devastation was to be as thorough as his father had explained it, then what would be the point? He had replied incredulously, "My roles? Father, if the destruction is to be total then who would want to survive?" Noah added plaintively, "We are not just talking about the people being destroyed, but all life."

"My son, the Creator has a plan and it has been revealed to me and soon the specifics will be revealed to you. I am here to assure you that whatever you learn, it is from Him who knows all and we must trust His will in this matter."

Noah had hoped that the ark his sons had been building for so many years would be unnecessary. Now it appeared that its use was inevitable. He had heard and seen first-hand the depths of degradation to which the people of the land had now sunk and the consequence could no longer be denied. "Father, what have you been told?"

Lamech gazed out upon the early morning sun and gloried in its beauty and tried to draw strength from it warmth. He took a few moments to gather his thoughts then he began to teach his son. "The use of water is both symbolic and necessary for our mother earth to be refreshed and renewed. Man has corrupted our world with acts of darkness and abominations; as a consequence, the earth is to be cleansed with water and all living things that walk, crawl or fly will cease. All life except that which has been preordained to live will have to begin anew following the event once the waters have receded. You and your family will assume the role of agents in this matter and the details of how this is to be done will be revealed to you in due time, but it occurs to me that the Creator has designated certain animal life that will survive the floods and they will come to you for eventual shelter and this is the purpose for the vast size of the ark."

Rather than a permanent home without a place to set aground, Noah now realized that the ark was merely a temporary means to an end and was relieved. He commented, "I had despaired that there was to be no reprieve for anyone to resume a normal life and now it appears my worst fears were unfounded. My family will survive and can live again a normal existence."

Lamech assented and added, "Your other role is equally important. For after you and your family have survived the trial that is to come, all your future descendants will need to be taught in the language of our fathers, including an understanding of their genealogy and history. This can only be done with the records that have been kept since the beginning of time. Therefore, you must insure these records are protected and safe from the destruction which is to come; the future progress of our family and subsequent civilization will depend upon it."

Noah, owing to his missions over the past fifty years, had made many notations of the works of darkness which Cain and his Society had spread throughout the land. All the same, they had yet to be recorded on permanent materials. He commented, "I have, of course, maintained some records and have hidden them from Cain and his agents, but the other records I am unaware where they have been kept."

Lamech continued, "Noah, my mission is to inform you that you will be required to secure the records and ensure they will be well protected from the waters. You must cross the kingdom of Cainan until you reach high mountains to the east. There is a long valley deep within this range surrounded on both sides by mountains and within the valley there are several settlements of our people who are direct descendants of Seth as are we. There is one, a woman, by the name of Sariah who will guide you to where the records are stored. She and others in the valley have been prepared and will assist you in the protection of the sacred writings and it is the Creator's will that these persons are to be spared from the great flood to come, but they must heed your counsel if they are to survive and the records are to be safeguarded."

Lamech reluctantly turned to the additional assignment that in many respects would be even harder than the completion of the ark. "After you make the journey into the mountains and have ensured the records are safe, you must then attempt to warn the citizens of Cainan one last time. Report to the King, Menahem, and declare unto him your message and attempt to call the citizens to repentance. If they reject you, then you must perform the ritual dusting off on your own people. I am sorry, I know that will be difficult and for this reason have I been sent to you so that you will know that His will be done in this matter. This is my final message to you. I will accompany you to your home to be with my grandchildren for the last time then later, you and I will meet again in the city of Cainan." Then father and son completed their walk northeastward through the kingdom of Cainan to Noah's home where the work of the ark was nearing completion.

Four days after leaving his father in the city of Cainan with some kinsmen, Noah found himself on a path winding through a long valley floor, his donkey carrying the weight of his own records. The trip through the mountains had been arduous and difficult to manage, even for a man having been used to walking for most of the past twenty years. He realized, now with aching limbs, that he was no longer middle-aged and there were probably more years behind him than in front. The past few days he had been anxious to know the location of the woman he was to meet and the message he was to deliver, but as of last night, the answer had still not come. His father had instructed him to meet a woman, Sariah, but he was still unsure where to begin his search. After some thought, he finally concluded that the anxiety he felt was creating a larger dilemma, so he decided that it was time to simply be still and wait. He found a suitable campsite for the night then after a light evening meal he simply sat, cleared his mind then stared intently into the fire and waited. After a few minutes, the night creatures were quiet and the air was still then slowly he had closed his eyes and in time the answer had come:

…with a faraway ringing and a slight, tingling feeling of being plucked away and thrust toward some unknown, yet familiar place in time. He was transported in mind or spirit, he was unaware, but inexorably he began to slow, slow until his senses became acutely aware and at one with the nature of the Earth. She was everywhere and the feel of Her and the smell of Her filled him with a sense of purpose and understanding of all things of the air, the water and land. All things growing and yet to be grown were visible and tactile. All things being born and yet to be born were present and discernable. She was both body and spirit and aggrieved. The time had come to be cleansed and refreshed from the corruption of Man and She anticipated the moment and longed to embrace it. Noah saw, perhaps sensed, the corruption and abasement of that which should have been held most precious and sacred, our home, an earthly abode for our eternal growth and fulfillment. Then the saving rain, the cleansing from above began to drop then fall until Man and beast and flying thing was no more to pollute and defile; a washing, an anointing, a baptism of grace…then relief and a chance to begin again.

He was then taken to a valley and understood its sacred nature and its connection to all things not yet borne. He walked among the people of the valley and revealed to them a plan and their means of survival. When all things seemed right and connected with all events past, present and the future, a feeling of warmth and gratitude came over him as his spirit *ka* was reunited with its human form and now he knew. With a smile, he slowly entered a dream state and slumbered peacefully through the night. In the morning he arose with the sunshine of a new day throwing its light slowly into the valley before him. With a smile he ate a simple breakfast and moments later was on his way down the path before him.

Presently, and by chance or not, Noah knocked on the door of Sariah and her family. A young lady answered the knock and Noah asked to see her parents. While he waited for an adult to return, he gazed about the farm and was impressed to note the degree of careful husbandry and attention to detail that abounded. Further, he observed that the farm had been built deliberately in the lee of the greatest mountain in the valley. A thought then a connection came to him as he heard the approach of steps to the doorway.

Sariah opened the door, and as her recognition of Noah was immediate, she rushed into his arms as though seeing a member of her family for the first time in many years. Now smiling broadly, she calmly looked him over and announced matter-of-factly, "I have been expecting a stranger to knock at my door for over a week now and last night when I was asleep I saw your face in such detail I can hardly consider you a stranger any longer. I know you are here to deliver a message and your name is Noah."

And Noah replied, smiling, "And you are Sariah."

At that the two broke into laughter as if coming to an obvious conclusion that had puzzled them both for some time. "Please come in Noah and rest. My family and I were just sitting down for our mid-day meal and would be pleased to have you join us."

Noah replied, now quite fatigued by his journey, "Thank you. I don't think I could have gone much farther. I feel as though I have walked for months instead of only a few days." As she accompanied him into the dining area of her home, he added, "You are quite correct. I have come to deliver a message, but let us first break bread together and talk of our families. There is still time before we must talk of serious messages." He spent the remainder of the day getting acquainted with Sariah and her family, but truly what he was doing was assessing her disposition and level of commitment.

The next morning Noah was leaning over a fence gazing up at the mountain when he heard someone approaching. He had arisen early, and wishing to greet the new day, had strolled around the farm trying to gather his thoughts. Inevitably his walk had led him to this spot where the mountain was so obviously predominant. Without having to turn around, he knew it was Sariah who was approaching. She joined him at the fence and both took in the singular majesty of the view before them. After a few minutes of quiet reflection a voice softly commented, "Legend has it the mountain is sacred. What do you think, Noah?"

Without hesitation, Noah responded, "My father seemed to think so. He passed by here some years ago with one of our distant kinsmen who was quite old at the time and what he saw had left a lasting impression upon him. His name is Lamech, but I think you already surmised as much." Turning toward her and leaning on the fence, he pressed, "Sariah, I have come to talk with you about a cave high in this mountain. I will need to know everything you know and then you must show me the location."

"You mean where the records are kept?" she asked, but it was really unnecessary. "I knew the moment you arrived what you were looking for." Her gaze was direct, and though she needed no confirmation, she asked the question anyway. "They are the records of our fathers, aren't they?" She was aware of the look of surprise on his face, so she continued, "Your father told me of this place many years ago when I was but a child. Before he arrived with Lamech, Seth had made several visits to our valley before my birth and my fathers had mentioned to me later of the reasons for his visits, though the reasons were more speculation than real. Later, I decided to see for myself, and after viewing the contents of the cavern, I made the connection that his travels here were connected with the records." Her response was direct and it encouraged Noah to proceed.

In the short time Noah had known this woman, he had grown not only to admire her directness, but respect her keen intellect as well. He reflected on his life experiences which had led him to this day and location and realized that her preparation for the task ahead had been no less than his own. With a smile Noah assented, "Indeed they are, Sariah. They represent the sum total of all the experiences, both good and bad, which our family has endured since our first parents Adam and Eve began it all. They describe a history and genealogy as well as a written Book of Remembrance of all the generations written by men called to perform this special work. They represent not only our accumulated knowledge, but moreover a written language of our people so that future generations may be able to build upon what we have started." The last remark seemed to diminish his enthusiasm.

Sariah noted the change in his voice. "There is something more you are not telling me. It has something to do with your special message, doesn't it?"

Noah seemed to change the subject slightly. "As soon as we have properly prepared ourselves for the trek, we must begin our climb. Along the way I will explain to you how it was that I came to your valley and why I now need to ascend your mountain." With growing excitement at finally beginning this next step of his mission, his eyes followed the gentle slope upward and made the mental ascension to the top, but, unsurprisingly, he discovered also that he was saddened that so little time remained.

The day was warm and brilliant as Noah and Sariah reached the point of their first rest stop of their climb. The dryer, thinner air made it necessary to eat and drink more frequently now, and while they drank from water gourds and ate dried fruit, Noah felt it was time to reveal some of his message. As he ate, he gazed out over the valley floor below and took in the majesty of the view. He then leaned back against a nearby tree and met her eyes then began with a personal reflection. "Sariah, the accumulation of knowledge over time can seem excruciatingly slow, but absolutely necessary. Our minds, for now, have a limited capacity to accept and process new information, so when our Creator deems it necessary to reveal more to us, he will do this a parcel here, a portion there, line upon line and precept upon precept. This is done to allow us time to ponder and analyze what we have received and finally decide whether we are ready for more. A person or a people cannot move this process along any faster than they are ready and willing to apply what they have learned. Unfortunately, we as a people have run out of time. Whatever knowledge that has been recorded and placed in this mountain will have to suffice for many years to come." He avoided her eyes as he scanned the horizon to the west. He added thoughtfully, "There is something ahead which will change our lives dramatically." Turning back to her, he noted the surprised frown on her face which indicated a deep foreboding.

"So this event, how bad will it be?"

With a deep regret felt so intensely that it caused him physical pain, he gazed at her troubled eyes and intoned, "It will be total and very few will survive. A continuous rain will cause a deluge that will cover the entire earth and anyone not securely covered will perish and no one will escape save those who serve a specific purpose for the Creator."

She replied, "Noah, I simply cannot comprehend that there will be no way to avoid this catastrophe. Surely there will be time for some groups to prepare and save themselves in boats?"

"Sariah," Noah sadly pointed out, "this will be a rain unlike men have ever experienced. The rain will not just fall, but it will literally drop from the sky." With that said, he slowly arose and Sariah quietly led the way and the trek up the mountain resumed.

Sariah and Noah stood looking over the records that had been stacked neatly throughout the inner rooms of the cavern. The records were all metallic and of a high, burnished quality, no doubt fashioned by an accomplished metallurgist; Noah had been told Seth was an accomplished artisan, but until now had never quite understood just how exceptional he was. He marveled at the size and scale of this feat and noted that each record he had seen had begun with a preamble by way of explanation and instruction. Noah then carried his own records wrapped in cloth from the leather bag strapped to his donkey then added his history to the larger collection in the depository.

Once Noah had completed his inspection of all the other records, the two climbers now stood outside, near the entrance to the cave and gazed over the valley floor laid out beneath them. Sariah began haltingly, "It seems hard to believe that all this will be destroyed. What of my family and those who live below?"

Noah wanted to ensure she completely understood her role in all this and remained undistracted by the horror that was to come. "Sariah, after we descend and are rested, I will counsel with your people of this valley. I cannot tarry with you for much longer for I, too, have a task that must be fulfilled, so it will be your responsibility to encourage all others to see that the records are safeguarded. Their safe keeping is the only reason you and the others are being spared this terrible ordeal."

A few days later, Noah was standing in front of a group of more than one hundred thirty-five settlers representing various farms and settlements in the valley. Sariah had met each family with an uncharacteristically somber face and had escorted each in turn to her courtyard as they had arrived. The group was silent, but restive as they sensed that the serious, staid stranger standing before them had brought portents of some unseen danger yet to be revealed.

Noah gazed around the assembled throng for a few moments then announced, "I am Noah, a descendant of Seth as are each of you. We have been given much so much has always been expected. This is the way of our God and Creator and it will always be thus." He cast his eyes around the gathered crowd, looking for any sign of doubt or astonishment at these pronouncements. Having observed none, he pressed on. "Some of you may have wondered over the years how your valley seemed to have had so few visitors. If you search your memories or recall anything which your parents may have said to you, you will remember that there was something peculiar at the circumstances that led you or your forefathers to this place. That same peculiarity has likewise prevented the valley from being infested by the influences of corruption which abound in the rest of the realm. Each family represented here has a special story and that story is meant to live with your posterity long after this generation passes away and it is also meant to be recorded and discussed among future generations. As descendants of Seth, that is the special nature of who we are and that same spirit of continuity is the reason why I have gathered you here today. If you are to survive the calamity that is to come, you will have to believe everything which I am about to say to you then act on it." Noah took notice of the signs of incredulity on the faces of many of the men and women as well as those who quietly murmured "calamity" under their breaths.

Noah looked around the settlers and recalled his fist impression of the valley. He continued. "As farmers and wise stewards of our properties we eventually arrive at the erroneous certainty that everything we work before us belongs to us and us alone. We sometimes forget that what we think of as our possessions, in reality, belong to our Creator and we are simply here to harness and control it, but never to own it." Noah's next statements hit them hard and pierced them to the very marrow of their being. "It is the Creator's will and judgment that all his possessions, including his sons and daughters, are to perish. Only those deemed worthy to fulfill a specific role will be spared and that task must take priority over all other considerations."

Deathly silence followed. Noah could see no one had exactly doubted, but once astonishment had receded, loud denial would soon replace it. Anticipating this, Noah moved closer to the point of his message. "I have been sent among you to leave a message of warning and to extend a special mission. As most of you already know, Sariah and I trekked up the mountain and I have seen the sacred records that have been stored therein. The safeguarding of those records is now your sacred duty, and after I leave, Sariah has been appointed the Creator's agent in this matter. I have appointed her and the Creator has appointed me and each of you should carefully consider this before you question her decisions on this subject."

There was more silence from the crowd, but a man near the middle of the group quietly asked, "Noah, you come as a man with power and authority and that is evident and no one doubts this, but what of this warning? What is to come?"

Noah, rather than directly responding with gloom and disaster, decided upon a different tact based in part from his own dream regarding the matter. "The world upon which we dwell is a living entity created with a spirit similar in nature to the one each of us has within us. She provides us with sustenance, a home to live, clothing on our backs and air to breath. Yet, many of our brethren have treated Her shamefully with the manner in which they have exploited Her resources and offended Her spirit with their degrading behavior. The rebellious attitude in which they refuse to acknowledge their Creator has led to such corruption that it has become irreversible and now their disdain is so complete and unrepentant that our world actually grieves and longs to be cleansed from the filth to which our brethren have subjected Her. Our God has heard Her cries and will send rains to cleanse Her completely from the stains of His greatest creation of all, Mankind." He paused slightly and added, "The rains will fall until there is no life left upon the land. Your survival will depend upon your recognition of your first priority which is to safeguard the sacred records."

Noah ended his remarks with, "Details of how and in what manner this task will be carried out will be provided before I leave. In the meantime, I suggest you retire to your homes and think about all that has been said and you, with your families, commit to this grand undertaking." The meeting broke up a few minutes later and as the farmers quietly filed out of the courtyard, each embraced Sariah and looked thoughtfully over at the man that had brought news of disaster and hope.

A week later, Noah reluctantly bid farewell to the people of the valley. Sariah accompanied him much of the way towards the pass that led to Cainan and the walk reminded her unsurprisingly of a similar one she had made many years earlier with Lamech. Noah had given much thought to what he might say to her before they parted company because he feared it might be final and did not want to leave her on a sad note. "Sariah, over the past few days I have tried to prepare you for what must come, but in parting there are a still a few things which must be said. The first thing is: I feel strongly the event will occur before the end of this year and you will know when the time is growing near, but you are to begin the work of preparation as soon as possible. The second thing is: You must avoid thinking that this responsibility is somehow too big for you to accomplish; it is important, but since we first met it has been evident to me you have been prepared for this event all your life. Moreover, I am in the way of knowing that you will receive assistance from an unexpected source; an old friend will appear to give you emotional strength and support. And third, which is probably the most important, when you are bothered by a problem, take a quiet moment to pause and listen then wait for the answer."

Now smiling, Sariah nodded and agreed with affection, "As always, I appreciate your words of counsel and, as usual, they were exactly what I needed to hear. Of course, I am curious to know this unexpected friend that will appear to provide me support, but I have discovered that some things must be taken on faith." Though she was reluctant to see him leave, but knowing it was inevitable, she asked, "Noah, to where will you go now?"

With sadness Noah replied heavily, "There is one more duty I must perform before finalizing the project with the ark. It involves a last effort to appeal to our people in Cainan."

Her isolation from the corrupting influence of the remainder of the realm had provided Sariah more optimism than Noah felt. Though she believed all that he had described, notwithstanding she said hopefully, "Surely you will be successful."

Noah's reply did give her some encouragement. "It is not for me to decide, but if I can persuade a few, I will have them join you in your valley."

Holding back the tears because she feared the finality of his response, nonetheless Sariah asked, "Will I ever see you again, Noah?"

He looked back over his shoulder to the north towards the mountain. His smile was quick. "That might be too far into the future to predict, but there will be someone else who will stop by. He will be of our lineage and he will come to climb the mountain."

"Will he be like you?"

Noah paused to consider the question. "No, he will be different."

Menahem and his four advisers were comfortably seated behind an ornately gilded table on a raised dais and were all sipping wine, enjoying the spectacle of watching the prophet Noah and making note of what he might say to incriminate himself. "Noah," began Menahem in a conciliatory tone, "I know your father as a great man and prophet, so I have allowed you this audience before me and my court, but now is hardly the time to preach your sermon to me or my people. These are unsettling times and I may have to get them ready for battle." Menahem's spies had just returned the day before from Shulon and had reported that Giddiel had invaded that land, but had yet to begin his usual work of destruction and murder. This news had left Menahem wondering about Giddiel's true intentions.

Noah heard the King's words, however, he would not be swayed from delivering his message. "Menahem, unless you and your people turn away altogether from the dark abominations that you have embraced, you will be destroyed. Your benign government, though admirable, falls very short of accepting the will of the Creator. You personally may have rejected the rites of the Clan, but your own court is riddled with its influence and their unbridled excesses have caused the citizens of your kingdom to wallow in abomination. Your women, young and old, walk the streets wantonly and many traffic with any man they meet. Your people continually indulge in riotous living, wearing costly apparel and persecute the meek." With open contempt, Noah pointed a finger at Menahem and declared, "Yours will be the greater condemnation than the other kingdoms because you were provided the light and now you openly reject it without regret. You all must turn your back on this life or feel the full wrath of our outraged Creator."

"Noah, you dare to condemn me and my people?" the king sputtered his absolute surprise at the disparaging insults. He looked over to a nearby adviser seated next to him and asked, "Who is this man to judge us so harshly?"

His adviser, actually a member of the Clan, saw Noah as a threat to his influence over Menahem. He had likewise heard of Lamech and if his son was cut from the same cloth, then indeed they would have a problem unless he was dealt with now. He declared heatedly, "Sire, the man is obviously addled. There is no fault here in Cainan. The problem lies with Noah!"

Shaking his head in arrogant denial, the King turned his attention back to Noah and declared menacingly, "I should have you publicly hung." He signaled to nearby guards and ordered, "Guards, seize this man and throw him out of the city." The guards grabbed Noah roughly by his arms and began dragging him from the court.

Menahem was riddled with anxiety over recent political and military matters and no doubt it was this fear that had driven him to strike out in anger, but his threat was real. "Noah," he shouted, "The only reason I don't hang you publicly in the square for your insulting threats is out of respect for your father. If you return again, I will execute you!"

Noah, in a last effort to reach the citizens and forestall their imminent destruction to come, climbed upon the highest wall in the city, near the market square, and now stood overlooking the passing throng. He raised his walking stick ominously over his head and shouted, "Citizens of Cainan, how long will you try the patience of an angry God who even now looks down upon you weary of your abominations? How long will you continue in your works of darkness until it is everlastingly too late for you to repent?" He paused to ensure everyone below was now attentive. Now pointing accusingly from the wall, he pleaded, "Even now, a great army has combined to destroy you and yet you persist in your blindness of mind and soul. Turn away from the darkness before it is too late!" he thundered.

There was now utter silence in the market square as the power and voice of a prophet of God had penetrated their souls. Each could feel their inner shame, but instead of allowing it to perform a change of heart, their collective anger galvanized their mood and they began hurling insults up at Noah. "Away with you old man and take your counsel with you! We will do as we please and seemeth us good. We are a great and powerful people! Our army is indestructible and can defeat our enemies easily. We don't need you to remind us of who we are!"

Noah shouted back at the incensed mob, "You must turn away altogether from your abominations or you will be destroyed!"

There were members of the Clan in the throng and they began to harangue the citizenry in the market place to take action against Noah. "Spear him, pierce him with your arrows, stone him!" they goaded the crowd. With the intent to knock Noah off the wall evident in their minds, armed guards began casting spears and those in the market began throwing anything they could find in his direction, but, in spite of so many spears, arrows and stones being cast at him, he still remained on the wall, steadfast and upright. No spears, no arrows pierced him and no stones found their mark. He gazed with despair upon the crowd below and reluctantly withdrew from their sight, never to be seen again in the land of Cainan.

Chapter 4 – The Invasion

All warfare is based on deception.

----- Unknown

Zadok now stood before the ruler of Cainan, King Menahem, and he was ashamed at what he must now reveal to the man he had grown to respect over the past several months. His worst fears had been verified by military advisers he had sent into the land of Shulon and Hesh. "Sire, we must talk," he began without preamble. "I apologize for the abruptness of that statement, but the circumstances require we must now speak bluntly and without the usual courtly mannerisms."

"Zadok, I too agree that the time has come for direct talk. Of course, I had been expecting to hear from you. My own spies had reported disquieting news from the west and, thus I was anxious to hear whether you would confirm what I already suspected, that Giddiel may have other reasons for being in Shulon. Please proceed."

"King Menahem, as you know, ostensibly to quell the uprising by King Nathaniel of Shulon, my father entered that kingdom a week ago. It grieves me to inform you that it is highly likely my father is even now invading your kingdom; his assistance to the kingdom of Hesh and his apparent invasion of Shulon was more ruse than reality. Of my five military advisers I sent to investigate this situation, only one was able to return safely, and based upon the intelligence which he brought back, I predict that Giddiel plans to combine his main army with that of Hesh and Shulon and launch a full-scale invasion so quickly that it will leave your army off-guard and on the immediate defensive. I assure you that if this was his plan, then he is even now prosecuting the invasion and within a week will be at the gates of your city. You and your kingdom will not survive the attack."

The news from Zadok that Giddiel had been planning to break the alliance did not surprise Menahem, but the former general's assessment of the military situation had caught him unprepared and his reaction, though naïve was understandable. "Zadok, that is simply impossible. My spies have reported no such preparations on the part of Giddiel. And even if he were, my army is quite capable of defending us."

"Sire, your spies were not trained in military matters as mine were and did not ask the right questions to the right soldiers. Mine were all former officers under my command in the field and recognized preparation of my father's army that only they would know and understand. All were captured, and of the five, only one escaped captivity; the rest were executed. The one survivor assured me of what I now report to you."

Menahem remained unconvinced that his army would crumble that quickly. "Zadok, my army is well trained and my men will defend our kingdom with their lives if need be," assured the king.

"Sire," he replied with regret, "It will make little difference what action you take with your army. Giddiel has a far superior force which is now thoroughly prepared and provisioned and has in all likelihood already struck a sudden invasion into the heart of your kingdom and he will destroy everything in his path. Believe me, I know him and he will do it. Moreover, it is quite likely that the forces of Hesh and Shulon have also combined with Giddiel, and if that is the case, your chances of victory are nil. If you wish, I could intercede on your behalf and ask him the terms of your surrender. I wish I could offer you hope, but I have witnessed personally his actions in the past and I know that he will want your blood as an offering to his gods. Though he may spare the remainder of the citizens of your kingdom, your family and court will meet a similar fate as you; that is the best that can be expected."

The words of Noah now began to haunt Menahem and he knew now just how doomed his kingdom was. With the dawning horror that awaits one who finally realizes the degree to which he has been damned, Menahem passed a hand across his face, and, as he lowered his head, he said simply, "Zadok, please do what you can."

Just as Zadok had predicted, the slaughter and destruction in Cainan had begun immediately after the border had been breached. The entire western reaches of the kingdom had been put to the torch by the invading army, and in its wake, each city and village had been razed to the ground and all inhabitants were systematically put to the sword. Giddiel's army moved so quickly that the fleeing villagers were unable to escape their approach and no one was left alive to witness what had occurred. Giddiel intended the campaign to be quick and ruthless and anything that could not be pillaged, ransacked and hauled off was burned or left to rot in the sun.

Zadok and his officers had ridden long and hard for five days in an effort to halt or at least reduce the slaughter, and because the smoke of the burning villages and cities could be seen easily from the east, they had little trouble finding his father's army. While the king was still resting from the previous day's victory celebration, Zadok met up with Giddiel later the next morning. Zadok and his retinue were permitted immediate audience to appear before his father, the King, in his personal tent.

Upon entering the tent they found Giddiel in a triumphant mood. "So, my Son what do you think of our chances for a total victory?" he boasted sarcastically. "Would you prefer to resume your old command and take the city of Cainan by force and share in the spoils?" Giddiel was feeling very replete and rubbed his hands together as though enjoying the bloodletting immensely. "I will pound Cainan and Menahem's useless army to dust then I will cut his throat and that of his entire family!"

Zadok doubted that his father was aware of his demented appearance or would care even if he was. He decided to appeal to Giddiel's vanity and so announced with false cheerfulness, "Father, there can be no doubt that you have accomplished what you have set out to do. Total victory is yours and so the killing and burning can now stop. King Menahem, in his wisdom, has decided that throwing his army at you would be a needless waste of lives on both sides. He wishes to talk terms of surrender and is willing to have a new king installed in his stead. Let us now put away our swords and machines of war and talk peace."

Giddiel shook his head in merry laughter. "Zadok you can stop the charade. Your role in the destruction of Cainan was masterful and we would have been unable to get this close to that old fool Menahem without your help. It is now time for you to take your rightful place next to mine. We will ride through the gates of Cainan as conquerors after my army has burned it to the ground and all its inhabitants slaughtered."

Zadok, a look of pained disappointment now on his face, realized that he not only had been duped by his father's machinations, but had been unsuccessful at mollifying his father's intent of annihilation of the populace of Cainan. "Father, what would you hope to accomplish by the slaughter of so many innocents?"

Giddiel's disdain was evident. "Zadok, do not play the diplomat with me! I know you sent operatives into my camp to ascertain my true intent for this campaign. I permitted one of your pathetic spies to return just so you and Menahem would know just how hopeless your chances were for success." Giddiel then screamed maniacally, "The arrogance of Menahem has offended me far too long! His snobbery at being so enlightened was a constant affront to my rule and now I will send a message in blood to all who would dare refuse to kneel before me in the future. I will have the head of that *effete* snob on a pike for all to spit upon." With this last statement, while he howled like a wolf, he pounded the table before him as if possessed and devoid of any human feelings of remorse and pity. This outburst of demented hatred had caused even his personal guards to draw back in astonishment.

Zadok had experienced feelings of contempt and even disgust for his father over the years, but until today he had never known such horror at being in the presence of one so consumed with hatred and blood lust. There was nothing he could say which would sway him from this course of action he had already decided; his insanity was all too obvious. Nevertheless, Zadok warned, "Father I fear that you are setting a dangerous precedent in attacking Cainan without provocation. I assure you that once Menahem understands your intentions, he and his army will resist you until the last man. I would in his place." He added with some caution, "May I be permitted to return to Cainan and remove my family from the battle?" he asked.

Giddiel beamed as though a delightful thought had just crossed his mind. "Of course, my son, but don't go too far," he boasted with glee. "I will want you to be on hand when I capture Menahem and his family. I intend to have his throat cut then I shall have him hung him upside down in his own courtyard. His family will, of course, be forced to witness his demise before they are similarly dispatched."

Now sickened at the destruction to come, Zadok took his leave and the realization that his father was quite insane had hit him with the force of a hammer. A thought occurred to him, however, that there might be a way to forestall the slaughter to come.

Cain watched as Zadok left the tent, obviously disgusted by his father's boorish behavior. He shook his head in bewilderment and remonstrated, "That was foolish. Your little performance shocked everyone, including myself. It's quite likely that the next time you meet Zadok, it will be on the field of battle arrayed in the colors of Menahem."

Giddiel carelessly shrugged his shoulders as if to dismiss Cain's rebuke. "It will do him no good. My army will carry the day and crush everything in its path. Instead of dying later because of an unfortunate accident in battle, my son will be trampled under the feet of my men in open combat. So be it," he added with a flourish of his hand.

Cain turned on him viciously, "That was not part of the plan. Zadok is far too clever in the field and it will slow our progress. I refuse to give Menahem time to think about why his kingdom is really being invaded. Those records must be mine and I will not have them moved about or squirreled away in some distant hideout. They will not slip through my fingers again."

Giddiel brooded momentarily over Cain's outburst. It was pure folly to be so concerned over some trivial records written by demented old fools about events that no longer concern anyone. Cain was becoming tiresome. So, Giddiel promised himself that soon, after this final victory, he would see Cain's head upon a pike, probably next to that of Menahem's. He smiled at the thought.

"So, this confrontation cannot be avoided?" asked Menahem. Zadok had just made his report from the field and the idea of losing his whole kingdom to Giddiel had made Menahem more angry than frightened.

This anger was what Zadok had wanted to see. If there was any hope at all of slowing down the army of his father, Menahem would have to suppress any fear he might have and throw himself and his army headlong into the fray; his sense of urgency might be the only thing which could reach his men. For when they see the approaching hoard that follows Giddiel, their first reaction may be to run. If that occurs, their defeat is assured and Giddiel will enjoy a complete rout.

Zadok had given much thought over the past few days of what he was about to ask. "My King, when the army of Giddiel appears you will need an experienced commander in the field to head your army who already knows the enemy. If I have earned your trust then I would be willing to assume command and give your citizens their best chance for survival."

Menahem was so despondent over the predicament he faced with the loss of his kingdom he nearly missed hearing Zadok's offer. He frowned as though completely unprepared for what Zadok had just proposed. He was incredulous, and his face showed it. "Zadok, your offer, if genuine, might reverse the inevitable outcome of the invasion, but why would you do this?"

Zadok had anticipated that Menahem would ask this question. He still wasn't sure of his motives except that the citizens of Cainan, in spite of all their pretentions of superiority, deserved a chance to live. If his father had his way, no one would be left alive. "Sire", he began with some uncertainty, "my father's cause is unjust. If you had given him a motive for offense, then I would have simply removed myself from further involvement, but, alas, no offense was given. I have served as a general for over thirty years and I have never seen him in this state of mind. He simply wants to destroy the land of Cainan to satiate his own bloodlust."

Zadok carefully considered his next words and commented, "I fear that once word reaches the other kingdoms of my father's depredations, it will set off an ever increasing escalation of similar actions all throughout the realm. If the other kings see my father's perfidy toward your people, then they may decide to settle old scores with their neighbors in the same manner, especially now that my father is occupied here in Cainan so far removed from his center of control. Sire, your army must put up a fight and sue for a peaceful surrender then perhaps your bravery can convince the realm that peace must be examined before anyone resorts to military action. If not, then chaos and anarchy will descend upon the land and there will be no one to turn off the violence, my father least of all."

Menahem pondered Zadok's remarks. He ventured reasonably, "If I committed my entire army to our defense, would it make any difference in the outcome?"

Zadok's response was immediate and negative. "You would have none. With the combined armies of both Hesh and Shulon, my assessment of the strength of his army is that he has a ten to one clear advantage in the field, but, if we can make a valiant stand and inflict more damage than Giddiel is willing to accept, perhaps we can push him for a conditional surrender."

Later that same day Zadok found himself in an argument with the only person who had ever successfully convinced him of reversing his decisions. Elisheba, now pacing back and forth in front of her husband was beyond angry and was throwing every verbal dart and arrow in her repertoire in his direction. "Zadok, you must look beyond your silly pride or sense of duty to these people. You must think of your family first. I absolutely forbid you to throw your life away in this manner."

Zadok, a man quite familiar with the anger of his wife, but still very much in love with her, allowed Elisheba to vent her anger and frustration without protest. When he felt she had sufficiently worn herself down, he interjected, "Elisheba, I am thinking of my family first. Unless I can convince my father to turn back his army, he will march through this city and raze every building and burn down every house, but he will not stop there. He will insist on a bloodletting that will consume everyone. This upheaval will overflow into the remainder of the realm and our children and their families will not be spared. I may be the only one who can stop it, but not because I am his son and might appeal to him for mercy, but because I know his army and if I can inflict enough damage, he may be forced to settle for a peaceful surrender from Cainan."

Slowly, the anger faded from her face and was replaced by sorrow. "My Husband, I know you are right, but I cannot bear losing you." She now wept openly, all the fear and frustration finally being released. Zadok held her close until the sobs diminished.

"Elisheba, you and all the children and their families should flee the city immediately. Even if I can convince my father to spare the city, he still intends to plant his standard here and govern Cainan with blood and terror. I refuse to allow my children to witness and be consumed by a barbaric occupation. You have mentioned before that your birth place is nearby. Is there anyone with whom you and the children can stay?"

Elisheba had been thinking more and more lately of her childhood home some miles to the east. She even wondered whether her childhood friend, Sariah, would still remember her. "Yes," responded Elisheba tonelessly, "but it has been many years and the journey over the mountains is arduous. I am unsure whether Sariah will even welcome me."

Zadok pressed his reasoning, hoping to prevail over her doubts. "Regardless, it is the only solution, so you must plan your departure as soon as possible. Once you leave do not return to Cainan and do not tell anyone from here where you are planning to go. There must be no one to follow you. I will send my two remaining military advisers to accompany you and the children then, once you are safe, have them return and bring me word."

She smiled ruefully at her husband. "Very well, Zadok, but I go under protest. You must promise to return to me."

Their eyes met and he replied, "I will." But, they both wondered if it was meant to be.

From the walls of the city of Cainan, Menahem and a detachment of guards watched intently as the armies of Giddiel engaged the Army of Cainan now commanded by Zadok. The fighting had been going on for almost an hour, but owing to its vastly superior size, Giddiel's force was winning the day. Then, incredibly, there appeared a contingent of horsemen riding through the middle of the attacking army, parting it to each side.

Zadok had hoped to cut his father's army in half by dashing through to the rear with a large detachment of cavalry. Meanwhile, his well trained and armored infantry were to forcefully attack the flanks and work inward, but though this tactic was inflicting many casualties, the attrition to the smaller army confronting Giddiel's onslaught was obvious. Zadok, with his selected cavalry, was cutting a terrible swath through the larger army, but by the time he reached the rear, near his father's tent, he was down to only seven men. Seeing his father's tent in sight, he spurred on his horse and along with his remaining men attempted to cut through the rear guard now protecting King Giddiel. One by one his men fell to a barrage of spears and arrows from Giddiel's personal guard posted in a tight perimeter outside the tent. The remainder of Zadok's men was cut down, some being pierced in the neck while still others had exposed parts of arms and legs gouged with spears. Zadok was now injured from an arm wound, but managed to charge forward to his father's tent and dispatch the remaining two guards at the entrance. He blundered through the tent flap, sword now drawn and intent on forcing Giddiel to recall his forces.

The sight of Zadok thrusting his way into the tent startled his father even then girding on his armor. "What is this intrusion Zadok? You dare draw your sword in my presence?"

Surprised that his father's personal guards seemed reluctant to offer any protection, Zadok lunged forward at his father who then attempted to flee, but he quickly pinned Giddiel from behind. His sword was now at his father's back, ready to plunge it through if his guard even attempted to rush him. "Father, you must recall your forces. This slaughter is unnecessary and will only lead to further bloodshed later."

"Never," screamed his father defiantly. "I will have your head for this insult. I have tolerated your disloyalty long enough. Guards, seize him and cut him down!"

From the shadows in the corner came a strident command. "Guards, ignore that order and stand down." Obediently the guards withdrew to the corner from whence the voice originated.

Giddiel was incensed that his order had been countermanded. "Cain, how dare you override my order? My men will obey me or I will have them publicly castrated!"

"Giddiel," countered Cain disdainfully, "they were never *your* men. They are members of my personal guard on loan and are of the Clan. They obey me and me alone. Did you really think I would ignore your ridiculous posturing and allow you to breathe out threats against me? My eyes and ears have been among your entourage for some time and now you will shut your mouth while I question your son." His gaze shifted back to Zadok. "If it pleases you, Zadok, you may continue to hold your father as hostage, though I assure you he is no longer a threat." He noticed the look of bright hate in the eyes of this fool he had left in charge of the realm and realized what an incredible mistake it had been. He berated himself, "*Yes, Giddiel had been easy to manipulate, but the man was a ruthless fool, without a fraction of the sense the Creator had given a goose.*"

Cain, always the dissembler, began to use his natural charm. "Now Zadok," he soothed, "we have never met, but I know you have heard of me. You are a reasonable, intelligent man, so there are a few questions I would like to ask you. After that you may dispatch your fool of a father at your leisure."

Giddiel lunged forward in an attempt to get at Cain, but, as the guards moved to surround Cain in a protective shield, Zadok held his father close. He shifted his gaze back to Cain and replied, "Cain, yes I have heard of you, but as you say we have never met. I suspect it was always because, unlike most other men, you walk in the shadows." The loss of blood from his wounded arm was beginning to make him understandably light-headed and he suspected that he would soon pass out making this heroic charge a moot point. He commented woozily, "We can talk all you like once my father calls off the attack on Cainan."

Cain turned to the chief guard. "Guard, bring my field general here immediately, unless of course he wasn't killed by Zadok as he plunged heroically through the ranks. I left him a few minutes before arriving here so he should still be in his tent."

Within minutes the General of the Army arrived running. He took in the entire scene, but was not at all surprised to see Zadok with a sword at his father's back. "General Zadok, I see you wear the colors of Cainan. What is the meaning of all this?"

"General Tubal," directed Cain, "I want you to communicate to your field commanders to sound retreat and remove your army from the field of battle. They will need their rest for the final push tomorrow."

"It will be done, Cain". The General saluted Cain and Zadok on the way out. In a few minutes the sound to withdraw from the field could be clearly heard.

Zadok, upon hearing the signal to withdraw, felt relief for the first time in days; Giddiel's reaction, however, was one of anger. "So, I finally realize my position in the realm was, in reality, hardly more than that of a martinet."

"Yes, and what of it?" Cain replied disdainfully. "You have the mentality of a head-breaker and deserve no less." He shifted his gaze back to Zadok and asked, "Will that suffice, Zadok?"

Zadok appeared woozy and began to weave as though about to pass out from the blood loss. As Cain was concerned he might faint before he had a chance to interrogate him, he glanced over at one of the guards and directed, "Guard, please restrain Giddiel while Zadok has a seat." He looked back at Zadok and with impatient politeness said, "Zadok, do rest. Your father is no threat, as you see, so please have some water or wine from the table."

Zadok reluctantly released his father to the guards. There was a struggle in which Giddiel attempted to lunge at his son, but one guard, anticipating the move, easily backhanded him and the King crumpled helplessly to the ground.

Cain gazed contemptuously at the thrashing, cursing figure on the dusty floor of the tent and ordered, "Guard, run him through with your spear." Without the least hesitation, the guard smiled as he brought the spear down hard and into the throat of the now cringing man, once the King of Nod. The blood flowed freely from the wound as the dying man attempted to speak, but could only croak feebly between gouts of blood, mucous and torn tissue. Within a few minutes, Giddiel laid dead, one hand still around his shredded throat.

Cain, uncaring at the results of his order, seemed impatient for the dying to be done and when it was finally over remarked casually, "That should have been done long ago. Now, where were we? Oh, yes, I had some questions for you. Do I now have your full attention?"

Zadok was frankly astonished at his sanguine tone. His father, now disposed of, was no longer of any use and therefore was beyond any further interest to this man. It was clear that Cain's reputation for brutality was well deserved, thus Zadok was curious as to why he removed the army from the field when it was obvious the army could have simply rolled over the smaller defenders. He was therefore intrigued by Cain's interest in what information he might have and he also wondered whether it could be used to his advantage. "I am listening", Zadok replied.

Cain was about to be seated when his eyes were drawn to the inert figure of Giddiel in the corner of the tent and, pointing to the corpse, he instructed the guard peremptorily, "Guard, remove that from my sight and have it burned. The stench now begins to distract me."

After the body was dragged away, Cain sat down opposite of Zadok at the table and watched Zadok for several moments, then said with honest admiration, "So, General Zadok, your reputation for bravery is well deserved. I would not have thought anyone capable of cutting his way through this army in such a dramatic fashion and getting this far to his goal. Your goal was, I assume, the withdrawal of my army from the field and the safety of Cainan, yes?"

Attempting to be unimpressed by the charisma of this man, Zadok casually replied, "So, it is now your army?"

Cain shrugged his shoulders absently as though the evidence was apparent. "It always was; you just never knew it. In all the years you served your father as a general in his army, you were never aware that you were actually serving me. It didn't have to be that way, but your record for integrity always made it difficult for me to completely trust you so your invitation to join our Fraternity was always delayed. I can assure you that this was not a problem for most of your comrades in the military. Most of them were always only too anxious to set aside personal morality and become loyal to my Order." With obvious contempt he added facetiously with a smile, "And of course, your dear departed father was one my most loyal members."

"Cain, I have witnessed first-hand how the loyalty of the Clan favors its members until they displease you."

With growing impatience, Cain replied, "Zadok, there are only two rules for measuring success within the Clan: competence and loyalty. Your father was highly successful, though stupid and even that could have been tolerated, but his disloyalty could not have been overlooked; he was planning to assassinate me the first opportunity. But, let's be honest. I have seen the contempt on your face in the presence of your father on a number of occasions. I seriously doubt that you will miss his winning personality", he added sardonically. "So, let us put such talk aside for now. While my army is resting, there is still a matter that we will need to discuss and we should hurry. My general assures me my soldiers will soon grow anxious to return to the field and finish the work of death to the army of Menahem."

"Cain, you seem to know everything. How is it that you need information from me?"

Cain gazed directly into Zadok's eyes and with total conviction demanded, "What I need and what I will have is all information relating to the whereabouts of the historical records that I know are hidden somewhere in the land of Cainan. These records must be found and remanded into my possession. Believe me when I say that the survival and well-being of the inhabitants of Cainan are secondary to my interest in those records. I would cut down every person in this kingdom that tried to get in the way of my goal." He paused and added reasonably, "You have been among the citizens of Cainan for several months now. Have you ever seen or heard any mention of these documents?"

Zadok's response was immediate. "Never, but the subject never arose so the opportunity to discuss them never occurred." Zadok now understood how he might manipulate this man to his advantage. "Though, I am aware, however, that two men came and talked to King Menahem over what they termed spiritual matters. They babbled on about how Menahem and his people should repent and return to the teachings of the God of their fathers. One even climbed upon the great wall of the city overlooking the market place and began to sermonize. The message was curious, even compelling, but not well received so he fled the city just ahead of an angry mob of citizens. Nonetheless, out of simple curiosity, I had the two men followed and it was reported back to me that they had had a conversation about some records. Since this information held no importance to my mission in Cainan, I simply dismissed it as idle prattle between two old men."

Cain was immediately interested and realizing he was closer to his goal, he asked, "Who were these two men and are they still in Cainan?"

"The elder of the two was named Lamech and the other Noah. It has been reported that Lamech occasionally visits in the old quarter of the city, but no one has seen the other, Noah, since his exile, so presumably he has left the area."

Cain broke into a mirthless grin. "Well, perhaps my old friend Lamech will introduce me to his young whelp of a son? We should all get re-acquainted. After all, we are family," he added reasonably.

His smile disappeared as he seemed to consider all Zadok had related to him. At some length, Cain decided, "Zadok, please take what remains of your army back to Cainan and encamp them to the north of the city. You will disband the army within the week. My army will occupy the other corners of the kingdom including all main roads and mountain passes. A contingent of soldiers and I will assume control and governance of the city. Any resistance from the populace will be met with the harshest of consequences. Please report this message to King Menahem immediately."

Zadok was astonished. "So, am I to report that the city will be spared including the King and his house hold?"

"Of course, Zadok," reassured Cain with his most winning smile. "As long as there is complete cooperation and support of my goals, there is no need to despair."

Chapter 5 – The Message

And God talked with Lamech, the prophet; and Lamech, knowing the Flood was near, warned Cain to flee Cainan to the land of Hesh. And there in the land of Hesh, Cain was given a boat and escaped the waters as they fell.

----- *The Abridgement, Chapter 15*

The city of Cainan was now near collapse. After nearly three months of military occupation the food supplies necessary to feed the citizens and the army of Cain were nearly exhausted. To complicate matters, Cain was still no farther along to achieving his goals than he had been before the occupation began. He thought bitterly, *"And I intend to stay until I have uncovered the records and if that means starving the city, then so be it."* He had sent for Menahem yet again to persuade him to give up Lamech.

Cain, now seated on the king's throne, received the former ruler with a resounding rebuke. "Menahem, you are being foolish. How many members of your family must I hang in the city square before you come to your senses? You are running out of sons and daughters! Shall I now see which one of your wives you love less than the others? As you know, this can be easily arranged."

With complete misery Menahem responded, "Cain, you have to understand that the moment you entered the city, Lamech simply disappeared. We have continuously searched the city from one end to the other and I have appealed to my people publicly to hand him over, but he is nowhere to be found. I beg you to end my life and let me die without seeing further deaths in my family."

Cain was unimpressed with Menahem's grieving concern for his family. "I am growing weary of your excuses. You still don't understand how important those records are to me. You will produce Lamech within two days or the head of another one of your children will decorate my courtyard; after that, I will turn my attention to your wives." Cain shouted with anger and frustration, "And If you can't persuade your citizens to help me, this will continue each day until either Lamech is found or you run out of family members. Now get out of my sight and do your job or I swear I will burn this city to the ground!"

Menahem despondently removed himself from Cain's presence. He, too, was worried that he would run out of wives long before Cain had been satisfied of his efforts to find Lamech. His personal guard would pay dearly if he lost any more relatives because they were unable to find that old man.

Presently, the chief adviser, Gilgal, entered the council room where Cain sat and fumed. With some trepidation he asked to speak. Cain, now impatient, shouted, "Well, get on with it: Report!"

Gilgal, now trembling, replied reluctantly, "Sire, I have spoken with several members of the Clan who have just arrived and they report mass defections of the kings throughout the land. Each who has ever received an offense against his brother is now taking revenge. One army is fighting another only to have it spill over into the next kingdom, which has sparked an open outbreak of violence spreading throughout the realm. Our advisers to each of their courts have been executed and those that have escaped report that without your guidance and immediate intervention, there will be anarchy and chaos." He added reluctantly, "You must leave Cainan and tend to these affairs."

Cain was livid. "You dare lecture me on my priorities? You think I care a whit what those brainless fools do to each other? Before I gave them their thrones they were lucky to be governing a pigsty in the worst backwater in the land. Whatever I created once, I can recreate. Let them destroy one another and then all will see how easy it will be for me to start over without them. Now, get out of my sight before I have my guards throw you from the tower!"

Once his adviser was dismissed, he brooded for the better part of the next hour over what could be done to quell these mass defections to his Society throughout the realm. Finally, angered at the disruption to his plans, he summoned his Field Officer, General Tubal. The General was an old, but loyal member of the Clan and now, awaiting his orders, he stood rigid and unblinking before his master. Cain gazed at him directly and asked, "Tubal, do you trust and give unfailing filial loyalty to me and to our Society?"

"Yes, Sire," Tubal responded immediately.

"Then take half of my army and march them to the west and put down all uprisings in the kingdom. Send out my spies and special agents to assassinate every king sitting on his throne who dares make war against the realm and the Clan. Can you do this or should I have you relieved and send someone else in your place?"

Tubal was unperturbed at the threat and stated, "No, Cain, as always, I am loyal first to you and to the Clan. It will be done as you say. My oath is my word."

Cain shook his head, quite pleased with his General's response. "Very well, Tubal, you and the main army will leave tomorrow morning and you will send me weekly reports by courier. You will leave your chief captain behind in nominal command of the remainder of the army here in Cainan and I will direct them as I see fit. " He added as an afterthought, "I have not seen Zadok in a week. Have your chief captain look for his whereabouts." He added, now suddenly concerned, "I don't like the idea of him running about free."

Two days later and again Menahem stood before Cain, but this time, however, he wore a smile of victory. "Well, Menahem, what have you to report or should I just send my guards to select one of your wives for the cutting table?"

With a desperate grin and flourish of his arm, Menahem was only too anxious to bring Cain the good news. "Sire, my agents have finally ferreted out Lamech and now have him in chains. Can I have him brought before you", he gibbered, now so relieved he could hardly stand up.

Cain happily banged his fist down on the arm of the throne. Beaming at the terrified, but now relieved ex-ruler, he exclaimed, "Well done, Menahem! It appears that finally I may have found a way to motivate you after all. I suspected that sooner or later I would find someone you really did care for; it was simply a matter of eliminating everyone else." With a sardonic laugh he quipped, "I must say, though, I was beginning to believe that you cared for no one. For your future edification, Menahem, I want you to listen and witness everything that is said."

Cain watched as the guards brought in a disheveled old man fettered in chains. It had been many years since he had last seen his brother Lamech and that confrontation had gone badly and clearly not to Cain's total satisfaction. Too many of the records this old fool had been hoarding were spirited away before he could arrive to destroy them all. He had had to settle for the few remaining records that had been overlooked. Cain suspected that the more damning records were those that Lamech had hidden away from him. Inconsequence, he had no intention of losing the advantage again; he was tired of finding only the left-overs.

Lamech, the prophet and patriarch, was thrown unceremoniously to the stone floor in front of Cain and the pain was obvious on his agonized face. "Guard," Cain shouted, and his concern fooled no one, least of all the guard, "who told you to throw the old man to his knees? Are you so blind that you can't see how feeble his decrepit legs are? Unshackle him and leave us." Although his voice displayed anger, the mirth never left his eyes. It was clear that Cain was enjoying Lamech's discomfort and he intended to have an audience wherewith he could boast and gloat over his victory.

"Well, Lamech, do arise and let us speak of old times." Cain's joyous tone assailed him breezily. "It has been many years since last we met and embraced as brothers."

Lamech tried to arise, then fell, but finally was able to stand upright. "Cain, I see your memory is no better than your hospitality," muttered Lamech between breaths of pain.

"My hospitality? Brother, whatever do you mean?" Cain responded with false innocence. His tone now turned to umbrage as he looked over at Menahem. "Explain yourself, Menahem! Have you had my dear brother shackled and languishing away in some dank dungeon somewhere? You know how such ill treatment can afflict the old and infirmed," he cried out in sanctimonious shocked outrage.

Menahem was about to protest this insinuation when Lamech interrupted, "Cain, save your regret for someone who doesn't know you that well," countered Lamech, now with more strength in his voice.

Cain opened his arms wide and replied in a conciliatory tone, "Lamech, we are all family here and there should not be such hostility between brothers," he smiled with a feral grin. "For my part, I am ready to bury our past differences and work together to help our poor brothers and sisters in our homeland of Cainan."

"Cain is there anything that proceeds from your mouth which carries any truth?" replied Lamech, now weary of Cain's charade. Lamech knew very well why he was here standing before this shadow of a man.

Cain was feeling now quite expansive as he felt he was now so close to his victory. "I must say, dear Brother, your old age has addled your civility as well as your mind." He turned to Menahem and in a confiding voice responded, "Well, what can be expected from the aged and infirm?" Turning back to Lamech he remarked gloatingly, "It's too bad the Creator has not seen fit to slow your aging down the way he has mine."

"Cain," countered Lamech simply, "we all serve the will of our Creator."

Cain, now tired of the repartee, shouted, "Spare me your useless homilies, you old fool! I know for a fact the records lie somewhere in Cainan to the east of here and some have even speculated that they lie deep in a mountain vault, but what I don't know is the exact location. So, you know why you are here and unless you divulge the location of your records, which you have squirreled away somewhere in Cainan, I will drag into this room every one of your kinsmen who have been hiding your worthless hide all these months." Cain, now relishing the tortures to come, began to describe the horrible mutilations. "Each will be thoroughly interrogated with whips at length for the whereabouts of the records before I have them publicly flayed alive. Each one will then be dragged through the city by horses and what is left will be hung upside down in the city square until their worthless life screams out of them." Cain's smile was beatific.

Lamech replied with sadness. "Cain there is an old rumor among our family that suggests you were always a lover of torture. You started as a young boy practicing on small, innocent animals then later on you would whip your brothers who worked the fields for you. I find this practice of yours distasteful and unworthy of a son of Adam. You will always have my deepest sympathy for your weakness."

Cain listened to Lamech with growing anger then his fury grew beyond his ability for speech. He slowly turned to Menahem and the guards. His anger was so deep he had trouble at first articulating, but finally he screamed, "Leave us!" Menahem and the guards stumbled over one another to get out of his sight.

"Why, you useless old goat!" he screamed. "I should have your tongue pulled out by the roots for those remarks! Lies, all damnable lies!" he sputtered impotently. He did not have the words to verbalize his depth of fury at the shame which he had carried around all these years. He thought,

"It must have been my worthless sister, Sariah, who spread those lies about me. I swear if she were standing before me I would split her head open!"

"Lamech, this will be enough of our family chat!" Cain bellowed. "You will tell me what I want to know or I will have your wagging tongue removed along with any other part of your body still capable of wagging, though in your addled condition, your tongue is probably the only thing left on your miserable old body that still does function."

"Cain, I am not here to listen to you rant on about your missed opportunities or tolerate your threats of torture to me or my kinsmen. Removing my tongue would not alter the course of the disaster that is inevitable, but it would seal your fate along with the rest of mankind."

"What are you babbling on about you old fool?" Cain spat.

Patiently Lamech replied, "I have not been in hiding these past months out of fear, but to give my son, Noah, as much time as possible to complete his work and prepare for the cataclysm to come. Menahem's men did not capture me. I surrendered because I knew eventually I would be brought before you and now I have a message for your ears alone. What you do with this message is up to you, but I urge you to heed it."

Cain arose from the throne and back-handed Lamech across the face, knocking him to the hard floor. Now standing over Lamech, the prophet, now in chains, he bellowed, "Look, you simple-minded, addle-brained old fool. The only message I want to hear is the whereabouts of the records!" Cain was now panting and trying to calm his anger. His voice, now roughened by his previous tirade, threatened menacingly, "After you tell me, perhaps I will allow you to return to your kinsmen unharmed, but my patience is wearing thin."

Lamech slowly arose from the floor and stood before his tormentor then replied implacably, "Cain you must forget about the records. My kinsmen know nothing about them and I refuse to divulge their location for obvious reasons. And even if I were to disclose that information, you would not be permitted to access them."

Cain realized he was too close to his goal to be frustrated by this old man. "What are you babbling about now, Lamech?"

Lamech tiredly related, "Cain, the records you seek lie within a mountain vault and have been stored on hallowed ground. The land has been consecrated for that purpose alone and no one can be allowed to destroy them or remove them once they have been safely deposited. The Creator has so decreed it."

Cain angrily pounded the arm of his chair and bellowed his anger and frustration, "What is this nonsense you say? I am permitted to destroy the records so long as they have not been hoarded in some filthy, bat-infested mountain cave?"

Now disgusted by the effort of trying to reason with this creature, Lamech replied wearily, "Cain, you were never going to be allowed to get at them once they were safeguarded in the mountain. You should forget them because you have other concerns to worry about. Listen: The Creator will soon send a great flood that will cover our world and destroy all living things that walk or crawl upon it. There will be only a few persons to survive. The agency of mankind will still remain a significant precept in the judgment of Man and the Creator intends to continue with that principle following the devastation to come."

He closed his eyes momentarily, his face clearly deploring the words that followed next. "The Creator and your adopted father of lies, Lucifer, have made a compromise regarding your fate. Lucifer wants you to remain his agent and provide the necessary justification for testing the agency of mankind. Following the flood to come, you will, of course, begin anew your filthy Order that you call the Clan. You will be allowed, for the sake of testing the agency of Man, to spread this falsehood throughout the earth once again until the end has been determined. That is the Creator's will on the matter of your fate. The rest of us are doomed to die within a few months."

Cain, now temporarily side-tracked by this new development sneered, "And just how, pray tell, am I to survive this calamity?" But, there was absolutely no doubt that he believed everything that Lamech had just told him.

"I don't know and frankly I don't care. You are to ask your father, Lucifer, and he will direct you". Lamech added contemptuously. "But, I suggest you refrain from wasting any more time torturing the populace of Cainan for the records. Your time is almost up. Even now, my son Noah is completing the project for saving his family and the creatures of the earth. He and his sons have been building an ark for over twenty years and it will be large enough to house every living creature the Creator has seen fit to allow to survive. When my son's work is complete, the rains will begin."

Cain angrily swore under his breath. "And what of the records?" he demanded.

With more patience than he thought possible, Lamech informed him, "Cain, the records have always been in the hands of the Creator and will so remain until the end of time several millennia from now. That is my message and it is for you to believe or disbelieve."

Cain resignedly realized his hope to discover and destroy the records had been dashed once again. "Oh, I believe you. If there are anything you pedantic prophets understand it is telling the truth; you never lie. I would keep one of you on permanent retainer in my court if I thought I could trust any of you to look after my welfare, which I don't."

"Guard," Cain yelled. Immediately a guard came running. "Escort this *prophet* to the gates of the city," Cain ordered with utter contempt. He looked toward Lamech one last time and said, "Don't return again, old man. There is nothing left for you here."

With a deep regret at having to be the messenger to this creature, Lamech nonetheless left a parting salutation. "Good-by, Cain, I wish I could say it has been a pleasure to see one of my distant kinsmen one last time, but I would be lying if I did, and as you have pointed out already, I don't lie."

Cain sat thinking for several minutes after Lamech had been taken away. While his left hand played nervously along the scar that ran down his left cheek, his agitation over what he had heard had caused a nervous tic in one eye and his fingers of his right hand were in constant motion, thumping the arm of his chair. Additionally, the news regarding his inability to access the records after so much resource and effort had been expended was especially galling. The longer he pondered the portent of what Lamech had described the more his agitation increased. Abruptly, to relieve some of the anxiety, he arose from the chair and began pacing about the room. He noticed the fire in the fireplace had burned down so he did what he always did when he was agitated: he started the tedious business of adding more wood, stoking the fire and rearranging the coals until he had a lively fire now re-warming the room.

At length he began to calm down. He was standing over the hearth looking deep within the fire when an unseen presence entered the room, immediately cooling everything within his surroundings. Cain was hardly surprised. He had been expecting his old mentor, and without turning, he bent down and continued to push the wood about the fireplace. "I knew there had to be a reason why I needed to get up and stoke the fire. It must be very cold where you live because you always manage to bring some of it with you when you arrive."

"My, aren't you glib today?" noted Lucifer facetiously.

Cain replied drolly, "An old friend of the family dropped by today and left me a few messages. He declared that an entire mountain of records is inaccessible to me because it has been designated hallowed ground, whatever that means, and oh, by the way, he mentioned that the world was going to end." Cain arose, turned around and strode back to his throne past the ephemeral figure standing in the middle of the room. After seating himself, he demanded, "Do you know anything about any of this?"

The voice of his mentor was smooth, as usual. "As it so happens, I do. I have just been informed that the ground on which the records are stored is hallowed and therefore off-limits. I considered this a clear violation of the rules under which we began this effort, but I so seldom am allowed access to the inner chambers where the decisions are made. So, we must live with it. In the future, you must plan your confiscations more thoroughly in order to bag the records before they are stored in that ridiculous safe-zone."

"What future do you mean?" Cain sneered contemptuously. "Haven't you heard? The world is going to end."

Lucifer refused to rise to the bait. "The Creator is displeased over our recent triumphs among men and now wishes to end it all and start over. I rightly pointed out to Him that this action signifies a clear victory on our part. If Mankind is so easily manipulated and deserving to be destroyed, perhaps agency is not as necessary as He once believed. As always, He was unamused as well as unreceptive to my arguments. He still remains unwilling to surrender His misplaced trust in that principle and concede us our victory. So, we must begin again. I insisted, of course, that you continue in your role as my chief agent."

"Lucky me", muttered Cain. The thought of all his efforts of the past millennium going to waste had cankered his enthusiasm at being saved. "And just how was that received?"

"Much better than I could have believed", Lucifer added lightly. He went on to add, "You are to be provided with an escape, but you must travel quickly because the time grows near the end."

"To where must I flee?" he countered curtly.

"To the west coast in the land of Cush", Lucifer responded breezily. "As you know, Samuel, one our most ardent supporters of the Clan has a castle near a large bay. He has an excellent shipwright who has built a special boat that can be used for your escape. Simply report to Samuel and take the boat out through the bay to the open sea."

"To Cush, you say? That is on the other side of the realm!" he shouted. "If what my advisers tell me is true, the whole countryside will be in conflict. I and my army will have to hack our way westward mile by mile. That is the great plan?"

"I must say, Cain, you show remarkably little gratitude for this boon I have provided for your survival," Lucifer responded, now somewhat ruffled by Cain's tone of voice.

"So sorry to have injured your delicate feelings," Cain added contemptuously. "Assuming you had any to begin with, that is." Cain began pacing about, spouting invective with every step. "You realize, of course, that my Council of Advisers will cease to exist. All my work and effort selecting only the best councilors and Clan members completely loyal to our cause will be obliterated along with everything else!"

"This bickering is pointless, Cain. You and whatever men you wish to accompany you must begin your journey posthaste." He warned, "Remember, the Creator has agreed to this compromise and He will keep His word in the matter of your continued survival, but you must make every effort to reach your destination on time. I assure you, He will not wait. He has decreed that each species of animal life upon the Earth is to be saved and housed on an ark being built by Noah, son of Lamech. Once he has completed the building of the ark and all the animals have been stored securely, the rains will begin." Lucifer paused and added soothingly, "Cain, this is simply a temporary delay. Once this tedious interruption is behind us, we can re-introduce our plans. As you know, I will need you to help me restart our Order." His smile, as always was false, but to Cain reassuring.

Chapter 6 – The Translation, continued

The two professors were deep in a heated discussion. Jasher walked into the living room and understood immediately that the argument was about the recent translation. They had just completed reviewing the records regarding the Great Flood and the subject of Cain had come up yet again. Levinson watched as Jasher entered the room and turned his attention to him. "Ah, Jasher, just the man we need to clarify a point of translation. In your record there is an entry that strongly implies that God and Lucifer came to a compromise over the matter of whether Cain should remain alive or suffer the same fate as the rest of mankind during the Great Flood. Clearly, as you say, he is still among us and you have skillfully, I might add, made a good case as to why that is so, but My God, man, the very idea of God and Lucifer working together on this as though they had made a deal? This I find extremely hard to conceive if not personally distasteful."

Jasher glanced over to Professor Bedford and asked, "William, will you bring us a Bible containing the Old Testament, please?" While William was in the study and busied himself rummaging around looking for the text, Jasher asked Professor Levinson, "Isaac, how well do you understand the calamities of Job as they now appear in the Old Testament?"

Isaac responded as any good scholar, "Job was a righteous man of God and was tested to determine whether he could remain so."

William reappeared with a Bible and sat down. He was about to hand it to Jasher, when he asked William to turn to Job 1: 7-12. When Bedford located the passage, Jasher said, "Now hand the Book to Isaac and leave it opened to that passage." William complied and once Isaac had the book in hand Jasher responded to Isaac, "You are quite right about God's test to Job, but, perhaps we should read the passage to determine if there was still more to learn here." Jasher quoted from Job from memory:

> *7   And the Lord said unto Satan, Whence comest thou? Then Satan answered the Lord, and said, From going to and fro in the earth, and from walking up and down in it.*

> *8 And the Lord said unto Satan, Hast thou considered my servant Job, that there is none like him in the earth, a perfect and an upright man, one that feareth God, and escheweth evil?*
>
> *9 Then Satan answered the Lord, and said, Doth Job fear God for naught?*
>
> *10 Hast not thou made a hedge about him, and about his house, and about all that he hath on every side? thou hast blessed the work of his hands, and his substance is increased in the land.*
>
> *11 but put forth thine hand now, and touch all that he hath, and he will curse thee to thy face.*
>
> *12 And the Lord said unto Satan, Behold, all that he hath is in thy power; only upon himself put not forth thine hand. So Satan went forth from the presence of the Lord.*

He finished quoting Chapter 1 of the Book of Job and asked, "Would either of you care to comment on the discussion recorded here between God and Satan?"

Bedford began, "There seems to be an argument as to just how faithful Job would be if he had been better tried instead of given so much comfort."

Isaac pointed out as well, "Job was clearly a righteous man of God and so He was rightfully proud of Job's commitment to the commandments."

"Gentlemen, you are quite right on both of your observations, but what you have missed in your analysis is the most intriguing aspect of the passage. To put it bluntly, Satan had complained that Job's life was easy and he had become a rich man and therefore hardly a fitting example of a righteous man that would use his agency to obey the commandments unconditionally. So, a wager was made and God allowed Satan to curse Job's life to prove a point to Satan. So, we have here a clear precedent of the two of them agreeing to wager that Job would or would not prevail in spite of his challenges. This would indicate a collaboration of sorts, a willingness to give both sides an opportunity to test their theories of the importance of agency and man's willingness to exercise it justly. So, what God can do once, he may have done many times before or since in a similar manner. Just because there is no written record available of these other events, does not make the possibility any less plausible or the principle any less acceptable once a precedent has been set." He paused momentarily to allow this logic of established precedent to register in their minds then pushed on with his final point.

"In the example of the recent translation from *The Abridgement*, God, our Creator and Lucifer the sworn enemy of mankind, put aside their avowed differences and collaborated on a course of action. They decided that, for the sake of a proper means of temptation whereby Men could be properly judged, that Cain would be allowed not only to survive the Flood, but be permitted to set up his business once again following the event."

Isaac sat pensively for a few moments digesting Jasher's correlation of the two events. "Jasher, getting back to the example of Job, if what you are saying is true then the wager was not whether Job could endure the hardships, but whether he would continue using his agency in the same righteous manner as he did before his trials and without rancor in spite of the hardships."

"Yes, and I will get you one step farther along that same road." Jasher reflected for a moment then proceeded with his point. "Suppose the story was recorded as an object lesson for all of us regarding the importance of using agency for positive behavior in spite of our mortal challenges? The Creator did not make a wager with Lucifer because he was fond of games. He used Job to emphasize a point to Lucifer and to us today about the correct use of agency. The story as recorded in the Old Testament was never really about Job."

Chapter 7 – The Ark

A few miles from the home of Noah and his family, a blue jay and its mate hopped about on a limb of a large, but ancient elm tree high above the landscape. Though their species is migratory, their coming to the land of Cainan was more than mere animal instinct designed into their nature. It was more a feeling of being called or directed, which they still managed to comprehend, though the experience was a new one. The male had been busy all morning gathering acorns and seeds and returning them to the nest that he shared with his female companion. They both had completed the building of their new home high in the fork of two interconnecting branches only the day before. In normal times it would be the time of mating, but the two creatures felt restrained as if awaiting a better time and location for the business of procreation. Though curious about the ark and eager to investigate it, they felt the time was not quite right, but soon when bidden, they would have to leave their nest. They sensed their time here would be temporary.

As he was the eldest, it had fallen to Japheth to feel the terrible burden of responsibility. Once Noah had carefully laid out the plans for the ark and had assisted in its initial framework, he had departed on his mission to the people of the realm and left the responsibility of completion in his hands as overseer of the work with his other two brothers, Shem and Ham and their families. Now that Noah was back, Japheth had been quick to allow his father to resume his patriarchal place in the family, however, Noah was so impressed with his sons' progress and attention to detail that he had surprised Japheth by allowing him to continue as the chief overseer of the final phase of the project. Now, almost complete, the ark had taken on gargantuan proportions and Japheth had felt the pride of workmanship well done.

Each morning, Noah walked up the two-mile pathway from their home to the construction site atop a nearby hill shaped much like a plateau. The local lake still provided ample water and food for his family, but the adjacent forest and hill had been denuded. On both sides of the path, one could see in every direction the effects of a long-time lumber extraction process. The once great forest had now been removed of its proud, tall trees, unusually thick from age. Since his vision, Noah had been especially sensitive to the voice and disposition of nature, accordingly, Noah shook his head disgustedly at the stark ugliness of the landscape, but knew it was unfortunately a necessary evil. High above his head he heard the chatter and fussing of two blue jays signaling to all others their territorial rights, and as he turned his head up to the elm and smiled, he marveled and envied the simplicity of their existence.

He arrived earlier than usual and so he had an opportunity to observe his sons and grandchildren who were hard at work and now anxious to complete the project. He had had misgivings at leaving Japheth with so much responsibility, but he had proven an able shipwright and overseer of the work. More important, he had the respect and love of his younger brothers Shem and Ham and they had all risen to the challenge. There was much for which he could be proud, so he greeted each one affectionately and settled into the day's tasks ahead.

After a few hours work, and now completing work on the top deck of the ark with his sons, Shem was looking to the west when he observed a distant cloud of dust that had been raised as a result of what appeared to be a large number of moving animals. Thinking that the movement was because of a large army on the move in their direction, he shouted to his father and brothers to join him. When they had all assembled, Shem pointed to the west and announced with his own conclusion, "Father, a large army of men has detected our ark and is now moving on us to destroy it or capture it for their own use."

Noah did not answer at first. He only stared. Then with dawning comprehension he realized that the dust being raised was not the result of any army of men, but the immigration of a large herd of animals that had traveled a great distance with a definite purpose in mind. With a smile of gratitude he announced, "My sons, we must finish quickly our preparation of the ark. The animals are arriving and once they have been properly watered from the lake nearby then they will need a place to rest after their long journey, and once in the ark, they will need to be fed, so please let us hurry, our time is short."

Chapter 8 – Before the End

Cain had begun his arduous journey westward with over one thousand men. The rest, he had left behind in Cainan to provide a rear guard in the event he had to retreat. After almost a month on the road, with the struggles of men trying to gain advantage over the other in open warfare, he realized that there would be no opportunity for retreat. The time for that option had come and gone because they were now cut off. His own envoy carrying his colors had seldom guaranteed him safe passage, and often as not, he and his men had to hack their way through one attack after the next. After five months of constant ambush and open assaults, he had been down to a handful of men, most of those wounded or sick.

The army he had sent westward with General Tubal was no more. That army had been cut to pieces by opposing armies thrown at them by desperate kings trying to hold on to whatever semblance of power they could still manage before they, too, fell under the sword. Tubal had been as good as his word, though. Cain discovered that wherever his general had been, the agents he sent out before him had indeed assassinated the ruling kings and their courts. The unfortunate side effect was that the successors or pretenders to the thrones were in a furious struggle to maintain their tenuous control and more times than not were themselves murdered which left the realm even more susceptible to unrest. Most of those now in power were not members of the Clan and were hardly in any mood or state of mind to take direction from Cain.

This had led to renegade armies roaming about the countryside, leaderless except for those strong enough to wrest temporary control. These robber armies descended upon every village and city, raping, pillaging and slaughtering whole populations and robbing whatever they could to support their army then moved on to the next city and kingdom. This condition was widespread and evident wherever Cain traveled on his way westward. His realm, once closely held together under the guidance of the Clan of the Scar, had been thrown into complete chaos and anarchy. As Zadok had predicted, there was no one alive willing to stop the machine

236

of death and any who tried soon found themselves ground under the same wheels.

Now alone and weary of nearly seven months of constant warfare and personal danger, Cain finally arrived at the castle of King Samuel of Cush. Ever anxious to please the Master Mahan of the Clan of the Scar, Samuel was shocked at Cain's disheveled appearance. Attempting to hide his surprise, he asked respectfully, "Cain, how may I serve you?"

Cain was so weary and hungered that he only managed to croak, "Food and a bed, then we can talk." He was led to a finely set table in the king's dining hall and with animal hunger he threw himself into consuming the food and drink as would a starved wolf. He never uttered a single word during the whole repast except *more food*. Finally, satiated, he staggered off in the direction of the bedroom, found a bed and slept for a whole day.

A day later and now rested and replenished in body, Cain sat before the King of Cush, an old associate of the Brotherhood. He knew his time was running short so he came quickly to the point. "Samuel, your hospitality is appreciated, but now I must ask for one more favor. A shipwright of note in your city has recently built a new craft of curious workmanship and I think you know to whom I make reference. I must have the boat". He watched the reaction on Samuel's face for any sign of denial. When he saw none, he embedded a small lie to conceal his real intentions. "My enemies have harried me for over six weeks and are now hot on my heels to murder me. I need the boat to make good my escape."

Samuel was well aware of the boat. The builder had completed it only this past year and it had caused quite a stir among his city because of its unusual design. "Of course, Cain, I will send for the owner and he can accompany you to the wharf on the bay where the boat is tied." A servant was sent to bring the shipwright immediately back to the palace. "Please, relax and tell me of your recent travels. You are very fortunate to still be alive. I understand control of the realm has unraveled like an old, rotted robe."

Especially since what Samuel had heard was far too close to the truth, Cain was hardly in the mood to dispute idle gossip, however, he would need this man for a few more days so he felt obliged to indulge him. He began talking, and to his surprise, he realized he needed to speak with someone about this harrowing, near death experience. He omitted matters regarding the defections of the rulers from the Clan and their subsequent murder by Tubal. He tried to minimize the description of devastation to the countryside and the cities through which he passed and he especially avoided any outward emotion of worry that would indicate his loss of control over the realm. He needed this man's support, not his sympathy, which might lead to his defection if he felt it in his best interest to do so.

"So, Cain" inquired Samuel, "What will you do now?"

Cain, now fully aware that Samuel's total loyalty might rest on his next response declared confidently, "The first order of business after escaping my enemies will be to re-establish the realm to its former glory and strength. I will, no doubt, need the trust and support of my closest allies to help me rebuild and since your loyalty has always been valued and your counsel priceless, quite rightly, you will figure highly in my plan for reconstruction."

Cain felt reasonably sure that Samuel's remote location from the rest of the realm would make it impossible for him to know the complete details of its devastation until it was too late to work in his favor. Within a week, perhaps days, the warfare will spill over into his kingdom and then he, too, will be under pressure to submit to the pillaging hoards now roaming unchecked throughout the country. If was now clear that the robbers infesting what was left of his realm would have their way because any show of defense was met with ruthless and savage retaliations.

Cain had given no thought that he might have set this scene of destruction in motion when he had placed ambitious cut throats in power to do his bidding. Now they and those who would wrest power from them were beyond his control. Three weeks earlier he had attempted to meet privately with one of the few rulers who had escaped assassination by Tubal, only because the General and his army had already been destroyed. Though still a member of the Clan, but highly suspicious of anyone, including Cain, who might relieve him of his hard fought position in the kingdom, this king had set his guards upon Cain and had killed the remainder of his retinue. He had barely escaped with his life and consequently he knew that he would be killed on sight if he were ever captured. If Samuel knew this, he would use Cain as a bargaining chip to broker a deal to save himself and his kingdom should his country be invaded. Cain intended to be far out at sea before that ever happened.

Cain had been deep in thought with these matters when Samuel uttered something and so he did not catch the entire statement. Cain commented apologetically, "Sorry, the matter of rebuilding my realm has been constantly on my mind lately. You were saying?"

Samuel actually knew more about what was truly happening in the realm than he had been willing to divulge. So, he was watching Cain carefully, trying to squeeze out an advantage. He was flattered, of course, by Cain's offer of promotion in his new kingdom, but he suspected that his offer might have as much substance as a wisp of cool air on a hot summer day. He responded by relating a piece of information he had received a month earlier. He watched intently for Cain's true reaction. "A man rode in from my northern province with an unusual story, one to which I could scarcely give credence. He reported the weather in the north had been unseasonably warm and in fact, the snows should have already begun, but have yet to fall. He went on to say that from the north and the west he viewed a large heard of animals of such magnitude and variety that at first he thought he must be imagining the whole scene. On closer inspection, he said, they showed hardly the least amount of fear of one another, even those who would have been natural enemies in the wild. Lions, tigers, wildcats all walked side by side with prey such as rabbits and deer; wolves and bears ignored sheep, goats and horses. Animals of which he had never before seen nor heard of could likewise be seen in the throng and they showed neither fear nor enmity in any way and they appeared to be absolutely unstoppable. The horde could be seen trekking from one watering hole to the next and the only reason they stopped was to take rest for the night. The next morning, the herd all awoke together and once again set out on a due easterly direction across the northern part of the realm, collecting more animals from the south as they proceeded along the way. This hoard included not only animals of the forest, but all manner of snakes, turtles and lizard-like creatures; likewise, birds of every variety were represented. This man reported to have followed them for a few days, but finally grew weary of the dust such a multitude had kicked up." Samuel smiled indulgently, "What do you think of that story? It does stretch the truth beyond normal limits, doesn't it?" Samuel watched him closely for any reaction that would signal his belief in the story or an indication as to why Cain had mysteriously appeared on his doorstep with his unusual request.

As his worst fears had just been confirmed, Cain found it difficult to remain emotionless, but Cain was anything if he was disingenuous. With so many years of practice at lying and deceit, he cleverly concealed his true feelings with an off handed remark, declaring, "The man was clearly drunk and prone to exaggeration." Shrugging his shoulders in dismissal and feigning any real interest, he side stepped any further discussion on the matter. With a question he hoped would appeal to Samuel's familial pride, he posed, "Samuel, how are your children? The last I heard your third daughter was to present you with new grandchildren, twins no less."

Cain had astutely divined Samuel's weakness, which were his grandchildren. Apparently, the old fool, though canny and ruthless as a fox when needed, was totally pliant to flattery if approached about his prolific family. Cain was able to avoid any further dangerous talk until the messenger arrived with the shipwright that same afternoon.

The valley had been abuzz with activity for the last month. Work parties loaded with foodstuffs had been making their way up the mountain from morning until evening until the rooms within the cavern were filled from the floor to half way to the ceilings. Knowing that the time was drawing near, Sariah had inspected the food reserves of the valley each day and she was afraid that their home supplies would be so low shortly that eventually they would have to start eating in the cave to survive. In any event, at least the stores would be in place when the end descended upon them.

Making her responsible for the lives of all those whom she knew as friends and family had been a constant fear of hers from the time that Noah had left the valley. She was thus in the act of second-guessing her preparations when a woman of striking beauty and effervescent manner walked up beside her. "Well, there you are again in a state of worry. My best friend the perfectionist!" remarked Elisheba. She put her arm around Sariah and gave her a quick hug. "You realize, of course that thanks to you, all is well and on schedule." Her smile and encouragement were contagious as always.

Remembering the final words of Noah, Sariah wondered how she would have ever accomplished so much without the love and support of her old friend. Sariah shook her head in admiration and laughingly commented, "Elisheba, without your encouragement and skill with those of the valley, my job would have been so much more difficult. Sometimes I even think we are going to be ready." *It was ironic,* she thought, *"Our success seems to dampen my spirits."* She was always saddened to realize that their complete readiness meant they would be closer to the end and eventually lose everything they had ever known and built.

Elisheba could always read Sariah's moods, even as young women. "I know there will be difficult days ahead, but we have our families and our friends and we will survive. The prophet has assured us and so it will be." Elisheba could say this with total conviction even though she had never met Noah nor heard a word of his message.

Sariah was always amazed at her friend's acceptance of this difficult undertaking. She had stepped in seamlessly to the challenges and had brought a sense of optimism and heightened readiness to them all. If asked how it was that she could unequivocally take their word for what was happening she would simply say, "I just know."

Sariah recalled as a child, even before ascending her mountain for the first time, Lamech had visited their valley and had made his way laboriously up to the summit. When he had returned, he had remarked to her that one day she would be an instrument in saving her people from destruction. "Of course!" she had remembered replying.

He looked at her quizzically and smiled, as if testing her conviction, "And how do you know I speak the truth?"

"I just know" she had replied.

He had shaken his head, as if in admiration and said, "All my life I have seen and I have known, but you are truly blessed because you know and yet have not seen. The greater blessing is yours and I envy you that gift."

Until the return of her childhood friend, Elisheba, she had always wondered what the old man had meant. She could never see how it might apply to herself, but now she understood and could see how this gift was evident in her friend as well. Sariah smiled and changed the subject somewhat. "Zadok seems to be embracing our project with more enthusiasm now." She now wore a mischievous grin as though a private joke had passed between them, which it had.

Elisheba smiled and countered, "What he lacks in belief, he more than makes up in enthusiasm. I think he is just happy to be reunited with us and to have a goal to think about, even if he is reluctant to accept the goal as authentic." Her smile faded as she tried to find the right words then she added, "He is not one of us yet, Sariah, but he is a strong, loving man and a role model to his sons and daughters and his grandchildren. I am content to hope for now. I know the Creator will provide."

The two women embraced and smiled. When the two smiled a stranger could have confused them for sisters. For all purposes of any importance they were.

Cain stood on the wharf looking at his boat the Creator had provided for his escape. The scowl of disapproval was finely etched upon his face as he turned to the builder and pointed, "So, this is it? This ugly scow looks more like a tomb," he groused.

The vessel was the size of a large fishing boat. There was no mast, no oars and no way to steer it, so there was no rudder either and there was only a short guard rail around the perimeter to prevent a person from slipping off. A small hatch had been cut into the deck just large enough for an average sized man to fit as he descended into the interior. The hatch was recessed into the opening for a snug, water tight fit, but since there were no seams, no joints nor hinges, the boat had been built as though it had been constructed entirely from one large tree trunk of lumber. Cain had correctly described it as a floating tomb.

The shipwright, whose name was Edom, was a jovial man and so he took no offense at Cain's disapproving insults to his boat. He merely smiled and declared, "Ugly she is, but this boat would float out into the open seas and would never tip nor turn over on you. Once you are securely inside, I will water seal it from the outside. She fits tight so there is no chance for water drip on you. A small opening for air opens on the deck and can be controlled from the inside. Open it up once a day and you should have no trouble getting enough air. When your *trip* is over, he was smiling now even broader, you simply turn the handle on the hatch from the inside and then you give it a good shove and pop it right out." If possible, his grin was even wider. "Now, would you like a tour of the interior?" he asked happily as though bestowing a great gift.

Cain was totally aghast at what he had just heard and his face scarcely reflected the look of one to whom a great gift had just been bestowed. His eyes played over the stark outlines of the boat. Inwardly he shouted, *"There has to be some mistake. This boat is the same thing as being dead. I would have to live inside for some ungodly period of time and just pop out again when perchance I finally ran aground on solid land? This is a cruel joke and I know just who to blame for it."*

Realizing he was to have no choice in the matter and that time was indeed short, Cain reluctantly decided there was no alternative. He grudgingly agreed to the tour, and seeing the grotesque grin on Edom's face, he impatiently signaled, "Well, show me the way. I don't have all day to stand around and listen to you boast about this floating atrocity you call a boat."

Edom merely smiled enigmatically. He jumped lithely from the wharf to the boat as Cain followed on his heels, trying to balance himself enough to prevent the inevitable soaking if he slipped. With practiced ease, Edom opened the hatch and descended first using the ladder that had been constructed just below the opening. As his eyes gradually got used to the dimness of light, Cain realized there was just enough room for an average-sized man to move about without striking his head from above. There were only two compartments, one presumably for eating and the other for sleeping. Over in the corner a rounded hole had been constructed inside a raised seat and this, he supposed, had been built for taking care of the inevitable by-products of the human body. *This is disgusting and utterly unacceptable*, Cain thought miserably.

Edom, though he could see little because of the dimness, assumed that Cain had finally become aware of the privy. With obvious pride he confided, "That toilet system is my own design, you know. It is all gravity driven. You drop the little turdie in the bottom, you throw the switch and water pushes it down into a cavity into the bottom of the ship where it is taken out to sea only to be replaced with just enough water to push through for the next special delivery", he added with a smiling flourish.

"Wonderful," croaked Cain facetiously with obvious disgust.

Edom went on as though he had been given the greatest complement a man could receive. "If this is going to be an extended *vacation*," again he abruptly turned and smiled, "you should lay up a good supply of dried fruit, vegetables and meat. I know a good supplier in town who will have everything you will need."

With obvious distaste for the attractions of the tour, Cain resignedly asked, "What about light? I suspect that once underway, natural light will be unavailable." Due to the dimness of light, there was not much to see, so unless he wanted to stumble around in the dark then this problem would have to be solved soon. Once underway and out to sea, he would be sealed inside tighter than a pearl in an oyster shell and it would be just as dark. Cain had no intention of wandering and bumping about inside this floating nightmare for months on end in total darkness.

Edom again quickly smiled, the obvious pride reaching his eyes. "The only natural light will be through the air vent. Aside from that, you will need lanterns which you will need to purchase along with oil. Flint strikers have been provided and I have built-in candle holders throughout the boat to store them, but give a care with their use. Candles and wood seldom provide a good mixture on a boat." He smiled as though he had made a delightful pun.

"And fresh water?" inquired Cain, still lacking enthusiasm.

Edom snapped his fingers as if overlooking the obvious. He led Cain over into the eating compartment and threw down a nearby switch. Immediately, fresh water began to fill up a small bucket hanging under a wooden spigot, and depending upon how much water was needed, it could be turned on and off as needed. "There is a small opening from the outside that collects the fresh water after a rain and sends it down inside a cavity built into the boat. You pull the lever and just enough water comes out to fill the bucket or turn the spigot to control the flow." He demonstrated the process to Cain. "Again, my personal design," he added with pride.

"And if it doesn't rain?" Cain asked with a crooked smile, being purposely maudlin.

"The rain water collects and is stored, so you will always have sufficient water if you use it carefully, assuming of course you don't hit too many dry days which I suspect you will not at first." Again, the enigmatic smile appeared, but this time it was followed by a wink.

Cain was growing weary of this smiling oaf and abruptly asked, "Edom, just what do you think you know about me?"

Cain's abruptly rude behavior never fazed him. His smile was still sunny although the conversation quickly turned wet. "I think when the time comes, you will be leaving in a big hurry and the haste will be caused by rains. Since you don't look like a man that appreciates a boat, I conclude that you will have no choice in the matter. The nature of my boat indicates that you will need it to be air and water tight with no possible way to steer it. You are looking for a boat whose only function is to float for an extended period of time and you are expecting things to be wet, very wet. Does that about cover it?" he asked, not the least bit peremptory and his smile, if possible, was even broader.

Cain refused to give him the satisfaction of hearing his speculation was true. He responded dryly, "Show me the shop where this trader in dry goods is located." With that, he turned around and ascended topside back into the sunlight.

Chapter 9 – The Flood

Then God said, "Let there be a firmament in the midst of the waters, and let it divide the waters from the waters." Thus God made the firmament, and divided the waters which were under the firmament from the waters which were above the firmament; and it was so. And God called the firmament Heaven. So the evening and the morning were the second day.

----- Genesis 1: 6-8

And God created the firmament for the good of Man to protect and preserve His children. And He divided these waters from above from the waters beneath and saw that it was good and thus was the evening and the morning of the second day.

----- The Abridgement, Chapter 1

From the end spring new beginnings.

----- Pliny, the Elder

The word "firmament" has been loosely translated in the Hebrew as raqia, or raqiya. Its root word raqa was a verb which meant to beat or spread out, as in the process of making a dish by hammering it into a thin lump of metal.

The ancient Hebrews, much like other ancient cultures, believed the sky was a solid dome with the sun, moon and stars embedded within it. The Hebrews saw the earth as a plain or a hill figured like a hemisphere, swimming on water. Over this is arched the solid vault of heaven. To this vault are fastened the heavenly lights, the stars. And so slight is this elevation that birds may rise to it and fly along its expanse.

Augustine of Hippo, an ancient Greek of the 4th century BCE, noted that too much learning had been expended on the nature of the firmament. It was his claim that "We may understand this name as given to indicate not it is

246

motionless, but that it is solid." According to St. Thomas Aquinas, 13ᵗʰ Century CE, the firmament had a "solid nature" and stood above a "region of fire, wherein all vapor must be consumed."

With the advent of 16ᵗʰ century mathematicians, there was a serious reconsideration of these matters. In 1554, John Calvin decided that "firmament" be interpreted as clouds. He wrote, "He who would learn astronomy and other recondite arts, let him go elsewhere. As it became a theologian, [Moses] had to respect us rather than the stars," Calvin wrote. Thus, Calvin's "doctrine of accommodation" allowed Protestants to accept the findings of science without rejecting the authority of scripture.

The firmament, normally translucent, lay heavily upon the earth in the lower troposphere. As it grew darker and pregnant with water, it had a corresponding diminishing effect on the sunlight. As the days continued, light, which normally shone through the atmosphere, was now slowly cut off leaving the land darker and increasingly more dismal. Most persons had seen the inclement conditions growing for a few days now and why it still had yet to rain, they were at a loss to say. They merely looked up and concluded that they were, indeed, in for a long, rainy downpour. Not having the benefit of sophisticated technology to warn them of dry lines and cold fronts, which generally preceded tempestuous weather, the citizenry simply went home to wait for the storm to pass as they always had in the past. They would remain blissfully unaware that no storm front had created this condition or that a super saturation point would soon be reached within the firmament itself and that after that point was reached, the heaviness of the aqueous solution would eventually burst it like an overfilled membrane.

Sariah led her company of villagers hurriedly up the mountain. Three nights earlier, her husband had noted with some irritation that that she appeared as restless as a willow in a windstorm. When the conditions of rain had begun to appear early that next morning, she felt strongly that the time had finally arrived. Without further hesitation, messengers had been sent riding to all parts of the valley to alert neighbors and family to meet at the prearranged point to start their climb. Each arrived with whatever was left from their homes to carry and each knew that whatever articles or keepsakes in their packs would be the only things left to remind them of what had been before this event.

As the sky had steadily darkened, Cain had been looking out of a window of Samuel's castle all morning long of the final day. If he had likewise been unaware at what was coming, he too, would have been as ambivalent as those around him. Unfortunately, as the sky had darkened with each passing hour of each of the last three days, for Cain this portent was all too conclusive. His boat had been ready for almost a week and from the castle he could see it floating quietly next to the wharf. With an inner fear he had never known, he quietly walked down the steps from the upper floor and through the inner quarters of the castle.

Samuel was waiting just inside the main doorway to the court yard gazing up at the ever darkening sky. He heard Cain approach from behind him, but did not turn. With seeming disinterest, he quietly commented, "An inclement day. Are you going out into the rain?"

Cain managed to remove the quiver from his voice. Years of practice had prepared him to dissemble quite convincingly. "I want to check the boat to ensure that it will be properly protected from the storm. I assume Edom will be nearby?"

The King merely glanced in his direction as Cain passed him out the door. He seemed unconcerned, almost resigned. "Edom is a boat man so he will be nearby." He looked up at the gathering storm. "This will be a good day to be off a boat, I believe, unless it is a special boat" he added off-handedly.

There was scarcely much left to say. Cain and Samuel had shared few words over the past two days and though the King might be one of the last men Cain would see for a long time, there seemed no reason to prolong his departure. Cain turned and with a sense of despair he had never before felt merely said, "Good bye, Samuel. You are right, only a man with the right boat would want to be out today." With that said, he turned and made his way down the pathway to the wharf.

King Samuel of Cush watched the man Cain as he walked steadily down the hill toward the wharf and his waiting boat. As it overlooked the entire bay, his castle had a good vantage point so he missed scarcely any boat traffic in and out of his fiefdom. Unlike many others his age, his eyes had been undimmed by the passage of years so he had never suffered that indignity of older men he had known. He watched as Cain met Edom in front of the boat and exchanged words then Cain hopped aboard and turned to the hatchway. Before descending, he seemed to be looking round about, and as if expecting to see the King for the last time, he turned his gaze upward toward the castle for a few moments then reluctantly he lowered himself into the bowels of his special craft. Samuel could see Edom seal the hatch and untie the boat from its mooring. Now speculative, while the boat rocked gently away from the wharf, he turned his gaze slightly upward and watched expectantly as the sky grew darker.

On the other side of the huge landmass of the Earth, inside a mountain, a large stone wheel was being slowly rolled into position over the opening to a cave. It had been noticed near the entrance to the inner cavern some months earlier and it had become clear that the wheel had been formed to provide a specific function and now it was simply waiting to be rolled out and used for that designed purpose. Corresponding grooves had been carefully cut out of the entrance to the cave and when the wheel was rolled into place in front of the opening and seated, it fitted perfectly. No one knew who had created the stone or even how it had made its way up the side of the mountain, but they all understood why it was to be used: it would cover and protect everyone inside from the oppressive weight and pressure of water.

From the entrance of the cave, high up in the mountain, a dark panoramic view of the entire western horizon could be seen. The dark was everywhere and still as death. It was now time to face the future in a way that none had ever anticipated. The valley had represented the endurance of the human spirit and the cycle of life. Each person had taken a final look at the valley floor below them where life had always existed in its myriad of forms. This was where children had been born and parents had been buried for over eight hundred years. It was a place where young people had found love for the first time and had consummated that love in marriage. The valley knew these same people when they had grown to middle age together and had aspired to grow old together. They all knew the valley and in their minds it was sacred and they were loath to destroy that connection, but if they could dream and hope then their life cycle would endure. It was now a time to give thanks and wait for a new beginning.

In the gloaming of the late afternoon hours of the last day, the saturation point had been finally achieved within the firmament. Those upon the land who had followed the darkening of the past few days with keen interest suddenly looked upward as a loud cracking noise reverberated across the land mass of the Earth. The sound, in consequence of what followed, would have seemed more like a death knell. Those gazing up at the time would at one moment have seen a most unusual sight and the next moment experienced death. Everyone has at one time observed rainfall in its various forms, from a light mist to drizzle, from a steady downpour to an outright tempest, but, unless a person has observed a large waterfall up close, then felt its absolute, irresistible power of vertically descending water, would they begin to comprehend the strength of the inimitable deluge of that day. It did not just rain. The water, trillions of tons of liquid, dropped straight-way, vertically to the earth impacting it with all the irrepressible force of gravity on a tremendous weight. The vast majority of the populace was pounded then consumed with water within seconds, the rest washed away in the wake of a tremendous wave that swept across the planet.

Epilogue – Attack in Austin

The first set of the abridged records had just been translated. They had contained the summary of Mankind's history from the time of Adam up to and including the Great Flood. Professors William Bradford and Isaac Levinson were relieved to have finally completed the preliminary translation. Though Jasher seemed reluctant to consider it his book, between the two of the professors they were now referring to it as *The Book of Jasher*; he continued to refer to it as *The Abridgement*.

The efforts of the last two weeks had proven exhilarating, yet not without its challenges. None of them knew how the outside world had learned of what they were doing, but suddenly, in the last few days, phone calls from news agencies, local and national television networks and even from colleagues had become a constant source of distraction. Eventually, Jasher had to jam all incoming calls with a device much like the one he had used to thwart the surveillance equipment in Israel. This proved to be only a temporary measure for, as of yesterday, the news media had descended upon Bedford's home and were now parked outside awaiting comments. In desperation, using Jasher's inexhaustible contacts, Bedford had hired two trusted security men that were present for crowd control as well as possible theft. What the two professors were unaware was that Jasher had had the neighborhood under constant surveillance and protection since his arrival by a retinue of men he had recruited surreptitiously in Israel to discourage infiltration of Cain's agents. They had quietly moved into the neighborhood and had provided a tight cordon of protection from thieves, trained assassins, and government operatives bent on halting the process of translation.

All three men were now standing over the records and the finished translated manuscript. "My friends," began Jasher. "You may have wondered why our work has suddenly received so much attention of late. Our security here in William's home over the past few weeks has been exemplary, but it was inevitable that Cain would learn of our collaboration. The result you see on your front lawn. Network and newspaper owners are some of the most powerful and most influential persons on the planet as well as their chief editors and behind them all is always the same man, Walker Caine. Their allegiance has been seldom to the public or freedom of the press or any other freedom they may purport to represent, but primarily to the agenda of the Clan. It is now time to reveal our activity and release the results of our joint effort. The longer we postpone this, the more the media will speculate and eventually pronounce its spin on our efforts. Their version, I can assure you, will be unfavorable. Therefore, it is imperative that we control how our working translation is released rather than in an off-handed manner to the media crew parked on your front lawn. In spite of our best efforts, there will be many of the yellow press who will report our results along the lines of their distorted program, but there will be a few willing to print exactly what we reveal, so we must focus our efforts to reach out to those who would print the truth. We must now review the parameters of our comments to the press."

The three had been working on this media release for the past day and now that the time had come to face the press, they needed to be absolutely sure of their strategy. Following their review, Professor Levinson made a few calls to the university and had spoken directly to the Campus President as well as the Dean over his department. The two officials had been informed of the clandestine nature of his short sabbatical over the past few weeks and with whom he had been working. Levinson requested that he be allowed to make an official press release from the University's Campus Public Relations Center as soon as possible and accordingly invited both university officers to be present for the release. The two men had quickly agreed and the President had made the campus facility available for their use on the next morning. After being notified of Levinson's intentions, the University President informed the news media services that there would be an official statement on the recent collaborations of Professors Bedford and Levinson for the following day at 10:00 am. The announcement would include a brief overview of the nature of the translation and the specifics of what it would reveal to the world. Although it still had to be properly edited and the artifact itself had yet to be thoroughly examined and carbon tested, nonetheless, there would be sufficient information to make a public statement.

Caine's agitated pacing was contagious. James Perkins, the personal CIA liaison to the office of Walker Caine, wanted badly to pace along with him. He had been recently transferred from the agency's Middle Eastern Office to New York City. Technically, he had no real official mandate to operate openly within the borders of the United States; that dubious privilege had been reserved for the Federal Bureau of Investigation and more recently to Homeland Security. He was here only because Walker Caine had requested it, and as he had discovered time and again, whatever Caine wanted, he was given.

Perkins often wondered what power Caine could wield over so many powerful men and women of the world. He instinctively knew that he would never know such secrets, not because he was incapable of keeping them, but because he was curious instead of pedantic. Caine invariably insulated himself with men who would take orders and concern themselves only for the reasons they were provided and never wonder why they needed to be carried out. They were highly tactical-minded and awaited Caine to provide the strategies to be completed. On the other hand, men curious by nature were meant to rise no higher than a need-to-know level of acceptance. In his opinion, in the rarefied air of Caine's inner circle, there was only room for the ruthless and blindly obedient. The rest would always be relegated to the ranks of messenger boy or spear-carrier. So, here he sat, waiting for Caine to make his deliberation that he would carry back to his superiors at Langley. From there, the final plan of action on Benjamin Jasher would be disseminated throughout the world.

Perkins was eager to assuage some of the anxiety he perceived from Caine by providing some hard news. "Mr. Caine, as you are now aware, our operatives on the university campus have confirmed that Levinson phoned the Campus President and a press conference has been set for tomorrow morning at 10:00 a.m."

"Perkins, do you have any idea what specifics Jasher and his *groupies* plan to reveal?" He snarled impatiently.

His reply was immediate. "Sir, we have none, but our agents are even now prepared and are standing by to breach Bedford's home. As soon as the press corps has been dispersed, and on your orders, we can move forward with our plan. As you know, sir, they have been a constant hindrance to our operation since we learned what Jasher was up to."

Cain reacted with an immediate shot of anger that Perkins would insinuate his lack of control over the media. He fumed, "Yes, I am quite aware of their meddling in this matter. It appears that I may have turned them loose prematurely upon Jasher and his *Merry Men*. I had hoped that it might draw them out, make them vulnerable and allow your team to move in on them and now I frankly admit that it had been a mistake. Jasher is deceptively cunning and no doubt he has briefed the absent-minded professors on my strategies."

Perkins was always amazed at how much Caine was troubled by this one man, Jasher. In his opinion, Caine's continual berating of Jasher and those who followed him was little more than a smokescreen for fear. Caine was normally the most coldly ruthless man he had ever known and he seemed always in complete control. Perkins knew he was in the presence of probably the most dangerous man in the world, yet the question persisted: *Exactly what did Jasher have over Caine to make him feel this worried?*

Cain continued with his rant. "I will not stand by impotently while that jackal tears my organization to threads with his lies. He has left me no choice but to act to protect myself. Perkins, your team goes in tonight. I want Jasher in handcuffs standing before me tomorrow morning with all his lying records and I want him alive!"

"And what of the other two?" inquired the agent.

Cain replied without hesitation. "I want them carried out in body bags."

"And what reason shall we give to justify our actions? The media will have a field day." Perkins was worried about the blowback such an incident might cause.

Cain replied coldly, "National security, what else?" As to the media, my spin control team will be notified, and as you know, they are highly competent." He offered a crooked smile to Perkins as he dismissed him.

It was a cool night so a fire had been lit in the fireplace. *There was always something inherently comforting about a lit fire in a hearth, thought Levinson.* It was late evening and Jasher had concluded briefing the two professors on a recent development. His security team had intercepted messages, which indicated that an attack on the residence was imminent.

The two had just been informed of their role that they would now need to play.

"So," inquired Levinson quietly, "There is no other way?"

Jasher replied apologetically, "Isaac, you and William have become more than just friends to me these past few weeks. I can only apologize for the danger that I have placed upon each of you, but you must realize by now that from the moment we met and you agreed to this collaboration that your lives were inextricably linked with my own and all its dangers. I can only say in my defense that the hallowed nature of this work obviated any other consideration."

The two professors reluctantly nodded their assent. "It will be hard on our families, though," added Levinson. He gazed thoughtfully into the fireplace at the dying embers.

It was 3:00 a.m. when the tactical insertion began. From time immemorial it had always been the hour of the club and the rough awakenings. Isaac Levinson's kinsmen in Europe could attest to this, assuming they had lived through the experience; most had not.

Perkins' insertion squad did not bother with subtle entry. Since any real resistance was unexpected, they simply battered down the front door and in moments half the team had scurried up the stairway, the other half had moved through the downstairs area. Finding no one downstairs, the second group moved carefully down the basement stairs. Instinct and training had taught them that this would be a perfect choke point for defense. With their special breathing masks now on, as they carefully descended, canisters of incapacitating smoke were tossed into the darkness. Through specially crafted lenses mounted on their face masks, the smoke posed no problem with their sight.

They must have felt overconfident when they encountered so little resistance to their initial breach which proved to be a tragic assumption. One of the intruders had overlooked a dimly lit sensor that, when tripped, set off a number of fragmentary explosives scattered about the circumference of the basement. The explosives were of professional grade and designed specifically to rip through even the most resistant body armor. Within the tight confines of the basement, the effect was lethal.

The leader of the basement team was immediately beheaded with an explosive that carried ball-bearing fragments placed at shoulder level. The other members of the team were simply blown apart as the concussion and pressure of the combined explosives ripped and tore their way through the enclosed room. Jasher's security team had reinforced the outside of the basement windows weeks before with sandbags so there was nowhere for the force of the blast to escape except back into the basement and upwards.

The upstairs team had heard the commotion from below as they were moving quietly down the hallway. It was probably the last thing they did hear because the explosion in the basement triggered incendiary explosives upstairs when the landing began to collapse from the destruction below. Within moments the entire structure was ablaze and the firestorm could be seen miles away.

The Learjet36 cruised at an altitude of 36,000 feet at just over 600 miles per hour in an easterly direction. It had taken off two hours earlier from a remote section of a mid-sized corporate airport near Austin, Texas. Jasher, Bedford and Levinson were seated comfortably, though the professors were hard pressed to remain calm in the face of their near-death evacuation from Austin. Jasher was calmly explaining their ease of escape. "One of the advantages of being so long-lived is that my contacts go back very far and they are especially reliable."

"It was still touch-and-go back there in Austin," commented Bedford. "The tunnel from my basement to the next street was unexpected. I know I was unaware of it."

"You were not meant to be aware of it, William," replied Jasher. "It was only to be used in the event of certain circumstances. When they arose, we were left with no choice. My intelligence team got wind of Cain's intentions and still I nearly underestimated his commitment to destroy the records and us at any cost."

Bedford, still shaken from their narrow escape, replied quietly, "It was a pity about the house, though. I had only two mortgage payments remaining. The fire destroyed everything, I suppose."

"The ruse had to give us enough time to make good our escape," Jasher pointed out. "You can be assured that Cain's men were first on the scene, however, it will be days before anyone can glean a full picture of how we managed to get away." Jasher retrieved tonic and seltzer waters from the icebox at the rear of the plane.

Levinson, in a slight state of retroactive shock, was more sanguine when he commented, "Those bodies from the morgue were a nice touch, I must say." Levinson accepted one of the bottles and sipped thoughtfully over their violent scrape with death.

"Yes, they had to have the exact appearance of you two gentlemen or there would always be some room for doubt. My men were fortunate to find the bodies in the morgue and switched the dental records," Jasher commented as he sipped the glass of tonic water he had just poured from the bottle. "They smuggled them into the house the same route we took to escape. Of course, Cain will never accept that we were all killed in the explosion and fire, but the diversion will buy us enough time to make good our escape."

Isaac glanced over to his friend who shook his head to indicate his concern. Levinson likewise seemed disturbed by the events. "Jasher, is this the way you have always lived?"

Jasher was silent for a few moments as if collecting his thoughts. "I have always had to live by my wits and plan for unforeseen circumstances. Of course it is more than just skill acquired over time. Without my contacts, I would be helpless in this fast-paced world we now live. Again, gentlemen, let me apologize for dragging you so deeply into my world for you will now have to live even as I do. This will be your lot in life now until we can complete the testing and preparation process of the records for publication."

William commented, "I suppose it's to be in for a penny, in for a pound. Though we would have wanted it differently, it is clear we must accept the reality of our situation and make the most of it."

"I agree, but what went wrong in Austin, Jasher?" asked Isaac. "We were just hours away from revealing our translation."

Jasher pondered over the question for a moment then replied, "Please understand gentlemen, that, though I have been in possession of the abridged records for over sixty years now, this was the first attempt to reveal them publicly before the media. It was imperative that I knew to what degree Walker Caine would react to this development. It is evident by this display of force that he intends to prevent us from disclosing our translation regardless of the repercussions, even if that means harming us and destroying the records in the bargain. Fortunately, I had a contingency plan prepared should we need to make a retreat and postpone our announcement for another day. In any event, this flight would have been needed eventually; there are more records to translate."

Both professors leaned forward as if not hearing correctly what Jasher had just revealed. Bedford was the first to voice his surprise. "You say there are more?"

Jasher again seemed apologetic. "Forgive me, my friends, but the plates I presented before you that we have just spent the last few weeks translating were only half of *The Abridgment*. The other half sit in my basement on Cyprus guarded closely around the clock by my best security team."

Isaac appeared stunned by what he had just heard. He stammered, "Then the announcement planned today before the media was a ruse to measure Cain's determination to stop us?"

Jasher replied, "Isaac, I did not plan for failure, but every plan must have a contingency for failure. Thus, even though our plans were halted, we now know what he is prepared to do to prevent any future announcements. That will give me time to develop a tighter security ring around us and the records for our protection. We will be better prepared next time."

Bedford's smile was hard; he didn't appreciate the deception. "We could have been better informed by these developments, Jasher."

Jasher was tired, but he felt a need to teach a short lesson he had learned by trial and error during his long life. "William, most of us, I included, learn our purpose and responsibilities the hard way, not because of our lack of intelligence or motivation, but because we can seldom apply more than we are prepared to understand. Unless you have lived in my world for more than a few weeks, it is very difficult to comprehend those dangerous demands. You two are academics, unaccustomed to living a life rife with danger. I have lived with it for so long, it has become second nature and I would prefer you never have to be concerned with it so that you may better focus on our translation needs. I had hoped that what you had just experienced tonight would not have been necessary, but now that you have seen and lived through the danger of my world, you will be better prepared the next time we are required to move quickly and, I assure you, in the future, I will not hesitate to bring you in on my contingency plans."

Bedford nodded his assent and asked, "Then Cyprus is to be our final destination?"

Jasher considered his question and after a moment replied, "There may be one more, but for now my plan is that Cyprus is the location where we can complete the translation of the other records and make our announcement to the world. For now, we will have to postpone our announcement of the translation of the first part of *The Abridgement.*"

"Perkins," muttered Caine through clenched teeth, "explain to me how you allowed this debacle to happen." He had just been briefed by his liaison, but he could have learned as much information from the 5:00 a.m. newscast. There was little information to be collected this early in the investigation because the rubble from the explosion was so extensive and the heat from the incendiaries was so hot, few firemen could get close enough to extinguish it. The entire block had to be cleared of people and there was a real fear that the fire might spread before it could be subdued.

Perkins replied defensively, "Mr. Caine, my people on the ground tell me that the insertion went by the book. They were in constant communication with the teams and by all reports there had been no defense of the residence. When Team B descended to the basement they popped smoke and proceeded forward without any resistance. Then all hell had broken loose."

"Perkins," spat Cain, "spare me your colorful speech and stick to the facts."

"Sorry, sir," replied Perkins, now more nervous than ever. He continued, "We think that fragmentation devices were planted in the basement and were remotely activated when Jasher and the others escaped. The windows had been blocked from the outside and the foundation, of course, was cement so the blast had only one way to travel, upwards. After the men were taken out in the basement, the force of the blast was directed up through the first and second floors of the house causing enough structural damage that the upper floors collapsed. Incendiary explosives had also been laid into the second floor set to be triggered by remote activation or perhaps by the collapsing motion of the floor. Whatever method was used, once the basement was destroyed, the second floor closely followed, taking out the other team as well. Even if the teams had not been killed by the explosions, they would have been taken out immediately by the resulting fire storm."

"Impossible!" shouted Cain, now completely irate at this missed opportunity to capture Jasher alive. "Are you suggesting that two old college professors and an arts dealer set up your team and led them into an ambush?"

"No, they had professional help", Perkins replied. "We suspect Jasher had a specially trained team of ex-Israeli Mossad operatives led by Dov Hacohen who helped them, but to what extent we have not yet ascertained." He ventured a personal comment. "Sir, we could have taken them all out weeks ago, including Jasher. I don't understand your reluctance to eliminate him once and for all. This waiting undoubtedly allowed them more time to prepare for our assault."

"Perkins," replied Cain with mounting fury. "I don't owe you any explanation. You are an errand boy whose only job is to communicate my commands to your superiors. The only reason I don't have you thrown out this window for your failure is because you already know more than any other errand boy in that bungling agency you represent. Since I have neither the time nor the interest in bringing someone else up to speed, I am stuck with you. Now, get out and report back to me when you have all the facts, not rumors and not innuendo."

With more dignity than he thought possible under the circumstances, Perkins turned quickly and half trotted out the door.

It was obvious, regardless of what they found at the destruction site, Jasher had made good his escape with Bedford and Levinson, and of course, the records and translation would likewise be in tow. Angrily, Cain turned and walked over to the window overlooking the river. As he heard Perkins retreat, he reflected on his last question, which was a good one, and perhaps deserved an answer, but one that he would never reveal.

He quietly reviewed the facts. The only purpose for ever keeping Jasher alive was that he knew the whereabouts of all the remaining records. If he had to drag the information from him one fingernail at a time then he would do it, but he had to have the man alive. Of course, there is much more to it than that and always has been. The entire mountain vault containing the records were off-limits as the area was considered hallowed ground and therefore unassailable; as a consequence, he would now have to wait until Jasher removes them before he could move on him.

Moreover, he knew those damnable rules of engagement with which he had been hamstrung since the beginning of all this would always give Jasher an unfair advantage just as it did his meddling brother, Seth. He could take the records and destroy them once in the open, but he couldn't injure the recorders, not even to extract the lying information they carry around with them bag and baggage.

He thought, *"And now, my old nemesis, Jasher, has resurfaced and was ready to make the end-game more interesting. Considering the heightened secrecy and with whom he was now associating, it was clear Jasher was planning something spectacular. Now I know that Jasher finally dragged out those dusty records he had once used to threaten me and has decided now to dangle them before me in a feeble effort to coerce me to postpone or change my plans."*

Cain swore by the oath of his Brotherhood that he would not permit any more delays, but as he considered his next move, he realized that he must have those damnable records Jasher was hoarding, and soon, or his plans would come to naught.

Cain resumed his pacing about the room. "Damn it," he cursed, not for the first time then murmured, "I need a fireplace in this room. It's always so bloody cold in here and I need a fire to relax and think."

THE END

34085960R00167

Made in the USA
Middletown, DE
07 August 2016